the twilight saga: the official illustrated guide

the twilight saga:
the official
illustrated guide

The publisher wishes to acknowledge
contributions by Lori Joffs and Laura Byrne-Cristiano
of the Twilight Lexicon

→‑ ‑←

Illustrations by
Rebecca Bradley, James Carey, Young Kim, Sarah McMenemy,
and Leah Palmer Preiss

Megan Tingley Books
LITTLE, BROWN AND COMPANY
New York   Boston

Little, Brown and Company
Hachette Book Group
237 Park Avenue, New York, NY 10017
Visit our website at www.lb-teens.com

Little, Brown and Company is a division of Hachette Book Group, Inc.
The Little, Brown name and logo are trademarks of Hachette Book Group, Inc.

The publisher is not responsible for websites (or their content)
that are not owned by the publisher.

First Edition: April 2011

Book Design by Georgia Rucker Design

ISBN 978-0-316-04312-0

10 9 8 7 6 5 4 3 2 1

RRD-C

Printed in the United States of America

⤜ TABLE OF CONTENTS

Humans

Dear Reader,

Working on this guide has given me a chance to reflect on how much this story has changed my life. One of the best ways things have changed is the opportunity I've had to get to know so many of my readers. I'm always impressed by the funny, caring, interesting people you are. I truly feel that with your enthusiasm and dedication you've brought as much to this series as I have. Little, Brown and I have been working hard to make this guide something special for you, and I hope that we've succeeded. I would never presume to expect that all the questions have been answered, but (fingers crossed) I think we got the big ones, plus many that no one's ever asked me before. Enjoy!

Much love,

Steph

A Note from the Publisher

Since the initial publication of *Twilight* in 2005, readers have asked thousands of questions about the Twilight Saga universe—everything from "Where do Stephenie Meyer's ideas come from?" to "How does vampire venom work?"

This guide expands upon the world of the Twilight Saga, adding histories for its characters and providing other details that might not have made it into the books themselves but are a key part of the people and stories that make up the Saga. You'll find outtakes from the books—such as the story of how Emmett was mauled by a bear—as well as never-before-seen background notes on main plots and subplots. We hope that these added details shed light on such favorite characters as the Cullens and Quileutes; on such new characters as Nahuel and Garrett; and even on the human residents of Forks, most of whom are unaware of the supernatural creatures all around them.

Also included in this guide are artistic interpretations of the series: everything from new art created just for this book to a gallery of art conceived by talented fans to the many covers that have appeared on different editions of the books around the world.

Because music is such an instrumental part of Stephenie's writing process, this guide also includes the official playlist for each book in the Twilight Saga, alongside quotes from the books that reveal what each song represents. Also featured is an extended conversation between Stephenie and Shannon Hale, award-winning author of The Books of Bayern and the Newbery Honor winner *Princess Academy*, during which they discuss how the Twilight Saga began and some of the challenges and surprises Stephenie encountered along the way.

Thank you for being a part of the world of the Twilight Saga—it wouldn't be the same without you.

A Conversation
with Shannon Hale

When Megan, my publisher, came to me with the idea of doing an interview for the guide, I started to come up with a list of reasons why I couldn't in my head. *Interviews always make me uncomfortable, and really, what question haven't I answered at this point? But then she went on, presenting her inspiration of having the interview conducted by another author, and I was intrigued in spite of myself. I love hanging out with authors, and I don't get a chance to do it very often. So I oh-so-casually suggested my "baffy" (Best-Author-Friends-Forever), Shannon Hale. And the upshot was, I got to hang out with Shannon for a whole weekend and it was awesome. We did find time to do our "interview," which was without a doubt the easiest and most entertaining interview I've ever done. This interview took place August 29, 2008, which affects some of the directions that our conversation went, but I was surprised when reading through it again at how relevant it still is.*

On How It All Began

SH: So, let's look at the four different books first. *Twilight*—it started with a dream.

SM: Right. Should I tell the story—and get it on record?

SH: Do you want to?

SM: I'd like to. This story always sounds really fake to me. And when my publicist told me I needed to tell it—because it was a good story for publicity reasons—I felt like a lot of people were going to say: "You know, that's ridiculous. She's making up this silly thing to try and get attention." But it's nothing but the cold hard facts of how I got started as a writer.

Usually, I wake up around four o'clock in the morning. I think it's a baby thing—left over from knowing that somebody needs you—and then I go back to sleep. That's when I would have the most vivid dreams—those morning hours. And those are the ones you remember when you wake up.

So the dream was me looking down on this scene: It was in this meadow, and there was so much light. The dream was very, very colorful. I don't know if that always comes through in the writing—that this prism effect was just so brilliant.

SH: The sunlight on Edward's skin?

SM: Yeah. There was this beautiful image, this boy, just glittering with light and talking to this normal girl. And the dream really was about him. She was also listening, as I was, and he was the one telling the story. It was mostly about how much he wanted to kill her—and, yet, how much he loved her.

In the dream I think I'd gotten most of the way through what's chapter 13 now. The part where he recounts how he felt in each specific previous scene was obviously put in later, because I hadn't written those earlier scenes yet. But everything else in that scene was mostly what they were actually talking about in the dream. Even the analogy about food was something that I got in my dream.

I was so intrigued when I woke up. I just sat there and thought: *So how does that end? Does he kill her?* Because it was really close. You know how, in dreams, it's not just what you hear, but you also kind of feel what's going on, and you see everything that the person in your head sees. So I knew how close it was. I mean, there was just a thin, thin line between what he was going to choose. And so I just wondered: *How would they have made that work? What would be the next step for a couple like this?*

I was so intrigued when I woke up. I just sat there and thought: So how does that end?

—⊷ 3 ⊶—

I had recently started realizing that my memory was going, and that I could no longer remember whom I had said something to yesterday. My youngest was just passing one, and the next one was two, and I had an almost-five-year-old. So my brains were like oatmeal—there was nothing left. And so I knew I was going to forget this story! That realization was something that really hurt me.

You know, when I was a kid, I always told myself stories, but I didn't write them down. I didn't have to—my memory was great then. So I could always go back and revisit the one about this, the one about that, and go over and refine it. But this one was going to get lost if I didn't do something about it. So after I got the kids' breakfast done, I only had two hours before swim lessons. And, even though I should have been doing other things, I started writing it out.

It wasn't the dream so much as that day of writing that made me a writer. Because the dream was great, and it was a good story. But if I'd had my memory [laughs] it would have stayed just a story in my head. And I would have figured out everything that happened, and told it to myself, but that would have been it.

But writing it down and making it real, and being able to go back and reread the sentences, was just a revelation to me. It was this amazing experience: *Wow! This is what it's like to write down stories.* I was just hooked—I didn't want to quit.

I used to paint—when I was in high school, particularly. I won a few awards—I was okay with the watercolors. My mom still has some hanging up in her house. Slightly embarrassing, but they're decent. I was not a great painter. It was not something I should have pursued as a career, by any stretch of the imagination. I could see a picture in my head, but I could not put it on the canvas the same way it was in my head. That was always a frustration. When I started writing I immediately had a breakthrough: *I can make it real if I write it, and it's exactly the way I see it in my head.* I didn't know I was able to do that. So that was really the experience that made me a writer, and made me want to continue being one.

SH: So you started out writing out the meadow scene. Where did you go from there?

SM: I continued to the end, chronologically — which I don't always do anymore.

SH: So you didn't go back to the beginning...because you wanted to know what was going to happen next.

SM: Yeah. I was just like any reader with a story — you want to find out what happened. The backstory was for later. I wasn't really that worried about it — I wanted to see where it was going to go.

So I kept writing. The last chapter just kept getting longer and longer — and then I made epilogue after epilogue. There were so many things I wanted to explore — like why this was this way, and why this was that way, and how Bella first met Alice, and what their first impressions were. So I went back and did the beginning, and found it really exciting to be able to flesh it out and give reasons for everything that had happened later.

I had lettered all my chapters instead of numbering them. So I went back and did A, and I think that I had chapter 13 being E. Because I thought, maybe, five or six chapters of material would cover the beginning...and then it was twelve, so I was surprised about that. [Laughs]

SH: You were surprised about how much had really happened beforehand?

SM: Yeah, it just kept going on. I was thinking: *Wow, this is taking a long time.* And that's where I finally ended, which was the last sentence in chapter 12. And I knew I had crossed the continent with the railroad, and this was the golden spike that was being driven. It was all linked together. And that was that moment of shock, when I thought: *It's actually long enough to be considered a book-length thing of some kind.*

SH: You really didn't even consider it like a book until then?

SM: No. [Laughs] No, I think if I would have thought of it as a book, I never would have finished it. I think if I would have thought, halfway in, *You know, maybe I can make this into a book...maybe I could do something with this,* the pressure would have crushed me, and I would have given up. I'm really glad I didn't think of it that way. I'm glad I protected myself by just keeping it about this personal story for me alone.

SH: And you were thinking of yourself as the reader the whole time.

SM: Yes, yes. Well, I'm kind of shy, and I obviously had to get over that in a lot of ways. But the essential Stephenie, who is still in here, has a really hard time with letting people read things that she writes. [Laughs] And there's a lot of enjoyment, which I'm sure you've experienced, in letting somebody read what you write. But there's also the fear of it — it's a really vulnerable position to put yourself in.

SH: I was in a creative-writing class once and the teacher asked us: If we were stranded on a desert island, what two books would we take? And one of the books I chose was a notebook — an empty notebook — so I could write stories. And there was a classmate who said: "If you were on a desert island by yourself, why would you write stories?" And I thought: *Why are you in this class?* [SM laughs] Because if the only purpose you have for writing is for someone else to read them, then why would you do this? It didn't make sense to me. But there is something extraordinary about writing for yourself and then sharing that.

sм: I've never thought of the desert-island story. But that would be the perfect writing conditions, as far as I'm concerned. That would be great. I wouldn't want a spiral notebook, though — I'd want a laptop. Typing is so much better. I can't read my own handwriting half the time.

sн: So you started immediately on the computer, when you started writing this?
sм: Yeah.

sн: Now, how long was it from when you wrote down the dream until you finished the first draft?
sм: I wrote down the dream on June second. I had it all marked on my calendar: the first day of my summer diet; the first day of the swim lessons. It's kind of funny to know exactly what day you started being a writer! And I finished it around my brother's wedding, which was — he just had his anniversary — I think it was the twenty-ninth of August?

sн: So this was done in less than three months — just an outpouring of words.
sм: Yeah.

It's kind of funny to know exactly what day you started being a writer!

SH: Was the story going through your head all day long, even when you weren't writing?

SM: Even when I was asleep—even when I was awake. I couldn't hold conversations with people. All my friends just thought that I had dropped them, because I lived in my own world for a whole summer.

But here was this really hot, muggy, nasty summer. And when I looked back on it later, it seemed like I'd spent the whole summer in a cool, green place, because that's how distant my brain was from what was really going on. I wasn't there—which is sad. [Laughs]

I was physically there for my kids, and I took care of them. And I had my little ones, one on my leg and one on my lap, most of the time I was writing. Luckily, the TV was behind me [laughs] so they could lean on my shoulder, you know, watch *Blue's Clues* while I was typing. But I don't think you can keep up that kind of concentrated effort for more than a summer. You have to find some balance eventually.

SH: You have to come up for air.

SM: Yeah.

SH: How did you? You're so busy as a mom. Every moment of the day, with three little kids, is occupied. Suddenly, you're inserting this huge other effort into it. How did you allow yourself to do that?

SM: A lot of the time it didn't feel like it was a choice. Once I got started writing, it felt like there was so much that I had been keeping inside for so long.

SH: Not just this story. But very active storytelling and creating, I'm sure, had been percolating in you for years.

SM: It was a creative outlet that was the best one I've ever found. I've done other creative things: birthday cakes and really great Halloween costumes, if I do say so myself.

It was a creative outlet that was the best one I've ever found.

I was always looking for ways to creatively express myself. And it was always kind of a frustrating thing—it was never enough. Being a mom, especially when kids are younger—when they get older, it's a lot easier—you have to be about *them* every minute. And a lot of who Stephenie is was slipping away.

SH: Yeah.

SM: The writing brought that back in with such force that it was just an obsession I couldn't...I couldn't be away from it. And that was, I think, kind of the dam bursting, and that huge surge at first. And then I learned to manage it.

SH: You would have to. But what a tremendous way to start!

SM: It was. It felt really good—it felt really, really good. And I think when you find something that you can do that makes you feel that way, you just grasp on to it.

SH: So you had never written a short story before.

SM: I had not ever considered writing seriously. When I was in high school, I thought of some stories that might be a good book, but I didn't take it seriously, and I never said: "Gosh, I'm going to do that." I considered it momentarily—the same way I considered being a professional ballerina.

SH: Right.

SM: Oh, and I was going to be so good [SH laughs] in my *Nutcracker*. I would have been fantastic—except that, obviously, I have no rhythmic skill, or the build for a ballerina, at all. [SH laughs] So it was like one of those nonsensical things—like wanting to be a dryad.

And then, when I was in college, I actually wrote a couple chapters of something... because I think it's the law: When you're an English major, you have to consider being an author as a career. But it was a ridiculous thing. I mean, there's no way you can make a living as a writer—everybody knows that. And, really, it's too hard to become an editor—that's just not a practical solution. If you're going to support yourself, you have to think realistically. You know, I was going to go to law school. I knew I could do that. I knew that if I worked hard, I'd be kind of guaranteed that I could at least get a decent job somewhere that would pay the bills.

There's no guarantee like that with writing, or anything in the publishing industry. You're not guaranteed that you will be able to feed yourself if you go down that path, and so I would have never considered it. I was—I still am—a very practical person.

SH: So you really had to go into it from the side... by fooling yourself that you're not actually writing a book.

SM: I think there was this subconscious thing going on that was protecting me from thinking of the story in a way that would keep me from being able to finish it.

SH: Right. But, of course, you were a reader. You've been an avid reader for your whole life.

SM: That was always my favorite thing, until I found writing. My kids and my husband used to tease me, because my hand would kind of naturally form this sort of bookholder [SH laughs], this claw for holding books. Because I had the baby in one arm and the book in the other—with the bottle tucked under my chin and the phone on my shoulder. [Laughs] You know, the Octopus Mom. But I always had a book.

I always needed that extra fantasy world. I had to have another world I could be in at the same time. And so, with writing, I just found a way to have another world, and then to be able to be a lot more a part of it than as a reader.

SH: I think it's part of multitasking. I wonder if most writers — I know moms have to be this way, but most writers, too — have to have two things going on at once just to stay entertained.

SM: Exactly. [Laughs]

SH: It's not that I'm unsatisfied, because I love my life. I'm a mom, too, of small kids — and I love my husband — but I also need something else beyond that. I need another story to take me away.

SM: You know, it's funny. As I've become a writer, I started looking at other writers and how they do things, and everybody's very different. I read *Atonement* recently, and I was interested in the way Ian McEwan writes about being a writer through the character's standpoint. . . . She's always seeing another story. She's doing one thing — but, then, in her head, it becomes something else, and it turns into another story.

> I always needed that extra fantasy world. I had to have another world I could be in at the same time.

It's kind of like what you were saying about writers needing that extra reality to escape to. I think that writers maybe do have just that need for more than one reality. [Laughs]

SH: You know, we're not really sure if it's insanity or it's a superpower.

SM: But it's an insanity that doesn't hurt anybody.

SH: Right. It's kind of friendly, cozy, fuzzy insanity.

SH: I think you must write much better first drafts than I do.

SM: I doubt that.

SH: Really? Are they pretty bad?

SM: I think so. I have to go over them again and again, because I don't always flesh it out enough. I write it through so quickly that I have to go back and add things. I tend to use the same words a lot, and I have to consciously go back and take out things like that. And I don't always get them. My first drafts are scary.

SH: How do you go about rewriting? With *Twilight*, did you send it off immediately, or did you go back and start revising it?

SM: I probably read it, I don't know, fifty to a hundred times before I sent it anywhere. And I cannot read a page of anything I've written without making five changes — that's my average. So even now that *Twilight* is "finished" — quote-unquote — oh, I'd love to revise it. I could do such a better job now. And I have a hard time rereading it. Because if I read it on the computer, I want to go in and change things — and it drives me crazy that I can't.

And I cannot read
a page of anything I've
written without making
five changes —
that's my average.

sm: Yeah. I try not to read anything that I've already published.

sm: If I read it in the book form, I can usually relax and kind of enjoy it. I like to experience the stories again, because I see it like I did the first time I saw it. But sometimes it's hard not to be like, "Oh, I hate that now. Why did I do it that way?" [Laughs]

sm: That would be writers' hell: You're continually faced with a manuscript that you wrote years ago and not allowed to change it.

sm: [Laughs] Well, then, that's every writer's reality, right? [Laughs]

sm: I don't know if you feel this way, but once a book is written and out of my hands and out there, I no longer feel like I wrote it. I don't feel like I can even claim the story anymore. I feel like now it belongs out there, with the readers.

sm: I feel that way about the hardbound copy on the shelf. There is a disassociation there. If I look at it on a shelf, and it seems very distant and cold and important, I don't feel like it's something that belongs to me. When I read it, it does.

sm: I guess I haven't reread my books. I listen to the audiobooks, actually — one time for each book — and I have enjoyed that. The people who did my audiobooks are a full cast, so it's like this play, almost.

sm: Oh, that's so cool.

sm: They say things differently than I would have, but instead of being wigged out by it, I actually like it. Because it's as though I'm hearing a new story, and I'm hearing it for the first time.

sm: See, I can't ignore my mistakes as much when I hear it on audio. I have tried to listen to my books on audio, and

I cannot do it. Because I hear the awkwardness in a phrase when it's spoken aloud, and I just think: *Oh, gosh! I shouldn't have phrased it that way.* And there'll be other things where I hear the mistakes a lot louder than when I read through it and kind of skip over them with my eyes.

sh: Now, by the time you finished *Twilight*, you thought, *This is a book*—and then you started to revise. Did you revise just to, like you said, relive the story? Or did you have a purpose?

sm: Well, while I was writing I would revise while I was going. I'd start and go back and read what I'd written up to that point before I started. And some days I'd spend the whole day just making changes and adding things to what I'd written. That was one of my favorite parts—reading it. That surprised me, you know.... But then it's the book that's perfect for you, because you wrote it for yourself, and so it's everything that you want it to be.

And when I put the "golden spike" into it, I looked at it and felt...kind of shocked that I'd finished it. And then I thought maybe there was a reason I'd done all this, that I was supposed to go forward with this. Maybe there was some greater purpose, and I was supposed to do something with it. Because it was such an odd thing for me, to write a book over the summer; it was so odd for me to feel so compelled about it.

The one person who knew what I was doing was my big sister Emily. But my sister's so: *Everything's wonderful! Everything's perfect! You shouldn't change a single word!* [SH laughs] She's so supportive; I knew that it was not a big risk to let her see it. So it was the combination of thinking, *I finished this!* and Emily saying, "Well, you have to try and publish it. You have to do it." I don't know how many times we talked when she'd say, "Stephenie, have you sent anything out yet?"

So then I revised with a purpose. And I revised with a

sense of total embarrassment: *Oh my gosh. If anyone ever sees this I'll be so humiliated. I can't do it.* And then Emily would call again, and again I'd feel this sense like: *Maybe I'm supposed to.* Then I started doing all the research, you know...like looking for an agent. I didn't know that writers had agents. I thought only athletes and movie stars did that.

So that was intimidating and off-putting: *I need an agent? This sounds complicated.* Then I had to find out how to write literary queries. And summing up my story in ten sentences was the most painful thing for me.

SH: Horrible.

SM: It does not work well. [Laughs] And it was also pretty painful having to put out this letter that says: "Hi, this is who I am; this is what I've written; this is what it's about. I have absolutely no experience, or any reason why I think that you should actually pick this up, because who am I? Thank you very much, Stephenie Meyer." [Laughs] That was hard.

And sending them out — I don't want to remember that often. Because you know how you kind of blank out things that are unpleasant — like childbirth and stuff? It was such a hard thing to do. Back in the neighborhood where I lived at the time, you couldn't put mail in your mailbox — kids stole it — so you had to drive out and go put it in a real mailbox. And to this day I can't even go by that corner without reliving the nauseating terror that was in my stomach when I mailed those queries.

That was one of my favorite parts—reading it.

SH: Wow.

SM: See, I didn't take creative-writing classes like you. I didn't take the classes because I knew someone was going to read what I would write. I didn't worry about the writing part — it was letting someone else read it. My whole life that was a huge terror of mine: having someone know what goes on inside my head.

SH: So how have you? Because, obviously, millions of people now have read what you wrote. Is it still terrifying for you, every time you put a book out?

SM: Yeah...and with good reason. Because the world has changed — and the way books are received is different now. People are very vocal. And I do not have a lot of calluses on my creative soul — every blow feels like the first one. I have not learned how to take that lightly or let it roll off of me. I know it's something I need to learn before I go mad — but it's not something that I've perfected. And so it's hard, even when you know it's coming. You don't know where it's coming from — a lot of them are sucker punches.

With every book, I always see the part that I think people are going to get mad about, or the part that's going to get mocked. With *Twilight*, I thought: *Oh gosh. People are just going to rip me apart for this — if anybody picks it up. Which they're not going to, because they're going to read the back and say: A book about vampires? Oh, come on — it's been so done.* So I knew it was coming.

But there were always some things I wasn't expecting that people wouldn't like. I mean, with everything you put out, you just have to know: There are

> With every book, I always see the part that I think people are going to get mad about, or the part that's going to get mocked.

going to be people who really like it, and that's going to feel really good. But there are going to be people who really dislike things that are very personal to me, and I'm just going to have to take it.

SH: But it's so terrifying. I don't know how you even have the courage to do it every time. The book of mine that I thought was going to be my simplest, happiest book, just a sweet little fun book that people would enjoy — that was the one that got slammed the hardest. Like you said, it was things I never could have anticipated that people didn't like.

As I look back on it, I think if I had a chance, I would take those parts out, or change those things that people hated. But I didn't know at the time. And so now, as I'm writing another book — I know there are things that people are going to hate. But I don't know what they are. [SM laughs] If I only knew what they were, I would be sorely tempted to change them to try and please everyone! I do the very best I can, but you can never anticipate what it is that people are going to react to.

SM: See, I have a very different reaction to that, because I *can't* change it — it is the way it is. I mean, there are things I can do in editing — and I can polish the writing. I know I can always do better with that. And I know that, even in the final form, if I could have another three months to work on it, I would never stop polishing, because I can always make every word more important.

But I just can't change what happens, because that's the way it is. That's the story: Who the people are dictates what happens to them. I mean, there are outside forces that can come in, but how the characters respond to them eventually determines where they're going to be. Once you know who they are, there's no way to change what their future is — it just is what it is.

And so my reaction, when the criticism is really bad and really hard, is: *I wish I would have kept this in my computer. I should have just held on to this work and have it be mine alone.* Because sometimes I wonder: *Is it worth it to share it?* But then you feel like you're not doing your characters a service with that—they deserve to live more fully, in someone else's mind.

Yes, I know I sound crazy! [Laughs]

SH: No. I totally, totally understand that. I remember hearing writers talk about how their characters are almost alive, and almost have a will of their own. And I thought they were kinda full of crap [SM laughs] but there is something to it. I think that it's a balance, though. There's the idea of these characters that are alive in my mind, and then there's me, the author. And I have some power to control the story, and to try and make it a strong story—but, then, the characters also have some power to say no.

SM: Yeah.

SH: For me, writing is finding a balance between that sort of transcendental story and my own power of writing—not letting myself overwrite them too much, and not letting them overrun me.

SM: Yeah. See, I find that difficult—because, to me, you create a character, and you define them, and you make them who they are. And you get them into a shape where they are final. Their story isn't, but they are who they are—and they

You can't change who they are to make the story go easier.

do feel very real. You can't change who they are t
story go easier.

So sometimes things happen in the story
character, being who he is, can't do anything d....
written him so tightly into who he is that I cannot change his
course of action now, without feeling like: *Well, that's not in
character — that's not what he would do. There's only one course now.*
And sometimes it's hard, when the course goes a way that's
difficult to write.

On Characters Coming to Life

SH: So how much did you know about Jacob and his future
when you were writing *Twilight*?

SM: Jacob was an afterthought. He wasn't supposed to exist
in the original story. When I wrote the second half of *Twilight* first, there was no Jacob character. He started to exist
about the point where I kind of hit a bit of a wall: I could
not make Edward say the words *I'm a vampire.* There was no
way that was ever coming out of his mouth — he couldn't do
it. And that goes back to what we were talking about with
characters. You know, he had been keeping the truth about
himself secret for so long, and it was something he was so . . .
unhappy about, and devastated about. He would never have
been able to tell her.

And so I thought: *How is Bella ever going to figure this
out?* But I had picked Forks already as the story's location,
and so then I thought: *You know, these people have been around
for a while, and they've been in this area before. Have they left
tracks — footprints — somewhere, that she can discover an older
story to give her insight?*

That's when I discovered that there was a little reservation

. Quileute Indians on the coastline. I was interested in them before I even knew I was going to work them into the story. I thought: *Oh, that's interesting. There's a real dense and different kind of history there.* I've always kind of been fascinated with Native American history, and this was a story I'd never heard before.

This is a very small tribe, and it's really not very well known, and their language is different from anyone else's. And they have these great legends — even one that's similar to the Noah's Ark story; the Quileutes tied their canoes to the tops of the tallest trees so they weren't swept away by the big flood — that I thought were really interesting.

And they have the wolf legend. The story goes that they descended from wolves — a magician changed the first Quileute from a wolf into a man, that's how they began — and when I was reading the legend I thought: *You know, that's kind of funny.* Because I know werewolf people and vampires don't get along at all. And how funny is it that there's that story, right here next to where I set my vampire story.

SH: That's so cool, that kind of serendipity that happens in storytelling.

SM: It felt like, *Now* it's on! Now I know how it has to be! What kismet to happen. And so Jacob was born — as a device, really — to tell Bella what she needed to know. And, yet, as soon as I gave him life, and gave him a chance to open his mouth, I just found him so endearing. He took on this personality that was just so funny and easy. And you love the characters you don't have to work for.

And Jacob was not an ounce of work. He just came to life and was exactly what I needed him to be, and I just enjoyed him as a person. But his appearance in chapter 6 was really it — that was all he was in the story. And then my agent loved this Jacob, and she's never gotten over that. She was one hundred percent Team Jacob all the time.

What a world it would be if we knew that all these little legends around us are absolutely real!

SH: [Laughs] And, you know, I am, too. I love Jacob.

SM: Oh, I love Jacob, too. So when my agent said: "I want some more of him," I thought: *You know, I would love to do that. But I don't want to mess with this too much.* I wanted to have my editor's input before I started making any major changes. And my editor felt the same way: "You know, I like this. Are you going somewhere with this wolf story?"

So when I started the sequel, I knew there were going to be werewolves in it. Because it just seemed like all these stories that are pure fantasy, that are myths, are coming true for Bella. And then there's Jacob. Here's this world that he just thinks is a silly superstition. Then I thought: *What if all of it were real? What if everything that he just takes for granted is absolutely, one hundred percent based in fact?* What a world it would be if we knew that all these little legends around us are absolutely real! I can't even imagine being able to wrap my mind around that.

And so I knew that the sequel I had already started on would be about finding out that they were werewolves. And it wasn't *New Moon*—it was much closer to *Breaking Dawn*. Because the story had originally skipped beyond high school fairly quickly. But my editor said: "Well, I'd like to keep the story in high school, because we are marketing the first book this way. And I just feel like there's so much that must have happened that we miss if we just skip to Bella being a grown-up." And I said: "Well, you know, I could always make my characters talk more—that's not a problem. Let's go back and have this kind of stuff happen earlier." So I had a chance to develop it.

By the time I got to *Breaking Dawn* the characters were so fleshed out—and their allegiances were so strong to whatever they hated or loved—that it made the story just a whole lot richer when I came to it the second time, because there was so much more backstory to it.

SH: I have to go back to the point that Jacob exists because Edward couldn't say, "I am a vampire." So Edward is what created the necessity for Jacob. Just as Edward's existence, and nearness as a vampire, made Jacob into a werewolf. I just think it's interesting that those two characters, who are sometimes friends and sometimes...

SM: Not.

SH: ...enemies, can't seem to live without each other. They completely are born from each other.

SM: Jacob was born from Edward... also because of—I guess you have to say it was a flaw—Edward's inability to be honest about this essential fact of himself. Although it was an understandable flaw—it was something that he was supposed to keep secret. You know, it wasn't something that you just say in everyday passing conversation: "By the way [laughs], I'm a vampire." It's just not a normal thing.

Jacob's character also became an answer to the deficiencies in Edward—because Edward's not perfect. There were things about him that didn't make him the most perfect boyfriend in the whole world. I mean, some things about him make him

> I think that, in reality, it's never one boy—there's never this moment when you know. There's a choice there, and sometimes it's hard.

an amazing boyfriend, but other things were lacking—and Jacob sort of was the alternative. Here you have Edward, someone who overthinks everything—whose every emotion is overwrought—and just tortures himself. And there's so much angst, because he has never come to terms with what he is.

Then here you have Jacob, someone who never gives anything a passing thought and just is happy-go-lucky: If something's wrong, well, okay—let's just get over it and move on. Here's someone who's able to take things in stride a little bit more, who doesn't overthink everything. Someone who's a little rash. He does seem foolish sometimes, just because he doesn't pause to think before he leaps, you know?

That was sort of the opposite of Edward's character in a lot of ways. It gave a balance to the story and a choice for Bella, because I think she needed that. There was an option for her to choose a different life, with someone that she could have loved—or someone who she does love. I always felt like that was really necessary to the story. Because when I write, I try to make the characters react to things the way I think real people would.

I think that, in reality, it's never one boy—there's never this moment when you know. There's a choice there, and sometimes it's hard. Romance and relationships are a tangle, and this messy thing—you never know what to expect, and people are so surprising.

SH: So for you, was the storyline inevitable? Or were there points when you were writing where you thought the characters might have made one choice or another?

SM: It's a funny thing—because it was inevitable. From the time I started the first sequel, I always knew what was going to happen. With *Twilight* I had no idea what was going to happen—it just sort of happened. But after I knew where it was going, I knew Edward and Bella were going out together. As you start to write stories you get twist-offs of things — there are three or four or five different ways it could have gone, and none of them were the right way. I knew what the real way was.

But I do know what would have happened if Edward hadn't come back. You know, I know that whole story — how it went down, and what their future was. I know what would have happened if this character had changed — when he did one little thing here, or that. There are always a million different stories — you just know which one it is that you're going to write. But that doesn't make the others not exist.

SH: And I think that comes through in the writing — that you are aware of these alternate realities. I think the reader becomes aware of these other realities, too. And that's nice, because then it's not predictable. You don't know exactly what's going to happen, because you can see there are other ways it can go.

SM: I think that's why the alternate stories develop — because you have to make it suspenseful; there has to be conflict — and there has to be, hopefully, some mystery about where it's going to go. If it's so clear that something specific is *obviously* going to happen, well, nobody wants to read that. So where's the suspense going to come from? It comes when you start to realize: Well, this other thing *could* have happened. Even though *you* know where you're going with it.

SH: I love that.

SM: It's all very circular. Something happens within something else, but the thing that happened is somehow the birthplace of the other one, too. It's very confusing [laughs] in the head of a writer. At least, for me.

SH: But it *is* like life, in that I think we are all aware of how if we'd made a different decision, we would be living in a different reality. And you can think about the other ones, but you live the one that you're in. The story has to live in the reality it's in.

sm: I think my fascination with that very concept kind of comes through in Alice's visions of the future, where there are fourteen million of them. As characters make choices, they're narrowing down which visions can actually happen. Alice sees flashes of the future possibilities coming from the choices they've made. But if they make different choices, it becomes a whole new future. And that's what happens to us every day. You choose to go to Target today [laughs] and you don't know how that's going to impact everything in your future, because of one decision. I'd always been really fascinated with that concept, and I enjoy science fiction that sort of deals with those strands.

> I do know
> what would have
> happened if Edward
> hadn't come back.
> You know,
> I know that whole
> story—how it
> went down, and
> what their
> future was.

sh: So, if you knew — that morning you woke up after having the dream of Edward and Bella in the meadow — if you knew the reality that would happen after you sat down and wrote it, would you still write it?

sm: You know... I wonder if I could have. The pressure would have been so immense. If I'd been faced with knowing: If you sit down and write today, eventually you're going to have to speak in public, in front of thousands of screaming people; you're going to have to travel around the world and live on Dramamine and Unisom; and you're going to have to be away from your family sometimes; and you'll be more successful than you could ever possibly have dreamed, but there's going to be more stress than you could have ever thought you were able to handle—I don't know what my decision would have been.

Probably, because I'm a coward, I would have jumped back under the covers and said: [high, squeaky voice] "I'm not ready!" [Laughs]

SH: I guess that's why it's good that we don't know what's going to happen in advance. I mean, if Bella had known everything that was going to happen...

SM: See, Bella would have gone through it exactly the same way. I know what my characters would do. They're very, very real to me. I know what they would say if I had a conversation with them. I know if I said this, Jacob would respond like this. And even if he knew exactly how it was going to end, and all of his efforts were going to be for naught, he would not change one tiny thing he did. Because he wouldn't be able to say to himself: *Well, at least I tried.* He needed to know that he did everything that he could—because that's who he is.

And Bella wouldn't change anything, either, because eventually, she was going to get what she wanted, and what she wanted her life to be. And if you're very sure about what you want from your life, if you're absolutely positive—then you can make that decision and say: "I won't make any changes, because this is what I want."

I never had that kind of absolute certainty and focus in regular everyday things when I was a teenager—I was never really sure where I wanted to be in ten years, but Bella knows. And so she walks through it the way a person walks across hot coals—because they know what they want on the other side. [Laughs]

I was never really sure where I wanted to be in ten years, but Bella knows.

SH: What's the most important thing for you to get out of the writing? Why do you do it?

SM: Originally, I wrote because I was compelled. I mean, it wasn't even like a choice. Once I started, it was just...I had to do it. It was similar to the way, when you start a book that's really good or extremely suspenseful, you can't put it down. At the dinner table, you have it under your leg—and you're peeking down there, so your husband won't catch you reading while you're eating dinner. It's like until you know what happens, you'll have no peace.

And there was a great deal of joy in that—although it wasn't a calm kind of joy. [Laughs] There was also some frenzy.

I wrote the rest of the books because I was so in love with the characters in the story that it was a happy place to be. But by then, I had to become a little bit more calculated about the writing process. I spent more time figuring out the best ways to proceed...like how outlines work for me, or is it better to write out of order, or in order? I'm still working on my ways. But it's still for the joy, when I actually sit down and write.

You know, there's a lot of other stuff you have to do as a writer—with editing and touring and answering a million e-mails a day...all of that stuff that's a grind and feels like work. But when I get away from that, and when I'm just writing again—and I have to forget everything else in the world—then it's for the joy of it again.

SH: And, you know, it's funny, because I totally agree. But you meet some writers who are not yet published—and they're so anxious and earnest and need to have that first publication come. What I want to say to them is: Don't hurry it.

SM: Yeah.

SH: The reason you're a writer is because you're telling stories. And everything that comes after publication has nothing to do with why you're a writer. The business stuff, like you said, and the anxiety of how the book is doing and the publicity—and, you know, dealing with negative reviews or negative fan reactions—all that stuff is not really what you're yearning for. What you're yearning for is the story. And the best thing to do is just enjoy that process and that journey.

SM: And you miss it when it's gone. You miss being able to write in a vacuum—where it's just you and the story, and there's no one that's ever going to say anything about it. I find that I can't write unless I put myself in that vacuum.

SH: But the characters have to almost come in on their own....

SM: I know. You have that experience of a character talking in your head, where you don't feel like you're giving them the words. You're hearing what they're saying, and it sounds like it's the first time you're hearing it, and you're just writing it down. Unless you have that experience, you can't understand that this is actually a rational way to be. [Laughs]

SH: I know, I know. Not that anybody who chooses to write books for a living is actually *rational* ...

You miss being able to write in a vacuum—where it's just you and the story, and there's no one that's ever going to say anything about it.

On Endings and Inevitability

SH: I think that, with certain kinds of stories, if you preplan a happy ending, it feels so false. I have had a couple stories like that, where I decided: *This is not going to be the happy ending people are going to want, but we're just going to have to live with it.* And then a character swoops in or something happens to change the problem and take it out of my hands. I think that kind of ending can feel more real and satisfying. You can't force it, though.

SM: No. Usually, the endings become impossible to avoid, because of whatever is growing in the story. There's nothing you can do after it's set in motion — it just keeps going.

Sometimes I don't see something changing at first. It's like... say, when you change direction by one degree, and you end up on a completely different continent, even though you turned just the slightest bit. Things like that'll happen that change the course. But by the time you get to the end, there's no... there's no more leeway for changes.

And so the endings, to me, are always inevitable. You get to a point where there's no other way it can go. If I tried to do something different, I think it would feel really unnatural. But I rarely try. [Laughs] It's like: Let's just let this be what it is. *This is the way the story goes.*

> And so the endings, to me, are always inevitable. You get to a point where there's no other way it can go.

SH: Now, with *New Moon*, there was a way that it could have ended that was very different. And what changed the course of those events was happenstance.

> ## It gets complicated because, as the author, I see the first-person perspective from more than one person's perspective.

sm: It wasn't altogether happenstance — whether you're referring to the paper cut or the cliff-jump or what have you. With the characters being who they are, it's only a matter of time before Bella bleeds near Jasper, and then the outcome is inevitable. It's only a matter of time before Bella finds a way to express her need for adrenaline in a way that nearly kills her, and it's pretty good odds that Jacob will be somewhere close to Bella at that time, clouding up Alice's visions.

It gets complicated because, as the author, I see the first-person perspective from more than one person's perspective. I started writing Bella in the beginning, but there are several voices that are first-person perspective for me while I'm writing. So I know everything that's going on with those people. Sometimes it's hard for me to write from Bella's perspective only, because Bella can only know certain things. And so much of that story was first-person-perspective Edward for me.

I knew it was going to be a problem if Edward took off. [Laughs] I mean, even though *Twilight* had not come out yet, I was aware enough at this point that this is not the way you write a romance. You don't take the main character away — you don't take the guy away. [SH laughs] But because of who he is, he had to leave — and because of the weakness that he has, he was going to come back. It was his strength that got him away, and it was the weakness that brought him back. It was a defeat, in a way, for him — but, at the same time, it was this triumph he wasn't expecting. Because he didn't see it going the way it does in the end.

He's such a pessimist — oh my gosh, Edward's a pessimist.

And one of the fun things about *Breaking Dawn* for me was working through that with him, till he finally becomes an optimist. That's one of the biggest changes in *Breaking Dawn*, that Edward becomes an optimist. So many things have lined up in his favor that he can no longer deny the fact that some good will happen to him in his life. [Laughs]

And so for me, *New Moon* was all about what Edward had to do to be able to call himself a man. If he hadn't tried to save Bella by leaving, then he would not have been a good person, in his own estimation. He had to at least try.

And it was really hard to write, because I had to live all that. Oh gosh — it was depressing! I was into listening to a lot of Marjorie Fair. [Laughs] But I was able to do some things as a writer that I was really proud of, that I felt were a lot better than what I'd done in *Twilight*. I was able to explore some things that felt really real to me — even though I'd never been in Bella's position. It didn't feel like sympathy; it was empathy. Like I was really there, like I really was her. And so that was an interesting experience . . . but it was hard. It does take up the majority of the book, and that was tricky. It's gratifying to me that, for some people — a minority — *New Moon* is their very favorite book.

SH: I have a book like that — *Enna Burning* — which has been my least popular book all around. But there is a core of people for whom that is their favorite. And it is tremendously gratifying, because that was a difficult book to write for me, too. It's a dark book, and I poured so much into it. I'm really proud of that book. But to find that it spoke to someone else besides me makes me feel not quite so lonely as a writer.

SM: As a writer I don't think you always realize how lonely it is to feel like you're in this world all by yourself. That's why you end up sharing it, because there are some people who will get it.

sm: What surprises me is not that there are people who don't get my book—because that seems really obvious and natural—but that there are people who *do*. And I do think that, as the series went on, the story started to get more specific, and possibilities were getting cut out. As you define something, all the "might have beens" die as you decide things. And so I'm not surprised that people had problems with wrapping it up, because it became more specific to me as time went on.

Every book has its audience.

Every book has its audience. Sometimes it's an audience of one person—sometimes it's an audience of twenty. And every book has someone who loves it, and some people who don't. Every one of those books in a bookstore has a reason to be there—some person that it's going to touch. But you can't expect it to get everybody.

sh: No.

sm: And you can't say: "Well, there's something wrong if this book didn't mean the same thing to everyone who read it." The book *shouldn't* make sense to some people, because we're all different. And thank goodness. How boring would it be if we all felt the same way about every book?

sh: I really believe that, as writers, we do fifty percent of the work—and then the reader does the other fifty percent of the work—of storytelling. We're all bringing experiences and understanding to a book.

When you start with *Twilight*, you've got one book and one story. There's still an infinite number of possibilities of where that story can go. So if you've got, maybe, ten million fans of *Twilight*, by the time you get to *New Moon*, you're narrowing what can happen, because these characters are making choices, and so maybe you've got seven million possibilities. By the time you get to *Eclipse*, you're down to, say, three million people who are going to be happy with the story. After *Breaking Dawn* . . .

SM: There are only twenty people who are going to get it. [Laughs] I think it's a weird expectation that if a story is told really well, everybody, therefore, will have to appreciate it. People bring so many of their own expectations to the table that a story can't really please everyone.

SH: But is it still hard for you? Do you still have a desire to please everyone?

SM: Of course. I would love to make people happy. It's a great thing to hear that your book made someone's day brighter. It's amazing to think that you're doing some good, with a thing that just brings you joy in the first place. It's not why I do it, but it's a great benefit. It's the frosting.

It's hard when people who really wanted to like it don't. That makes me sad, because I know that there was a story for them, but it's just not the one that I could write. I think that sometimes for people who are that invested, it's because they're storytellers themselves. And maybe they need to cross that line — cross over to the dark side . . . join us! — and start creating their own stories.

> People bring so many of their own expectations to the table that a story can't really please everyone.

SH: That is an impossible situation, though. Because here you've created these characters in *Twilight*, and then readers are creating their own versions of those characters. So then you go on and write another book, and what your characters did...isn't necessarily what their characters would do. Maybe from their point of view, you're manipulating their characters into doing things they wouldn't do, even though of course you're not.

SM: It *is* funny....I mean, it's hard because I am very thin-skinned. I don't take anything lightly. When I read a criticism, I immediately take it to heart and say: "Oh my gosh—maybe I *should* have done that! Oh, I *do* do this wrong!" I question myself very easily. I don't question the characters, which is why I'm able to maintain my voice when I write—because that, to me, is the one thing that's rock-solid. It doesn't matter what my doubts are—they are who they are. And that's a good thing.

> I don't question the characters, which is why I'm able to maintain my voice when I write—because that, to me, is the one thing that's rock-solid.

SH: It is. And despite all of the criticism, there are so many more fans than there are people who are angry about the books, but you hear the negative stuff so much louder.

SM: Oh, always loud. You know, it reminds me of the movie *Pretty Woman.* Whenever that comes on TV, for some reason I can't change the channel. [SH laughs] And there's the one part where she says: It's easier to believe the bad, you know.

SH: Yeah.

SM: That's one of the things that I think is a constant struggle: to make the negative voices not as loud as—or at least just equal to—the positive voices. I know a lot of people who feel the same way. It's easy to doubt yourself.

> But if you kill off your characters—
> even minor characters—you still sob
> for everything that they were
> and could have been.

Maybe the answer is not to write a sequel. I'm considering that. You know, write one-shots—just one contained story, which I have a hard time doing. I guess I'll just have to end it by killing the characters—because then it'll be over, right? [Laughs] But if you kill off your characters—even minor characters—you still sob for everything that they were and could have been.

SH: In the book I'm writing right now, there is a death—a major death. And every time I do a rewrite, as I get near that scene, and I know I have to face it again, my stomach just clenches and I get sick with dread. And as I go through that scene, I'm sobbing the entire time. It is not easy....

SM: No. When you know in advance that you're going to put yourself through that, it gives you some pause. And then you also have to know that it's a different story than what people are expecting. That's also the trouble with sequels.

SH: The most letters I get from fans is for one book called *Princess Academy*, and the most requests I get from fans is for a sequel to that book. And then they tell me what happens in the sequel, you know? [SM laughs] And that's how I know that I shouldn't write it.

SM: Right.

SH: Because they've already told their own story. And that's what I want, anyway...because I didn't tie everything up completely. I just gave them an idea of where they might go in the future.

SH: I loved *Breaking Dawn*. It's hard to pick a favorite, but it might be my favorite. It was so the book I wanted, and so what it felt like it needed to be for me. And I have to say I loved the pregnancy and birth stuff, because I love the horror. Your books are romance, but there's also this real, wonderful undercurrent of horror that's different from any kind of horror I've read. And I love what horror can do: shine a light on what is real. And you make it bigger and more grotesque — just so you can see more clearly how grotesque what really happens is.

SM: I do think that sometimes I put horror in unusual places for horror to exist, and I take it out of places where it might have been easy to have it. You know, that birth scene really was horror for me. We live in a time where having a baby is not much more dangerous than giving blood. I mean, it's horrible, but it's unlikely that you're going to die.

But that's something new for this century. You know, there was a time when childbirth was possibly the most terrifying thing you could do in your life, and you were literally looking death in the face when you went ahead with it. And so this was kind of a flashback to a time when that's what every woman went through. Not that they got ripped apart, but they had no guarantees about whether they were going to live through it or not.

You know, I recently read — and I don't read nonfiction, generally — *Becoming Jane Austen*. That's the one subject that would get me to go out and read nonfiction. And the author's conclusion was that one of the reasons Jane Austen might not have married when she did have the opportunity . . . well, she watched her very dear nieces and friends die in childbirth! And it was like a death sentence: You get married and you will have children. You have children and you will die. [Laughs] I mean, it was a terrifying world.

And Bella's pregnancy and childbirth, to me, were a way to kind of explore that concept of what childbirth used to be. That made it very specific for readers who were interested in that, and it did take it away from some of the fans who were expecting something different. I was aware that it was taking Bella in a new direction that wasn't as relatable for a lot of people. I knew that it was going to be a problem for some readers.

SH: Yeah.

SM: My agent and my editor and my publisher all said: "Um, can we tone down the violence here? It's making me a little sick." [Laughs] But I was kind of proud of myself. I was thinking: *I actually wrote something violent enough to bother anybody? I'm such a marshmallow. Wow—you go, Stephenie!* [SH laughs] And I toned it down for them, and I made it a little bit less gruesome. Although I kept some of the gruesome stuff in, too.

SH: I know you hate spoilers. You don't want any leaks.

SM: You know, though, I wonder with this last book...I wonder if it would have been an easier road for readers who have difficulties with *Breaking Dawn* if they'd known more in advance. If people had asked me, "Can vampires have babies with humans?" And, instead of saying, "I can't answer questions about those crazy things that might or might not happen"—which is what I said because I didn't want to make it super-obvious it was going to happen; I mean, that just seems wrong—I could have just said, "Yeah, they can."

> I was aware that it was taking Bella in a new direction that wasn't as relatable for a lot of people.

Maybe it would have been easier for them if they'd been expecting it.

SH: So you knew, even before *Twilight* was published, that in your world a vampire and a human would have a baby?

SM: Oh yeah. I've got it all worked out in my head. My scientific reasoning works for me, but for people who don't buy into it, I can only agree. It's true. Vampires cannot have babies...because vampires aren't real. [Laughs] And vampires can't have babies with humans, because humans can't actually copulate with vampires—because vampires are not real. [SH laughs] It's a *fantasy*.

> My scientific reasoning works for me, but for people who don't buy into it, I can only agree.

SH: Right. And yet people believe those characters, and the possibility of those vampires is real enough that they have to say: Wait—those aren't the rules.

SM: It's flattering in a way, that this is so real to them that they feel like there are things that can't happen in this fantasy.

SH: Now I have a nerd-girl question. Does Nessie's bite do anything? Did it do anything to Bella, when Nessie bit her?

SM: Nessie is not venomous.

SH: You did say in the book that Nessie wasn't venomous. I mean, it's just about food. [Laughs] Extreme nursing. [Laughs] But I guess when Bella did so well with the transition, as the new vampire, I was thinking: *I wonder if Nessie's bite did that for her*.

SM: [Laughs] I hadn't even thought of that. No, Bella's transition was unique among new vampires, in that she knew what was coming. None of the other Cullens had any warning. It was just, all of a sudden, this overwhelming need to drink blood—just without any kind of readying. You know how sometimes you have to brace yourself for something? Bella was braced—she was ready. And it wasn't like it was easier for her than it was for them. She'd just already made up her mind that that's the whole key to everything. She's the only person in the entire history of the Twilight universe who chose beforehand to be a "vegetarian" vampire.

SH: I liked that Jasper had a hard time with that. His personal struggle was that it wasn't inevitable.

SM: You know, when you're really used to giving in to instant gratification, that makes it harder not to. If you've never given in, it's easier to keep it that way.

SH: I remember when you were writing *Breaking Dawn*, you told me that this story made you happy. What is it about this story that made you happy?

SM: Well, it goes back to what we were talking about before, about Edward. And it's an interesting thing to me, how I worry about my characters like they're real people. Like how after I wrote *Eclipse*—even though I knew exactly what was going to happen in *Breaking Dawn*—until I actually got to the part where Jacob sees Renesmee for the first time, and his life comes together for him, I worried about him all the time.

And Edward, this whole time, has had a lot of happiness—and, yet, he's not trusting any of it to last. He's feeling like he's doomed, and there's no abating it—that something bad is going to happen to him because of who he is. And now I could finally watch that change and watch him come to accept happiness—even more than Bella does. Because Bella sees the end coming and sort of loses hope, but he never does.

After he accepts that he can have happiness, he just clings to it. And I really enjoyed that, and I enjoyed writing the end. I had to write all four books to get to those last two pages. Just to have Bella and Edward really be able to understand each other—that made it worth writing four books.

sh: And he really makes the journey—even though vampires, as you've said, are frozen sort of in that moment when they first become vampires. But he changes so much in *Breaking Dawn*, and so quickly in becoming a father. What was it like to take him through that journey, as well?

sm: You know, all that really changes is his outlook—which, of course, changed everything. But who he is, what he loves, how he does things—it all stays the same. He did get a lot of things that he hadn't even let himself think about wanting, though. I mean, getting to have this daughter that he had never envisioned—that he never could have conceived of—was this unbelievable thing for him, you know. And he accepts it pretty quickly. But the bigger wonder for him is Bella being happy. He thought he was going to ruin her life, and he made her happy. And that really was everything for him.

> Just to have Bella and Edward really be able to understand each other—that made it worth writing four books.

sh: So when you were writing, you'd have a literary classic that helps inspire your books. With *Breaking Dawn* you said it was *A Midsummer Night's Dream*, and you couldn't say the second one.

sm: *Merchant of Venice*—which I do say in the story. You know... [SH gasps] It's the book Alice pulls a page from to leave her message for Bella.

sh: I wondered about that.

sm: And, you know, originally it was *Jane Eyre* that Alice tore a page from. But *Jane Eyre* had nothing to do with the story. It just got in there because Jane Eyre was one of my best friends growing up. She was a really big part of my life. [Laughs] That's why it was in there, because that book was such a big part of my growing-up experience and the way I view the world.

Because, actually, I do think there's a Bella–*Jane Eyre* relationship. Jane Eyre's a stoic. She does what she thinks is right, and she takes it—and she doesn't mouth off about it. You know, in her head, maybe, she suffers, but she never lets that cross her lips. And I do think that there's some of that stoicism—not in the same way, but there's a little bit of that—in Bella.

The real story that I felt tied to was *A Midsummer Night's Dream*, where, in this lovely fantasy, the heartbreak of people not loving the right people—which happens all the time—is made right in this glittery instant of fairy dust. I love that book—and that's the part I love about it. I enjoyed the character of Bottom in the play, but that's not what I read it for. I read it for the magic.

That really is sort of where the imprinting idea came from, which existed in *Forever Dawn* (the original sequel to *Twilight*). And I introduced it earlier, so that it would be something already explained, and I wouldn't have to go into it later. It was about the magic of setting things right — which doesn't happen in the real world, which is absolutely fantasy. But if we can't have things made right in fantasy, then where do we get them made right?

So here's where *The Merchant of Venice* comes in. The third book of *Breaking Dawn* — which is a full half of the novel — was a lot longer than I thought it would end up being. And the whole time I had to have tension building to the final confrontation . . . but I wanted to give the clue that this was not going to be a physical confrontation. This was a mental confrontation — and if one person loses, everybody dies.

SH: Yeah.

SM: There's no way to win this one with a physical fight. Everyone's going to lose if that happens. So it's a mental battle to survive, and it's all about figuring out the right way to word something. Figuring out the right proof to introduce at exactly the right time, so that you can force someone into conceding — just trapping them in their own words.

SH: Because in *The Merchant of Venice*, Portia stayed with her beloved by being clever.

SM: Exactly. And just with her cleverness and by using the right words, she's averting bloodshed and murder from legally happening right in front of her and ruining her life.

SH: When *The Merchant of Venice* came up in the story, I immediately started going through my mind: What's the story of *The Merchant of Venice*? What does it mean to this book?

SM: And in the end of *The Merchant of Venice*, all the lovers get their happy ending. That's one of the reasons I like it. [Laughs]

SH: *The Merchant of Venice* and *A Midsummer Night's Dream* — I like that.

SM: Can you tell I like the lighter side of Shakespeare? I mean, I like the tragedies, too, and *Romeo and Juliet* is probably my favorite. Which is probably very immature of me, but that's the one that always gets me, and I think that's part of who I am. [Laughs] That's why my books are the way they are — because those are the stories that come alive for me.

SH: It works so well in *New Moon*. I did also identify with *New Moon*, though, because there's something a little Rochestery about Edward for me.

SM: Yeah.

SH: And then Edward leaves — and in *Jane Eyre*, Jane is the one who leaves.

SM: Yeah.

SH: And she's with St. John, but you know Jane and Mr. Rochester need to be together. And you don't know: Are they going to be together? And then there's that little bit of the mystical — when she hears him call her name. And she returns to him, and she saves him. And I love that in *New Moon*, too. I never get tired of it.

SM: I have never thought of it in that context, and there is so much that works with that comparison. I mean, I'm going to have to think about this some more later. Because, wow — there is a lot. I have never written a book where I said: "This one has a *Jane Eyre* emphasis." But I think you're absolutely right.

You know, isn't it funny how books influence us? They become a part of who you are. I mean, how much of my childhood that I remember has actually happened to me, and how much of it is the events that were in *Anne of Green*

Can you tell I like the lighter side of Shakespeare?

Gables? You know, I'm not really sure, because reading was so much of who I was. And those stories were every bit as real — and much more exciting — than the day-to-day boringness that was my life.

But Jane Eyre was this person that I felt like I knew. I think that there's a lot of Mr. Rochester in Edward, and I think there's a lot of Jane in Edward. Because he would take himself away from a situation that's not right, just like she does! And then she's like Bella, coming home at the end. But, my goodness, how close that is. I thank you, Shannon Hale. You have enlightened me.

SH: [Laughs] Well, you're welcome.

SM: You know, I think…maybe readers who aren't writers might look at something like that — using inspiration from other books — as kind of a form of plagiarism. But, actually, the more you get into writing, I think you realize that there is no new story.

SH: Every story has been told, so you're just telling it in a new way. One big reason why it's so important to be well read when you're writing is because when you write, you can dialogue with everything else that's ever been written. The more you read, the more you get to converse with all these other great works. And that makes them more exciting.

SM: Right. I really do believe that, you know, there are no new

But, actually, the more
you get into writing, I think you
realize that there is no new story.

stories — except maybe Scott Westerfeld. [Laughs] He's, like, the one person who always makes me think: *No one has ever done exactly that before!* [Laughs] But, you know, every story has a basis in all the stories of your life.

SH: I think the most common question any writer gets is: Where do you get your ideas from? And that's the impossible question to answer, because, like you said, they come from...
SM: A million places.

SH: Everything: everything you experienced or imagined or thought or smelled or read or...
SM: A person you walked by in the airport once that just — you know, you saw a look in their eye, and you started spinning a story about what was going on in that person's head.

SH: And, of course, a story isn't just one idea. The more you write, the more you're drawing on a million different pieces of things. That's why it takes so long to write a story, because I start out with an idea...but the more I write, I realize it's just the kernel — because I'm adding more and more depth and intrigue. And along with the characters, it builds to a whole universe.
SM: It really does. I was trying to describe this recently, about how you have this universe of possibilities. And every time you pick one thing for your story — like Bella is brunette — all her blond and redheaded possibilities disappear. And then, when you pick the kind of car somebody drives, there are a million other vehicles, makes, and models that suddenly die. And as you narrow it down, you're just taking pieces of it and destroying whole worlds that could have been. It's a very interesting process.

SH: I've got chills.

SH: So when you were writing *Eclipse*, *Twilight* hadn't come out yet.

SM: *Twilight* was not yet in stores. I had finished the rough draft of *Eclipse*. I still had a lot of editing to do, but it stayed pretty much in its present form.

SH: Was *Twilight* successful immediately?

SM: Yes—more so than I thought it would be. I mean, nothing, obviously, to what's going on right now. But when I was out on tour, it did, for one week, hop onto the *New York Times* list—which, for me, was like the epitome of everything. It was like: *For the rest of my life, I get to say I'm a* New York Times *bestselling novelist.*

SH: [Laughs] Right.

SM: So, for that one week, it felt like that was it—that was all I ever needed. [Laughs] So it started out really well. Booksellers were really great about getting the word out and hand selling it—which is awesome. Before *New Moon* came out, I had a couple of events with like a hundred people—and they were all excited and ready for what was coming next. That was really, really gratifying.

SH: So at what point did you have to start balancing the success and the pressures from the outside while you were still writing?

SM: I think the first real pressure was with *New Moon*, when the advance reading copies came out. *New Moon* had those two spoilers. Edward leaves, Jacob's a werewolf. Once you know that, most of the suspense is gone from the book. Whether you figure it out or not, it's still huge. So those two things ruin any possibility of suspense in the story, pretty much. Then a review written by someone who had an advance reading copy was put online and it gave away every plot point of the whole book six months before the book came out.

That was the first time, I think, my publisher started to realize the power of the Internet with this particular series. Because it just started this huge outpouring of letters and people were so upset. Has this really happened? Why did this person tell us this? Can we read the book now? Is it out? What's going on?

So I felt pressure then—but the book was already written. And then, with *Eclipse*, it started to feel like a lot of people had their specific ideas about what should happen. That was the first time I was really conscious that people were writing the story differently in their heads. I had also started to get that people-didn't-like-Jacob vibe, which really took me by surprise. I think it's because they weren't hearing his first-person the way I was. So then they got to, later.

> I had also started to get that people-didn't-like-Jacob vibe, which really took me by surprise.

SH: I don't know if you felt this way . . . but I never thought I would write from the point of view of a boy. Maybe because I read a lot of books where men wrote from a woman's point of view, and I found them unrealistic characters.

SM: Yes, yes!

SH: Especially, you know, books written in the last century. But I was like: That is such crap! A woman wouldn't think that—wouldn't do that—and it bothered me. So I thought I would never write from the point of view of a boy.

But then I met a character—almost exactly the same way

you did. With *Goose Girl* there was a minor character named Razo. And then the book after that, *Enna Burning*, he was in it again — a minor character. And so by the time I got to the third book in the series, and I started to write from his point of view, I'd already known him for two books. And I was thinking: *I'm not writing this from the point of view of a boy; I'm just writing this person that I know.* And the gender wasn't an issue. Was it sort of like that with Jacob?

SM: Yeah. You know, I felt a little presumptuous when I started working on writing *Twilight* from Edward's perspective, because I'm not a boy. But Edward was so much a part of the story, and such a strong voice, that it didn't seem to matter. So I'd kinda gotten that out of my system by the time I decided that I needed to write from Jacob's point of view. But, again — I wasn't writing a boy, I was writing Jacob. It was not like a universal male thing.

I do think that I have a sense of boys, because I have three brothers; I have three sons; I have a husband and my father and my father-in-law. I've seen a lot of teenage boys in action, and they're actually very fascinating, hilarious, and heartbreaking creatures. I mean, they can beat the crap out of each other, and then be laughing with their arms around each other with black eyes five minutes later. I do think that I've observed enough to be able to get the outside right, and that I knew Jacob enough that I could get the inside right.

SH: I love the Jacob chapters in *Breaking Dawn*. But I need to go back to *Eclipse*. You've talked about *Wuthering Heights* influencing *Eclipse*.

SM: Yeah. You know, and that's one of the ones that's interesting to me, because *Wuthering Heights* is not a book that I like. There are characters in it that fascinate me, but, as a whole, I don't enjoy reading that book. I enjoy reading the very end of it, and I enjoy reading a couple pieces in the middle, but

Either one could have been the one that was wrong for her, and either one could have been the one that was right.

most of the time I just find it really depressing. When Edward speaks about it, he has my opinion being spoken through him: It's a hate story — it's not a love story.

The pull between Edgar and Heathcliff is strong — and, you know, Cathy makes the wrong choice. Both of them had something to offer, and she chose the part that didn't matter. Even though I don't like to read *Wuthering Heights*, I think about that part a lot. It's one of those things that stays with you.

You could look at Edward and Jacob from one perspective and say: Okay, this one is Heathcliff and this one is Edgar. And someone else might say: No, wait a second. Because of this reason and that reason, that one is Heathcliff and the other one is Edgar. And I thought that was great, because either one could have been the one that was wrong for her, and either one could have been the one that was right. I like that confusion, because that's how life is.

SH: And when we're reading *Wuthering Heights*, we're reading it from an outsider's perspective. From the future looking back. So, as a reader, we know who she should choose. And we see her choose the wrong one, and that's why it's a tragedy. But with *Eclipse* we don't know who she will, or maybe even should, choose.

SM: Well, in *Wuthering Heights* we see who Cathy should choose. But we also see the person that she should choose is a horrible person.

SH: [Laughs] Right.

SM: And so, maybe, she should choose the nice guy, but, you

know, Heathcliff was who she loved. But, at the same time, was he really healthy for her? What would have happened to them if they had gone off together?

SH: Now, this reminds me of something that I'm really interested in. We're talking about who she should or shouldn't choose. I think sometimes readers assign a moral to a story, and think that, from the outside, we're writing the story in order to teach people how to live. [SM laughs] But I can't think about a story's moral when I'm writing—I can only think about whether this story is interesting to me.

SM: And when I write stories, they're very specific—it's about this one situation, and one person who's not like anybody else in the world. So that person's decisions and choices are not a model for anyone else. And it bothers me when people say: Well, this story is preaching this, or the moral is this. Because it's just a story. It's about an interesting circumstance and how it resolves. It's not intended to mean anything for anybody else's life.

> And when I write stories, they're very specific—it's about this one situation, and one person who's not like anybody else in the world. So that person's decisions and choices are not a model for anyone else.

SH: I do think there are some writers out there who are trying to teach something through their stories. And I've read moralizing books that just don't work.

SM: Well, you have to be really talented to make it work. You know, C. S. Lewis does it well. I love his books, and he is very much out to put a message into his stories. But he's so good that he gets away with it.

SH: I think it's really important as

readers to expand our understanding of the world, to get really close to characters that are different from us — and watch them make mistakes, or make good choices, and then think: *Would I do it that way?*

SM: Sometimes people tell me: "So girls are coming away from your books with this fill-in-the-blank impression." Maybe something like: "You should hold out for the perfect gentleman." In which case I could say, "Well, that's a positive message: You should not let people treat you badly. If you're dating somebody who doesn't put your well-being first, if they're being mean or cruel to you — get away from that." And that's a great message: If you're with a mean, nasty boyfriend, run away right now. [Laughs]

SH: Right.

SM: But that's not the message of the book. Just because Edward's a gentleman, and he cares about Bella more than himself — and maybe that's something that you would wish for in a romance — it doesn't mean that that's a message I was trying to write.

SH: On the flip side, if someone comes away thinking that the moral of the story of *New Moon* is that there's only one person who's right for you in the whole world, and if they leave you, then life is not worth living...

SM: Exactly! Some things you could take away from books could be turned into a positive thing in your life, but you could also make them into something negative, and that would be horrible. So I think it's easier just to look at the books as: This is a fictional account — I wasn't trying to teach anyone anything — I just wanted to entertain myself. And I did. I was really entertained. [Laughs]

SH: I'm always trying to figure out where the line is with author responsibility. What we write and then send out there is going to affect people's lives. But I have absolutely no control about how people will *interpret* what I write. If readers need to find a moral, or a lesson, in it, they teach it to themselves. And I don't think I can control what it is that the readers teach themselves. Do you think that reading does more for you than just provide entertainment?

SM: It does a lot for me—but I don't hold the writer responsible for what I get out of it. When I read about someone like Jane Eyre, I say: "I want to be stronger. I want to know myself so well, and to know right and wrong so well, that I can walk away with nothing." I just loved her moral sense. But I don't think that Charlotte Brontë meant for me to use that as a guide to life. If you can find something inspiring in characters, that's awesome, but that's not their primary purpose.

SH: And it can't be, or it kills the story. The primary purpose has to be telling the story.

SM: It has to be entertainment.

When I read about someone like Jane Eyre, I say: "I want to be stronger. I want to know myself so well, and to know right and wrong so well, that I can walk away with nothing."

On Finding Story Ideas

SH: People often ask me—and I'm sure you get this, too: How do you come up with so many ideas? Once you start writing, the ideas just keep multiplying.

SM: Yeah. I hate to travel, but I see so many stories in airports. We were in, I think, Chicago, waiting for a flight, and this whole story just played out right in front of us. There was a man and a woman, and she kept leaning toward him and touching him, and he was always shifting away from her just a little bit, and not meeting her eye. And it was so clear, the inequality in their feelings, and where I imagined their future was heading, I felt I could just run with it. When you spend time around people, you know, there are so many stories that it just can make you crazy when you want to write them all down.

> When you spend time around people, you know, there are so many stories that it just can make you crazy when you want to write them all down.

SH: Yeah, there's never a problem with finding ideas; it's just finding the time to write it, and the words to tell it.

SM: For me, it's time. I don't usually experience the kind of writer's block that people talk about. My kind of writer's block is when I know what needs to happen, and I just have a stumbling block—some transition that I can't get past.

The longest part of writing *Breaking Dawn* was writing right after all the action sequences. Bella becoming a vampire—that was very easy—but after that section I had to skip four months ahead. And that transition took me more time than any other section of the book. It's only half a chapter long—it's not very many words—and the amount of time per word put into that section is probably ten times what it was in any other part of the book.

There are just some things that are not exciting, but I like to write minute by minute. And when I have to write, "And then three months passed," it kills me.

SH: [Laughs] I don't believe in writer's block. I sort of embrace it, which feels good. And it doesn't mean that writing isn't hard, and sometimes I can't come up with the right way to do it. The way I get over it is by allowing myself to write really badly, and then I rewrite a lot. The first draft for me is the worst. I hate writing first drafts—it's so painful for me—but the story time for me comes in the rewrite. I already have some clay there to work with, and then I rewrite. But your first drafts, I think, are different for you.

SM: I love writing first drafts. I don't think about what I'm doing. It's hard for me to go back and reshape it. I can see it needs help, so I have more trouble—maybe because it doesn't feel like clay anymore. It's more like marble—I have to chip it off.

SH: Then you know what we need to do? [Laughs] You need to write first drafts, and then I'll rewrite them. And then we'll be happy.

SM: We'll combine forces.

SH: But then you'll see the book that I've turned it into, and you'll be like: *What?!*

SM: Well, then you'll get the rough draft and think: *I don't want to do anything with this!* [Laughs]

SH: Would you ever collaborate with another writer? Do you think you could do that?

SM: I don't know if I could. You know, sometimes I wonder,

because it looks like a whole lot of fun. I really enjoy other writers, and their ideas and their processes. It's fascinating. Maybe if it were something where we were switching off voices... But I just don't think I could write another person's character,

If I don't care about the character, I can't finish it.

because I have to really care to be able to write. If I don't care about the character, I can't finish it. Or if, for some reason, the character has become an unhappy place for me, then I just can't go there.

I had one draft of about five chapters of a story that really was human — no fantasy, which is always a drawback for me — and then something happened in my family that made it a very painful place to be. It wasn't something I had seen coming. I didn't think it would ever have any relevance in my life that way. And it became too painful a place to work.

So I have to be in just exactly the right place to be able to write. With someone else's character... I just don't think I could care deeply enough about them to put out the effort that it takes to write a story.

ON CELEBRITY AND SUCCESS

SH: The person who you are naturally — when you're at home with your family, and you're working — is going to be different than the person signing books and greeting fans. How do you balance those two personas? Have you created two different personalities?

SM: I had to. The person who I am at home, with my family,

is shy, not comfortable around strangers, kind of a homebody. And so to be able to speak to large groups—to be able to meet a bunch of strangers, which is hard for me; to be able to travel outside of my comfort zone—I had to get stronger. I had to do things that weren't fun for me and just suck it up, you know. [Laughs] Because the real me couldn't even imagine having to do that, so somebody else had to do it. [Laughs]

SH: Is it exhausting to live that public persona?

SM: It is. It's funny....Just recently—I've got some friends who are friendly with some fans, and they had a party, and I was invited to it. And they're like: "It's just going to be really mellow. Don't worry about it—you know, it's just for fun." But I knew I would have to go and be Stephenie Meyer. I couldn't just be Stephenie. And I'd just gotten off the tour, and I just couldn't face it right then. I needed to just stay home and be me.

SH: I've found it's hard for some people to understand that. For me, there's nothing as exhausting as doing a book signing or a school presentation or something. And I think part of it is that I don't think I am interesting enough to make it worthwhile for anybody to hear me talk—or to stand in line to meet me. And so I'm pouring my energy out onto these people, and trying to give them as much as I can. I mean, I'm sure you've had this, too—more than I have—where people will fly in from several states away just to meet you for those few seconds in line. And I think: *How on earth could I make this worth their time?*

And, in fact, I felt so much pressure not to be a letdown that, on my last tour, I brought along a rock star.

SM: Exactly. And, in fact, I felt so much pressure not to be a letdown that, on my last tour, I brought along a rock star. And I felt so much better. [Laughs] Justin Furstenfeld from Blue October came and played some of the music that inspired my writing, and we interviewed each other onstage. I enjoyed what he did so much that I thought: *You know what? These kids are getting an amazing show. This is special—this is something that is worth them coming out for.* If I ever tour again, I will not leave the house without a rock star by my side. [Laughs] That is the new rule. Or . . .

SH: A juggling act—a magician.

SM: A magician would be good! Because, well, honestly, in person, there's nothing really that great either of us can do. We write books, so our big finale is sitting in front of a little computer, in a little room. And it's not something exciting to watch. It's the story that's the exciting part, and anybody can get that at the bookstore.

I've had the experience where I got to meet one of my personal idols, just because a friend pulled some strings and I got backstage at a concert. I lived off that for months. So I try and remember that, and think: *You know what? It means something to them, even though I can't understand why it would be anything special.*

SH: You know, it is true. I really can be such a fangirl. And I get so excited when I meet with writers. . . .

SM: On the last tour I got to go out to lunch with Terry Brooks. The first real book I ever read was *The Sword of Shannara.* I was sitting next to this man who has so much experience—and so many years of doing this—and I'm thinking: *This book opened the entire world of reading to me. The gift that this man has given me, unconsciously, is nothing I could ever, ever repay.* It was just this really amazing experience.

SH: It took me a long time to admit that I was a writer. I wouldn't give myself permission to take the time—or to take it seriously—for a long, long time. But you started off in a different way. You already had three kids.

SM: I did not call myself an author without making some kind of snide comment for at least two years after the book was sold.

SH: Two years?

SM: I had this really strong sense of paranoia—like it wasn't real, that the whole deal was a practical joke—for a very long time. Because the contract negotiation took a good nine months, so for all of that time someone could have been stringing me along. It wasn't until the check came—and didn't bounce—that I really started to believe it.

SH: Have people changed toward you—family, friends, and acquaintances?

SM: You know, because when I started writing I had a bunch of little babies, we've moved a couple times. And you lose track of people, anyway, so I haven't held on to many of my friends from before I started writing, just because of location.

It's the same way with my college roommates. We're lucky if we get a phone call in once a year anymore. Then I've gotten enormously busy—I've changed—I don't have as much time for social things. And I do think that I probably lost some friends just out of sheer neglect. Because I wasn't going to neglect my kids.

SH: Yeah.

SM: And that summer with *Twilight*, I couldn't do anything social. Why would I spend my time away from Forks when I could be there? I'm getting better at balancing it, and I have some really great friends now, which is nice. I have a lot of extended family, too, and they've all been very cool and supportive. But because there are so many of them, we haven't been able to spend a lot of time together.

I have seventy-five first cousins on one side of my family, so it's not like we can get together and party very often. Most of us have several kids. My dad had a stepmom with five kids; his dad had seven.... It's just a really big family. [Laughs] A big warm family, and nobody's been uncool about it. It's all been very nice.

> And that summer with *Twilight*, I couldn't do anything social. Why would I spend my time away from Forks when I could be there?

SH: I think family is good....They knew you as an obnoxious young person. [Laughs]

SM: Very obnoxious. Yeah, I'm just Stephenie to them.

SH: I don't think any success I've had has gotten to my head, because I can't really take it seriously, or absorb it, anyway. But if I ever got close, I think my family would be there to tear me back down. [SM laughs] Which is what family's for.

SM: Yeah, my husband's really good at keeping me humble, you know? Because he's such a math person. If something's not quantifiable — if it doesn't fit into an equation — it can't possibly be important. And so, to him, books are like: *Oh, you know...isn't that nice? Little fairy stories.* To me, books are the whole world, and it's such a different viewpoint. So that helps. And then, like you, I don't trust this to last for a second.

SH: Yeah.

SM: And when negative things happen with my career, I kind of expect them — more than I expect the positive. It's almost like: *Yes, this is what I thought was going to happen! I saw this one coming!* Because I am a pessimist — raised in a long tradition of fine pessimists [SH laughs] who have never expected anything good for decades. So I come by it naturally. [Laughs] So with every book that comes out, I think: *Oh, this is it. This is the last time anybody's going to want to publish me.* And maybe it's healthier than thinking: *I am the best! I'm so amazing!* I don't think that's a healthy way to be. It'd probably be nice to be somewhere in the middle, but... [Laughs]

SH: In some ways, I would love to have that armor — the wonderful author's ego — that I am right, and I know what I'm doing, and I'm brilliant.

SM: Yeah, that might be nice.

SH: So, we're both mothers. And I think that mothers are famously guilt-ridden creatures. [SM laughs] I mean, we never succeed — we're always failing at something. So have you had to deal with guilt of, you know, taking the time — allowing yourself to take the time to be a writer, and to pursue this?

SM: Occasionally. It doesn't bother me that often. I think it's because my kids are really, really great. They're good and they're happy. I've seen kids who are treated like the center of the universe, and I don't think that's entirely healthy. I think it's really good for my kids to see that I have my own life outside of them — that I'm a real person. I think that's going to help them when they grow up and have children — to realize that they're still who they are.

> I think it's really good for my kids to see that I have my own life outside of them — that I'm a real person.

And then I am pretty careful about *when* I write. Now it's mostly when they're in school. When they were little, though, I never shut myself away in an office—I'd always written in the middle of their madness—so I'd be there, and I could get whatever they needed. They know I'm listening. And they're also pretty good about saying: "Okay, Mommy's writing right now. Unless I'm bleeding, I'm not going to bug her."

And I also write at night. When they come home from school, we do homework and I hear about their day and I make them snacks. The nice thing about writing is, you can do it on your own schedule. But you do lose sleep. You know, I feel like I haven't slept eight hours in ten years.

SH: It's like having a newborn, writing a book, isn't it?

SM: It is. Well, because you lie there in bed—and, oh, heaven help you if you start thinking about plotline. If you start getting a little bit of dialogue in your head, you're doomed—you'll never get to sleep.

SH: It is so true. I can sleep pretty well at the beginning of the night. If, for whatever reason, I wake up—or my son comes in and wakes me up anytime between the hours of two and five—and if my mind, for one second, goes back to the book I'm writing right now, I'm done for the rest of the night. I can't go back to sleep, because my mind starts working over and over it. I've had to train my brain to do that, on purpose, so that I'm always writing, even when I'm not.

> If you start getting a little bit of dialogue in your head, you're doomed—you'll never get to sleep.

SM: You at least put things in the back of your head, so that you're solving the problems.

SH: Exactly—so when I sit down to write it's more productive, because I've been working over it in my brain. But, like you say, when you do that in the middle of the night, you're doomed.

SM: Well, one of my problems right now is that I have not committed to a project at this point in time, and I'm waiting to be done with the publicity. And that's never *really* going to happen, so I need to just commit to one. I have about fourteen different books, and every night it's a new one. And I'm coming up with solutions for this one point that really bothered me in one story. I thought maybe I couldn't write it because of this one point. But then I'll wake up at four o'clock in the morning with a perfect solution, and then I can't go back to sleep.

SH: I have found if I just write it down, then my mind can stop working over it.

SM: Exactly.

ON READING AND WRITING FOR YOUNG ADULTS

SH: So far, all of your stories have something of the fantastic in them. You don't read only fantasy, though.

SM: Oh, I love mainstream fiction, and there are a lot of books that I really love that are without absolutely any fantasy elements. But, for me, the fantasy ones are for writing. There's an extra amount of happiness, that extra oomph, in getting to make your own world at the same time that you're writing it. I like that part.... Megalomania...You know, having control over an entire world? [Laughs]

SH: That's funny. Like we were talking about earlier, when you're a writer there's so much that can happen to ego, both good and bad and everything in between. But young-adult authors tend to be pretty down-to-earth, don't you think?

sm: Well, I think writing YA keeps you humble. Because everybody says to you: "Oh...you write for children. Isn't that nice?" It can be so patronizing sometimes, and, absolutely, it keeps you humble. It makes it so you can't possibly become the "I am an author" author. There's no way to do that when you write for children. [Laughs]

sh: I think there's also an element of: *It isn't all just about me.* We've both written adult books. I think, when you're in the adult market, it's all about how many books you sell and what awards you get. But when you're writing in the children's market, it's about the children, too. And you're part of this team — with librarians and booksellers and parents and teachers — and you're promoting literacy and some good stuff beyond just: *I'm writing a book, and now pay me for it.* So I think people tend to be more even-tempered and more balanced in the children's world.

sm: Because I didn't set out to write for children, I would never have thought that my books would promote literacy. Someone would have to be a real reader to ever pick one of these up, just because they've run out of everything else. [Laughs]

And one of the little "icing things" of this career is to have these kids come up to tell me that this is the first book they've ever read for pleasure, and that they've moved on. Now they've read this other one, and they've read that one, and now they're so excited about some other book

> And one of the little "icing things" of this career is to have these kids come up to tell me that this is the first book they've ever read for pleasure.

they've found. And to have written the first book that got them excited to be a reader—oh, that's an amazing gift.

sh: It is. The best compliment that I ever get is not that my books are their favorite, but that mine was the first that made them fall in love with reading.

sm: And now they've gone on. You know, I had a great childhood, and one thing that made my childhood so special was that because I loved to read, I lived a thousand adventures—and I was a thousand heroines, and I fell in love a thousand times. And now, to open up those worlds for somebody else...I know how great it is, and I wish I could give everybody that gift—to find the book that does it for you.

I wish I could give everybody that gift— to find the book that does it for you.

I did an interview for *The Host* once, and the camera guy who was setting everything up said: "So this book is about aliens?" I said: "Yeah, kind of." And he said, "Well, you know, I think I've read three books in my life. I hate reading, ever since school—it was such a torture." And I just thought: *How sad! There's some book out there that's perfectly tailored for him, and he doesn't know.*

sh: Right.

sm: But he's not going to pick it up, because he had a bad experience. I really feel like one of the important things you can do for kids in school is not just give them the classics that teach them about excellent form and really great writing style, but also throw in a couple of fun things that teach them that reading can be this amazing adventure. Let them love some story, so at least they know not all books are "hard" or "difficult," but that they can just be fun.

SH: I agree so passionately about that. And I think some of the key is to have a lot of variety. Because not every genre, or every storytelling style, is going to be right for everyone.

SM: Some people are going to latch on to Shakespeare, and they're going to be like: [gasps] "The insights!" And then some people are going to need an action story with car chases and gunfights—they're going to need that to get them started.

SH: Every student should have a chance to find at least one book they fall in love with. Then they'll be more likely to go on and keep reading for life.

SM: Exactly. When I was in school I had some really great teachers. And lucky for me, I had already discovered books that I really liked. The classics came easily to me—I read them early, and so it was familiar ground: *Oh, good. I'm doing Jane Austen again. Whoo!* But a lot of kids come into it and they're hit in the face with a great big difficult-to-understand text—if they don't have the background to appreciate the experience, it just sours them on the whole thing. And it's sad.

SH: I meet so many adults who stopped reading for years. And they tell me that a friend pressed them to read a book, and more often than not it was *Twilight* . . . and then they find that they do like to read, after all, and they go on to read other books.

So, Stephenie Meyer, thank you. For changing the world—making it a better place—and reminding so many people that we love to read.

SM: I do what I can. [Both laugh]

VAMPIRES

ampires, the central supernatural creatures of the Twilight Saga, have existed in myths and local lore for centuries. While the Saga's vampires share certain similarities with the vampires of legend, they have many more unique characteristics and supernatural abilities that are specific to the world of Twilight.

PHYSICAL CHARACTERISTICS

n the Twilight universe all vampires were originally human. As vampires, they retain a close physical resemblance to their human form, the only reliably noticeable differences being a universal pallor of skin, a change in eye color, and heightened beauty.

REACTION TO SUNLIGHT:

In direct sunlight, the disparity between human and vampire becomes more obvious. The cellular membrane of the vampire is not as soft or permeable as in a human cell; it has crystalline properties that cause the surface of vampire skin to react prismatically, giving the vampire a glitter-like shimmer in sunlight.

> "EDWARD IN THE SUNLIGHT WAS SHOCKING. . . . HIS SKIN, WHITE . . . LITERALLY SPARKLED, LIKE THOUSANDS OF TINY DIAMONDS WERE EMBEDDED IN THE SURFACE."
> —Bella (*Twilight*, Chapter 13)

BEAUTY:

The common factor of beauty among vampires is mostly due to this crystalline skin. The perfect smoothness, gloss, and even color of the skin give the illusion of a flawless face. The skin reacts differently to light, creating an angular effect that heightens the perception of beauty. Additionally, the stone-like firmness of the vampire body creates a look similar to muscle, making any size human appear more fit as a vampire.

Like humans, vampires are drawn to beauty. When choosing a human for the transformation process, vampires are as likely as humans to be motivated by a beautiful face and body.

PALLOR:

Pale vampire skin is a product of vampire venom's transformative process. The venom leeches all pigment from the skin as it changes the human skin into the more indestructible vampire form. Regardless of original ethnicity, a vampire's skin will be exceptionally pale. The hue varies slightly, with darker-skinned humans having a barely discernible olive tone to their vampire skin, but the light shade remains the same. All forms of skin pigmentation — freckles, moles, birthmarks, age marks, scars, and tattoos — disappear during the transformation.

EYE COLOR:

While all vampires have similarly pale skin, they can have a certain variety of eye colors. Vampires who haven't fed for a few weeks will have solidly black irises. Recently fed vampires will have deep red eyes if they drank human blood, and medium gold–colored irises if they drank animal blood. Vampires who have been newly transformed will have very bright red irises, regardless of diet. It is possible to disguise this feature with colored contact lenses, but the lubricant in vampire eyes breaks the contacts down quickly. One pair will

"While vampires are frightening and deadly, they are also alluring. They can be beautiful; they can be sophisticated; they have qualities that we actually aspire to: eternal youth, strength, and intelligence.
The dual side to vampires makes them hard to resist." —Stephenie

last only a few hours. Vampires also universally exhibit dark circles under their eyes. These circles, like the changing irises, denote thirst in a vampire. They appear darker and more obvious when the vampire has not recently fed.

TEETH:
Vampire teeth appear the same as human teeth; the canines are not longer or more pointed than human canines. However, vampire teeth are unbreakable, razor sharp on their edges, and strong enough to cut through almost any substance, including vampire skin.

MOVEMENT:
Less noticeable than these physical features is the vampire's tendency toward stillness. Unlike humans, who grow uncomfortable after holding one physical position for a time, vampires are most comfortable when perfectly motionless. A common vampire reaction to stress is a statue-like immobility.

Vampires breathe reflexively, as do humans, but they have no need for oxygen. They are able to consciously stop breathing for an indefinite period, but they find the sensation uncomfortable. Vampires rely on their sense of smell above other senses, similar to many animal predators. The lack of smell is what causes the discomfort from not breathing.

PETRIFICATION:
Some very old vampires are visibly different from others because of this stillness. If a vampire remains unmoving often enough over thousands of years, dust actually begins to petrify in response to the venom-like liquids that lubricate his eyes and skin. Eventually, a vampire's skin begins to appear thin and translucent, like the skin of an onion — though the strength of the skin is not compromised. A milky film covers the eyes, making the irises appear pink in color. Again, the vampire's eyesight is not compromised.

FLUIDS:

Internally, the vampire's system contains many venom-based fluids that resemble, and in some cases perform the same function as, the human fluids that were replaced. Only the saliva-like liquid in the vampire's mouth is venomous. A fluid similar to this venom works as a lubricant between the hard cells of the skin, making movement possible. Another lubricates the vampire's eyes so they can move easily in their sockets. However, vampires do not produce tears, as tears exist to protect the eye from damage by small foreign objects, and those objects would not be able to harm a vampire's eye. Throughout the body, this pattern is repeated, with venom-like fluids performing the functions that are still necessary to the vampire. Most notably absent is the circulatory system.

PHYSICAL CHANGE:

Vampires are frozen in the state at which they are transformed. They do not grow older, taller, or wider, or experience any other physical change, including unconsciousness (vampires never sleep). Their fingernails and hair do not grow. Their hair does not change color.

ABILITIES AND LIMITATIONS

A vampire's physical and mental abilities far exceed those of a human being. Vampires can run in excess of a hundred miles per hour. They are able to lift objects hundreds of times their own weight. Their senses are similarly boosted, giving them the ability to see, hear, and smell things imperceptible to humans. Their skin is harder than granite, rendering their bodies nearly indestructible. Their minds work many times faster than humans' are capable of, and all vampires have perfect recall.

Vampires are frozen in the state at which they are transformed.

IMMORTALITY:

Vampires do not age from the moment their transformation is complete. Vampires have no natural life cycle; they exist in this progressionless status indefinitely. This is a conditional form of immortality, as they *can* be permanently destroyed by fire. However, their speed and strength make it necessary to incapacitate them before burning them. Only another supernatural creature has the ability to incapacitate a vampire, by tearing her limbs from her body (thus vampires are in no danger from human beings). A vampire who is incapacitated but left unburned has the ability to reconstitute herself.

One facet of the absence of aging is that vampires do not develop emotionally or mentally past the age at which they are transformed. A transformed child would remain childlike forever, unable to mature in any aspect.

NUTRITION:

Vampires do not have a circulatory system. Their bodies are harder than human bodies, but their cells are selectively porous. They receive nutrition only from blood, which, once drunk, is absorbed throughout the body. Blood satiates their thirst and makes them physically stronger, but it is not necessary for life. Vampires cannot starve to death; they only get progressively weaker and thirstier as time goes on. They are not able to digest solid food. If a vampire swallows a solid as a subterfuge, that substance will sit in his stomach until he forces it back out through his mouth.

Human blood is the most appealing to vampires—and hardest to resist. However, they can receive the same nutritional strength from animal blood. Vampires do not need to feed as often as humans do; drinking the blood of one human is enough to satiate a mature vampire for a week or two.

Supernatural Abilities

ost vampires find their key personality characteristics intensified by the vampire transformation in the same way their physical abilities are strengthened, but relatively few have abilities that can be classified as supernatural. More common would be a human with a love of learning becoming a vampire with an insatiable scholarly curiosity, or a human with a deep value for human life becoming a vampire with the strength to avoid human blood.

But a few vampires do develop additional abilities that go beyond the natural. These extra abilities are due to psychic gifts in the original human that are intensified in the resulting vampire. For example, a human who was very sensitive to other people's moods might develop the vampire ability to read thoughts or influence emotions. A human who had some limited precognition might develop into a vampire with a strong ability to see the future. A human with a good instinct for hunting might become a powerful vampire tracker.

The proportion of supernaturally talented vampires to "normal" vampires is greater than the proportion of psychically gifted humans to "normal" humans. This is due to the same factor of temperament that results in more beautiful humans being selected to become vampires. Vampires are also drawn to gifted humans when they look to create companions. Some vampires actively seek out the gifted in the hope of utilizing that extra ability in their coven.

"I've always loved superheroes,
so the vampires I created actually have
a lot more in common with superheroes than
with horror-genre vampires." —Stephenie

Newborn Vampires

A newborn vampire—defined as any vampire who is less than one year from his date of transformation—is different from a more mature vampire in behavior and appearance. The newborn is plagued by an unrelenting thirst and will feed as often as possible. The thirst is so maddening in the first year that most newborns are more animalistic and wild than their older counterparts.

They are marked as physically different by their vibrantly crimson irises, though in other ways they look the same as mature vampires. Their behavior is more diverse than their appearance. As they age, their behavior generally becomes more rational and constant.

The Transformation Process

The transformation from human to vampire begins with a vampire bite. Once the venom coating the vampire's teeth enters the bloodstream of a human, it moves through the human's body, changing each cell as it passes. The spread of the venom is swift, but the reconstruction of the cells takes time. This process is excruciatingly painful, comparable to the feeling of being burned alive. The process lasts for roughly two to three days, depending on how much venom is present in the circulatory system and how close to the heart it entered. There is no way to circumvent the burning with painkillers; the most narcotics can do is immobilize the body.

One benefit to the human is that vampire venom is capable of repairing all kinds of damage to the body. A human who had sustained a crippling injury would be made whole again as a vampire. Venom does have limits, though; it could not, for example, regrow a lost limb.

The transformation is difficult from the vampire perspective as well. Even mature vampires have trouble resisting flowing human blood. The scent affects them as it does sharks; they can go into a feeding frenzy. For this reason, vampires tend to not hunt in packs. During the irrational frenzy, members of a coven are likely to turn on one another in competition for the blood. The taste of human blood makes it even harder for the vampire to resist. It is nearly impossible for a vampire to not drain the human — thus killing him or her — once the vampire has tasted blood. Only vampires with a great deal of self-control are able to remain focused enough to bite a human and then let him live long enough for the venom to effect the change.

Only vampires with a great deal of self-control are able to remain focused enough to bite a human and then let him live long enough for the venom to effect the change.

SINGERS:

There is another factor that can compli-
cate this process for the vampire. The smell of each human is different, and certain humans can smell more appetizing than is usual to vampires. The more appealing any human's scent (and taste) is to a vampire, the more difficult it will be for that vampire to bite the human and still leave him alive.

Infrequently, a specific human will smell nearly irresist-ible to a specific vampire. That human is known as a "singer" among vampires, because his or her blood "sings" for the vampire in question. Singers are individual phenomena; a person whose blood sings for one vampire will not have the same effect on all vampires. While there are some humans whose scents are more appealing to vampires in general, that appeal does not reach the level of a singer. Singers are considered by most vampires to be a great find, the drinking of whose blood is an experience to be savored.

VAMPIRE HISTORY

The oldest known vampire history is that of the Romanian coven (named for the location in which they originated, which would later be known as Romania), the most powerful coven during the time before 400 A.D. Their power resulted from their numbers; the Romanians were the first to expand their single coven beyond the normal two or three vampires. They had to cooperate in a way unusual to vampires to accomplish this (see "The Transformation Process" for information about feeding frenzies), but their self-control extended only to their fellow vampires. The Romanian coven made no secret of its existence and both preyed on and enslaved humans indiscriminately. The Romanians were overthrown by the Volturi coven between 400 and 500 A.D.

The Volturi coven originated in Greece during the Mycenaean Era. It began with three original members — Aro, Caius, and Marcus — and then grew to a core of six as the members found romantic partners: Sulpicia, Athenodora, and Didyme. Ambition was their bonding element, much the same as with the Romanians. The Volturi actively recruited gifted humans into their coven. Eventually, using the basic argument that vampires should conform to simple laws of mutual convenience, the Volturi launched a successful war against the Romanians, who would not conform to these laws. The Volturi hunted the Romanians until there were only two survivors of the original coven, Stefan and Vladimir.

The Volturi preserved ruling status over the years through coven strength and a policy of general noninterference. The Volturi coven is both the largest and easily the most talented group of vampires in existence, but they could still be overthrown if they gave the other vampires of the world a

The Volturi coven is both the largest and easily the most talented group of vampires in existence.

reason to unite against them. For this reason, the Volturi do not get involved with other vampires frequently, and act against other covens only when there is a complaint that could negatively affect other vampires. Consequently, they are commonly perceived by vampirekind as a positive force.

There are very few vampires alive who predate the Volturi. Most have been born into a world where the laws constructed by the Volturi are an accepted fact of life. This protects the Volturi from the realization that their laws are merely an excuse to exert control over the vampire world.

THE SOUTHERN WARS:

One notable event during the modern rule of the Volturi was the war that engulfed most of the southern part of North America during the early 1800s. Precipitated by a vampire known as Benito, the conflict began when Benito created a small army of newborns in order to conquer the older covens that controlled the majority of what is now Mexico and Texas. His tactic was so successful that most covens in the area created their own armies of newborns to defend against him and the other covens that were also reacting. The resulting disappearance and death toll was so alarming to the humans in the area that supernatural causes were suspected and reported (though the epidemic was later blamed on cholera). The Volturi eventually descended in force on the area and exterminated every coven that had experimented in the creation of newborn armies.

Vampire Law

he basic law of the vampire world is that all vampires must protect the secret of their existence. This affects vampire life in a variety of ways. Vampires must be circumspect enough in their hunting and behavior that humans do not become aware of them. Or, if a human were to become aware, the vampire at fault would be responsible for silencing that human. Neither of these is a particularly difficult task.

As long as a vampire's interaction with humans does not garner wide attention, there is no consequence to the vampire. Many vampires have relationships with humans to varying degrees, and as long as these stay within boundaries, the Volturi are not aware. However, if something suspicious—something that might indicate the existence of vampires—was known widely enough to appear in the human news, or even in human fiction, the Volturi would hunt the rumor to its source.

TEACHING THE LAW:
Vampire laws are not written down; to write them would in itself be an infraction. Vampire laws are passed by word of mouth from creator to newborn, and each creator is responsible for the behavior of his creation. If a newborn is abandoned by his creator (a rare occurrence, given the difficulty of creating a new vampire), the newborn, though ignorant of the law, is still punishable for any rash acts.

IMMORTAL CHILDREN:
Sometimes group behavior will bring on a stronger response from the Volturi. The Southern Wars are one example. Another example would be the outlawing of immortal children.

Immortal children were humans who had been transformed into vampires at a very early age. There was no absolute age limit set as to what constituted an immortal child;

it was a subjective definition, based on the child's ability to behave himself in a way consistent with vampire law.

Like all vampires, immortal children were frozen at the mental and physical age at which they were transformed. Post-transformation, these small children continued to exhibit childish behaviors, including impulsive acts, tantrums, irresponsible activities, and a general lack of circumspection. These behaviors were incompatible with the law of secrecy, and immortal children often attracted the notice of humans.

Another aspect of immortal children was their appeal; they were both beautiful and endearing. Covens were utterly devoted to their immortal children, and would protect them at all costs.

The Volturi found themselves punishing individual covens for the behavior of their immortal children with a much greater frequency than other occurrences of lawlessness. Because of the devotion inspired by immortal children, the Volturi were forced to destroy full covens in order to destroy an immortal child. After some study into the matter, the Volturi decreed that immortal children were not capable of following the law, and therefore it was no longer legal to create an immortal child. Anyone responsible for creating such a child would be destroyed whether that child had broken the law or not.

The Volturi continued to experiment with and study immortal children for centuries, but has never reversed its decision.

"The only time I really did any research on vampires was when the character Bella did research on vampires. Because I was creating my own world, I didn't want to find out just how many rules I was breaking." —Stephenie

VAMPIRE MYTHS

There are many myths about vampires, most of them created and put into circulation by the Volturi. Their purpose is to disguise the existence of vampires behind stories that could never be proven to have a basis in truth—and to make it possible for a vampire to easily "prove" that he is not a vampire to a human who believes the myths (by touching a cross or standing in front of a mirror, for example). Additionally, these myths give humans a sense of control over the supernatural. Though vampires are never in any danger from humans, the Volturi contend that human ignorance makes hunting more convenient for all.

MYTHS CIRCULATED BY THE VOLTURI INCLUDE:
- Vampires are burned by the sun.
- Vampires are always unconscious during daylight hours.
- Vampires have no reflection.
- Vampires can be harmed by crosses, holy water, and garlic.
- Vampires have visible fangs.
- Vampires can assume the form of a bat.
- Vampires must have permission to enter a house.
- Vampires can be killed by a wooden stake stabbed into their hearts.

TRUTHS THE VOLTURI WERE ABLE TO ERADICATE OVER TIME:
- Vampires have red or black eyes (gold wasn't a known option at the time).
- Vampires reflect sunlight prismatically.
- Vampires never sleep.
- Vampires are nearly indestructible.

➤ Vampires are flammable.

➤ Vampires are pale.

➤ Vampires drink blood.

➤ Vampires are beautiful.

➤ Vampires are immortal.

One benefit of the surviving truths is that there are humans who actually seek out vampires in an attempt to gain beauty or immortality. This benefits the Volturi when they want a human front as a façade.

VAMPIRE LIFESTYLES AND PSYCHOLOGY

Though there are a range of vampire lifestyles, the most common is nomadic. The majority of vampires move frequently, never settling permanently in one place. This pattern is partly an attempt to hide from the notice of humans. If too many humans disappear from one area, suspicion might be aroused and the Volturi might take notice. Also, if a vampire interacts regularly with humans, eventually the humans will notice that the vampire isn't aging. Another aspect is boredom. Vampire lives are so long that many keep up a continuous search for novelty.

A few covens are exceptions to this rule, and maintain semipermanent or permanent homes. Doing this requires a great deal of subterfuge — if the coven wants to avoid suspicion and keep the Volturi from becoming involved — and most vampires don't care for the hassle.

BONDING FACTORS:

Most commonly, a coven is made up of two members. One feature of the unchanging nature of vampires is that they mate for life. Once they fall in love, that feeling never fades. As a general rule, only the bond between mates is strong enough to survive the competitive drive for blood. Larger covens are less stable, and usually end because of internal violence.

The second bonding force, and one that is — unlike romantic love — able to keep a large coven stable, is ambition. Vampires are competitive by nature, and some vampires have been able to evolve this competitive disposition into a greater cause capable of uniting many individuals into a secure whole. The pursuit of power is that bonding cause for vampires. The Romanians were the first to do this successfully for a significant length of time.

The third, and rarest, bonding force is the vampire conscience. Very few vampires are born with or develop a value for human life. The consumption of human blood is such a known aspect of vampire life that few ever question it; the driving thirst for human blood seems irresistible. However, those who do learn to value human life in spite of this reality are able to subsist on animal blood. Vampires who live this way are sometimes referred to as "vegetarians." Animal blood is unappealing to vampires, and thus a difficult diet to maintain. Those who make the sacrifice, though, experience related benefits. In the absence of human blood, the competitive drive disappears. Vampires are able to form bonds of love in addition to the bond between mates. The weak coven alliance is replaced by a strong, family-style union.

VENGEANCE:

Another prevalent vampire trait, along with strong romantic bonds and the intense competitive streak, is that of a vengeful nature. Related again to their unchanging state, vampires are not forgiving; they do not move past an insult or injury. The most common example of vampire vengeance is the aftermath of the loss of a mate. When a vampire loses his mate, he never recovers from it. He cannot rest until the party responsible (usually another vampire, given the strength necessary to destroy a vampire) is eradicated. Centuries can pass without lessening the ferocity of his need for vengeance.

VAMPIRE HYBRIDS

The biological passing of vampire traits is one of the least common exceptions to normal vampire life. Out of the thousands of vampires on the planet, there are only five known hybrids in existence, and these five all originated from only two sources.

Male vampires do have the capacity to pass on genetic material with a human female partner. However, it is beyond the ability of most vampires to be so close to a human physically and still resist the lure of her blood. Also, vampires are so much stronger than humans that any loss of self-control at such close proximity can quickly lead to mortal injury to the human.

Female vampires still carry ova similar to human ova, but the unchanging state of their bodies results in a total absence of a reproductive cycle. Even if the female vampire could somehow continue this cycle, her frozen body would be unable to grow and change to accommodate a growing and changing fetus.

One hybrid, Renesmee Cullen, was created by accident as the result of a rare romantic bonding between a vampire and a human. The other four hybrids, Nahuel and his three sisters, were all purposely created as an experiment by a vampire named Joham.

Vampire hybrids have both vampire and human traits. They are much stronger and faster than humans, with sharper senses, but not as strong, fast, or sharp as a pure vampire.

They are strong enough, however, that human females are rarely able to survive the gestation period. The movement of a hybrid fetus causes extreme injury to the more fragile mother. If the gestation is survived, the birth is not. The usual method of delivery for a hybrid is for the hybrid to make her own escape from the womb. The hybrid must utilize her teeth, which have more in common with vampire teeth than human teeth, to pierce the amniotic sac—a membrane nearly as durable as vampire skin. This is too traumatic to the human body to be survived. Only the introduction of vampire venom to the mother's system can heal the injuries incurred; only one mother has ever survived to become a vampire.

Like the amniotic sac, a hybrid's skin is almost as durable as her vampire parent's skin, but it does not have the same prismatic reaction to sunlight. Hybrids can also have supernatural abilities, though not all do. Like humans, hybrids have a circulatory system and are warm-blooded. They can eat solid food, but generally find blood more appealing. They also sleep. Their irises come in the usual range of human colors, and do not change in response to diet. In the first few years of their lives, hybrids grow and change like humans do, though at an extremely accelerated pace. After roughly seven years, the hybrid reaches physical adulthood and settles into the same unchanging state and conditional immortality that vampires enjoy. The hybrid mind develops much faster than the physical body; a hybrid has the mental capacity of an adult human by the time of her birth. Hybrids learn quickly to communicate with their caretakers, picking up their first language mere weeks after birth. This capacity for physical and mental maturation is what sets the hybrid apart from the immortal child.

Covens

The Cullen Coven

The Cullen coven, one of the largest stable vampire covens, is also one of the few that does not drink human blood. The Cullens call themselves "vegetarians" because they instead choose to drink the blood of animals, putting more value on human life than do most of their peers. They consider the Denali clan their cousins, as that coven shares a similar philosophy. Abstaining from human prey takes the competitive aspect out of the hunt, and as a result they are able to form stronger family bonds than traditional vampires.

The Cullens prefer to stay in one place as long as possible, choosing cloudy climates where they can go outside during the day without revealing their inhuman nature. But after six or seven years in one location, they are usually forced to move on, before their lack of aging is noticed.

They own several residences so that they can return to places they have especially enjoyed—but only after enough time has passed that they won't be recognized as the same people who once lived there.

Each member of the coven maintains several well-tended identities, complete with the documents to support them, which allows the Cullens to establish themselves in new locations as necessary.

Each time the Cullens move, the relationships they claim to share with one another may shift, too. In one place, two members might pose as father and adopted son; in another, brothers, or uncle and nephew. Regardless,

> Each time the Cullens move, the relationships they claim to share with one another may shift, too.

the bonds of love and respect between members of the coven are immutable.

The Cullen family began when Carlisle transformed Edward. They then traveled across the United States together, gradually adding other members to the coven. The family is currently made up of eight vampires—four of whom have supernatural abilities beyond those of a normal vampire—and a vampire hybrid, who also has psychic gifts.

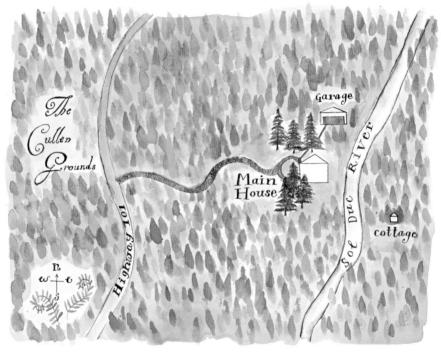

"AND THEN, AFTER A FEW MILES, THERE WAS SOME THINNING OF THE WOODS, AND WE WERE SUDDENLY IN A SMALL MEADOW, OR WAS IT ACTUALLY A LAWN? THE GLOOM OF THE FOREST DIDN'T RELENT, THOUGH, FOR THERE WERE SIX PRIMORDIAL CEDARS THAT SHADED AN ENTIRE ACRE WITH THEIR VAST SWEEP OF BRANCHES. THE TREES HELD THEIR PROTECTING SHADOW RIGHT UP TO THE WALLS OF THE HOUSE THAT ROSE AMONG THEM, MAKING OBSOLETE THE DEEP PORCH THAT WRAPPED AROUND THE FIRST STORY."

—Bella, on her first impressions of the Cullen grounds (*Twilight*, Chapter 15)

NAME: Carlisle Cullen

DATE OF BIRTH: circa 1640

DATE OF TRANSFORMATION: 1663, at approximately age 23

SOURCE OF TRANSFORMATION: An ancient vampire living in the sewers of London

PLACE OF ORIGIN: London, England

HAIR COLOR: Blond

EYE COLOR: Blue (human); gold/black (vampire)

HEIGHT: 6'2"

PHYSICAL DESCRIPTION: Carlisle has a well-toned medium frame, collar-length hair, and movie-star good looks. He has a slight English accent from his youth, although he can speak with a flawless American accent.

SPECIAL ABILITIES: He does not possess a quantifiable supernatural ability.

EDUCATION/OCCUPATION: He has attended many universities, both as a student and as a professor. He has studied a variety of subjects, ranging from science to music, and typically works as a doctor.

HOBBIES: He collects art and books.

VEHICLE: A black Mercedes S55 AMG

FAMILY/COVEN RELATIONSHIPS: He is married to Esme Cullen and considers Edward Cullen, Rosalie Hale, Emmett Cullen, Alice Cullen, and Jasper Hale his children; Bella Cullen his daughter-in-law; and Renesmee Cullen his granddaughter.

PERSONAL HISTORY:

Carlisle's father was his only family. His mother died giving birth to him, and he had no siblings.

An Anglican pastor, Carlisle's father was a crusader against evil, leading hunts through London and the surrounding areas for witches, werewolves, and vampires. Self-righteous and compassionless, Carlisle's father caused many innocent people to be burned.

When he grew too old, he put Carlisle in charge of these raids. However, Carlisle had a very different temperament. He was not as quick to see evil where there was none. He was smart and persistent, though, and he eventually discovered an actual coven of vampires living in the sewers. He gathered a group of hunters and they waited for darkness to fall, suspecting that this was when the vampires would come out.

When a thirsty vampire did emerge, he attacked the hunters. Two were killed and Carlisle was wounded. Knowing that anything infected by the monster would be burned, Carlisle hid himself in a nearby cellar. During the transformation he never cried out, despite the agony he felt. When it was finally over and he realized what he had become, he was horror-struck. He tried to destroy himself by jumping from great heights and attempting to drown himself. When these methods didn't work, he tried to starve himself to death.

A newborn vampire's thirst is overwhelming, but Carlisle found the strength to resist. Months passed, and Carlisle, filled with self-loathing, kept to the loneliest places he could find, places where he wouldn't stumble across a human. He understood his willpower was weakening.

The vampires of this coven
were very different from the
sewer-dwellers of London.
They were refined and cultured,
and Carlisle admired their civility.

One night a herd of deer passed by and, crazed with thirst, Carlisle attacked without thinking. After feeding, he felt his strength and sense of self return, and he realized he could live without killing human beings. He would feed on animals, just as he always had, drinking their blood now instead of eating their flesh.

Knowing that his father would hate him no matter how he lived his new life, Carlisle never returned home. He watched his father a few times from a distance but never made contact.

Carlisle had always been eager to learn, and now he had unlimited time. By night he studied music, science, and medicine in the universities of Europe. During his travels Carlisle encountered others of his kind. Most vampires Carlisle crossed paths with responded to his natural amicability; in this way he is a novelty among vampires.

While studying in Italy in the early 1700s, Carlisle was discovered by the Volturi, an ancient coven of vampires founded by Aro, Caius, and Marcus. The vampires of this coven were very different from the sewer-dwellers of London. They were refined and cultured, and Carlisle admired their civility. But Aro, Caius, and Marcus never stopped trying to change Carlisle's aversion to what they called his "natural food source," and Carlisle never stopped trying to persuade them of the value of his pro-human philosophy. Over time, a legend formed among the humans in Italy of a *stregoni benefici*, or "good vampire," who was the avowed enemy of evil vampires, though Carlisle was always on friendly terms with the Volturi. After about two decades in Italy, Carlisle decided to travel to the New World. He was growing increasingly lonely and longed to find other vampires who believed there was a life for them that didn't involve murder.

When Carlisle reached America, things didn't change for him the way he'd hoped. He didn't find other vampires like him. He was, however, able to begin a career in medicine. He felt that by saving human lives he could compensate in some measure for the existence of vampires.

Carlisle couldn't risk more than a cordial acquaintance with his coworkers, for fear of exposing what he was, and his enforced solitude and lack of intimacy pained him. So he began to deliberate creating a companion. However, he was reluctant to steal a life the way his had been stolen.

For decades he debated with himself about whether or not it was right to doom another to the life of a vampire. The plea of a dying woman, Elizabeth Masen, helped him make his decision. In 1918, Carlisle was working nights at a hospital in Chicago as an epidemic of Spanish influenza raged through the city. Elizabeth's husband died in the first wave of the epidemic, but Elizabeth and her teenage son, Edward, managed to stay alive for a while longer. Carlisle was with Elizabeth on her

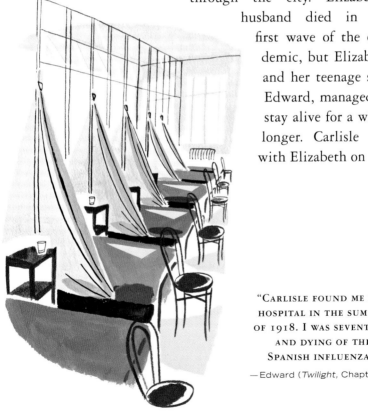

"CARLISLE FOUND ME IN A
HOSPITAL IN THE SUMMER
OF 1918. I WAS SEVENTEEN,
AND DYING OF THE
SPANISH INFLUENZA."

—Edward (*Twilight*, Chapter 14)

last night. She begged him to save her son, intuiting that Carlisle was more than what he seemed. She died less than an hour later. Her son lay in the room with her, his own death imminent. The goodness and purity in Edward's face finally convinced Carlisle to take action. Carlisle bit Edward, effecting his transformation.

Both Carlisle and Edward were surprised to discover Edward's ability to read minds, but due to his experience with the Volturi, Carlisle quickly understood the phenomenon.

Carlisle and Edward began traveling together, using the cover story that Edward was the younger brother of Carlisle's late wife. In 1921, they moved to Ashland, Wisconsin, and there the Cullen coven gained another member. While working in a local hospital, Carlisle was called to the bedside of a young woman grievously injured in a suicide attempt. Carlisle was surprised to recognize Esme Evenson, whom he had treated for a broken leg about ten years earlier, when she was a teenager. It was almost impossible for him to believe that that vivacious, beautiful girl had come to this tragic end. Carlisle knew he could not save her life through conventional methods.

> The goodness and purity in Edward's face finally convinced Carlisle to take action.

Influenced by his memory of the happy girl Esme had been, Carlisle bit the dying woman and took her to the home he shared with Edward to wait for the transformation to be complete. When it was over, Carlisle apologized for what he had done, but Esme was not unhappy with the situation. She remembered their first meeting, too, and had always considered Carlisle her ideal of a gentleman. Carlisle and Esme soon fell in love and were married.

The coven's cover story now changed: Edward began to be introduced as Esme's brother. In many ways, however, Edward regarded Carlisle as his father and Esme as his mother. Carlisle now had more than the companion he'd longed for; he had a family.

Carlisle wasn't expecting the coven to get any bigger, but one night while on his way to work at a hospital in Rochester, New York, he discovered the nearly lifeless body of Rosalie Hale lying in the road. She had been beaten, sexually assaulted, and left for dead. Struck by the waste of a beautiful young life, Carlisle brought Rosalie home and transformed her, hoping in the back of his mind that one day she might be a companion for Edward.

Two years later, Rosalie had only reluctantly assimilated to vampire life. The relationship Carlisle had hoped would spark between her and Edward hadn't happened. So when Rosalie carried the dying Emmett McCarty to Carlisle and begged Carlisle to change him, Carlisle did as she asked. Rosalie wanted a companion of her choosing, and Carlisle felt he could make amends to her in this way.

At this point Carlisle and his family moved to Washington State, west of the Olympic Peninsula. To his surprise, he discovered a local Native American tribe who had the ability to transform into wolves. The Quileutes had previous experience with vampires, whom they called the cold ones, and they considered it their sacred duty to protect humans from them.

Unwilling to harm the werewolves, Carlisle brokered a treaty with the leader of the pack, Ephraim Black, utilizing Edward's mind-reading abilities to communicate. The treaty established boundary lines for both the Cullens and the Quileutes. The Cullens agreed never to hurt a human, which included never transforming a human into a vampire, since the Quileutes considered transformation the same as killing.

Both the vampires and the werewolves promised to keep the true nature of the other secret from humans.

The family continued to move when necessary, and in Denali, Alaska, Carlisle found what he'd been looking for when he set off for America—a coven of vampires who shared his philosophy and drank only animal blood. The two covens ended up close friends, viewing each other as extended family.

The Cullen family grew when they were joined by Alice Brandon and Jasper Whitlock, who had been traveling together as a couple. Since the family was now quite large, a new cover story was devised. Edward, Alice, and Emmett were now said to be the adopted children of Carlisle and Esme. Jasper and Rosalie, who looked alike, were passed off as Esme's twin orphaned cousins.

Eventually, the Cullen family returned to Washington State, this time to Forks, somewhat north of their previous location. Carlisle took a job at Forks Hospital and became well regarded in the community as a doctor and a citizen.

FAMOUS QUOTES

"I look at my. . . son. His strength, his goodness, the brightness that shines out of him . . . How could there not be more for one such as Edward?" New Moon, Chapter 2

"I've never been to veterinarian school." Eclipse, Chapter 25

"I can imagine what you think of me for that. But I can't ignore her will. It wouldn't be right to make such a choice for her, to force her." Breaking Dawn, Chapter 12

"She hasn't gone for his throat even once." Breaking Dawn, Chapter 22

"It's an interesting twist. Like she's doing the exact opposite of what you can." Breaking Dawn, Chapter 34

NAME: Edward Anthony Masen Cullen

DATE OF BIRTH: June 20, 1901

DATE OF TRANSFORMATION: 1918, at age 17

SOURCE OF TRANSFORMATION: Carlisle Cullen

PLACE OF ORIGIN: Chicago, Illinois

HAIR COLOR: Bronze

EYE COLOR: Green (human); gold/black (vampire)

HEIGHT: 6'2"

PHYSICAL DESCRIPTION: Edward is thin and lanky but muscular. He has untidy bronze hair and boyish looks.

SPECIAL ABILITIES: He can read the thoughts of anyone in close proximity to him, with the exception of Bella Cullen.

EDUCATION/OCCUPATION: He has two medical degrees but has never worked as a doctor. His other graduate degrees are in literature, mathematics, law, mechanical engineering, several languages, art history, and international business. Edward owns his family's house in Chicago, and about every fifty years or so, he "inherits" his family fortune from himself.

HOBBIES: He loves music—he plays a variety of instruments, sings, and has an extensive vinyl and CD collection. He also enjoys collecting cars.

VEHICLES: A silver Volvo S60R and a silver Aston Martin V12 Vanquish

FAMILY/COVEN RELATIONSHIPS: He is married to Bella Cullen and has a daughter, Renesmee Cullen. He is the natural son of Edward and Elizabeth Masen, and the "adopted" son of Carlisle and Esme Cullen. He thinks of himself as a brother to Alice and Emmett Cullen, as well as to Rosalie and Jasper Hale.

Edward was born to Edward and Elizabeth Masen on June 20, 1901. He was their only child. His father, a successful lawyer, provided Edward with many advantages, including music lessons and the opportunity to attend private school; however, although his father provided for Edward in material ways, he was emotionally distant and often away from home on business. This absence was made up for by Edward's close relationship with his mother; he was the center of her life.

Edward excelled at his studies and became an accomplished pianist. As he grew older, Edward became enamored of the life of a soldier. World War I raged during most of his adolescence, and Edward dreamed of the day he could join the battle. His mother's greatest fear was that she would lose Edward in the war. Every night she prayed that it would end before her only son turned eighteen and was old enough to enlist.

Nine months before his eighteenth birthday, the Spanish influenza hit Chicago, infecting all of Edward's family. Gravely ill, they were treated in the hospital where Dr. Carlisle Cullen worked. Edward's father quickly succumbed to the disease. On her deathbed and fearing for her son's life, Elizabeth Masen begged Dr. Cullen to do what was necessary to save her son. Somehow she seemed to know Dr. Cullen had a supernatural means to save Edward.

"Unfortunately Edward isn't based on anybody—he is all imagination and wishing. I think his allure is partially due to his old-fashioned manners. He's a gentleman, and those are hard to come by these days." —Stephenie

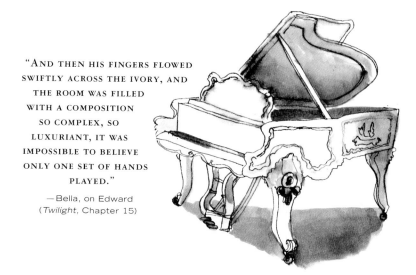

"AND THEN HIS FINGERS FLOWED
SWIFTLY ACROSS THE IVORY, AND
THE ROOM WAS FILLED
WITH A COMPOSITION
SO COMPLEX, SO
LUXURIANT, IT WAS
IMPOSSIBLE TO BELIEVE
ONLY ONE SET OF HANDS
PLAYED."

—Bella, on Edward
(*Twilight*, Chapter 15)

Moved by Elizabeth Masen's plea and having already thoroughly considered the idea of creating a companion, Carlisle took Edward from the hospital late that night, carrying the unconscious boy to his home. There Edward became the first human Carlisle changed into a vampire.

Edward formed a deep bond with Carlisle, who became a father to him, gaining Edward's trust and love the way his natural father never had. It was Carlisle who first realized that Edward possessed mind-reading abilities; he noticed Edward answering questions that Carlisle had not asked aloud. Edward had always had a knack for reading people; after his transformation, this ability blossomed into a true psychic talent.

Edward's new family gained a member when Carlisle transformed Esme to save her life after her suicide attempt. Edward was still young enough to appreciate a mother's care, and Esme gave it to him. Edward grew to love his new "father" and "mother." But as much as he respected Carlisle's ideals and valued Esme's gentleness and tenderness, he couldn't help questioning what it meant to be a vampire.

After almost a decade of living with Carlisle, Edward decided to leave his new parents and experience an alternate style of vampire life. He began drinking human blood instead of animal blood. Rather than become a true villain in his own estimation, he became a vigilante. Edward used his mind-reading abilities to target serious criminals as his victims—murderers, rapists, abusers, pedophiles, and the like. For his first victim, he tracked down Charles Evenson, Esme's abusive ex-husband. In the end, though, he couldn't accept taking so many human lives, no matter the justification, and in 1931 he returned home to Carlisle and Esme and their way of life.

"I like that Edward's not so clean-cut, that he has a dark side, that he's doing things that are not clearly legal or illegal." —Stephenie

Edward knew from hearing their thoughts that Carlisle and Esme were sometimes concerned that he had no romantic love in his life. When Carlisle transformed Rosalie Hale and brought her into the family in 1933, Edward knew that Carlisle and Esme hoped she and Edward would become a couple. But as stunningly beautiful as Rosalie was physically, Edward was not attracted to her somewhat shallow and self-absorbed mind. The feeling was mutual. Edward and Rosalie always treated each other as brother and sister, and were not always on the best of terms.

When the Cullen family lived in Alaska, Edward had another opportunity to find romance, this time with Tanya, the leader of the Denali coven, a group that also practiced a "vegetarian" lifestyle. Though Tanya was interested in Edward, he did not return that interest. It wasn't until the Cullen family returned to Forks in 2003 that anyone captured Edward's attention. There Edward met a human girl named Bella Swan. Bella was markedly different from every other

person he'd ever met in two impossible-to-o\
First, her blood "sang" for him the way no o\
had; second, her mind was the first he'd encount\
entirely closed to his mind-reading abilities.

FAMOUS QUOTES

"On the contrary, I find you very difficult to read." Twilight, Chapter 2

"No blood, no foul." Twilight, Chapter 3

"What if I'm not a superhero? What if I'm the bad guy?"
Twilight, Chapter 5

"Honestly — I've seen corpses with better color. I was concerned that I might have to avenge your murder." Twilight, Chapter 5

"I've decided that as long as I was going to hell, I might as well do it thoroughly." Twilight, Chapter 5

"Your number was up the first time I met you." Twilight, Chapter 8

"You aren't concerned about my diet?" Twilight, Chapter 9

"Hadn't you noticed? I'm breaking all *the rules now."*
Twilight, Chapter 10

"Be safe." Twilight, Chapter 12

"Yes, you are exactly *my brand of heroin."* Twilight, Chapter 13

"I may not be a human, but I am a man." Twilight, Chapter 14

"It will be as if I'd never existed." New Moon, Chapter 3

"Amazing. Carlisle was right." New Moon, Chapter 20

"Marry me first." New Moon, Chapter 24

"Well, I'm nearly a hundred and ten. It's time I settled down."
New Moon, Chapter 24

"I was all braced for the wrath that was going to put grizzlies to shame, and this is what I get? I should infuriate you more often."
Eclipse, Chapter 8

s that boy, *who would have—as soon as I discovered that*
u were what I was looking for—gotten down on one knee and
endeavored to secure your hand. I would have wanted you for eternity,
even when the word didn't have quite the same connotations."
Eclipse, Chapter 12

"The way you regard me is ludicrous." Eclipse, Chapter 19

"Would you please *stop trying to take your clothes off?"*
Eclipse, Chapter 20

"I lived through an entire twenty-four hours thinking that you were
dead, Bella. That changed the way I look at a lot of things."
Eclipse, Chapter 21

"But if I had been able to take your place last night, it would not
have made the top ten of the best *nights of my life. Dream about*
that." Eclipse, Chapter 23

"I just beheaded and dismembered a sentient creature not twenty
yards from you. That doesn't bother *you?"*
Eclipse, Chapter 25

"I love you. I want you. Right now." Eclipse, Chapter 27

"You're awfully small to be so hugely irritating."
Breaking Dawn, Chapter 4

"I'm not ready for you to kill me yet, Jacob Black. You'll have to
have a little patience." Breaking Dawn, Chapter 9

"Even you, Jacob Black, cannot hate me as much as I hate myself."
Breaking Dawn, Chapter 9

"I am truly sorry for the pain this causes you, Jacob. Though you
hate me, I must admit that I don't feel the same about you. I think
of you as a . . . a brother in many ways. A comrade in arms, at the
very least. I regret your suffering more than you realize. But Bella is
going to survive and I know that's what really matters to you."
Breaking Dawn, Chapter 17

"Now it's your turn to not break me." Breaking Dawn, Chapter 20

"It goes against the grain, letting you wrestle with lions. I was having an anxiety attack the whole time." Breaking Dawn, Chapter 21

"Maybe I'm hoping she'll get irritated and rip your head off." Breaking Dawn, Chapter 22

"I am her father. Not her creator — her biological father." Breaking Dawn, Chapter 30

"Don't be sad for him. He's happy now. Today, he's finally begun to forgive himself." Breaking Dawn, Chapter 39

"THIS IS ISLE ESME....
A GIFT FROM
CARLISLE — ESME
OFFERED TO LET
US BORROW IT."
— Edward, to Bella
(*Breaking Dawn*,
Chapter 5)

ESME ANNE PLATT EVENSON CULLEN

NAME: Esme Anne Platt Evenson Cullen

DATE OF BIRTH: 1895

DATE OF TRANSFORMATION: 1921, at age 26

SOURCE OF TRANSFORMATION: Carlisle Cullen

PLACE OF ORIGIN: Columbus, Ohio

HAIR COLOR: Caramel brown

EYE COLOR: Brown (human); gold/black (vampire)

HEIGHT: 5'6"

PHYSICAL DESCRIPTION: Esme has a heart-shaped face. Her body is small and slender, but curvy.

SPECIAL ABILITIES: She does not possess a quantifiable supernatural ability.

EDUCATION/OCCUPATION: She has degrees in architecture and art, and has also studied photography.

HOBBIES: She loves to restore old houses.

VEHICLE: None; she borrows one of her family members' cars whenever she needs a vehicle.

FAMILY/COVEN RELATIONSHIPS: Before her transformation, she was married to Charles Evenson and had a son who died shortly after birth. She is currently married to Carlisle and considers Edward Cullen, Rosalie Hale, Emmett Cullen, Alice Cullen, and Jasper Hale her children; Bella Cullen her daughter-in-law; and Renesmee Cullen her granddaughter.

PERSONAL HISTORY:

Esme Anne Platt grew up on a farm outside of Columbus, Ohio. As a child, she lived a happy life, although in her teen years she found it hard to conform to the behavior that was expected of a respectable young lady at the time.

In 1911, Esme fell and broke her leg while climbing a tree. The local doctor was away, and she ended up being treated by Dr. Carlisle Cullen. Although she mentioned it to no one at the time, meeting Carlisle affected her deeply. He was unlike anyone she had ever met—genuinely thoughtful, and truly interested in what she had to say. Unfortunately, he was in town only briefly and soon left, but she never forgot him.

Esme's friends began to marry, and before long she was the only one still unwed. Esme wanted to fall in love herself, but she never found anyone who measured up to her memory of Carlisle. Esme tried to persuade her father to allow her to pursue a teaching position in the West, but he didn't think it was respectable for a lady to live alone in the wilds. Instead, her father pressured her to accept the son of a family friend who wanted to marry her. Several years Esme's senior, Charles Evenson had good prospects. Esme was indifferent to Charles, but not opposed to him, so she agreed to the marriage to please her father.

Although she mentioned it to no one at the time, meeting Carlisle affected her deeply.

Esme quickly discovered that the marriage was a mistake; Charles's public face was very different from his private one. He physically abused her. Her parents rejected her plea for asylum; they counseled her to be a "good wife" and keep quiet. When Charles left to fight in World War I, it was an enormous relief. When he returned unscathed in 1919, it was a nightmare.

Soon after his return, Esme became pregnant. The baby was Esme's motivation to escape—she would not bring a child into Charles's home. Esme ran away and went to stay with a cousin in Milwaukee, Wisconsin. When her husband discovered her whereabouts, she fled to Ashland, Wisconsin, where she posed as a war widow. In order to support herself, Esme pursued her old dream of being a schoolteacher.

Esme began building a life for herself and her baby. She loved the unborn child more than her own life. But two days

ESME'S CHILDHOOD
HOME IN COLUMBUS,
OHIO, IN THE EARLY
1900s

after her son was born, he died of lung fever. Feeling as if she had lost everything, Esme walked to a cliff outside of town and jumped.

Esme regained consciousness in excruciating pain. Despite the pain, Esme was amazed to see Carlisle again, not sure if she was in heaven or hell. When the transformation was over, Carlisle explained that he'd turned her into a vampire in order to save her life. Esme was not as upset as he had expected. Adjusting to her new vampire nature had its challenges, and there were times when the call of human blood was too strong for her to resist; still, she was happy to be with the man she'd always idolized. Her youthful crush transitioned easily into full-fledged love.

Before long, Carlisle and Esme married. She never lost her maternal instincts, and as the oldest of the Cullens, she automatically fell into a mothering role with Edward and, later, the other members of the family.

FAMOUS QUOTES

"Well, I do think of them as my children in most ways. I never could get over my mothering instincts—did Edward tell you I had lost a child?" Twilight, Chapter 17

"He's been the odd man out for far too long; it's hurt me to see him alone." Twilight, Chapter 17

"I prefer to referee—I like keeping them honest." Twilight, Chapter 17

"We'd never allow anything to happen to you, sweetheart." Eclipse, Chapter 4

"They ended up being vampires in the way they are because I have strong opinions on free will. No matter what position you're in, you always have a choice. So I had these characters who were in a position where traditionally they would have been the bad guys, but, instead, they chose to be something different—a theme that has always been important to me." —Stephenie

✈ Rosalie Lillian Hale

NAME: Rosalie Lillian Hale

DATE OF BIRTH: 1915

DATE OF TRANSFORMATION: Late 1933, at age 18

SOURCE OF TRANSFORMATION: Carlisle Cullen

PLACE OF ORIGIN: Rochester, New York

HAIR COLOR: Golden blond

EYE COLOR: Dark blue, almost violet (human); gold/black (vampire)

HEIGHT: 5'9"

PHYSICAL DESCRIPTION: Rosalie has strikingly beautiful features and a stunning, statuesque physique. Her wavy blond hair falls halfway down her back.

SPECIAL ABILITIES: She does not possess a quantifiable supernatural ability.

EDUCATION/OCCUPATION: She has earned degrees in electrical engineering, business, and astrophysics, and has studied medicine (the last as a favor to Carlisle, to help keep him up-to-date with the latest advances).

HOBBIES: She enjoys enhancing cars and doing anything mechanical.

VEHICLE: Red BMW M3 convertible

FAMILY/COVEN RELATIONSHIPS: She is married to Emmett Cullen. She considers Carlisle and Esme Cullen to be her parents; Edward Cullen, Alice Cullen, and Jasper Hale to be her siblings; Bella Cullen to be her sister-in-law; and Renesmee Cullen to be her niece. Before her transformation, she grew up with her biological parents and two younger brothers.

PERSONAL HISTORY:

Rosalie Hale was born to a banker and his wife in Rochester, New York. Luckily, the bank her father worked at stayed solvent through the stock-market crash and resulting economic downturn. The Great Depression did not seriously impact

Rosalie's family the way it did many less fortunate families. Her parents were eager to do better, though — to move in higher social circles. As Rosalie grew and her beauty increased, they hoped her loveliness would open doors for them.

Rosalie enjoyed her parents' pride in her looks, her father's pleasure in buying her beautiful clothes, her girlfriends' envy, and the admiration of every man she passed. The result of all this attention was that Rosalie tended to be self-absorbed and rather shallow, with a focus on the material.

"I WAS THRILLED TO BE ME, TO BE ROSALIE HALE. PLEASED THAT MEN'S EYES WATCHED ME . . . HAPPY THAT MY MOTHER WAS PROUD OF ME AND THAT MY FATHER LIKED TO BUY ME PRETTY DRESSES."

—Rosalie, on her human life
(*Eclipse*, Chapter 7)

At eighteen, Rosalie was considered the most beautiful girl in Rochester, and possibly the state of New York. Her family was moderately wealthy and she wanted for nothing. Rosalie envied no one . . . except for her friend Vera. Vera had a husband who loved her and the most adorable baby boy, Henry. Rosalie longed for a husband and a baby of her own. When Rosalie caught the eye of Royce King II, the son of the richest man in Rochester, she felt that she was on her way to having absolutely everything she'd ever wanted. Her parents were overjoyed; a whirlwind courtship and plans for an extravagant wedding quickly followed.

One night, a week before the wedding, Rosalie was walking home after a visit with Vera. A few blocks from her street she heard the drunken laughter of a group of men. A moment later, she realized one of them was Royce. She'd never seen Royce drunk before, and didn't know the dark side of his character. Royce and his friends brutally assaulted and raped Rosalie. Thinking her dead, they abandoned her in the road.

Moments later, Carlisle Cullen found Rosalie and transformed her to save her life. He hoped that Rosalie might make a suitable companion for Edward, but they never viewed each other in that way, though they did come to love each other as brother and sister.

One of the first things Rosalie did as a vampire was to take revenge on Royce and his friends. She hunted her attackers down one by one, saving Royce for last because she wanted him to suffer psychologically from the fear of knowing that something was coming for him. She tortured all of her attackers to death, but she didn't drink their blood; she was repulsed by the idea of having any part of them inside her. She and Carlisle (and, later, Bella) are the only vampires in the Cullen clan who have never killed humans for blood.

Though vengeance was satisfying in its way, Rosalie remained deeply unhappy in her vampire life. She missed her human family greatly. More than that, the chance to have what she most longed for—a husband who loved her, a baby of her own—had been taken from her along with her humanity.

Two years later, Rosalie's life changed. While the Cullens were living in Tennessee, she discovered a man, Emmett

"There are characters that I have to work for a little bit harder, and sort of get down to their motivations. A few of them—Rosalie, for example— were difficult. It took me a while to figure out what her thing was." —Stephenie

McCarty, being mauled by a bear in the woods. Something about the man reminded Rosalie of her friend Vera's young son, and Rosalie didn't want him to die. She rescued Emmett and took him to Carlisle. She asked Carlisle to transform him, even though she hated her own vampire existence and knew her request was selfish.

But Emmett didn't see Rosalie as selfish; he fell in love with her, and he easily adapted to vampire life. He and Rosalie soon married—and did so repeatedly over the decades. Rosalie loved being the center of attention as the bride, and Emmett loved making her happy. The two have sometimes lived as a couple apart from the rest of the Cullen family.

FAMOUS QUOTES

"I'm so very sorry, Bella. I feel wretched about every part of this, and so grateful that you were brave enough to go save my brother after what I did. Please say you'll forgive me." New Moon, Chapter 22

"It's just that...this is not the life I would have chosen for myself. I wish there had been someone there to vote no for me."
New Moon, Chapter 24

"Would you like to hear my story, Bella? It doesn't have a happy ending—but which of ours does? If we had happy endings, we'd all be under gravestones now." Eclipse, Chapter 7

"Over my pile of ashes." Breaking Dawn, Chapter 10

"Oh, wonderful. I knew I smelled something nasty."
Breaking Dawn, Chapter 15

"You. Got. Food. In. My. Hair." Breaking Dawn, Chapter 15

"I'll help him toss you, dog. I owe you a good kick in the gut."
Breaking Dawn, Chapter 22

NAME: Emmett McCarty Cullen

DATE OF BIRTH: 1915

DATE OF TRANSFORMATION: 1935, at age 20

SOURCE OF TRANSFORMATION: Carlisle Cullen

PLACE OF ORIGIN: Gatlinburg, Tennessee

HAIR COLOR: Dark brown, almost black

EYE COLOR: Blue (human); gold/black (vampire)

HEIGHT: 6'5"

PHYSICAL DESCRIPTION: Emmett has an imposing frame; he is both tall and extremely muscular. His hair is curly and nearly black. He has dimples when he smiles, and his face has an innocent quality not often seen in a grown man.

SPECIAL ABILITIES: He does not possess a quantifiable supernatural ability.

EDUCATION/OCCUPATION: He has attended high school and college multiple times. He's never finished any particular degree, preferring instead to move quickly from one subject that interests him to the next.

HOBBIES: He loves competitive sports and games, especially anything that involves a physical challenge.

VEHICLE: Red Jeep Wrangler modified for off-roading

FAMILY/COVEN RELATIONSHIPS: He is married to Rosalie Hale. He considers Carlisle and Esme Cullen to be his parents; Edward Cullen, Alice Cullen, and Jasper Hale to be his siblings; Bella Cullen to be his sister-in-law; and Renesmee Cullen to be his niece.

PERSONAL HISTORY:

Emmett grew up in the small town of Gatlinburg, Tennessee, part of a large Scotch-Irish family. He had what his parents considered a wild adolescence; never one to worry about consequences, Emmett ran with a wild crowd that drank, gambled, and womanized. Emmett was always a help to his family, however. He was an excellent hunter and woodsman, and always kept the McCartys supplied with game. When he was twenty years old and out on a routine hunting trip in the Smoky Mountains, he was attacked by a large black bear. Emmett was close to losing consciousness when he thought he heard a second bear fighting with the first. He figured they were battling over who would get his corpse.

Then the growling stopped and Emmett felt like he was flying. He managed to open his eyes and saw what he thought was an angel. When the transformation began and the fiery agony spread through his body, he was sure he'd died and gone to hell.

When the pain left him, Emmett learned what had really happened to him. In his delirium, he'd seen Rosalie as an angel and Carlisle as God, but in fact they were both vampires—and now he was a vampire, too. He took the truth in stride; Emmett was never one to worry about situations outside of his control. He continues to think of Rosalie as his angel.

With his naturally happy nature, Emmett adjusted easily to the idea of being a vampire. Learning to control himself, however, was a more difficult challenge. In the years just after his transformation, Emmett was often unable to resist human blood. The Cullens were forced to move often until Emmett learned to restrain himself.

In his delirium,
he'd seen Rosalie as an angel
and Carlisle as God,
but in fact they were both vampires—
and now he was a vampire, too.

"IT WAS ONLY TWO YEARS LATER THAT SHE
FOUND EMMETT. SHE WAS HUNTING—WE WERE
IN APPALACHIA AT THE TIME—AND FOUND A BEAR
ABOUT TO FINISH HIM OFF. SHE CARRIED HIM BACK
TO CARLISLE, MORE THAN A HUNDRED MILES...."

—Edward, on Rosalie (*Twilight*, Chapter 14)

He genuinely bonded with all the members of his new family and, aside from his dietary lapses, also made their lives more comfortable. Emmett's easygoing nature brought out Edward's more optimistic side, and Rosalie became a different person altogether. When Emmett, ever practical, wanted to provide for his human family, Edward gave him a small fortune, which Emmett left in a bag on their doorstep. Even though he knew he could never again be a part of their family, he wanted to ease the burden of losing a strong, hardworking son. After doing what he could for them, he didn't look back.

Eventually, Emmett and Rosalie married—and have remarried more than once over the years, because Rosalie enjoys the process and the attention so much. At various times they have lived apart from the rest of the Cullen family as a married couple.

FAMOUS QUOTES

"Hell, yes!" New Moon, Chapter 24

"I'm really glad Edward didn't kill you. Everything's so much more fun with you around." Eclipse, Chapter 4

"Nice to have toddlers guarding the fort." Breaking Dawn, Chapter 11

"Did ya get in a couple of good swipes?" Breaking Dawn, Chapter 22

"So it's still standing? I would've thought you two had knocked it to rubble by now. What were you doing last night? Discussing the national debt?" Breaking Dawn, Chapter 25

"I'm sure you'll ace your classes . . . apparently there's nothing interesting for you to do at night besides study."
Breaking Dawn, Chapter 25

"'Bout time somebody scored around here." Breaking Dawn, Chapter 25

"She's too tame." Breaking Dawn, Chapter 26

"Not much wild about you, *is there? I bet that cottage doesn't have a scratch."* Breaking Dawn, Chapter 26

NAME: Mary Alice Brandon Cullen; preferred name: Alice

DATE OF BIRTH: 1901

DATE OF TRANSFORMATION: 1920, at age 19

SOURCE OF TRANSFORMATION: An unnamed vampire who worked in a mental institution

PLACE OF ORIGIN: Biloxi, Mississippi

HAIR COLOR: Black

EYE COLOR: Dark brown (human); gold/black (vampire)

HEIGHT: 4'10"

PHYSICAL DESCRIPTION: Alice is tiny and graceful. Her hair is very short and spiky because her head was shaved in a mental hospital and her hair was in the process of growing out when she was transformed.

SPECIAL ABILITIES: She can see into the future, although what she sees is based on decisions being made; thus, she must wait for a decision to be firmly rooted in the mind, or acted upon, before she can see the end result. Her talent is limited to humans and vampires because she has been both; she cannot see the futures of werewolves or hybrid vampires.

EDUCATION/OCCUPATION: She has attended high school and college several times. She has degrees in fashion design and international business. One of the ways she makes money is by using her gift for seeing the future to predict windfall investments in the stock market.

HOBBIES: She plays the stock market and loves designing and shopping for clothes.

VEHICLES: A canary yellow Porsche 911 Turbo

FAMILY/COVEN RELATIONSHIPS: Alice is married to Jasper Hale. She considers Carlisle and Esme Cullen to be her parents; Edward Cullen, Rosalie Hale, and Emmett Cullen to be her siblings; Bella Cullen to be her sister-in-law; and Renesmee Cullen to be her niece. She had a human sister named Cynthia, and she has a human niece who still resides in Biloxi.

PERSONAL HISTORY:

Mary Alice Brandon—or Alice, as she was commonly known—lived in a middle-class home in Biloxi, Mississippi, with her parents and her sister, Cynthia, who was nine years younger. Her father was a jeweler and a pearl trader. He bought the pearls from local divers and then moved the pearls inland to be sold in more profitable markets away from the coast. His job kept him away from the family for days at a time. Alice's mother tended to their home and the orchard on their property, and took care of Alice and Cynthia. The girls were fairly close despite the wide age difference between them.

Alice had the gift of foresight even as a little girl, but her premonitions were not nearly as strong as they would be later in her life. They came to her more as feelings than visions. At first her parents thought her premonitions were

"Alice was a character who just
popped into existence fully formed—so easily.
It was like if Edward existed,
then he must have a sister named Alice,
and she would be this person.
And she was one of the things that was sad for me
with the book, because I wanted her to be real so much.
Oh, I would love to have a friend like that.
There must be someone just like her somewhere,
because it seemed so obvious that
she must exist." —Stephenie

amusing. "Alice is always right," they would say when the five-year-old dressed herself in a slicker even though the sky was blue; later, of course, the rain would begin. "Grandma will be here soon," she would announce. They would laugh and put out an extra plate.

As Alice grew older, she became more hesitant to share her predictions. She hated looking ridiculous when her premonitions turned out to be wrong. (Weather was the easiest for her to predict correctly, because it didn't involve people and their tendencies to change their minds.) By age ten, she rarely voiced her predictions at all, but those she did give came true often enough that people started to talk. "That uncanny child of the Brandons" was seldom asked to other children's birthday parties. Alice's mother loved her deeply and counseled her to keep quiet about her premonitions.

By the time Alice turned eighteen, she'd learned to ignore her gift, for the most part, but occasionally she felt compelled to speak. When she did, it sometimes turned out badly, such as when Alice warned a friend not to marry a certain man; the friend ignored her, and it was revealed that the man's family had a history of insanity. Rather than blame herself or her husband, the friend whispered to others that Alice had put a curse on her. On another occasion, one of Alice's favorite cousins planned to go west to seek his fortune, and Alice begged him not to. The cousin died in an accident on the road, and his parents — Alice's aunt and uncle — blamed Alice for jinxing his trip. People started to use the words *witch* and *changeling* when talking about her.

> By the time Alice turned eighteen, she'd learned to ignore her gift, for the most part, but occasionally she felt compelled to speak.

Then Alice had her most terrifying vision. She saw her mother being murdered by a stranger in the woods on her way into town. She told her mother what she had seen, and her mother listened to her. Alice's mother kept her daughters in the house with the doors locked and a pistol loaded. Mr. Brandon returned home from a trip two days later to a dirty house full of terrified women and empty of food. On Mrs. Brandon's insistence, he searched the woods near the road but found nothing. He was angry with Alice's "damned stories" and ordered Alice not to put everyone in a panic again.

> People started to use the words *witch* and *changeling* when talking about her.

Alice began to be haunted by flashes of the stranger, still stalking her mother. When she told her parents what she'd seen, her father was furious with Alice's hysteria. He insisted that the family go about their usual routine. But he was often gone, and when he was, Alice's mother followed Alice's desperate warnings as much as possible. Still, she had to shop for supplies and tend her orchard. When a month passed and no one had seen the man, Mrs. Brandon grew less wary. She began returning her friends' visits and attending sewing circles. She took the pistol with her every time she left the house — at first. After two months, she started to forget.

One night Alice had a perfectly clear vision of the man in a Model T running her mother's buggy off the road just outside of town, where there was a steep drop. Alice's mother had already left home in the buggy. Alice ran after her, seeing in her mind the stranger watching the crashed buggy to be sure there was no movement inside. Next she had a vision of the man driving away from the scene of the accident. Alice knew she was too late, but she kept running.

The death of Alice's mother was declared accidental, and

Alice's protestations to the contrary were met with disdain and suspicion. Alice's father ordered her to be silent.

Mr. Brandon remarried within six months of his wife's death. The woman was a blond Yankee from Illinois who was only ten years older than Alice; Mr. Brandon had frequently sold pearls to her jeweler father in the past. The new Mrs. Brandon was quite cold to Alice, though she made a pet of the younger Cynthia.

Even unguided by visions, Alice was bright. Careless, offhand comments by her new stepmother and evidence of longer preparations for this marriage than should have been possible made Alice suspicious. She took her suspicions to her father, who raged at her for suggesting ill of his new wife.

The night after her confrontation with her father, Alice had a vision of him and the stranger who had killed her mother. Her father was giving the man money. Then Alice had a vision of the man standing over her with a knife. Too late, she realized that she'd confided in exactly the wrong person. Alice rushed out into the night and ran five miles to the home of her aunt and uncle, her only living relatives. Alice beat on the door until they answered, then gasped out her story: Her father had arranged to have her mother murdered and was sending the killer after her next. The aunt—who still blamed Alice for her son's death—shoved Alice off the porch and told her husband to get the dogs and drive Alice away.

Both her aunt and her father were already there, and the marshal had been informed that Alice had gone mad.

Alice hurried ten more miles back to town and arrived at the town marshal's house to find it lit and busy. Both her aunt and her father were already there, and the marshal had been informed that Alice had gone mad. Alice accused her father of his crimes and her stepmother of complicity, but no one listened. Most people already thought Alice was crazy — or possessed by the devil. The marshal was paid well to have Alice put quietly into an asylum two counties away. Few people knew what had actually happened, and everyone who did know the truth was very understanding about the Brandons' desire to pretend that Alice had died.

In the mental asylum, Alice's head was shaved during the threat of a typhoid outbreak. She also endured electroshock therapy. The treatment caused her to lose her memory, but it also allowed her naturally cheerful and humorous disposition to return, since she no longer remembered the sadness and horror of her recent life.

Unknown to Alice, a vampire was working as a groundskeeper at the asylum where she was incarcerated. This vampire, who was taking advantage of this pool of humans who could die without much notice being taken, formed an attachment to Alice. He kept her from the shock treatments and other horrors whenever he could. He learned of Alice's abilities; she always knew when he was coming to visit her. He would bring hidden objects with him, to see if she could guess what he had. She always got it right.

Then Alice had a vision of James.

Then Alice had a vision of James.

It occurred the moment he caught her scent, old and faded, in her hometown two counties away. She saw James find her. She told her only friend, the vampire, and he knew that what she was seeing was fact. He planned to escape with her, but Alice saw James catching up to her anyway. He offered other options, but every choice ended with James. Then the groundskeeper decided to change

"She was there—
expecting me, naturally....
'You've kept me waiting a long
time,' she said."

—Jasper, on Alice (*Eclipse*, Chapter 13)

her. Alice saw that this would be very close. There might not be time for her blood to transform sufficiently for James to gain nothing in killing her. The vampire had heard enough. He bit Alice immediately and took her away to hide her. Knowing this would barely slow James, he put himself in James's path to delay him. From Alice's vision, he knew James was a strong hunter, and that it was a fight he would not win.

She was able to see the best future for herself.

After her transformation, Alice awoke alone. The pain of the transformation had the same effect on Alice as the shocks; she remembered nothing of her life in the asylum, or of the vampire who had transformed her. She was unaware of James as the reason for her change. Fortunately, Alice's psychic gifts were now greatly enhanced and strengthened. She was able to see the best future for herself.

Alice's first clear vision as a vampire was of Jasper Whitlock. She knew that Jasper was her future mate, but she also knew that he wasn't ready for her yet. Instead of going to look for him, she waited for him to find her. In the meantime, she practiced — with sporadic success — living a "vegetarian" lifestyle, knowing that in time she and Jasper would end up with the Cullen family.

In 1948, Alice went to the small diner in Philadelphia where she knew she and Jasper were destined to meet. Though her greeting was characteristically cryptic, Jasper's ability to feel the emotions of those around him allowed him to appreciate the magnitude of the occasion. Alice was already in love; Jasper quickly learned to reciprocate.

To please Alice, Jasper began practicing a "vegetarian" lifestyle as well. By 1950, when they joined the Cullens, Alice was able to control her thirst as well as the rest of the family did. Jasper continues to have more difficulty with self-restraint than the others. Alice and Jasper were married sometime after joining the Cullen family.

Alice loves all of her adopted family, but has a special bond with Edward. Thanks to his mind-reading abilities, he is the only one who truly understands what it is like to live with constant visions of the future.

FAMOUS QUOTES

"You do smell nice, I never noticed before." Twilight, Chapter 15

"It sounded like you were having Bella for lunch, and we came to see if you would share." Twilight, Chapter 16

"Do you think any of us want to look into his eyes for the next hundred years if he loses you?" Twilight, Chapter 20

"I will always tell you the truth." Twilight, Chapter 20

"Edward, you have to do it." Twilight, Chapter 23

"Would you like to explain to me how you're alive?"
New Moon, Chapter 17

"Honestly, I think it's all gotten beyond ridiculous. I'm debating whether to just change you myself." New Moon, Chapter 19

"How strongly are you opposed to grand theft auto?"
New Moon, Chapter 19

"I think she's having hysterics. Maybe you should slap her."
New Moon, Chapter 22

"Who invited the werewolf?" Eclipse, Chapter 17

"Please, Bella, please—if you really love me…Please let me do your wedding." Eclipse, Chapter 21

"No one dressed by me ever looks like an idiot." Breaking Dawn, Chapter 1

"Bella gets in the way. She's all wrapped around it, so she's…blurry. Like bad reception on a TV—like trying to focus your eyes on those fuzzy people jerking around on the screen." Breaking Dawn, Chapter 14

"Esme, give her a few pointers on acting human." Breaking Dawn, Chapter 25

NAME: Jasper Whitlock Hale

DATE OF BIRTH: 1844

DATE OF TRANSFORMATION: 1863, at age 19

SOURCE OF TRANSFORMATION: Maria

PLACE OF ORIGIN: Houston, Texas

HAIR COLOR: Honey blond

EYE COLOR: Brown (human); gold/black (vampire)

HEIGHT: 6'3"

PHYSICAL DESCRIPTION: Jasper is tall with a medium build, and his hair falls to just above his collar. He has many scars from years of dealing with newborn vampires, but these scars are easily visible only to others with supernaturally good eyesight.

SPECIAL ABILITIES: Jasper has the ability to both feel and manipulate the emotions of those around him.

EDUCATION/OCCUPATION: He has attended high school and college several times. He has degrees in philosophy and history.

HOBBIES: He is a natural scholar and an avid reader. He has a shrewd mind for both business and battle tactics.

VEHICLE: Jasper has the silver Ducati motorcycle given to him by Edward.

FAMILY/COVEN RELATIONSHIPS: He is married to Alice Cullen. He considers Carlisle and Esme Cullen to be his parents; Edward Cullen, Rosalie Hale, and Emmett Cullen to be his siblings; Bella Cullen to be his sister-in-law; and Renesmee Cullen to be his niece. He also feels brotherly affection for nomadic vampires Peter and Charlotte.

PERSONAL HISTORY:

Jasper Whitlock grew up in Houston, Texas. When he was almost seventeen, he lied about his age and volunteered to join the Confederate Army. He rose quickly through the ranks, being promoted over older, more experienced men. People thought of Jasper as charismatic. This was likely due in part to early traces of the psychic ability Jasper would develop after his transformation. Even as a human, Jasper had a gift for empathizing with and influencing the emotions of those around him.

By the time the Battle of Galveston began, Jasper was the youngest major in the Confederate army. After leading a group of refugees from Galveston to Houston, he encountered three extraordinarily beautiful women—Maria, Nettie, and Lucy. Maria—a vampire and head of her coven—decided to transform Jasper into a vampire for the newborn army she was creating.

"I WAS ALMOST SEVENTEEN YEARS OLD WHEN I JOINED THE CONFEDERATE ARMY IN 1861."

—Jasper (*Eclipse*, Chapter 13)

Maria chose her newborns more carefully than was usual. She'd chosen Jasper first because of his rank—which meant he'd had success in a military system—and second because of that charismatic quality that had always drawn other humans to him. Jasper was naturally gifted as a warrior and a leader. His ability to control the emotional environment around him, although not yet fully developed, made Maria's army more effective.

A bond formed between Jasper and Maria. She came to depend on him more and more and grew quite fond of him. For Jasper, Maria's army was the only vampire life he had known, and he had no idea anything else was possible for him.

One of Jasper's regular tasks was to execute members of the coven who had outlived their newborn strength and developed no other skills that made them valuable to the army. Eventually he had help in this task from Peter, another former newborn who had proved himself worthy of being kept around. Jasper liked Peter for his oddly civilized nature. They became friends.

One night as he and Peter were carrying out the grim task of dispatching age-weakened newborns, Jasper could feel the unusually difficult emotional toll it was taking on his friend. When Jasper called out a newborn named Charlotte, Peter suddenly erupted in fear and fury. He yelled for Charlotte to run, then bolted after her. Jasper could easily have caught them, but he chose not to.

As the years passed, Jasper became depressed, tired of always being surrounded by the devastating emotions of those he killed. Maria was not pleased with this alteration. He began to notice a change in her emotions around him; sometimes she was fearful, sometimes malicious. He knew Maria was thinking about getting rid of him, and Jasper began planning how he would destroy her first.

At this critical moment, Peter came back to find Jasper. He told Jasper of an alternative he had never imagined: Peter and Charlotte had been living peacefully in the North for the last five years, meeting several other covens that coexisted amicably. Jasper left with Peter immediately.

He traveled with Peter and Charlotte for a few years, but even in the more peaceful North, his depression didn't lift. Though he was killing only humans now, he was still subject to their emotions as they died.

Jasper's misery stayed with him, and eventually he left Peter and Charlotte. He tried to kill less often, but the thirst always grew overwhelming.

In 1948, Jasper encountered Alice. She approached Jasper as if they were close friends and told him he'd kept her waiting a long time. Jasper was puzzled and wary, but Alice's joyful emotions impacted him greatly. When Alice held out her hand, he took it. And he felt an unfamiliar emotion: hope.

Alice explained her vision of the Cullens, and she described the lifestyle of Carlisle and his family. Jasper found it all hard to believe, but he and Alice set off to find them. Once they did, Alice and Jasper were quickly welcomed into the family. Jasper started using the last name Hale because he and Rosalie looked related, and people assumed they were siblings. It made sense to go along with what humans already seemed inclined to believe. At Carlisle's suggestion, Alice and Jasper were married shortly after joining the Cullens.

Jasper became fond of the members of his new family but never developed the deep bonds with them that Alice did. Jasper chose to live with the Cullens in order to stay with Alice, and because the "vegetarian" lifestyle, though exceptionally difficult for him, freed him from the negative emotions that had so depressed him.

> When A held out her hand, he took it. And he felt an unfamiliar emotion: hope.

FAMOUS QUOTES

"*I can feel what you're feeling now — and you* are *worth it.*"
Twilight, Chapter 19

"*You held out your hand, and I took it without stopping to make sense of what I was doing. For the first time in almost a century, I felt hope.*" Eclipse, Chapter 13

"*I've never seen a newborn do that — stop an emotion in its tracks that way. You were upset, but when you saw our concern, you reined it in, regained power over yourself.*" Breaking Dawn, Chapter 20

NAME: Isabella Marie Swan Cullen; preferred name: Bella

DATE OF BIRTH: September 13, 1987

DATE OF TRANSFORMATION: September 11, 2006, at age 18

SOURCE OF TRANSFORMATION: Edward Cullen

PLACE OF ORIGIN: Forks, Washington

HAIR COLOR: Brown

EYE COLOR: Brown (human); red (newborn vampire), which will change to gold/black

HEIGHT: 5'4"

PHYSICAL DESCRIPTION: Bella's dark brown hair is long, thick, and straight. She has a wide forehead with a widow's peak, and a narrow jaw with a pointed chin. Her eyes are large and widely spaced, her cheekbones prominent, her nose thin. Her lips are out of proportion, a bit too full for her slim jawline. Her eyebrows are darker than her hair and are straighter than they are arched. She's slender but not muscular. As a human, Bella was very fair-skinned, with chocolate-brown eyes. As a vampire, she is even paler, and her eyes are bright red. They will change to gold/black as her human blood leaves her system. Bella's features were heightened and perfected by her transformation.

SPECIAL ABILITIES: Her mind is impenetrable; no one can read her thoughts unless she allows it. She can shield herself from all types of psychic attacks and learns to shield those around her.

EDUCATION/OCCUPATION: She is a graduate of Forks High School. As a human, she held a part-time job at Newton's Olympic Outfitters.

HOBBIES: Bella enjoys reading, especially the classics, and listening to music.

VEHICLES: Red 1953 Chevy pickup truck, a 1960s Honda

motorcycle, a 2006 Mercedes Guardian, a red Ferrari F430

FAMILY/COVEN RELATIONSHIPS: She is married to Edward Cullen, and Renesmee Cullen is her daughter. Her father is Charlie Swan. Her mother, Renée, is married to Phil Dwyer, Bella's stepfather. Bella views Carlisle and Esme Cullen as her father- and mother-in-law, and Alice Cullen, Rosalie Hale, Emmett Cullen, and Jasper Hale as her sisters- and brothers-in-law.

PERSONAL HISTORY:

Isabella "Bella" Swan was born in Forks, Washington. Her parents, Renée and Charlie, divorced when she was still a baby. Bella lived with her mother, growing up mainly in Riverside, California, and Phoenix, Arizona. Up until 2002, Bella visited her father in Forks for a month every summer. The climate in Forks was unpleasant to Bella, though, and when she was old enough, she insisted that Charlie meet her in California for a few weeks in the summer instead.

Bella didn't fit in with her peers in California or Arizona. She had the feeling of being a little out of sync with everyone — even the person she was closest to, her mother. Renée was a very extroverted, impractical, and absentminded mother who liked to dabble in a multitude of hobbies; from necessity, Bella turned out quite the opposite. At an early age she took over most of the household responsibilities. When not being the adult, she preferred quiet pastimes like reading, in part because she was

"It was a sweet, kind of tender moment. But there was this dark side to it because he was also admitting how much he had wanted to kill her from the first day he met her." —Stephenie

"EDWARD POINTED
TO THE COUPLE IN THE MIRROR
DIRECTLY ACROSS FROM US. . . .
THE NARROW SHEATH OF THE
SHIMMERING WHITE DRESS FLARED
OUT SUBTLY AT THE TRAIN ALMOST
LIKE AN INVERTED CALLA LILY,
CUT SO SKILLFULLY
THAT HER BODY LOOKED
ELEGANT AND GRACEFUL. . . ."

—Bella, on wearing her wedding dress
(*Breaking Dawn*, Chapter 4)

BELLA'S WEDDING DRESS,
DEPICTED ON A MANNEQUIN

extraordinarily clumsy. Her naturally responsible nature carried over into her schoolwork, where Bella usually received A's. Her plan for the future was to get a degree in education and teach, like her mother. Renée's career was the one thing Bella truly respected about her mother. However, she intended to teach at the high school level.

When Renée fell in love with and married minor-league baseball player Phil Dwyer, Bella chose to move in with her father in Forks so Renée could go on the road with her new husband during baseball season. Bella arrived in Forks in January 2005 to finish high school in the town where she was born. On her first day at Forks High School, she met Edward Cullen.

FAMOUS QUOTES

"About three things I was absolutely positive. First, Edward was a vampire. Second, there was part of him — and I didn't know how potent that part might be — that thirsted for my blood. And third, I was unconditionally and irrevocably in love with him."
Twilight, Chapter 9

"I don't speak Car and Driver.*"* Twilight, Chapter 11

"You said that Rosalie and Emmett will get married soon. . . . Is that . . . marriage . . . the same as it is for humans?"
Twilight, Chapter 14

"Well, it's no irritable grizzly. . . ." Twilight, Chapter 15

*"Rosalie *is jealous of* me?"* Twilight, Chapter 15

"I'm betting on Alice." Twilight, Chapter 24

"Oh, I'm with the vampires, of course." Twilight, Epilogue

"Which is tempting you more, my blood or my body?"
New Moon, Chapter 2

"Nothing. I just hadn't realized before. Did you know, you're sort of beautiful?" New Moon, Chapter 8

"Could you . . . well, try to not *be a . . . werewolf?"*
New Moon, Chapter 13

"My mortality. I'm putting it to a vote." New Moon, Chapter 23

"I would want . . . Carlisle not to have to do it. I would want
you *to change me."* New Moon, Chapter 24

"Am I the only one who has to get old*? I get older every
stinking day!"* Eclipse, Chapter 5

*"We're a bit sensitive to blood around here. I'm sure you can
understand that."* Eclipse, Chapter 10

"I punched a werewolf in the face." Eclipse, Chapter 15

"Show me the damn ring, Edward." Eclipse, Chapter 20

"Kiss me, Jacob. Kiss me, and then come back."
Eclipse, Chapter 23

"Edward, I know who I can't live without." Eclipse, Chapter 27

*"It's a good thing you're bulletproof. I'm going to need that ring.
It's time to tell Charlie."* Eclipse, Chapter 27

"Does this screw my total? Or do we start counting after *I'm a
vampire?"* Breaking Dawn, Chapter 13

"It feels . . . complete *when you're here, Jacob. Like all my family
is together."* Breaking Dawn, Chapter 15

*"Huh. I can see what everyone's been going on about. You stink,
Jacob."* Breaking Dawn, Chapter 22

"You nicknamed my daughter after the Loch Ness Monster*?"*
Breaking Dawn, Chapter 22

*"We're going to tell her I spent hours in there playing dress-up.
We're going to* lie.*"* Breaking Dawn, Chapter 24

"It's over. We've all been sentenced to die."
Breaking Dawn, Chapter 28

"I am all *over this."* Breaking Dawn, Chapter 38

"Now you know. No one's ever loved anyone as much as I love you."
Breaking Dawn, Chapter 39

FAMOUS CONVERSATIONS WITH EDWARD

"Please tell me just one little theory."
"Um, well, bitten by a radioactive spider?"
"That's not very creative."
"I'm sorry, that's all I've got."
"You're not even close."
"No spiders?"
"Nope."
"And no radioactivity?"
"None."
"Dang."
"Kryptonite doesn't bother me, either." Twilight, Chapter 5

"I smelled the blood."
"People can't smell blood."
"Well, I can — that's what makes me sick. It smells like rust . . . and salt. . . . What?"
"It's nothing." Twilight, Chapter 5

"THEY WERE ALL WAITING
IN THE HUGE WHITE LIVING ROOM;
WHEN I WALKED THROUGH THE DOOR,
THEY GREETED ME WITH A LOUD CHORUS OF
'HAPPY BIRTHDAY, BELLA!'
WHILE I BLUSHED AND LOOKED DOWN."

—Bella (*New Moon*, Chapter 1)

"THE WOODEN FLOOR, THE LIGHT BLUE WALLS,
THE PEAKED CEILING, THE YELLOWED LACE
CURTAINS AROUND THE WINDOW—THESE WERE
ALL A PART OF MY CHILDHOOD."
—Bella, on her bedroom (*Twilight*, Chapter 1)

"I dazzle people?"
"You haven't noticed? Do you think everybody gets their way so easily?"
"Do I dazzle you?"
"Frequently." Twilight, Chapter 8

"How old are you?"
"Seventeen."
"And how long have you been seventeen?"
"A while." Twilight, Chapter 9

"Don't laugh — but how can you come out during the daytime?"
"Myth."
"Burned by the sun?"
"Myth."
"Sleeping in coffins?"
"Myth. I can't sleep."
"At all?"
"Never." Twilight, Chapter 9

"And so the lion fell in love with the lamb...."
"What a stupid lamb."
"What a sick, masochistic lion." Twilight, Chapter 13

NAME: Renesmee Carlie Cullen; nickname: Nessie

DATE OF BIRTH: September 11, 2006

DATE OF TRANSFORMATION: Born a vampire/human hybrid

PLACE OF ORIGIN: Forks, Washington

HAIR COLOR: Bronze

EYE COLOR: Brown

HEIGHT: 3'5"

PHYSICAL DESCRIPTION: Renesmee has fair skin, pink cheeks, dimples, and bronze-colored ringlets.

SPECIAL ABILITIES: She can show people her thoughts by touching their skin. So far, no one has been able to block her talent.

EDUCATION/OCCUPATION: She is taught at home by her parents, extended family, and friends.

HOBBIES: She likes to hunt with Jacob, read, study, and spend time with her parents and the other members of the Cullen family.

VEHICLE: She doesn't have a vehicle yet.

FAMILY/COVEN RELATIONSHIPS: She is the natural daughter of Edward and Bella Cullen. Charlie Swan and Renée Dwyer are her natural grandparents. Carlisle and Esme Cullen are her adoptive grandparents through their relationship to Edward. She thinks of Rosalie Hale and Alice Cullen as her aunts, and of Jasper Hale and Emmett Cullen as her uncles. Jacob Black has imprinted on her.

BORN HEALTHY, "MORE BEAUTIFUL THAN HER FATHER" (*Breaking Dawn*, Chapter 19), AND STRONG, RENESMEE NEEDED A CRIB MADE OF WROUGHT IRON.

Renesmee has both vampire and human characteristics. She has inherited many physical gifts from her vampire heritage; her teeth are nearly as strong as vampire teeth, her skin is almost as durable as vampire skin, and her muscles perform with supernatural strength, though not quite at vampire level. Mentally, she learns with vampire speed and retains with vampire perfection. Due to her human side, she has a beating heart and a functioning circulatory system. She also can eat human food and sleep. She maintains a body temperature greater than that of a normal human, at around 105 degrees Fahrenheit. From conception, she has grown at a greatly accelerated rate. It is expected that she, like other hybrids, will stop growing when her body reaches its adult size. Her physical growth is greatly outstripped by her mental development.

FAMOUS QUOTES

"But I can show you more than I can tell you."
Breaking Dawn, Chapter 30

"I'm not dangerous at all....I love humans. And wolf-people like my Jacob." Breaking Dawn, Chapter 30

"Momma, you're special." Breaking Dawn, Chapter 31

"I love you too, Momma. We'll always be together."
Breaking Dawn, Chapter 35

Mentally, she learns
with vampire speed and
retains with vampire perfection.

"THE HOUSE WAS TIMELESS, GRACEFUL, AND PROBABLY A HUNDRED YEARS OLD. IT WAS PAINTED A SOFT, FADED WHITE, THREE STORIES TALL, RECTANGULAR AND WELL PROPORTIONED. THE WINDOWS AND DOORS WERE EITHER PART OF THE ORIGINAL STRUCTURE OR A PERFECT RESTORATION."

—Bella, on her first impressions of the Cullen home (*Twilight,* Chapter 15)

The Cullen Home

The Cullens' house in Forks is more than a hundred years old. Painstakingly restored by Esme, it is painted white, is three stories tall, and features a deep porch that wraps around the front of the house. The back, south-facing wall is three stories of glass.

The inside of the first story is open and bright, with few internal walls. To the left of the front door is a wide central staircase. To the right is a raised area with a grand piano in the center. Also to the right are a dining room and kitchen, but these are more for show than for actual use. Behind the stairs is the office of C.E.E. Inc., the Cullens' personal company, where they manage all of their business dealings.

At the top of the staircase on the second floor is the room that Rosalie and Emmett share. Moving around the central stairs clockwise, first comes Jasper's study, then Alice and Jasper's room, with an attached closet that is larger than the room itself. Carlisle's office is next, with an area inside for Esme's study and Carlisle's personal library. During Bella's pregnancy, the library was converted into a combination exam and delivery room.

The room that Carlisle and Esme share is at the top of the staircase on the third floor. Edward's room is also on this floor, facing south. The remainder of the third floor is called the library and is used for any technically illegal activity, such as forging birth certificates and hacking into computer systems, which the Cullens must do in order to maintain the various identities needed to live unnoticed in human society.

The Volturi Coven

The equivalent of royalty in the vampire world, the Volturi coven consists of five core members: Aro; Caius; Marcus; Aro's wife, Sulpicia; and Cauis's wife, Athenodora. Marcus's wife (and Aro's sister), Didyme, was also a member of the Volturi before she died.

The Volturi reside in their city — Volterra, Italy — which they have secretly controlled for three thousand years, since the time of the Etruscans. They prefer to stay indoors, out of sight of humans, using other vampires as subordinates to serve their coven. Occasionally, they also use human minions.

Between 400 and 500 A.D., the Volturi launched an offensive against the most powerful coven in the world, the Romanians. Rather than simply attack the Romanians, the Volturi first cleverly demanded that the Romanians conform to laws that the Volturi claimed benefited all vampirekind. When the Romanians scornfully refused, the Volturi were able to categorize (and publicize) their strike as a move for the good of all vampires, rather than a standard territory dispute.

The main portion of the war lasted for nearly a century and — due to the fact that there are still two remaining survivors of the original Romanian coven — was never officially concluded. In the end, the Volturi were able to defeat the Romanians because of Aro's intentional creation of talented vampires. The Romanians had created vampires for their empire with less foresight, and their physical skills were not a match in the long term for Aro's psychically gifted choices. Aro called his soldiers "the Volturi guard," making it clear that they were subservient to the actual coven of five.

After the Volturi had defeated the greater part of the Romanian coven, they began spreading their doctrine throughout the world. Their basic operating premise was that keeping the existence of vampires a secret was beneficial to all; anyone who would not keep this secret was an enemy to the vampire public.

While many vampires questioned the validity of this premise at the time (after all, what could a human do to a vampire, despite any knowledge that human might have), none of them wanted to take on the Volturi fresh off their victory over the Romanians. As time passed, more vampires were born into a world where the Volturi existed as benevolent governors, and slowly the Volturi became accepted by their own positive, self-created definition. Many of these new vampires were created by the Volturi themselves, indoctrinated, and then let loose into the world. This was the first incarnation of the Volturi's human recruitment program; they found humans who sought the power and immortality of vampire lore and introduced them into that world with a set of preconceived ideas about vampire society—ideas that those new vampires eventually introduced to their own "offspring" and other covens they came in contact with. After the Volturi became an accepted force, they continued with the human recruitment on a smaller scale; they utilized humans hopeful of becoming vampires as servants in order to create a human façade for their ancestral home. The majority of these humans were eventually killed for their blood, and only those with potential for useful psychic talents were transformed.

"There aren't very many bad guys in my novels. Even the bad guys usually have a pretty good reason for the way they are, and some of them come around in the end. I don't see the world as full of negatives." —Stephenie

> If a human
> were to discover
> the truth about
> vampires and
> remain silent, it
> is probable that
> the Volturi would
> never know.

As time passed, the Volturi became more and more powerful as Aro discovered more humans and vampires with formidable gifts and added them to his "collection." In the twentieth century, the advances in human weapons technology came to be viewed by many vampires as a validation of the Volturi's now inspired-seeming laws.

The present-day Volturi guard stands at nine permanent members and ten to twelve additional transitory members. The foremost members are Jane and Alec, twins changed around 800 A.D. Jane and Alec had psychic abilities as humans that were greatly intensified in their vampire forms. After their inclusion, the Volturi's power became virtually unassailable.

Rank in the guard is decided by power; the guard members who are merely physically strong do not rank as high as those with extra abilities. Rank is marked by the color of the individual's cloak; the darker the cloak, the higher the vampire's rank. Jane and Alec wear the darkest cloak, outside of the true black of the actual coven members. The only guard who wears a darker cloak is Chelsea.

Generally, the Volturi do not keep the vampires of the world under close supervision. If a human were to discover the truth about vampires and remain silent, it is probable that the Volturi would never know and would leave the vampire responsible—and the human who possessed the new-found information—alone. The Volturi are concerned only with breaches that lead to widespread awareness in the human world. Certain news stories, books, or movies about vampires occasionally pique the interest of the Volturi. Members of the guard then trace the information to its source, assess the threat, and silence it if need be.

Many vampires around the world aspire to be accepted into the Volturi, as vampires are drawn to power. However, most of them have nothing to offer the Volturi that the Volturi don't already have. Vampires with powerful skills unmatched in the Volturi's current coven are invited to take the place of older, less skilled vampires. Depending on the circumstances, a demoted vampire might go off on his or her own, join another coven, or be executed.

"As I STARED AT THE ANCIENT SIENNA WALLS AND TOWERS CROWNING
THE PEAK OF THE STEEP HILL, I FELT ANOTHER,
MORE SELFISH KIND OF DREAD THRILL THROUGH ME."

—Bella, on her arrival in the city of Volterra (*New Moon*, Chapter 19)

ARO

NAME: Aro

DATE OF BIRTH: Around 1300 B.C.

DATE OF TRANSFORMATION: Around 1260 B.C.

SOURCE OF TRANSFORMATION: Unknown

PLACE OF ORIGIN: Greece

HAIR COLOR: Black

EYE COLOR: Red/black, with an overlying milky film (vampire)

HEIGHT: 5'10"

PHYSICAL DESCRIPTION: Aro has an average build and is incredibly graceful in his movements. He has shoulder-length jet-black hair and perfect features. His skin is translucent white, slightly resembling the casing of an onion.

SPECIAL ABILITIES: When he touches someone, he can read every thought the person has ever had.

EDUCATION/OCCUPATION: He is one of the three leaders of the Volturi coven, along with Caius and Marcus. He usually acts as the Volturi spokesperson.

FAMILY/COVEN RELATIONSHIPS: His mate is Sulpicia. His closest coven members are Caius, Marcus, and Athenodora. His natural sister, Didyme, is deceased. He and the other original Volturi are served by members of the Volturi guard.

PERSONAL HISTORY:

Aro was born in Greece just after 1300 B.C. All his life, he was ambitious; power was always his primary goal. It was in the pursuit of this goal that he was transformed into a vampire in his mid-twenties. During the first century of his vampire life, he joined forces with two other vampires, Marcus and Caius, and transformed two humans into vampires: his sister, Didyme; and his future wife, Sulpicia. Aro formed this coven (which also included Caius's wife, Athenodora) in order to further his ruling ambition, seeking strength in numbers to augment his own powerful mind-reading talent. Originally, Aro, Caius, and Marcus agreed to rule jointly, but Aro was always the decision-making force behind the threesome. It was Aro who devised the plan on which the Volturi ultimately founded their reign over the vampire world: the concept of vampire laws of mutual convenience.

Over time, Marcus lost interest in the coven due to personal tragedy, and Caius grew obsessed with solely the punitive side of governing. Aro handled every other aspect of the Volturi rule.

Aro was the last of the coven to form a romantic attachment. After Marcus and Didyme fell in love, Aro felt that the balance of power had swung away from him (before this, he would have counted his sister an infallible ally; now he assumed she would side with Marcus in any difference of opinion in the coven). Aro decided in advance that he would rather choose a human and create a mate than look for his match in another vampire, who might have ties to her own creator or other relationships that would complicate his plans. He had a certain type of woman in mind, and he found what he was looking for in Sulpicia: a lovely young orphan with few ties to her human community. He courted her successfully, and she agreed to be transformed into a vampire and join Aro as his wife. She remains totally devoted and loyal to Aro.

> *Aro was the last of the coven to form a romantic attachment.*

Aro had chosen to transform his sister because he hoped she might have a gift similar to his own powerful mind-reading gift. He was disappointed in this, and later disposed of her when she got in the way of his plans by distracting Marcus—her mate—from Aro's goals. One unintended consequence of this action was the near total debilitation of Marcus by the loss of his mate. Aro and Caius were both disturbed to realize that they were vulnerable to a similar devastation; they immediately sought safeguards for their own wives. Over time, as Aro and Caius increased security in every way they could devise, Sulpicia and Athenodora became virtual prisoners in their home. Part of their confinement, however, included a vampire talented at making them feel content. With Corin as part of their personal guard, Sulpicia and Athenodora never objected to their incarceration.

Despite his failure with Didyme, Aro never stopped seeking out talented vampires who could add to his power. He created the Volturi guard out of gifted vampires who shared his desire for authority. The guard were never fully part of the coven or the ruling body, but they gained prestige and protection by joining them in a subordinate position. After Aro acquired Chelsea (then Charmion)—who had the ability to bind people to one another and break any bonds that already existed—he was able to influence vampires to join the guard who would not otherwise have been motivated by power or prestige.

He created the Volturi guard out of gifted vampires who shared his desire for authority.

Aro made one of his best discoveries around 800 A.D.: the young twins Jane and Alec. Having already created a prohibition against immortal children, Aro left the talented humans to grow up in their native village, planning to transform

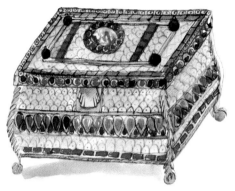

them when they reached adulthood. Unfortunately, Jane's and Alec's psychic gifts were very pronounced for mere humans, and drew the notice of the other humans around them. Though still children, Jane and Alec were condemned as witches and burned at the stake. Aro arrived immediately upon hearing the news and found them still alive, but barely. He freed them and set the transformation in motion at once. Then, having revealed his true nature in a rather dramatic way, he was compelled to destroy the entire village in order to obey his own law. He left no witnesses, and brought home his two most valuable assets.

Just because a human or a vampire has a special talent doesn't guarantee that Aro will add him or her to the coven. Aro seeks out talents that will make him more powerful, especially on the battlefield. For example, in Aro's mind, Alice Cullen's ability to see into the future — a skill he's never had access to — is far more useful than Jasper Hale's ability to manipulate emotions, as he already has Chelsea and Corin, whose gifts are similar to Jasper's, but more suited to Aro's purposes. Aro is deliberate and patient by nature. When he locates a desirable new talent, such as Alice's, he plans carefully the best way to acquire it. He doesn't make a move if he believes that doing so might destroy that talent. Instead, he bides his time and explores other avenues toward his goal. For example, he might convert human psychics in the hope of duplicating the talent. If a vampire's talent is no longer needed — if Aro finds a vampire with a superior version of the same talent or, as in the case of Didyme, one vampire's presence interferes with another vampire's needed talent — Aro will restructure the guard. Sometimes, as with Didyme, he will do so by execution. However, Aro will allow an amicable separation when he sees no possible threat from releasing the talent, or if he thinks he might need access to that gift in the future but has no way to hold on to it now. This was the case with Eleazar.

Occasionally, vampires approach the Volturi directly to seek a position in the coven. Usually, Aro already has a better version of the gift or skill being offered, but if not, the applicant is gladly accepted. Vampires who are not satisfactory are allowed to leave in peace. Other vampires visit the Volturi simply out of curiosity. Aro encourages such pilgrimages, as it gives him a chance to read their minds. More than just a tactical advantage or a chance to locate other talented vampires, these readings provide Aro with much-needed entertainment throughout the millennia. Aro is endlessly interested in any kind of curiosity.

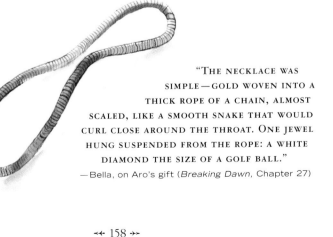

"THE NECKLACE WAS
SIMPLE — GOLD WOVEN INTO A
THICK ROPE OF A CHAIN, ALMOST
SCALED, LIKE A SMOOTH SNAKE THAT WOULD
CURL CLOSE AROUND THE THROAT. ONE JEWEL
HUNG SUSPENDED FROM THE ROPE: A WHITE
DIAMOND THE SIZE OF A GOLF BALL."
— Bella, on Aro's gift (*Breaking Dawn*, Chapter 27)

When Carlisle Cullen arrived in Volterra in the early 1700s, Aro was impressed and intrigued by Carlisle's "vegetarian" philosophy. Aro tried to convince Carlisle that drinking human blood was natural. He continually teased, prodded, and tested Carlisle (for example, by having a member of the guard deliver a profusely bleeding human body to the library where Carlisle was studying, just to see what Carlisle would do).

Aro was torn between wanting Carlisle to stay strong — the limits of Carlisle's resolve fascinated him — and wanting him to surrender to his true nature. After about two decades, Carlisle left the Volturi coven on good terms to travel to America. Before he left, his visit with the Volturi was captured in a painting by Francesco Solimena, an Italian painter who favored the Baroque style. Aro intended to drop in on Carlisle later in his life, in four or five hundred years, to see how things had turned out for him.

FAMOUS QUOTES

"I love a happy ending. They are so rare." New Moon, Chapter 21

"But still — la tua cantante! What a waste!"
New Moon, Chapter 21

"I certainly never thought to see Carlisle bested for self-control of all things, but you put him to shame."
New Moon, Chapter 21

"Besides, I'm so terribly curious to see how Bella turns out!"
New Moon, Chapter 21

"I doubt whether any two among gods or mortals have ever seen quite so clearly." Breaking Dawn, Chapter 36

"Oh well, we're all together now! Isn't it lovely?"
Breaking Dawn, Chapter 37

NAME: Caius

DATE OF BIRTH: Sometime before 1300 B.C.

DATE OF TRANSFORMATION: Unknown

SOURCE OF TRANSFORMATION: Unknown

PLACE OF ORIGIN: Greece

HAIR COLOR: White

EYE COLOR: Red/black, with an overlying milky film (vampire)

HEIGHT: 5'9"

PHYSICAL DESCRIPTION: Caius has an average build and is extremely graceful; he almost appears to be floating when he moves. He has shoulder-length snow-white hair. His white skin is translucent and looks insubstantial.

SPECIAL ABILITIES: He does not possess a quantifiable supernatural ability.

EDUCATION/OCCUPATION: He is one of the three leaders of the Volturi coven, along with Aro and Marcus.

FAMILY/COVEN RELATIONSHIPS: Caius's mate is Athenodora. His closest coven members are Aro, Marcus, and Sulpicia. He and the other original Volturi are served by members of the Volturi guard.

PERSONAL HISTORY:

Caius was born at least a century before Aro, and was transformed into a vampire when he was in his late forties. Before he met Aro, he'd run afoul of the Romanian coven. Caius escaped with his life but developed a great hatred for the powerful Romanians. He met a female vampire named Athenodora and they began to travel together as a bonded pair. Caius met Aro for the first time when Aro was only a few years into his vampire life. Young though he was, Aro was already formulating his plan to dominate the vampire world. He had formed a coven with another talented vampire, Marcus. Caius was immediately attracted to the idea of joining forces with the gifted vampires. He didn't like feeling weak, knowing that the Romanians—or anyone stronger than him—would be able to destroy him at will. He wanted to be powerful and strong as much as Aro did. Though Caius had no psychic gift, Aro was drawn to Caius's ambition and passionate capacity to hate; he saw a great potential for manipulation in what could be both a weakness and a strength.

> **Caius was immediately attracted to the idea of joining forces with the gifted vampires.**

Caius and Athenodora doubled Aro's numbers, and then they were quickly joined by Aro's sister, Didyme, and later Aro's romantic interest, Sulpicia. Aro and Caius worried about diluting their power further, and from then on brought vampires into the coven as subordinates only.

Aro and Caius were in agreement again after Didyme's death devastated Marcus: The wives must be protected at all costs. Thanks to the unchanging nature of the vampire, Caius is still as devoted to Athenodora as he was when they first fell in love. He is able to reconcile this love with her prisonlike circumstances by telling himself that it is the only way to protect her.

Caius was not as patient as Aro, but was willing to follow Aro's long-term plan because he could see that doing so gave him a better chance of getting what he wanted than seeking it head-on would. He supported Aro's cause, enforced vampire discretion, because it brought him to his ultimate goal: war against the Romanian coven.

After the Romanians were mostly destroyed, Caius was

satisfied to spend his time punishing offenders of Aro's law, while leaving the rest of the decision-making to Aro. Caius wouldn't have been quite as satisfied without Chelsea's influence, but Aro made sure that she kept him tightly bound to the coven.

After the Romanians were all but extinct, Caius kept himself occupied with other crusades. One was his campaign to wipe out the werewolf population. Similar to his response to the Romanians, Caius had once felt vulnerable and powerless during an attack by a werewolf. His characteristic reaction was to attempt to destroy the entire species that had made him feel helpless. (The werewolves he hunted to near extinction are also known as the Children of the Moon. They are not related to the Quileute wolves.)

Caius led most of the hunting parties and always participated in the destruction of offenders.

Another crusade was the offensive against the immortal children. Caius led most of the hunting parties and always participated in the destruction of offenders. He also oversaw the clean-up after the Southern Wars, making sure the newborn armies and their creators were utterly annihilated. Caius is always at the head of any Volturi punishing expedition, leaving Aro free for more important projects.

FAMOUS QUOTES

"And we will visit you as well. To be sure that you follow through on your side. Were I you, I would not delay too long. We do not offer second chances." New Moon, Chapter 21

"Now she has taken full responsibility for her actions."
Breaking Dawn, Chapter 37

MARCUS

NAME: Marcus

DATE OF BIRTH: Around 1350 B.C.

DATE OF TRANSFORMATION: Unknown

SOURCE OF TRANSFORMATION: Unknown

PLACE OF ORIGIN: Greece

HAIR COLOR: Black

EYE COLOR: Red/black, with an overlying milky film (vampire)

HEIGHT: 6'0"

PHYSICAL DESCRIPTION: Marcus has an average build and, like Aro and Caius, is incredibly graceful in his movements. His black hair is shoulder length, and his white skin is translucent, with a papery texture.

SPECIAL ABILITIES: He can see the relationships or connections people have to one another. For example, in a group situation he can easily pick out the leader, or sense the strength of the bond between mates or friends. He can also see where those bonds are weak.

EDUCATION/OCCUPATION: He is one of the three leaders of the Volturi coven, along with Aro and Caius.

FAMILY/COVEN RELATIONSHIPS: His mate, Didyme, died long ago. His closest coven members are Aro, Caius, Sulpicia, and Athenodora. He and the other original Volturi are served by members of the Volturi guard.

PERSONAL HISTORY:

Marcus is physically the youngest of the Volturi. He was transformed into a vampire before he was twenty. Aro found Marcus soon after his own transformation. Marcus was a solitary nomad at the time, but he quickly grew fond of enthusiastic young Aro. Aro was the first friend Marcus had as a vampire. When Aro wanted to form a coven with Caius and Athenodora, Marcus was hesitant. He didn't trust the very intense and bitter newcomer, but Aro talked him into the partnership. With his gift, Marcus could see the growing ties between Aro and Caius, but he never truly understood what Aro saw in Caius.

Marcus's life changed dramatically when Aro brought home his newly turned younger sister, Didyme, along with the first members of the guard — vampires who were drawn to Didyme's aura of happiness. None of these early subordinates lasted more than a few centuries; they were still experimental at that point. Didyme's gift had always been with her, though subtler during her human years, and so she was used to many suitors. She did not take these suitors seriously; her true allegiance was to her brother. After her wild newborn years were over, however, she came to admire Marcus greatly. They fell in love with the strongest romantic bond of any of the Volturi, as Marcus was in a position to know.

They were so happy together that soon Aro's ambition to dominate the vampire world became increasingly less important to them. After a few centuries, Marcus and Didyme discussed leaving the Volturi to live on their own. Aro, having read both their thoughts, knew these plans. He wasn't pleased, but he pretended to give his blessing.

Marcus's power was much more valuable to Aro than was Didyme's. On the battlefield, Marcus could easily determine the leader and key members of the opposition by the bonds between them and the other fighters. He could tell which person would die for another, which would turn traitor given incentive. In a diplomatic situation, Marcus could see how foreign vampires felt about the Volturi if they would not allow contact with Aro. Within the coven, Marcus could see if someone's loyalty was wavering, or if someone's feelings for another had become stronger than their bond to the coven. He was also quite dangerous in a fight—a skill Didyme did not share.

Aro waited for an opportunity, and when he knew he would not be caught, he murdered his sister, despite the fact that he truly loved her. Aro's grief was genuine, and Marcus never found out that he was responsible. Aro seemed to do everything in his power to discover the culprit, but of course all of his efforts, combined with those of Marcus and Caius, came to nothing. Once he'd given up hope of vengeance, Marcus became incapacitated by grief. He lost interest in the coven and began to consider suicide. Aro had sacrificed his beloved sister in order to keep Marcus's valuable gift in his coven, and he was aghast at the possibility of losing Marcus after all. Aro discovered Chelsea and used her gift to keep Marcus tied to the fortunes of the Volturi; he was unable to abandon the coven, even through suicide. Chelsea's gift kept Marcus loyal to Aro, but it was not enough to make him show any enthusiasm for the Volturi. Aro tried to make Marcus more amenable through Corin's gift, but Marcus refused to accept her comfort. He did not want to forget his pain. Corin's gift proved more useful with the wives.

⤙ OTHER MEMBERS OF THE VOLTURI COVEN

ATHENODORA Caius's mate

DIDYME The deceased mate of Marcus, and sister of Aro

SULPICIA Aro's mate

The Volturi Guard

 ## Alec

NAME: Alec

DATE OF BIRTH: Prior to 800 A.D.

DATE OF TRANSFORMATION: Exact date unknown; around the age of 12 or 13

SOURCE OF TRANSFORMATION: Aro

PLACE OF ORIGIN: England

HAIR COLOR: Light brown

EYE COLOR: Red/black (vampire)

HEIGHT: 5'0"

PHYSICAL DESCRIPTION: Alec is taller than his twin sister, Jane, but not by much. He is boyish in appearance and resembles Jane, although his lips are not as full.

SPECIAL ABILITIES: Alec cuts off all physical senses — sight, touch, hearing, etc. — from anyone, human or vampire. He is also able to extend his power over a large group of humans or vampires at the same time. His gift manifests as a mist, nearly invisible, that moves slowly away from himself toward his object, blanketing all the space in between. He is able to project this mist several hundred meters. He can also control who his mist affects, allowing the other Volturi soldiers to kill his senseless victims easily.

EDUCATION/OCCUPATION: He is a member of the Volturi guard.

FAMILY/COVEN RELATIONSHIPS: Alec's twin sister, Jane, is also a member of the Volturi guard. Guard members show the Volturi the loyalty they would family.

PERSONAL HISTORY:

Alec was born in England around 800 A.D., son of an Anglo-Saxon woman and a Frankish soldier. He was born a few minutes after his fraternal twin sister, Jane. Both Alec and Jane had strong psychic abilities that were evident even in their human state. Aro was made aware of Alec and his sister through the thoughts of a visiting nomad. Aro visited the twins but decided they were too young to transform immediately (the Volturi had already instated its rules about immortal children). Aro left them in the care of their parents, planning to return in a few years. Though the twins' gifts were obvious to anyone paying attention, Aro observed no menace toward them. They were only toddlers at the time, however, and Aro did not foresee how public opinion toward them would change as they grew. If he'd had any suspicion of the villagers' eventual reaction to them, he would have taken them back to Volterra and raised them himself.

Alec and Jane grew older. As they got bigger, the villagers found their unsettling natures more and more disturbing. Their talents had not taken a focused shape at that point, but bad things tended to happen to people who were unkind to the twins or their family, and good luck followed those who were friendly to them. Eventually, the superstitious locals found the twins too frightening to endure. They were accused as witches and condemned to be burned at the stake. Aro was apprised of the situation by a nomad who knew of Aro's interest in the twins. Aro hurried to the village, arriving just in time to interrupt the execution.

Eventually, the superstitious locals found the twins too frightening to endure.

The horrible pain of burning affected both of the twins deeply, and shaped the way their psychic gifts manifested themselves after the transformation. As Alec burned, his entire focus was on escaping the pain. As a vampire, this focus translated into an ability to totally anesthetize any human or vampire. Because he could project this sensory deprivation over many targets at the same time, he became the single most valuable weapon in Aro's arsenal.

FAMOUS QUOTE

"They send you out for one and you come back with two... and a half." New Moon, Chapter 21

 CHELSEA

NAME: Chelsea, born Charmion
DATE OF BIRTH: Before 1100 B.C.
DATE OF TRANSFORMATION: Around 1100 B.C.
SOURCE OF TRANSFORMATION: Aro
PLACE OF ORIGIN: Greece
HAIR COLOR: Light brown
EYE COLOR: Red/black (vampire)
HEIGHT: 5'3"
PHYSICAL DESCRIPTION: Chelsea is short, with an hour-glass figure.
SPECIAL ABILITIES: Chelsea can influence the emotional ties that people feel toward one another by either strengthening their bonds or breaking them apart.

EDUCATION/OCCUPATION: She is a member of the Volturi guard.

FAMILY/COVEN RELATIONSHIPS: Her mate is Afton, another member of the Volturi guard. Guard members show the Volturi the loyalty they would family.

PERSONAL HISTORY:

Chelsea was born not long after the original Volturi members. She was originally named Charmion, but as she frequently interacts with humans and vampires outside the city of Volterra, she has changed her name a few times over the millennia in order to keep it from attracting attention. She chose the name Chelsea in the 1950s and will use it until it becomes uncommon.

Aro discovered Chelsea in the midst of a very difficult time for the Volturi. He had recently murdered his sister, Didyme, in order to hold on to his talented partner, Marcus. Unfortunately, after Marcus had exhausted his search for Didyme's killer, he became suicidal. Aro did what he could to keep Marcus from finding a way to end his life, but he could tell he was losing the battle. When he discovered Chelsea, he was quick to utilize her abilities. He had her bind Marcus tightly to Aro so that he couldn't disobey Aro's wishes. Later Aro added Corin, hoping to help Marcus become more interested in the goals of the Volturi, but that was less effective; Marcus refused to let Corin's gift erase his pain.

Chelsea became the linchpin in Aro's organization. Her ability to both make and break emotional ties is the power that keeps the guard unified and the coven functional. She

Chelsea became the linchpin in Aro's organization.

is also able to dissolve the loyalties between coven members, with the exception of a romantically bonded pair; those ties are stronger than her power. The attachments she creates are nearly as strong as a romantic union. It was her ability that kept the powerful twins, Jane and Alec, from ever questioning their subordinate position to Aro and the rest of the coven, and that allowed Aro to recruit many gifted vampires—like Demetri and Heidi—who initially had no interest in the prestige of belonging to the Volturi. Her gift is long lasting; it does not fade immediately when she is not present. It does wear off over a matter of time—decades or centuries—depending on how long a person has been exposed to it before separating from her.

Because of her vital role, Chelsea is the vampire Aro is most dependent on and most vulnerable to.

Knowing this, Aro has a special relationship with Chelsea that is unlike any other among the guard. Chelsea wears the pure black robe of the coven leaders, and she always gets what she wants. For example, her mate, Afton, though not exceptionally skilled, holds a prestigious place with the guard. Chelsea enjoys all the perks of living with the Volturi, plus perfect job security—unless Aro finds someone with a better version of her talent.

> Because of her vital role, Chelsea is the vampire Aro is most dependent on and most vulnerable to.

Aro is nothing if not cautious, however, and he doesn't leave himself vulnerable for long. Aro made sure that Chelsea was often exposed to Corin's gift throughout the centuries; Chelsea is not aware of the true strength of Corin's addictive talent, but she would have a very difficult time leaving the Volturi.

→→ DEMETRI

NAME: Demetri

DATE OF BIRTH: Around 1000 A.D.

DATE OF TRANSFORMATION: Around 1000 A.D.

SOURCE OF TRANSFORMATION: Amun

PLACE OF ORIGIN: Greece

HAIR COLOR: Black

EYE COLOR: Red/black (vampire)

HEIGHT: 6'3"

PHYSICAL DESCRIPTION: Demetri is tall and lean. His pale skin has a faint olive tone. His wavy, dark hair is shoulder length.

SPECIAL ABILITIES: He is a skilled tracker. He catches the essence of a person's mind and then follows it like a scent over any distance.

EDUCATION/OCCUPATION: He is a member of the Volturi guard.

FAMILY/COVEN RELATIONSHIPS: Guard members show the Volturi the loyalty they would family.

PERSONAL HISTORY:

Demetri was originally discovered by the Egyptian coven's leader, Amun. Amun worked with Demetri to develop his tracking ability, and the two were very close. At the time, the Volturi had a tracker. However, when Aro heard that Amun had a more talented tracker than his own, he hurried to Egypt and offered Demetri a place with the Volturi. Demetri had no interest in leaving Amun, but Aro had Chelsea dissolve the bonds between the members of that coven, and then tie Demetri to the Volturi. Demetri joined them immediately.

Demetri is a permanent member of the guard and a part of

all of the Volturi's important missions. Though tracking gifts are more common than any other kind of psychic gift, Demetri is by far the best-known tracker in the vampire world. With the rare exception of strong mental shields, Demetri's gift is unstoppable and allows the Volturi to find anyone, anywhere. Demetri can link to a target once he has physically met that person, or he can pick up a person's trail from anyone who has met them in the past.

FAMOUS QUOTE

"Nice fishing." New Moon, Chapter 21

 FELIX

NAME: Felix

DATE OF BIRTH: Unknown

DATE OF TRANSFORMATION: Unknown

SOURCE OF TRANSFORMATION: Aro

PLACE OF ORIGIN: Unknown

HAIR COLOR: Black

EYE COLOR: Red/black (vampire)

HEIGHT: 6'7"

PHYSICAL DESCRIPTION: Felix is very tall and muscular. His pale skin has a slight olive cast. He has short, cropped black hair.

SPECIAL ABILITIES: He does not possess a quantifiable supernatural ability.

EDUCATION/OCCUPATION: He is a member of the Volturi guard.

FAMILY/COVEN RELATIONSHIPS: Guard members show the Volturi the loyalty they would family.

PERSONAL HISTORY:

Felix is one of the few members of the Volturi guard with no psychic talent. Instead, he is physically the strongest vampire that the Volturi have encountered. Felix wears the lighter gray cloak of a lesser member of the guard, but he does have a permanent position with them. Felix is a part of most of the Volturi's punitive missions. When there are larger threats, he is accompanied by other physically dominant members of the guard, like Santiago, or any of a number of other transitory guard members.

⤚ HEIDI

NAME: Heidi

  DATE OF BIRTH: Before 1550

  DATE OF TRANSFORMATION: Before 1550

  SOURCE OF TRANSFORMATION: Hilda

  PLACE OF ORIGIN: Germany

  HAIR COLOR: Mahogany

  EYE COLOR: Red/black (vampire), although she often wears blue contacts that make her red eyes appear violet.

  HEIGHT: 5'10"

  PHYSICAL DESCRIPTION: Heidi is tall and strikingly beautiful.

  SPECIAL ABILITIES: She is overwhelmingly physically appealing to men and women, humans and vampires. Resisting her allure is possible but also very difficult, especially if she is trying hard to attract.

EDUCATION/OCCUPATION: She is a member of the Volturi guard.

FAMILY/COVEN RELATIONSHIPS: Guard members show the Volturi the loyalty they would family.

PERSONAL HISTORY:

Heidi was originally changed by a vampire named Hilda, and belonged to her coven for several years. Hilda was later accused of attracting too much notice with her large coven. All but two of the vampires were destroyed: Heidi was considered penitent and so was spared, and the other — Victoria — was able to escape. Thanks to Chelsea, Heidi is totally loyal to the Volturi.

Heidi became a key member in the day-to-day existence of the Volturi. Her primary duty is orchestrating elaborate ploys to bring human victims to Volterra for the sustenance of the coven. She is required to bring them from far away, without leaving a trail. Heidi might arrange for a contest where the prize is an all-expenses-paid vacation to Turkey (or another random location), or a job interview for a position with an amazing salary. The victims never hear the word *Volterra*, and usually are unaware that they are even being taken to Italy. She has more than one jet and other vehicles and props to use in her efforts to attract humans to the Volturi's private city. Once an intended victim meets Heidi, it is difficult for him or her to refuse any invitation she extends.

> Her primary duty is orchestrating elaborate ploys to bring human victims to Volterra.

⇢ JANE

NAME: Jane

DATE OF BIRTH: Prior to 800 A.D.

DATE OF TRANSFORMATION: Exact date unknown; around the age of 12 or 13

SOURCE OF TRANSFORMATION: Aro

PLACE OF ORIGIN: England

HAIR COLOR: Pale brown

EYE COLOR: Red/black (vampire)

HEIGHT: 4'8"

PHYSICAL DESCRIPTION: If not for her girlish face and full lips, Jane could be mistaken for a preteen boy. She is quite short, and her childlike voice is high and thin. She usually speaks with an air of apathy or boredom. Despite all this, she has a commanding presence.

SPECIAL ABILITIES: She can cause people to experience excruciating pain that instantly incapacitates them. She can inflict this pain on only one target at a time; she must be able to see her victim to use her gift on him or her.

EDUCATION/OCCUPATION: She is a member of the Volturi guard.

FAMILY/COVEN RELATIONSHIPS: Her twin brother, Alec, is also a member of the Volturi guard. Guard members show the Volturi the loyalty they would family.

PERSONAL HISTORY:

Jane was chosen by Aro while she was still a human child. Aro's plan to let Jane and her brother mature with their human family backfired when superstitious locals condemned them as witches and sentenced them to death by fire. Aro arrived barely in time to save Jane and Alec from their accusers. While Alec focused his psychic powers on escaping his own pain, Jane was consumed with the desire to inflict her pain on those who were hurting her. This desire shaped her vampire talent into a very effective weapon.

While Alec—with his ability to use his gift on a great number of targets concurrently—is more advantageous in open battle, Jane's talent is more often used. As evidenced during Edward, Alice, and Bella's visit to Volterra, Jane's talent is frequently utilized to control potentially aggressive vampires. Just having her on hand usually guarantees Aro a polite and compliant audience.

> In the field Jane inspires a great deal of fear, which is helpful to the Volturi attack strategy, as well as to their reputation.

In the field Jane inspires a great deal of fear, which is helpful to the Volturi attack strategy, as well as to their reputation. Also, Caius enjoys using her talent to punish vampires before they are executed. Over the centuries, Jane has absorbed some of Caius's sadistic enjoyment in the process.

FAMOUS QUOTES

"We're not used to being rendered unnecessary. It's too bad we missed the fight. It sounds like it would have been entertaining to watch."
Eclipse, Chapter 25

"Caius will be so interested to hear that you're still human, Bella. Perhaps he'll decide to visit." Eclipse, Chapter 25

NAME: Renata

DATE OF BIRTH: 1240s

DATE OF TRANSFORMATION: 1260s

SOURCE OF TRANSFORMATION: Luca

PLACE OF ORIGIN: Malta

HAIR COLOR: Black

EYE COLOR: Red/black (vampire)

HEIGHT: 5'0"

PHYSICAL DESCRIPTION: Renata is slight in build.

SPECIAL ABILITIES: She can shield herself and others, repelling physical attacks and confusing the attacker and making him forget his purpose.

EDUCATION/OCCUPATION: She is a member of the Volturi guard and Aro's personal bodyguard.

FAMILY/COVEN RELATIONSHIPS: Guard members show the Volturi the loyalty they would family.

PERSONAL HISTORY:

Renata was born into an unusual, vampire-friendly family that has produced several vampires over the centuries, including, many years after Renata, a nomad named Makenna. Renata was changed by her great-uncle Luca (with a few dozen *great*s added) on her twentieth birthday. She originally intended to help her uncle protect and perpetuate their family line, but Renata was very talented. She quickly caught the attention of the Volturi and was invited to join. Luca, wanting no trouble with the Volturi—the way he interacted with his human relatives was already a gray area—encouraged her to go.

Thanks to Chelsea, Renata became exceptionally loyal to the Volturi, particularly Aro. On Aro's instructions, Chelsea attached Renata to Aro alone, rather than to all the leading Volturi together. Renata is so tightly bound to Aro that she would rather die than see him harmed. When Aro leaves Volterra, she is always at his side. She is able to repel attackers from herself and anyone in close physical proximity to her. Her gift causes assailants to become confused as they approach her. They find themselves moving in a new direction, with a blurred memory as to what they were trying to accomplish. She is able to push her shield several meters out from herself. She will also shield Caius and Marcus if they are nearby, but her primary concern is to protect Aro.

OTHER MEMBERS OF THE VOLTURI GUARD

AFTON: Chelsea's mate

Afton has a minor shielding skill, but it is limited by the fact that he cannot project it outside of himself. He has the ability to make himself invisible to attackers, but someone with a strong focus can see through the illusion. A person standing directly behind him can be hidden, too, but this is not a very reliable safeguard. Afton is not gifted enough to earn a place with the Volturi on his own merits; he owes his inclusion to his much more talented mate, Chelsea.

CORIN: A guard

Officially, Corin's primary job in the Volturi is to protect the surviving wives, Sulpicia and Athenodora. In reality, she does not protect them so much as soothe them into complacency while other, more physically impressive vampires do the actual job of guarding the wives. The wives are so closely protected that they have become virtual prisoners in Volterra. However, Corin's gift keeps them satisfied with life—even happy.

Corin is able to make anyone feel content in his or her circumstances. There is a druglike side effect to her skill, however. A person can become addicted to the feeling she produces, and be unable to feel well without it. Aro has been careful not to expose himself too greatly to Corin, while using Chelsea to keep her tied to the coven. Marcus has always refused to let her relieve his never-easing pain over Didyme's death. Caius, on the other hand, frequently uses Corin's gift to alleviate his boredom between battles and punishing expeditions.

> A person can become addicted to the feeling she produces, and be unable to feel well without it.

SANTIAGO: A guard

Like Felix, Santiago is a physical enforcer. He has no psychic gift, only tremendous physical strength.

✈ OTHERS WHO SERVE THE VOLTURI

NAME: Gianna

DATE OF BIRTH: Late 1970s

PLACE OF ORIGIN: Italy

HAIR COLOR: Black

EYE COLOR: Green

HEIGHT: 5'6"

PHYSICAL DESCRIPTION: Gianna was tall, with long, dark hair and olive-toned skin. She was beautiful, for a human.

EDUCATION/OCCUPATION: Gianna served as the receptionist and assistant to the Volturi coven.

FAMILY/COVEN RELATIONSHIPS: As a human, Gianna was not considered a member of the Volturi, although she was loyal to them.

PERSONAL HISTORY:

Gianna knew the Volturi's secret and kept it, serving them in the hope of one day being turned into a vampire. She knew that if she was not found helpful enough, she would be killed, but she chose to take the risk. Unfortunately, the Volturi decided her skills were less valuable than her blood.

The Volturi Lair

The Volturi maintain a permanent home in Volterra, Italy, which most of the actual coven—Caius being the exception—rarely leaves. The Volturi founded the town of Volterra three thousand years ago, during the time of the Etruscans. The Volturi still own almost all of the property in the vicinity.

The main structure of the Volturi's actual home is a castle constructed during medieval times, built into the walls of the ancient city. The most noticeable feature of the castle is the large turret that rises above the rest of the structure. Most of the living space is located below ground, in tunnels that run three stories beneath the town.

There are several entrances to the Volturi castle. The front door is located at street level. It opens to a reception area, where there is always a very polite human to receive visitors, as well as several inconspicuous surveillance cameras. All the doors in the room lead to dead-end, innocuous offices, and the elevator is heavily secured. This door is never used by the Volturi, their guard, or anyone who has real business with them. The elevator leads to another reception area, with even higher security.

> Most of the living space is located below ground, in tunnels that run three stories beneath the town.

The castle can also be accessed from Volterra's sewers. Several drainage holes in the stone-paved streets lead to often-used Volturi passageways. These drains are covered by iron grilles that are too heavy to be lifted by several human men together. These passages also lead to the second reception area, where the human in charge is aware of the nature of her bosses.

The most often used door is not actually located within the city. Rather, this door is located in the cellar of an ancient church outside the walls, somewhat hidden in the hills. Heidi's tours always end in this quaint, concealed historical landmark located beside a small private landing strip (owned by the Volturi). Just in case someone were to recognize the Tuscan landscape, there is no cell-phone service available. Thanks to Heidi's gift, when she asks her tourists to follow her into the beau-tiful, ancient tunnel that leads to an amazing castle, none of them refuse. This tunnel bypasses both reception areas and leads directly to the Volturi turret.

The turret contains the main meet-ing room of the Volturi, and also the dining room. They have made no attempt to make it comfortable for humans; the stone walls are not insulated, and there is no heat or cool-ing or artificial lighting. The room is lit by the arrow slits high above. The lone furnishings are three massive throne-like chairs that belong to Aro, Caius, and Marcus. They use these thrones when they are acting as magistrates, hearing cases against vampires who have infringed on the law. In the center of the room is a slight depression that contains a drain-age grate. The Volturi dispose of the bodies of their victims through this hole, which sits above a very deep cavern. Rou-tinely, these remains are reduced en masse by acid.

> Thanks to Heidi's gift, when she asks her tourists to follow her into the beautiful, ancient tunnel that leads to an amazing castle, none of them refuse.

"EDWARD WILL BE UNDER THE CLOCK TOWER,
TO THE NORTH OF THE SQUARE."

—Alice, to Bella (*New Moon*, Chapter 20)

"THE REUNITED AMAZONS HAD BEEN ANXIOUS TO RETURN
HOME AS WELL — THEY HAD A DIFFICULT TIME BEING AWAY
FROM THEIR BELOVED RAIN FOREST. . . ."

—Bella (*Breaking Dawn*, Chapter 39)

The Amazon Coven

The Amazon coven consists of three sisters, Kachiri, Zafrina, and Senna, all natives of the Pantanal wetlands. The sisters never interact with humans except when hunting; they do not associate with them or make any pretense of behaving in a human way. They are feral in appearance and rarely leave the unpopulated wetlands except to hunt. Few vampires — including the Volturi — have ever heard of this coven.

KACHIRI

NAME: Kachiri

DATE OF BIRTH: Unknown

DATE OF TRANSFORMATION: Unknown

SOURCE OF TRANSFORMATION: Unknown

PLACE OF ORIGIN: South America

HAIR COLOR: Black

EYE COLOR: Red/black (vampire)

HEIGHT: 6'4"

PHYSICAL DESCRIPTION: Kachiri is very tall, with thick black hair. Her features and limbs all appear unnaturally long.

SPECIAL ABILITIES: She does not possess a quantifiable supernatural ability.

FAMILY/COVEN RELATIONSHIPS: She is part of a coven with her sisters, Senna and Zafrina.

PERSONAL HISTORY:

Kachiri belonged to an ancient native tribe located on the

Their self-sufficient way of life has kept them a secret from most other vampires.

fringe of the Pantanal. After she was changed, she went back for her two closest friends. They've been together ever since, rarely leaving the wetlands, hunting in the habitations along the fringes. Their self-sufficient way of life has kept them a secret from most other vampires. Carlisle and his family discovered them in the 1940s while on a hunting trip; the Cullens' interest in large animal game brought them to an area other vampires dismissed for its lack of human prey. The Amazons were quite taken with Carlisle's gentle, friendly manner.

 SENNA

NAME: Senna
DATE OF BIRTH: Unknown
DATE OF TRANSFORMATION: Unknown
SOURCE OF TRANSFORMATION: Kachiri
PLACE OF ORIGIN: South America
HAIR COLOR: Black
EYE COLOR: Red/black (vampire)
HEIGHT: 5'11"
PHYSICAL DESCRIPTION: Senna is the shortest of the Amazons, but still very tall. She has the same long limbs and facial features as Kachiri and Zafrina. She wears

her black hair in a braid, and her clothing is home-made from animal skins.

SPECIAL ABILITIES: She does not possess a quantifiable supernatural ability.

FAMILY/COVEN RELATIONSHIPS: She is part of a coven with her sisters, Kachiri and Zafrina.

 ZAFRINA

NAME: Zafrina

DATE OF BIRTH: Unknown

DATE OF TRANSFORMATION: Unknown

SOURCE OF TRANSFORMATION: Kachiri

PLACE OF ORIGIN: South America

HAIR COLOR: Black

EYE COLOR: Red/black (vampire)

HEIGHT: 6'1"

PHYSICAL DESCRIPTION: Zafrina shares the same long limbs, fingers, and facial features as Senna and Kachiri. Like Senna, Zafrina wears her long hair in a braid, and her clothing is made out of animal hide.

SPECIAL ABILITIES: Zafrina has a strong illusory talent. She can make her target see any illusion she wants, or see nothing at all. Her range includes anyone in her eyesight.

FAMILY/COVEN RELATIONSHIPS: She is part of a coven with her sisters, Kachiri and Senna.

The Denali Coven

The Denali coven was originally founded by Sasha, who was responsible for transforming Tanya, Kate, and Irina into vampires. They considered Sasha their mother and one another sisters. After Sasha was executed by the Volturi for creating an immortal child, Vasilii, Tanya assumed leadership of the coven. The sisters often amused themselves by romancing local human men. Such trysts usually ended in a meal; their lovers never survived long. After a few centuries, the sisters began to regret their actions. They felt real affection for some of these men, and losing them was depressing. They tried to spare the men they associated with while hunting other humans, but this didn't work; the human blood was too hard to resist in such close proximity,

"DENALI WAS WHERE
THE ONE OTHER BAND
OF UNIQUE VAMPIRES—
GOOD ONES LIKE THE
CULLENS—LIVED."

—Bella (*New Moon*,
Chapter 3)

and eventually they would slip up. The longer one of them spent with a man, the more devastating it was when the man died. Finally Tanya devised a plan to give up human blood altogether. She had a similar experience in the woods as Carlisle did with his first vampire meal: She realized that unappetizing animal blood could quench her thirst. Her sisters decided to follow her example, and after many years of practice, they developed self-control to rival Carlisle's.

Around the time that Tanya and her sisters became comfortably settled into their "vegetarian" lifestyle, they met Carmen and Eleazar. The newcomers were very taken with the Denali coven's compassionate choice. Tanya invited them to stay and try out the "vegetarian" life. Both parties enjoyed one another's company so much that they made the situation permanent.

The coven was devastated by Irina's execution—again at the hands of the Volturi. At this difficult time they were joined by the nomad Garrett, who had formed an attachment with Kate.

CARMEN

NAME: Carmen

DATE OF BIRTH: 1700s

DATE OF TRANSFORMATION: 1700s

SOURCE OF TRANSFORMATION: Unknown

PLACE OF ORIGIN: Spain

HAIR COLOR: Dark brown

EYE COLOR: Gold/black (vampire)

HEIGHT: 5'5"

PHYSICAL DESCRIPTION: Carmen has a slight olive tone to her pale skin. Her hair is long and dark. Although she speaks flawless English, Spanish is her native language.

SPECIAL ABILITIES: She does not possess a quantifiable supernatural ability.

FAMILY/COVEN RELATIONSHIPS: She is part of a coven with Garrett, Katrina, and Tanya, and formerly Irina. Eleazar is her mate.

PERSONAL HISTORY:

They adopted the sisters' philosophy and were welcomed into the coven.

When Carmen fell in love with Eleazar, he was a member of the Volturi. Carmen had no talent to interest the Volturi, so she was not invited to join. For a while Eleazar worked for the Volturi while living with Carmen, but he felt the strain between his two worlds. Carmen was troubled by the violence of Eleazar's everyday life. Eventually he asked for and was granted permission to leave. Carmen and Eleazar spent several years traveling together and living as traditional vampires. But they sought a more peaceful existence and were pleased to meet the Denali sisters, who lived a "vegetarian" lifestyle. They adopted the sisters' philosophy and were welcomed into the coven.

FAMOUS QUOTE

"*May I hold you,* bebé linda?" *Breaking Dawn,* Chapter 30

✎➤ ELEAZAR

NAME: Eleazar

DATE OF BIRTH: 1700s

DATE OF TRANSFORMATION: 1700s

SOURCE OF TRANSFORMATION: Unknown

PLACE OF ORIGIN: Spain

HAIR COLOR: Dark brown

EYE COLOR: Gold/black (vampire)

HEIGHT: 5'11"

PHYSICAL DESCRIPTION: Eleazar's pale skin has a light olive cast. His hair is dark. Spanish is his first language.

SPECIAL ABILITIES: He has the ability to sense the type and strength of gifted vampires' talents.

FAMILY/COVEN RELATIONSHIPS: He is part of a coven with Garrett, Katrina, and Tanya, and formerly Irina. Carmen is his mate.

PERSONAL HISTORY:

Eleazar was once a member of the Volturi guard. A gentle person by nature, he wasn't entirely happy with their methods, but he felt he was serving the greater good by working with those who would uphold the laws he respected.

After Eleazar fell in love with Carmen, he asked Aro's permission to leave the Volturi, knowing that Carmen was not happy with his involvement. Aro didn't like the idea but nonetheless gave his blessing. He felt there was a good chance that Eleazar would come back to the Volturi if needed, and he did not want to destroy a talent that he had no backup for. The Volturi were not actively recruiting as they had before the acquisition of the twins, but the future was never certain, and Aro might need Eleazar again.

Following his departure from the Volturi guard, Eleazar, together with Carmen, sought a more compassionate lifestyle. They were elated upon discovering the Denali sisters and readily adopted the "vegetarian" philosophy.

FAMOUS QUOTES

"A very talented family." Breaking Dawn, Chapter 31

"No one can stand against them." Breaking Dawn, Chapter 31

 GARRETT

NAME: Garrett

DATE OF BIRTH: Mid-1700s

DATE OF TRANSFORMATION: Around 1780

SOURCE OF TRANSFORMATION: Unknown

PLACE OF ORIGIN: New England

HAIR COLOR: Sandy blond

EYE COLOR: Red/black (vampire)

HEIGHT: 6'2"

PHYSICAL DESCRIPTION: Garrett is tall and has a lanky build. He wears his long, sandy-colored hair tied back with a leather thong.

SPECIAL ABILITIES: He does not possess a quantifiable supernatural ability.

FAMILY/COVEN RELATIONSHIPS: He has recently joined the Denali coven with Carmen, Eleazar, Katrina, and Tanya. Kate is his mate.

PERSONAL HISTORY:

Garrett was transformed during the American Revolutionary War. A hotheaded patriot who willingly fought for the colonies' right to self-govern, he was a true believer in the American dream. His transformation occurred by accident in the aftermath of a battle.

Local vampires took advantage of the war's massive death toll to feast frequently. Garrett was with an isolated group of ten soldiers when a vampire attacked them, knocking Garrett unconscious at the beginning of the attack. The vampire drained the other nine soldiers. By the time he came to Garrett, he was so sated that he didn't drink much of Garrett's blood. Given the blow to Garrett's head, the vampire didn't expect the soldier to survive. Creating another vampire was not his intent.

After the transformation was complete, Garrett's quest to understand what had happened to him turned into a permanent characteristic. He is always curious and willing to investigate a mystery.

FAMOUS QUOTES

"Here's to freedom from oppression." Breaking Dawn, Chapter 34

"I have witnessed the bonds within this family — I say family *and* not *coven."* Breaking Dawn, Chapter 37

"Do you wish me to call you master, *too, like your sycophantic guard?"* Breaking Dawn, Chapter 37

"If we live through this, I'll follow you anywhere, woman." Breaking Dawn, Chapter 37

 IRINA

NAME: Irina

DATE OF BIRTH: 1000s

DATE OF TRANSFORMATION: 1000s

SOURCE OF TRANSFORMATION: Sasha

PLACE OF ORIGIN: Slovakia

HAIR COLOR: Pale blond

EYE COLOR: Gold/black (vampire)

HEIGHT: 5'2"

PHYSICAL DESCRIPTION: Irina had straight, chin-length, pale blond hair.

SPECIAL ABILITIES: She did not possess a quantifiable supernatural ability.

FAMILY/COVEN RELATIONSHIPS: She considered Kate and Tanya her sisters, even though they were not biologically related. All three were transformed by Sasha. Irina considered Sasha her mother. Carmen and Eleazar were also part of her coven. Irina was building a relationship with Laurent before his death.

PERSONAL HISTORY:

Irina was the third vampire added to Sasha's coven, after Tanya and Kate. As a human, Irina was a pretty peasant girl living in a small farm community. She physically resembled Tanya and Kate quite a bit, and Sasha liked the idea of adding a new sister for her other girls. Sasha considered the girls, including Irina after she was changed, to be her daughters, and they in turn loved her as a mother. They were a close-knit coven, so it came as a great surprise to Irina when she discovered that her mother had created an immortal child despite the Volturi law prohibiting them.

Irina and her sisters were devastated when the Volturi executed their mother and the child, though they did not fault the Volturi for their decision. Sasha knew the law as well as Irina did, and none of the sisters could understand what she'd done. They did, however, understand her decision to keep them in the dark; the sisters' total innocence of Sasha's act was the only reason the Volturi spared them.

All of the Denali sisters enjoyed the attention of men, both human and immortal, though — flirtatious by nature — none of them ever settled with one mate. As there were always more human men than vampire men, their relationships most often involved humans. In the beginning, these relationships with humans were short-lived and usually ended in a meal for one of the sisters. Their behavior earned them a place in human legend as the succubus. The myth varies from source to source, but at its essence is a tale of a beautiful demon who first seduces her prey and then drains him of life.

After a while, Irina and her sisters began to feel remorse; they were genuinely fond of many of the men they formed brief relationships with and regretted their deaths, though those deaths seemed inevitable. They tried to pursue such relationships without killing the man involved, but eventually they would make a mistake and he would die. The regret and guilt became too difficult to bear. For a long

After a while, Irina and her sisters began to feel remorse; they were genuinely fond of many of the men they formed brief relationships with and regretted their deaths, though those deaths seemed inevitable.

while, the sisters avoided human men completely—except as meals—but found this lonely. Tanya began to wonder if she could train herself to resist human blood altogether, and thereby make it possible to have human friends without killing them.

While testing her ability to go without drinking any blood, Tanya had a similar experience to Carlisle's; animal blood suddenly began to smell better than nothing at all. Tanya experimented with living on animal blood and came to the conclusion that abstaining did make it easier to be around humans. Irina and Kate were excited by this breakthrough and joined their sister in her experiment. After a few decades, all three sisters grew adept at this new diet, and at enjoying intimacy with humans without injury.

Over a century later, a nomad couple named Eleazar and Carmen crossed paths with Irina and her sisters. Both unusual among vampires due to their compassionate natures, Eleazar and Carmen were immediately intrigued by the sisters' choice to forgo murder. They stayed with the sisters to learn their way of life, and grew closer and closer. Soon, they asked to join Irina and her sisters permanently. The sisters were pleased to enlarge their family.

By the time the Denali clan encountered Carlisle, they all as good at vampire "vegetarianism" as he was. They quickly bonded with the Cullens over their shared lifestyle, and considered one another extended family from that time forward.

> After a few decades, all three sisters grew adept at this new diet, and at enjoying intimacy with humans without injury.

When Laurent came looking for the Denali sisters on Carlisle's instruction, Irina was intrigued by his interest in her family's way of life. She began to have romantic feelings for him, and he seemed to return them. Before their relationship could progress beyond this early stage, Laurent was killed by the Quileute wolves. Irina never really forgave the Cullens for defending the wolves' action, until she realized she was guilty of a much greater offense against them. Before she was killed, Irina had time to recognize how wrong she'd been to betray the Cullens to the Volturi without first asking them for their story.

FAMOUS QUOTE

"There was no crime. There's no valid reason for you to continue here." Breaking Dawn, Chapter 37

 KATRINA

NAME: Katrina; preferred name: Kate

DATE OF BIRTH: 1000s

DATE OF TRANSFORMATION: 1000s

SOURCE OF TRANSFORMATION: Sasha

PLACE OF ORIGIN: Slovakia

HAIR COLOR: Pale blond

EYE COLOR: Gold/black (vampire)

HEIGHT: 5'6"

PHYSICAL DESCRIPTION: Kate is tall and graceful, with long, straight hair the color of corn silk.

SPECIAL ABILITIES: She has the power to cause a painful, electric shock–like jolt in anyone she touches.

FAMILY/COVEN RELATIONSHIPS: She considers Irina and Tanya her sisters, even though they are not biologically related. All three were transformed by Sasha. Kate considered Sasha her mother. Carmen and Eleazar later joined the coven. In addition, Kate has become romantically interested in the nomad Garrett; he recently settled with the Denalis.

PERSONAL HISTORY:

As a human, Kate was an attendant — basically a bodyguard — to a highborn female in a warlike tribe of proto-Slavic people. She was well trained in the martial arts of her people. When Sasha and Tanya attacked a small caravan transporting Kate's charge, everyone but Kate was slaughtered. Sasha was impressed by Kate's courage and determination to save her mistress. Kate also resembled Tanya physically. On a whim, Sasha decided to create a sister for Tanya.

Kate's strongly developed sense of loyalty resulted in her becoming quickly bonded to her new family. Within a decade, Kate's ability to defend her mother and sister with more than normal physical means began to develop. She had the ability to create a sensation like an electric shock by touching someone else — vampire or human — with the palm of her hand. Although the shock was strongest in her hands, gradually she learned to control the intensity and to project it from any part of her body, though she always needed direct skin-to-skin contact.

> She had the ability to create a sensation like an electric shock by touching someone else — vampire or human — with the palm of her hand.

Kate had a deep sense of respect for authority, stemming from her early training with a ruling family. This respect transferred to the Volturi when she joined the vampire world and Sasha explained its laws to her. She was horrified when it was revealed that Sasha had broken those laws so egregiously in creating an immortal child. Despite her loyalty to her mother, Kate could not ignore the fact that the Volturi were in the right. When the Volturi spared her and her sisters' lives, Kate was grateful for their kindness. She never questioned their motives, and her respect for their authority did not waver.

Always lonely after the destruction of their mother, Kate and her sisters explored different kinds of company. All three were flirtatious and enjoyed the attention of men, whether human or vampire. The human relationships invariably ended in death for the man, and over time, the sisters began to feel remorse for killing these humans they'd felt a genuine fondness for. Kate was eager to try Tanya's solution — avoiding human blood altogether, with animal blood as a substitute. After a few decades, all three sisters grew adept at this new diet, and at enjoying intimacy with humans without causing injury.

A few centuries later, a nomad couple named Eleazar and Carmen crossed paths with Kate and her sisters and eventually joined the family permanently.

By the time the Denali clan encountered Carlisle, they were all as good at vampire "vegetarianism" as he was. The Denali coven came to bond with the Cullens over their "vegetarianism," and considered them extended family.

When Kate met Garrett, she found something she'd never found in another male. She is currently attempting monogamy for the first time in her long life.

FAMOUS QUOTES

"Keep the dream alive." Breaking Dawn, Chapter 4

"Nessie, would you like to come help your mother?"
Breaking Dawn, Chapter 32

"Jane's mine. She needs a taste of her own medicine."
Breaking Dawn, Chapter 38

TANYA

NAME: Tanya

DATE OF BIRTH: 1000s

DATE OF TRANSFORMATION: 1000s

SOURCE OF TRANSFORMATION: Sasha

PLACE OF ORIGIN: Slovakia

HAIR COLOR: Strawberry blond

EYE COLOR: Gold/black (vampire)

HEIGHT: 5'5"

PHYSICAL DESCRIPTION: Tanya is very beautiful, even for a vampire.

SPECIAL ABILITIES: She does not possess a quantifiable supernatural ability.

FAMILY/COVEN RELATIONSHIPS: She considers Kate and Irina her sisters, even though they are not biologically related. All three were transformed by Sasha. Tanya considered Sasha her mother. Carmen, Eleazar, and Garrett are also part of her coven.

PERSONAL HISTORY:

Tanya was the first of Sasha's adopted daughters. She was Sasha's biological great-niece, and when Sasha decided she'd like some companionship in her vampire life, she chose Tanya to join her. Sasha enjoyed having the company of another female so much that she added two more "daughters" to her coven in the first century after changing Tanya.

Tanya was the closest to Sasha, so she was even more shocked than the others when Sasha's crime was revealed. She could never understand why Sasha would act in such a way, but once the Volturi had tested Tanya and her sisters' innocence, she *did* understand why her adoptive mother would keep it a secret from her.

Losing Sasha was a tremendous blow to Tanya and her sisters. Tanya always felt like there was an immense hole in her life. She tried to fill the emptiness with a long line of flirtations, which were enough to frequently distract her from her loss. Tanya was the first of the sisters to become sensitive to the deaths of her human companions as she inevitably killed them for their blood. Over time, these smaller losses of short-term friends began to remind her too much of Sasha's death. When the pain of these losses became greater than her entertainment in the liaisons, she gave up human men for a time. Frustrated by the return of her nagging loneliness, Tanya tried to think of a way she could go back to her romantic pursuits without killing her human friends. After much thought, she decided it was the steady diet of human blood that made it so difficult for her to resist the blood of specific humans she wished to spare. Eventually, she discovered that substituting animal blood took care of her nutritional needs without weakening her ability to resist

> Losing Sasha was a tremendous blow to Tanya and her sisters.

human blood. Her sisters enthusiastically mimicked her new behavior, and in a few centuries they had perfected their "vegetarianism."

When Tanya met Eleazar and Carmen, she was happy to explain her dietary choices. As the newcomers became closer and closer to Tanya and her sisters, Tanya naturally took her place as the leader of the whole family. She was delighted to meet Carlisle when the Cullens finally encountered them, seeing him as her peer in many ways. She also was intrigued by Edward, mostly because he showed no interest in her advances despite the fact that he had no partner. Tanya never gave up her lighthearted pursuit of Edward, which is one of the reasons the Cullens did not settle in Alaska with the Denalis.

FAMOUS QUOTE

"We'll get to know each other later. We have eons of time for that!"
Breaking Dawn, Chapter 4

→→ OTHER MEMBERS OF THE DENALI COVEN

SASHA Creator of Irina, Kate, and Tanya. Sasha was killed by the Volturi for creating an immortal child, Vasilii.

VASILII The immortal child created by Sasha, Vasilii was physically three years old when Sasha transformed him. He was killed by the Volturi, along with Sasha, when his existence was discovered. He didn't meet the other members of Sasha's coven until the day he died.

The Egyptian Coven

The Egyptian coven is one of the oldest covens — if not the very oldest — in existence. The remaining coven is just a fraction of the size of the original, but they still hunt on their traditional lands.

AMUN

NAME: Amun

DATE OF BIRTH: Before 2500 B.C.

DATE OF TRANSFORMATION: Unknown

SOURCE OF TRANSFORMATION: Unknown

PLACE OF ORIGIN: Egypt

HAIR COLOR: Black

EYE COLOR: Red/black (vampire)

HEIGHT: 5'8"

PHYSICAL DESCRIPTION: Amun's pale skin has a slight olive cast, indicating the darkness of his skin before transformation.

SPECIAL ABILITIES: He does not possess a quantifiable supernatural ability.

FAMILY/COVEN RELATIONSHIPS: He is the leader of his coven, which includes three others: his mate, Kebi; Benjamin, whom he created; and Benjamin's mate, Tia.

PERSONAL HISTORY:

Members of the Egyptian coven, including Amun, existed as individuals for centuries before the Romanians' rise to power. After the Romanians began to grow as a coven and dominate their part of the world, several solo vampires and vampire couples joined forces to protect their dominance in the Nile River Valley. Unlike the Romanians, they did not form a guard of subordinates or try to overthrow other vampire covens. Similar to the Romanians, they kept many human slaves and lived as gods. Also, none of them possessed psychic gifts.

The Egyptians and the Romanians coexisted; they were cordial to one another, though not friendly. Had the Romanians continued the expansion of their empire, eventually they probably would have tried to overthrow the much smaller Egyptian clan. Before the Romanians had time to move that far south, however, the Volturi attacked.

> The Egyptians and the Romanians coexisted; they were cordial to one another, though not friendly.

A century later, after the Volturi had soundly won the war against the Romanians, they continued their march against other covens that lived ostentatiously. Their next target was Egypt. Again, the Volturi began with an attempt at diplomacy. They sent ambassadors to the Egyptian "gods," explaining their cause and asking the Egyptians to comply. For the most part, the Egyptians were furious and refused to grant the Volturi any power over them. Only one Egyptian pair changed sides — Amun and Kebi. Amun knew that if the Volturi were able to overthrow the Romanians, the more peaceful Egyptian coven would be easy prey. He was right; the Egyptians were totally decimated in only five years.

Amun had a very strong survival instinct, and he was willing to bow to the Volturi if it kept him alive. Kebi followed Amun's choice without question. However, Amun was always bitter at having to surrender his former lifestyle. He loved the worship, the towering desert monuments, and the excess. He knew he could not plot against the Volturi, because Aro would find out. But he hoped that, over time, he could gain the strength to oppose them. He had learned from the Volturi methods, and he sought out talented humans and vampires.

Unfortunately for him, Aro was well aware of Amun's true desires. Aro felt the need to let Amun survive in the first place as an example to other covens, so they could see the truth of the Volturi's offer: As long as they did as the Volturi commanded, they could live. Aro always kept a close eye on Amun's movements afterward, so Aro was able to identify individuals Amun was trying to integrate into his coven and—if they had a valuable talent—invite them into the Volturi guard first. Sometimes he was too late, and Amun found a good prospect first. Demetri was one of Amun's acquisitions. But with Chelsea on his side, it was not hard for Aro to woo people away from Amun. In many other cases, Aro would simply accuse a coven of a crime when he wanted one of their talented members. He'd kill the rest and save the special one. But Aro enjoys toying with Amun too much to end his life that way.

Over the centuries, Amun gave up trying to create his own talented force. However, when he stumbled across Benjamin—who, as a human, was performing "magic" tricks in the streets of Cairo—he began to dream again. He became a total recluse, keeping Benjamin a deep secret by avoiding contact with any vampire or human who might possibly cross paths with the Volturi. He treated Benjamin

> Over the centuries, Amun gave up trying to create his own talented force.

as a son, and Benjamin viewed him as a father. The only big falling-out they had in the early years of their coven was when Benjamin left briefly to create his own mate, against Amun's wishes. Benjamin was quickly forgiven when he returned, with no harm done.

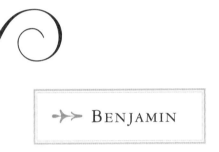

✈ BENJAMIN

NAME: Benjamin

DATE OF BIRTH: Between 1790 and 1800

DATE OF TRANSFORMATION: Between 1805 and 1820, at age 15

SOURCE OF TRANSFORMATION: Amun

PLACE OF ORIGIN: Egypt

HAIR COLOR: Black

EYE COLOR: Red/black (vampire)

HEIGHT: 5'7"

PHYSICAL DESCRIPTION: Benjamin appears to be a teenager, and his pale skin has the slight olive tone that is evidence of his much darker human skin.

SPECIAL ABILITIES: He can influence the elements — water, earth, fire, and air. He is able to physically manipulate the world around him with his will, similar to telekinetic powers.

FAMILY/COVEN RELATIONSHIPS: He was created by Amun, the leader of his coven, which also includes Amun's mate, Kebi; and Benjamin's mate, Tia.

PERSONAL HISTORY:

As a human, Benjamin grew up in the slums of Cairo. As a young child, he lost his mother, and he had no knowledge of his father. He was raised by his mother's extended family, handed around from grandmother to aunt to cousin — whoever was able to feed him at the time. Eventually he ended up in the hands of his mother's uncle, a street performer who took in unwanted young members of the family and taught them to dance and sing for money, sell trinkets, or pick pockets — whatever they were most adept at doing. Sometimes, he also profited from selling the children if they were no good at earning him money. The uncle discovered Benjamin's strange ability to control fire and taught him to do tricks with his gift. Benjamin became the most profitable member of the uncle's family, and therefore very dear to him.

> The uncle discovered Benjamin's strange ability to control fire and taught him to do tricks with his gift.

Among the children in the uncle's care was a girl named Tia, a distant relative of Benjamin's. Tia was an intelligent, serious child, and she and Benjamin grew very close. They watched out for and confided in each other. When Benjamin was fifteen and Tia was twelve, they decided that someday soon they would run away together.

Benjamin's audience was growing; more and more people heard about the amazing boy who could control fire. One night as he was performing for a large audience, Amun observed the show.

After so many frustrating losses to Aro, Amun did not hesitate. He snatched the boy from the street that night, in the process killing the uncle, whom Benjamin was walking home with.

Amun kept Benjamin hidden in his undiscovered, buried temple for five years. He and Kebi took turns hunting and bringing food home to Benjamin. Benjamin was never allowed to leave, so there was no chance someone would see him and mention him to the Volturi. Amun was honest with Benjamin to an extent; he told Benjamin that the Volturi existed and would want to steal him for themselves. He explained that the Volturi would use their gifts to enslave Benjamin, to take away his free will. However, Amun did not tell Benjamin why he himself wanted the boy — as a talent that could be added to his own coven in the hope of one day defying the Volturi. Amun treated Benjamin as his son, and never let on that Benjamin's talent was what he was really after. Benjamin responded to Amun's apparent kindness. He respected Amun and loved him as a father. His response to Kebi was less strong, mostly because Kebi did not show much affection for the boy. Amun was the center of her world, and all she really cared about.

Amun spent a great deal of time developing Benjamin's talent. He was overjoyed that the promise he'd seen in the human boy was more than answered in the young vampire. Benjamin was not only able to control fire easily; he also developed the ability to manipulate other elements. Wind came to him first after fire, then earth, and finally water. It was clear to Amun that Benjamin was an

> Benjamin was
> not only able to
> control fire easily;
> he also developed the
> ability to manipulate
> other elements.

unprecedented find. No one else like him existed in the vampire world. Amun was cautiously hopeful that his luck had finally turned.

After Benjamin had completely outgrown the newborn madness, he began to think more and more of Tia. Though his memories of her were dim, he remembered enough to worry about what would become of her without his protection, or his uncle's. Amun tried to convince Benjamin that human problems no longer applied to him, without success. Amun kept him as busy as possible, developing his talents and educating him in the arts and sciences, but Benjamin still found ample time to privately agonize over Tia's fate. He asked permission to look for her, but Amun was adamant. He told Benjamin it was far too dangerous to risk discovery, and that the Volturi would destroy Amun and Kebi to get to Benjamin.

About five years after his transformation, Benjamin disobeyed. One night when Amun was hunting, Benjamin briefly trapped Kebi with a small cave-in, and then escaped. Though it was his first time aboveground in five years, Benjamin remained totally focused. He was determined not to be responsible for putting Amun in any danger. He searched at night, questioning anyone connected to Tia, himself, or his uncle. He was careful to hunt inconspicuously, leaving no traces that might be reported to the Volturi. To avoid notice during the day he hid underground, in crevices he created himself.

It was clear to Amun that Benjamin was an unprecedented find. No one else like him existed in the vampire world.

"HE'D STREWN PILES OF
BOULDERS IN NATURAL-
LOOKING, NOW SNOW-
COVERED HEAPS ALL ALONG
THE BACK OF THE MEADOW.
THEY WEREN'T ENOUGH
TO INJURE A VAMPIRE, BUT
HOPEFULLY ENOUGH TO
DISTRACT ONE."

—Bella, on Benjamin
(*Breaking Dawn*, Chapter 35)

Eventually he found clues to Tia's trail, which led him to the port city of Suez, where she had been sold for a modest dowry to a much older man. She'd been fifteen at the time; she was now seventeen. Benjamin was conflicted. Tia was safe. She had a home and a husband. His plan to save her seemed unnecessary now. He watched her for two nights, wondering what the right course would be. Finally he decided to ask Tia.

He waited until an evening when her husband stayed late in the city, and then he called to her from her small garden. He was afraid to have her see him in the lamplight inside, afraid that she would be horrified by the changes in him. When Tia saw him through the window, she raced downstairs to meet him. Though she was momentarily shocked by his pale, hard skin, she was overjoyed to see him again, having thought for five years that he was dead.

Benjamin told her the truth right away, and explained why he'd come to find her. He said he realized now that she did not need rescuing, and told her he would go away. Tia was awestruck by the revelation that her best friend was an actual vampire, and yet still so compassionate and so much the boy she remembered. She asked for more details. As they talked, they walked away from Tia's house, through the dark city streets, so that her husband would not discover Benjamin when he returned. Benjamin told her all the details about his vampire life, Amun, Kebi, and hiding from the Volturi. They talked all night. When dawn was close, Tia worried that Benjamin would die. Benjamin told her about the sun's real effect on vampires. He offered to take her home before he had to hide, but Tia didn't want to go home—she'd already made up her mind. Benjamin needed her; she wasn't going to leave him to face the dangers of the Volturi alone. Benjamin warned her of the pain, but she would not be dissuaded.

Benjamin guessed that it would be wiser to convert Tia before taking her back to Amun. He created a deep fissure in the desert outside Suez and carried Tia inside. There he bit her, and then waited with her through the three days of her transformation. As soon as she was transformed, Benjamin took her hunting. When she was satiated, they went back to Amun's temple.

Benjamin guessed that it would be wiser to convert Tia before taking her back to Amun.

Amun was at first enraged, but quickly calmed down as Benjamin explained. Clearly, no harm had been done. Having Tia with him as a vampire would remove Benjamin's one tie to the human world. And Benjamin had proved that he could be relied upon in the outside world. Amun's coven began to live a little more normally, though always with the greatest secrecy possible. Benjamin was very happy in his coven, with Tia as his mate. He did not question Amun's motives.

"It's a pity you couldn't replace my will with your own in the process; perhaps then you would have been satisfied with me."
Breaking Dawn, Chapter 34

"Apparently, I'm a hot commodity. It appears I have to win the right to be free." Breaking Dawn, Chapter 34

✈ KEBI

NAME: Kebi
DATE OF BIRTH: Before 2500 B.C.
DATE OF TRANSFORMATION: Unknown
SOURCE OF TRANSFORMATION: Amun
PLACE OF ORIGIN: Egypt
HAIR COLOR: Black
EYE COLOR: Red/black (vampire)
HEIGHT: 5'3"
PHYSICAL DESCRIPTION: Kebi has long, curly black hair and a faint olive cast to her pale skin, denoting the darkness of her human skin.
SPECIAL ABILITIES: She does not possess a quantifiable supernatural ability.
FAMILY/COVEN RELATIONSHIPS: She is Amun's mate. Benjamin and Tia are also part of their coven.

PERSONAL HISTORY:

Kebi was chosen by Amun from his human slaves because of her beauty and total loyalty to her master. Even after her conversion, their relationship was never one of equals. When Amun decided to bow to the Volturi's demands, Kebi followed his lead without question. She would have done the same had he decided to defy the Volturi and end both their lives.

Kebi has little emotion for anyone besides Amun. Benjamin she tolerated because he made Amun happy, but she was somewhat jealous of the boy. When Benjamin brought Tia home, Kebi was pleased; she hoped Amun would be less entranced with the boy when it was clear he loved Tia more than Amun. Kebi's hopes about that rift were not entirely fulfilled, as Benjamin continued to love Amun as a father. But Amun's jealousy of Benjamin's affections, though well concealed, was enough to make Kebi content.

> Kebi has little emotion for anyone besides Amun.

➤➤ TIA

NAME: Tia

DATE OF BIRTH: Between 1790 and 1800; three years after Benjamin

DATE OF TRANSFORMATION: Five years after Benjamin's transformation, at age 17

SOURCE OF TRANSFORMATION: Benjamin

PLACE OF ORIGIN: Egypt

HAIR COLOR: Black

EYE COLOR: Red/black (vampire)

HEIGHT: 5'4"

PHYSICAL DESCRIPTION: Tia has heavy, straight black hair and pale skin with a slight olive tone, indicating the darkness of her skin before transformation.

SPECIAL ABILITIES: She does not possess a quantifiable supernatural ability.

FAMILY/COVEN RELATIONSHIPS: She is Benjamin's mate. They are in a coven with Amun and Kebi.

PERSONAL HISTORY:

Tia had a very large family; she was one of many children. Her overwhelmed and financially distraught mother began placing her children in the care of her second cousin (Benjamin's great-uncle) when she could no longer feed them. Tia was given away when she was five. She had a good singing voice and nimble fingers, so the uncle kept her with him. When she was about seven, Benjamin came to live with the uncle. Though Benjamin was three years her senior, he became her best friend and confidant. Tia was the first person to whom Benjamin revealed his gift with fire. It was Tia who suggested he show the uncle; she knew that a special ability like this would ensure that the uncle would hold on to Benjamin, thus keeping them together. As the years passed, their close friendship became more serious, and they planned to someday run away together. They held back small amounts of money instead of turning all their earnings over to the uncle, saving for that future.

> Tia was devastated when Benjamin disappeared.

Tia was devastated when Benjamin disappeared. When the uncle's body was found, everyone assumed that Benjamin was dead, too. Tia searched out her mother, whom she found in slightly better circumstances. Tia had all the money she and Benjamin had saved, and her mother was happy to let her stay with such a contribution. Tia continued performing and stealing to help her family. After a few years, Tia's mother was offered a dowry for the girl, which she accepted. Tia was married to a clerk for a shipping company and taken to Suez. Her circumstances were more comfortable than at home, and she was not unhappy. However, she did not love her husband.

When she saw Benjamin in her garden, Tia didn't question for a second that she would be leaving with him. Though she was totally unprepared for his changed appearance or revelations, none of it made a difference. When she realized that she couldn't effectively stay with him as a human, she was willing to become a vampire.

When she realized that she couldn't effectively stay with him as a human, she was willing to become a vampire.

Tia never embraced Amun or Kebi as fully as Benjamin had. She could see that, like the uncle, Amun was interested in Benjamin because of what he could get out of him. But as long as Amun's goal was the same as hers—to keep Benjamin safe—she had no problem staying with his coven.

The Irish Coven

The three members of the Irish coven are old friends of Carlisle Cullen's. Siobhan is the leader, but she and her mate, Liam, trust the judgment of their newest member, Maggie, who has a gift for knowing a lie when she hears one.

✈ LIAM

NAME: Liam

DATE OF BIRTH: Around 1615

DATE OF TRANSFORMATION: 1651, at approximately age 36

SOURCE OF TRANSFORMATION: Unknown

PLACE OF ORIGIN: Ireland

HAIR COLOR: Dark brown

EYE COLOR: Red/black (vampire)

HEIGHT: 6'5"

PHYSICAL DESCRIPTION: Liam is tall and lean, with an imposing countenance.

SPECIAL ABILITIES: He does not possess a quantifiable supernatural ability.

FAMILY/COVEN RELATIONSHIPS: Liam's mate is Siobhan. Maggie is the other member of their coven.

PERSONAL HISTORY:

Liam was an Irish warrior who fought in the Irish Rebellion of 1641 and later against Cromwell's reconquest of Ireland. Liam became a vampire through one of the most common types of accidental transformation: battlefield excess. After the Volturi came to power, vampires were unable to kill as recklessly as before, and most were forced to curb their appetites to avoid notice. The circumstances of war, however, gave them an opportunity to kill large numbers of humans at once without attracting attention from either humans or vampires. It became common among nomads to seek out human wars as an opportunity to feast. One of the consequences of this practice was the occasional unplanned transformation. Once a vampire was totally sated, she might continue to drink blood for enjoyment rather than need. In such situations, she might not drain enough blood from her victim to kill him. If she left him in that state without any further violence, he would begin the transformation process.

> Once a vampire was totally sated, she might continue to drink blood for enjoyment rather than need.

After Liam's conversion was complete, he went through the normal period of newborn behavior. He met Siobhan during his first six months of vampire life. She instructed him on the vampire laws, which kept him from drawing negative attention from the Volturi. Liam was very taken with Siobhan's strength and beauty. They joined forces quickly. Though it was never discussed, from the beginning Siobhan was the coven's leader.

When Liam was no longer a newborn, he became selective about his prey. For centuries he would kill only Englishmen. English soldiers are still his preferred victims.

Liam and Siobhan were well aware of the Volturi and their rules, and always behaved circumspectly. For Liam, as long as the Volturi did not become corrupted by their power and attempt to control more aspects of vampire life, he had no problem with them. He was born into a world where their laws of mutual convenience were accepted fact, and he did not question them.

Liam was not as fascinated as Siobhan by the stories of the Volturi guard's special talents. When Siobhan discovered Maggie and wanted to try to create her own talented vampire, Liam was opposed. He was concerned that the Volturi would resent the imitation, if they found out. More than that, he didn't want to share Siobhan's attention with anyone else. Siobhan transformed Maggie regardless, leaving Liam quite unhappy with her decision. Siobhan pled with him to give Maggie a chance, and he grudgingly agreed. It didn't take long for Liam to see the benefits of having a talented coven member, and over time he became quite fond of Maggie. He learned to consider her a younger sister.

 MAGGIE

NAME: Maggie
DATE OF BIRTH: 1832
DATE OF TRANSFORMATION: 1847, at age 15
SOURCE OF TRANSFORMATION: Siobhan
PLACE OF ORIGIN: Ireland
HAIR COLOR: Red
EYE COLOR: Blue (human); red/black (vampire)
HEIGHT: 5'2"
PHYSICAL DESCRIPTION: Maggie is short and very thin, and has bright red ringlets.
SPECIAL ABILITIES: She is able to tell if a person is lying.

FAMILY/COVEN RELATIONSHIPS: She is in a coven with Siobhan and Liam.

PERSONAL HISTORY:

Maggie always had difficulty dealing with authority, on a parental level and on a community level. The normal everyday hypocrisy that most people expected was always foreign to her. If someone said something that did not correspond with their true feelings, Maggie was instinctively aware of that discrepancy. In those situations, she felt compelled to point out the lie. Though this often led to punishment, sometimes quite severe, she was unable to let the lie pass. Her accuracy made people uncomfortable, and the closer someone was to her, the more uncomfortable she made them.

In the mid-1840s the Great Famine decimated her village. Everyone who could afford to immigrate to America left. This included her family, who had not quite enough to buy passage for every member. Maggie's maternal grandparents, who were already in poor condition, were left behind. Maggie was left, ostensibly to care for them as best she could. In reality—as Maggie was well aware—she was sacrificed because her parents did not love her as much as they loved her siblings. She was a trial to them, and they sometimes wondered if her abilities were demonic.

> In reality—as Maggie was well aware—she was sacrificed because her parents did not love her as much as they loved her siblings.

Siobhan and Liam found Maggie alone on the road to Cork, nearly dead from starvation. Naturally, when Siobhan questioned Maggie, her answers were the whole truth.

After Maggie's transformation, her ability became even

more pronounced. A person did not have to speak aloud for Maggie to know if he was behaving in a way contrary to what he believed. If a person misrepresented himself in either appearance or action, she knew.

Because Siobhan and Liam were routinely honest with each other and themselves, having Maggie join their coven was not the strain it might have been. It was easier for Maggie to be with them than it would have been otherwise; after her transformation, any kind of deception made her physically uncomfortable.

FAMOUS QUOTE

"I know truth is on Carlisle's side. I can't ignore that."
Breaking Dawn, Chapter 34

 SIOBHAN

NAME: Siobhan

DATE OF BIRTH: Around 1490

DATE OF TRANSFORMATION: Around 1510, at approximately age 20

SOURCE OF TRANSFORMATION: Sancar

PLACE OF ORIGIN: Ireland

HAIR COLOR: Black

EYE COLOR: Violet-blue (human); red/black (vampire)

HEIGHT: 6'2"

PHYSICAL DESCRIPTION: Siobhan is very tall, muscular, and voluptuous, with thick black hair and exceptionally beautiful facial features.

SPECIAL ABILITIES: Though Siobhan does not believe she has any talent, some suspect she can affect the outcome of a situation through willpower alone.

FAMILY/COVEN RELATIONSHIPS: Her mate is Liam, and Maggie is also in her coven.

PERSONAL HISTORY:

Siobhan was the only daughter of a blacksmith and his wife. This made her unusual in a village where most families were very large. She had a strikingly attractive face. Large violet-blue eyes, surrounded by incredibly long lashes, were her dominant feature. She also was known for her perfect fair skin. Aside from these things, however, she was unlike the other village beauties. By the time she was fourteen, she was taller than any other woman in the village. By the time she was sixteen, she was taller than all of the men, except for her father. She was also stronger than many of them; as an only child, she'd always helped her father at the forge. He died in an accident when she was seventeen, and by then she was strong and knowledgeable enough to take over his craft. This was unheard of, and disapproved of by many.

However, it was what she wanted, and the village needed a blacksmith. Eventually, she became an accepted part of village life and grew famous in the surrounding areas as the big blacksmith girl.

Despite her beautiful face and generous hourglass figure, Siobhan did not have suitors. Her height, strength, and profitable occupation were intimidating to the village men. This did not bother Siobhan, who saw no need for a husband. She was able to

> Eventually, she became an accepted part of village life and grew famous in the surrounding areas as the big blacksmith girl.

comfortably support herself and her mother, and she did not want anything else.

The physical size and strength that awed the locals, however, brought her to the attention of a Turkish vampire named Sancar. Sancar was creating a vampire harem, and he desired unusual women for his collection. Sancar traveled through all of Europe with human servants, seeking the exceptional. He heard of the beautiful Irish woman who was stronger than a man, and sought her out. She was like no one he'd ever seen before, and he decided to add her to his assortment of females.

Sancar gave Siobhan no warning or explanation. He abducted her in the night, raped her, bit her, and then carried her back to his home while she was still in the painful throes of the conversion process. Sancar had a difficult time dealing with the newborn Siobhan. She was incredibly strong, even for a newborn vampire. She also had no love for Sancar. For a while he was able to keep her distracted with plenty of blood, but before her first year as a vampire was over, she killed Sancar. She was then forced to destroy the three members of his harem coven who were devoted to him. The four others were not upset by Sancar's demise, and they all went their own ways.

She was intrigued by the amazing things they were rumored to be capable of, and by the warriors in the bunch.

Siobhan spent a few years traveling and learning the way vampires lived before she returned to Ireland. She was more widely nomadic for her first century, hunting across most of Europe and Asia. During that time, she met a few members of the Volturi guard. She was intrigued by the amazing things they were rumored to be capable of, and by the warriors in the bunch. She wondered if she was strong enough to be accept-able. But she never went to the Volturi to be considered. She didn't want to belong to anyone but herself.

On one of her return trips to Ireland, she found the newborn Liam. She was attracted to his fierceness and focus, both of which were appar-ent despite his newborn wildness. She could see that he was totally uneducated, and so she took him under her wing. After they joined forces, they stayed mostly in Ire-land. Liam was most comfortable there, though he did travel occa-sionally with Siobhan.

Siobhan and Liam had just finished hunting one night when they came across Maggie. Siobhan was startled when the delirious child

Siobhan was sure she had discovered one of those special humans who would have an extra ability as a vampire. She was excited to proceed.

accused them of not being human. Intrigued, Siobhan asked her how she knew, and Maggie explained the curse that had led to her abandonment.

Siobhan was sure she had discovered one of those special humans who would have an extra ability as a vampire. She was excited to proceed, but Liam was upset. He didn't under-stand why she would want to add someone to their coven. Weren't they happy as they were? Siobhan overruled him, and invited Maggie to join them, promising that she would never be hungry again. Maggie could sense that Siobhan was telling the truth, and that Siobhan did not mean her harm, so she agreed.

Siobhan asked Liam to trust her, and he reluctantly agreed to see how things would work out. Siobhan made it clear that Liam was her first priority, and he became reconciled to Maggie's presence more quickly than Siobhan had expected.

Siobhan also enjoyed Maggie's company more than she expected. She felt very maternal toward the girl, and fell naturally into the kind of close relationship she'd had with her own mother. She also enjoyed the advantage Maggie's talent gave her in any kind of interaction. Maggie learned to control her vocalizations, so she was able to simply nod or shake her head slightly to communicate whether or not someone was being honest. As long as she knew Siobhan was hearing the truth, she was comfortable.

While Siobhan was happy with her choice to include Maggie in her coven, she felt no desire to seek out other talented humans. Her curiosity about that world was satisfied.

FAMOUS QUOTE

"Shall I visualize the outcome I desire?" Breaking Dawn, Chapter 34

James's Coven

James, a tracker who loved the hunt, sought out the company of a few other vampires in order to use their help in his ongoing tracking games. His coven was nomadic. The members, all of whom are now deceased, drank human blood, as do most vampires, and they spent the majority of their lives outdoors. Because they never made the attempt to blend in with humans, they did not see the need to pay close attention to personal appearance; they looked feral to other vampires and to humans.

NAME: James

DATE OF BIRTH: Around 1780

DATE OF TRANSFORMATION: Around 1805, at approximately age 25

SOURCE OF TRANSFORMATION: A French vampire

PLACE OF ORIGIN: Present-day northwestern Pennsylvania, near Lake Erie

HAIR COLOR: Light brown

EYE COLOR: Red/black (vampire)

HEIGHT: 5'10"

PHYSICAL DESCRIPTION: With an average build and nondescript features, James was not as beautiful as most vampires.

SPECIAL ABILITIES: He was a skilled tracker, able to sense in advance the most likely moves of his prey.

FAMILY/COVEN RELATIONSHIPS: His mate was Victoria. Laurent also traveled in his coven for a short while.

PERSONAL HISTORY:

James was born near the end of the American Revolution. His father was a French trapper and his mother was an English girl who had come to the Americas as an indentured servant and subsequently run away from her master. They lived a nomadic lifestyle, spending most of their time on the trail and occasionally returning to Montreal or Pittsburgh to trade.

James was raised to track and trap, and he learned quickly. The Iroquois killed his parents before his eleventh birthday, but already his skills were developed enough that he was able to survive on his own. He gained a measure of fame during his late teens and early twenties as the best tracker on the frontier, as well as sometimes being called the ugliest. He didn't care about his face; all he cared about was winning. He was boastful about his prowess, and always up for a challenge. He won all contests of skill, until one night in Montreal, when he met a mysterious Frenchman — also claiming to be a tracker — who found James's confidence amusing. The Frenchman offered to best him in any test, his only condition being that the competition had to be at night. James was unimpressed by the dandified appearance of his competitor, and he agreed without hesitation, even when the Frenchman — seemingly in jest — upped the stakes to life or death. James's test was to release a marked deer into the wild, allow it an hour to run or hide, and then track it. Of course, the Frenchman found the deer in a matter of minutes. He returned the carcass to James, who had just begun his search, and reminded James that his life was forfeit. James — who had witnessed the speed with which the Frenchman moved and also saw no evidence of traditional hunting methods on the deer's body — cried foul. He said the Frenchman obviously had an undisclosed advantage, perhaps witchcraft or demonic help. If James were given the same advantage, he was sure he could beat the Frenchman.

He was quite pleased with his heightened abilities, and surprised that he was no longer considered ugly.

The French vampire was entertained by James's brash confidence. He agreed to give James the exact advantage he himself had, thinking it a good joke to end the bet by taking James's life in a different way. He bit James and left, laughing, offering a rematch in a decade or so.

James adjusted to vampire life fairly easily. He was quite pleased with his heightened abilities, and surprised that he was no longer considered ugly. But that didn't soften him toward the Frenchman. It was only about six months after the newborn madness had faded when he found the French vampire and killed him — James's idea of winning the bet.

Being a vampire made normal tracking — James's lifelong pursuit — somewhat boring. His senses were so developed that it was child's play to track any animal or human. To liven things up, James began giving himself harder and harder challenges. He would pick someone on a crowded city street, allow himself one sniff, and then walk away from the chase for a week or a month. Then he would return to the scene and track that individual. When that became too easy, he would do the same thing on a crowded dock, follow the ship a few months later, and search for his victim in another country. Sometimes these hunts took years, but James always found his prey. Because of his success, this got boring, too. He looked for bigger challenges, and began moving away from the practice of tracking for food. Instead he tracked vampires, a more worthy prey. This practice nearly cost him his life a few times, when he'd killed one member of a coven and then been set upon by the vengeful remnants. These dangerous experiences did not stop him; he enjoyed the escalated consequences of his game.

James met Victoria in England while playing this game. He caught the vampire scent, and though he had no idea whom he was tracking, he tried to hunt her down. It was the longest hunt he ever embarked on. No matter how fast he moved, she was one step ahead. He realized quickly that she somehow knew he was after her, though she'd had no warning. He got close enough a few times to catch glimpses of the beautiful redhead, but she always escaped. After a few years of

Victoria's super-developed sense
of self-preservation made teaming up
with such a lethal vampire look promising.

endless chasing, James was intrigued. He knew his tracking abilities went beyond just having excellent senses. He had a gift: He could predict his prey's moves in advance. But this vampire seemed to have a similar ability to know his own plans. He no longer wanted to kill the vampire; he wanted to learn more about her.

Unbeknownst to him, the less he meant her actual harm, the less effective her own skill became. She could feel the shift and eventually allowed him to catch up with her—in a place she'd chosen for its easy escape routes, just in case. She was also curious about this dogged pursuer who could somehow always find her trail again.

His own desires were always more important to him than Victoria was.

There was an immediate attraction between the two. They teamed up for more reasons than attraction, however. Victoria's super-developed sense of self-preservation made teaming up with such a lethal vampire look promising. James knew his ongoing search for the next big challenge was only going to get him into more dangerous circumstances as time went on; joining forces with a vampire so good at escaping would be a definite benefit. After a time, Victoria was totally bound to him; he was her mate. However, James was never as committed to the relationship. His own desires were always more important to him than Victoria was.

James did not view Victoria's survival as a failure, because he had found her and—in a way—claimed her life. He considered Alice Cullen his only failure.

While pursuing a different hunt, James came across Alice's scent. She was what the Volturi call "a singer" for James. The scent was very old, but James had tracked older. So, not abandoning his other hunt, James paused for a snack. Victoria, always the cautious one, was the first to be aware of the other vampire involved when James found the asylum where Alice had been incarcerated. She made James pause to get the lay of the land, thinking there might be more than one vampire; possibly this area was their hunting land, the asylum their headquarters. James never truly forgave her for making him hesitate in light of what happened.

The second James caught her scent, Alice saw a vision of him coming to kill her. She confided in her only friend, the old vampire who worked nights in the asylum. This vampire knew Alice was special and cared about her like a daughter. He decided to save her from James, but she foresaw failure after failure, and he started to realize what he was up against. He stole her from the asylum and hid her as well as he could, biting her before he left her alone. He went back to try to delay James, knowing he was no match for the strong tracker but hoping to give Alice the time she had foreseen might be enough to keep her alive. James easily overpowered the older vampire. As a precaution, Victoria questioned the old one, using rather extreme measures to extract all information about Alice and anyone else involved. James found the vampire's concern for Alice and interest in her baffling but intriguing. He paid attention to the story—until he found out that the old one had bitten Alice. He left Victoria with the still-living vampire and continued on to his prize. He was disappointed to find Alice clearly in the last throes of the vampire conversion—though she made no sound, an aftereffect of the shock treatments. All of her blood had been changed by the transformation, and there was no satisfying snack to be had. Alice was totally vulnerable, too lost in the pain of the process to even notice James's presence. He watched her wake and scramble away to look for blood, in the typical newborn fashion. He wondered if she would be special, as the old one believed. He decided to give her time to develop into a worthy adversary, though she looked too tiny and weak to give him much hope. Irritated by the loss of her blood, he returned and destroyed the old vampire.

As James grew more and more ambitious in his games, Victoria grew more cautious. She was the one who suggested teaming up with expendable allies just for the sake of numbers. They did this successfully a few times, letting the additions act as the canary in the mine during potentially dangerous situations, cannon fodder in others.

Laurent was wilier and more skilled than some others James and Victoria had chosen, so he lasted longer. He enjoyed the novelty of James's lifestyle. They all worked together easily through a couple of uneventful hunts.

James and Victoria heard rumors of large clans of vampires claiming areas in the Pacific Northwest, and James was attracted to the rumors of these unusually large covens. Victoria was wary; she wanted to find more backup, but James didn't want to waste time. He thought Laurent was more than enough.

James had no immediate objective in mind when they first met the Cullens. This was just an information-gathering trip. He let Laurent lead the way so that

As James grew more and more ambitious in his games, Victoria grew more cautious.

if the coven was hostile, Laurent would be their first priority. James was shocked and then thrilled by Bella's presence and Edward's protectiveness. Here was a hunt that would combine the best of both worlds: a delicious prize (though Bella was not a singer for James, she smelled much sweeter than the average human), and a huge coven bent on protecting her. He was determined to get to the prize before she was ruined, as Alice had been. The surprise of seeing Alice there only fueled this desire to win at last. He hoped that as they had not turned the girl so far, they had a reason for not acting, but he couldn't be sure.

"I THOUGHT THIS ROOM WOULD BE VISUALLY DRAMATIC FOR MY LITTLE FILM. THAT'S WHY I PICKED THIS PLACE TO MEET YOU. IT'S PERFECT, ISN'T IT?"
—James, to Bella (*Twilight*, Chapter 22)

James was furious when he learned of Laurent's defection, but in his hurry to get Bella before someone thought to change her, he postponed vengeance until after the hunt.

The hunt proved a huge disappointment. Rather than keeping Bella physically under his protection, as James would have preferred, Edward opted to try misdirection. Following his hunches, James wound up in the same city as Bella, and then struck upon a successful lure to separate her from the vampires. He was hopeful, however, that Edward and his family's search for revenge would prove more exciting.

> The surprise of seeing Alice there only fueled this desire to win at last.

He lied to Bella just once, in the dance studio. Of Alice, he said, "So I guess her coven ought to be able to derive some comfort from this experience. I get you, but they get her." In fact, he had no intention of letting Alice live. Now that Alice was able to care for herself and had the support of a strong coven, James planned to finish that hunt, too.

FAMOUS QUOTES

"You brought a snack?" Twilight, Chapter 18

"To be quite honest, I'm disappointed. I expected a much greater challenge." Twilight, Chapter 22

"I never will understand the obsession some vampires seem to form with you humans." Twilight, Chapter 22

NAME: Laurent

DATE OF BIRTH: 1700s

DATE OF TRANSFORMATION: 1740s, at approximately age 40

SOURCE OF TRANSFORMATION: Boris

PLACE OF ORIGIN: Paris, France

HAIR COLOR: Black

EYE COLOR: Red/black (vampire)

HEIGHT: 5'9"

PHYSICAL DESCRIPTION: Laurent had glossy black hair and pale skin with a slight olive tone. He had a medium, slightly muscular frame and an easy smile.

SPECIAL ABILITIES: He did not possess a quantifiable supernatural ability.

FAMILY/COVEN RELATIONSHIPS: He was once part of a coven with James and Victoria. He later formed an attachment to Irina in Denali.

PERSONAL HISTORY:

Laurent was born into an aristocratic but financially embarrassed family during the reign of King Louis XIV. He was the third son, and he had little in the way of prospects. Thanks to his older brother's marriage into a more prosperous family, Laurent was recommended for a minor position in the court of the Sun King. Laurent loved being a part of the court and had ambitions to rise. He was always attracted to people with power, and curried their favor. He had a knack for discerning who the most important person was in any given grouping, and then attaching himself to that person. There was a certain way about Laurent that made anyone he singled out feel more important. So he did well among the other aristocrats, and had a promising future.

His life changed when a mysterious ambassador, purportedly from the Romanov court in Russia, made a diplomatic visit to the French court. The ambassador's strange behavior was attributed to cultural differences. He came out of his quarters only at night, kept a retinue of mute servants and soldiers who were totally obedient, and always put off discussions of matters of state. He did seem to enjoy the entertainments of the French court immensely and was very interested in King Louis's art collection.

Laurent was irresistibly drawn to the Russian ambassador, who seemed to Laurent to exude true power. More even than the king himself, the Russian ambassador had no fear of any man.

> Laurent was irresistibly drawn to the Russian ambassador, who seemed to Laurent to exude true power.

The ambassador — a fun-loving Russian vampire named Boris who enjoyed human revelry — was flattered by the eager and admiring Laurent. He struck up a friendship with the French boy. When it was time for the Russian ambassador to leave (the number of vanished serving men and women was beginning to alarm many), he invited Laurent to go with him. Laurent's love of the powerful made this an easy decision; his instincts told him that Boris was more powerful than anyone he'd ever met.

Boris and Laurent became so close that eventually Boris told Laurent the truth about himself. Laurent begged to have the gift of power and immortality for himself. Boris was happy to comply.

For a while Boris and Laurent were companions, but Laurent quickly grew tired of Boris's jovial habits. Once Laurent was introduced to the vampire world, it was clear to him that there were others much more powerful than Boris.

The next relationship that changed Laurent's life was

with Vladimir, one of the surviving Romanians. Vladimir still radiated some of the power he had once held, and Laurent's reaction to that power was predictable. He did not follow Vladimir for long — Stefan was opposed to adding any new vampires to their number, favoring mobility and secrecy over everything else — but it was long enough. When he at last came in contact with the Volturi, he was already tainted. The Volturi were the epitome of vampire power, exactly the kind of vampires Laurent wanted to be with. But when he was brought to Aro as a prospective lesser-guard applicant, Aro saw the brief encounter with the Romanians and sent him away as untrustworthy. Laurent was unaware that members of the Volturi followed him for a few decades, hoping he would lead them to Vladimir.

Laurent always hoped that someday he would get another chance to join the Volturi. He wandered the world, allying himself with anyone who seemed to have power until he found someone more powerful. In this way he joined James and Victoria: James's aura of invincibility was very attractive to Laurent.

Another change occurred in Laurent's life when he, James, and Victoria clashed with the Cullens. His instincts told him he was on the wrong side of that conflict, and he quickly jumped ship to ingratiate himself with the Cullens by warning them about James. Laurent was confused by Carlisle, who had a very different kind of authority than he was used to. He was happy to stay out of the way

> Laurent always hoped that someday he would get another chance to join the Volturi.

until James was no longer an issue, hoping to study Carlisle's strength later.

The Denali sisters proved an interesting distraction. Tanya had a similar kind of influence as Carlisle. Laurent let their peaceful life envelop him for a short while, and enjoyed a passing flirtation with Irina, though he did not take it as seriously as she did. When Victoria sought him out—and after he was sure she was not there to kill him—he was seduced anew by the old kind of command. He decided to keep the lines of communication open with her, and do her the one favor she asked of him.

FAMOUS QUOTES

"Nothing stops James when he gets started." Twilight, Chapter 19

"I'm surprised they left you behind. Weren't you sort of a pet of theirs?" New Moon, Chapter 10

"Sometimes I cheat." New Moon, Chapter 10

NAME: Victoria

DATE OF BIRTH: 1550s

DATE OF TRANSFORMATION: Late 1560s, at approximately age 18

SOURCE OF TRANSFORMATION: Anne, her sister

PLACE OF ORIGIN: England

HAIR COLOR: Brilliant orange

EYE COLOR: Green (human); red/black (vampire)

HEIGHT: 5'6"

PHYSICAL DESCRIPTION: Victoria had a feline quality in the way she moved. Her eyes were fierce, and her orange hair was long and tousled, giving it the appearance of a flame. Her voice was unusually high-pitched, like that of a child.

SPECIAL ABILITIES: She was exceptionally good at evading enemies.

FAMILY/COVEN RELATIONSHIPS: She was James's mate, and after his death she created her own coven of newborns.

PERSONAL HISTORY:

Victoria was born in London in the mid-sixteenth century. Her mother was a scullery maid and her father was the master of the house. Victoria was the second illegitimate child, after her sister, Anne. They were raised as servants and worked hard from early childhood. Neither of them had much in the way of education. Anne had the misfortune of being quite pretty, with mahogany hair and a cream and rose complexion. Like her mother, Anne was subjected to the attentions of the men of the house beginning early in her adolescence. Victoria, on the other hand, had bright red hair, freckles, and eyes a shade of green that people called "witchy." Though her features were actually quite fine, she was still thought of as ill-favored. Eventually the sisters were able to get jobs together in a very fine establishment, Anne as a lady's maid, Victoria as a kitchen drudge. The master of the house was not a kind man, quick to beat a servant for any perceived fault—and lecherous as well. Both sisters, along with the other help, grew adept at disappearing whenever possible. With her shockingly bright hair, it was more difficult for Victoria to avoid notice than most, and she received extra beatings simply for being visible. She grew better at hiding, but when the master did catch her, he seemed irritated that she'd evaded him for so long and was more vicious in his punishments.

> With her shockingly bright hair, it was more difficult for Victoria to avoid notice than most, and she received extra beatings simply for being visible.

Though the jobs kept them fed, the sisters decided to flee when Victoria was twelve. Anne was very fond of her sister and feared for her life. It proved to be a bad decision. Without references, the girls were unable to find employment. They had no food and no shelter, and the cold season was coming. Anne finally agreed to work for a local pimp, on the condition that her sister could have free lodging with the other working girls. This situation was worse for Anne and nearly as bad for Victoria as the house they'd run from; however, it was better than the streets of London. Thanks to the heavy-handed pimp, Victoria perfected her ability to disappear despite her hair.

One night Anne went out to find a client and never came home. Victoria was heartbroken. The pimp, angry at losing one girl, was determined that the remaining sister would earn her way. The pimp kept her virtually a prisoner while she "learned her place." With her ability to escape, however, it wasn't long before she broke free. This put her back in the cold. To keep from freezing or starving, she became a kind of cat burglar: sneaking into houses at night, curling up in small, hidden places to sleep, and stealing as little food as possible to keep her theft from being noticed. She moved from house to house, leaving no trace of her existence. Even dogs did not react to her presence.

When she was fifteen, she was able to get a real job again. Having overheard the firing of a scullery maid, she presented herself at the opportune time and her lack of references was overlooked. It was hard work, but stable, and she was not hit often. She was content with her position for the most part. Trouble didn't start again until the pimp spotted her one day, buying groceries, and tried to follow her home. She evaded him easily, but she realized that now that he knew she was alive, he would keep looking. She thought of leaving the city, but she wasn't sure she could make a living in the country.

It was at that time that Anne found her. Victoria woke in the night to see Anne in her tiny attic room, standing over her. Anne was more beautiful than ever, though she'd lost all the pink in her cheeks. Victoria was ecstatic to see her sister alive and wanted to embrace her, but Anne kept her distance, moving at a speed that shocked and silenced Victoria.

Victoria was ecstatic to see her sister alive and wanted to embrace her, but Anne kept her distance, moving at a speed that shocked and silenced Victoria.

Anne wanted to know if Victoria was happy and safe. Slowly at first, Victoria began to answer all of Anne's questions. Anne was not satisfied with Victoria's predicament. She pondered aloud killing the pimp, but decided that he was only a small part of the problem. Victoria would never be safe until she was stronger than those who would hurt or control her. Anne asked Victoria if she would trust Anne's judgment. Victoria agreed. Anne picked Victoria up as if she were a doll and carried her out the attic window.

Apologizing first, Anne bit her sister. When Victoria revived from the transformation, she found herself in a beautiful country house, surrounded by four of the most beautiful women she had ever seen, including her sister. The other three were named Hilda, Mary, and Heidi, Heidi being by far the most beautiful of them all. Anne explained that Hilda, a nomadic German vampire, had saved her from her hard life out of pity, and then allowed her to go back for Victoria when she was able. The women, all with pasts similar to Anne's, were strong enough now to live as they wished, free from fear and abuse. For a short while, Victoria was perfectly happy. The coven of women coexisted easily because none of them craved power or authority. Two years after Victoria joined them, Hilda "rescued" another woman, Noela, who caught her fancy in the streets of Lisbon.

When Noela was still a newborn, the coven received a visit from the Volturi, led by Aro himself. With him were Caius, Jane, Chelsea, and a few of the more physical guards. Caius accused them of attracting too much human notice with their big coven of young, unruly newborns. Hilda defended her coven, maintaining that they had never introduced more than one newborn at a time, to be sure they could control

For a short while,
Victoria was perfectly happy.

them. Aro asked for evidence. Hilda agreed to prove her case with a handshake. After reading all her thoughts, Aro sadly claimed that the coven was guilty. Hilda angrily accused him of lying and was immediately slaughtered by the guards. Jane inflicted pain on each of the others in quick succession, halting their instinctive attack. Aro wanted to know if anyone was willing to live by the law — or would they all have to be destroyed? Almost as if in a dream, Heidi got to her feet and moved forward. Aro smiled and welcomed her while her former covenmates watched in shock.

> Victoria did not understand any of what she was watching, but she sensed that she and her sister were about to die whether they surrendered or not.

Victoria did not understand any of what she was watching, but she sensed that she and her sister were about to die whether they surrendered or not. She screamed for the others to run. Anne, Mary, and Noela all scattered in different directions than the one she took. Victoria was surprised when Jane did not attack again, not knowing that the Volturi guard enjoyed a good chase. Anne, Mary, and Noela were all quickly caught and dispatched. None of the Volturi worried much when the red-headed girl proved impossible to find. She was unimportant; they could deal with her some other time. For now, Aro was happy to go home with his prize.

That was the end of Victoria's peaceful vampire life. Now suspicious of other vampires, she avoided them all. With her gift, it was not difficult, until James. In James she found someone who was honest in his intentions and confident in his abilities. She was attracted to his gift, which was like a mirror of her own. Eventually she fell in love with his self-assurance. It felt safe to her, stable in an odd way. She was never aware that his feelings did not entirely reflect her own. While she was happier with James, her life definitely was not peaceful or easy. The way he liked to live constantly put her into situations that, on her own, she would have avoided.

When the Cullens killed James, Victoria lost her mate and her stability. She felt vulnerable. She quickly created a companion, choosing a strong young human man. She made sure Riley was totally loyal to her, and was surprised at how readily he believed she had changed him out of love. Then she made more vampires, feeling that if she could surround herself with allies, she would be safe. At the same time, she hid herself from these new allies, aside from Riley. She was extremely paranoid for a time, setting up layers of protection for herself. She was loosely copying what she'd seen with the Volturi guard, but waiting for her newborns to be old enough to train. In the meantime, she had Riley control them with carefully constructed lies — most notably, the myth that vampires were destroyed by the sun.

> She was extremely paranoid for a time, setting up layers of protection for herself.

In the first six months after James's death Victoria created fifteen newborns — and killed roughly four humans to every one that survived as a vampire. One of the first was Diego; one of the last — of this period — was Raoul. Fred was also created during this period. About half of this first wave did not survive during Victoria's absence.

Victoria's gift forewarned her when Edward was hunting her, just as it had with James. She left Riley behind to mind the other newborns she'd created. Passing through Texas,

Victoria ran up against a territorial coven with a small force of newborns. Victoria had no interest in a pitched battle over land and escaped easily. The encounter gave her new ideas for her newborns, though. When she was sure she'd thrown Edward off her trail, she headed back to the Pacific Northwest.

Victoria had not tried to avenge Anne; it wasn't in her nature to choose to put herself in danger.

Victoria had not tried to avenge Anne; it wasn't in her nature to choose to put herself in danger. However, her time with James had changed her in some ways. She was able to take slightly greater risks now. The newborns in Texas had inspired her to think beyond just protecting herself, to actively repaying Edward for what he'd done to her. Her plans in regard to the newborns shifted: They were no longer to be a guard for her, but an army.

The more plans she put into motion, she thought, the more likely one of them would succeed. The newborns were one option, but one that—were she to use them that way—would require more of a head-on confrontation than she was totally comfortable with. Another of her plans included Laurent. She traced him to Alaska and, feigning friendship (like James, Victoria had not forgiven the defection), she was able to glean all the information he'd learned about the Cullens from the Denalis. She asked him to do her a favor: Visit the Cullens and see if they were all still with the girl. It was win-win for Victoria; if Edward was back in Forks, she assumed he would kill Laurent when he saw the connection to Victoria in Laurent's head. If not, Laurent would bring back news of the girl's location and how many protected her.

Meanwhile, she created more newborns, leaving them under Riley's care, in case she ended up having to go through the full coven to get to the girl. After thinking carefully about Alice and her gift, Victoria put Riley in charge of making all the decisions about the newborns' movements. She made no plans to use the newborns for anything concrete. In fact, she thought about them as little as possible.

Laurent called Victoria once to report that the Cullen house was empty and he would look around to see if the girl had gone with them. She heard nothing more from Laurent. Very carefully, she went to investigate, and discovered the wolves. This was an unforeseen problem. James had tracked a werewolf once, for the challenge of it. He'd been successful, as usual. But werewolves were supposed to be nearly extinct, not traveling in large packs. Nor should they be able to maintain their wolf forms in the daylight. This was worrying, but secondary to the fact that Victoria had crossed a fresh trail left by the girl. The Cullens were gone, and all she had to do was get past the werewolves to find the girl totally alone.

This proved frustrating. With Victoria's powerful self-preservation instincts, it was nearly impossible for her to physically make a bold move. The wolves were able to drive her off again and again. She was patient, for she thought she had plenty of time. Then one night she caught Alice's scent and knew her hopes for an easy kill were over.

Riley and the newborns became her first priority. She created more and more of them, until Seattle was nearly overrun. Meanwhile, she continued making feints into the area around Forks, gathering information and hoping that the Cullens would believe these fruitless attacks were all she had up her sleeve.

FAMOUS QUOTE

"He's the liar, Riley. I told you about their mind tricks. You know I love only you." Eclipse, Chapter 24

The Mexican Coven

The Mexican coven was formed in the 1850s, its main purpose being to win back the land Maria had lost during the lesser hostilities that continued after the Volturi put an end to the Southern Wars. The coven lived on human blood and consisted mostly of often-replaced male newborns. Only Maria is presently a part of this coven.

LUCY

NAME: Lucy

DATE OF BIRTH: Unknown

DATE OF TRANSFORMATION: Unknown

SOURCE OF TRANSFORMATION: Unknown

PLACE OF ORIGIN: Northern Texas

HAIR COLOR: Blond

EYE COLOR: Red/black (vampire)

HEIGHT: 5'6"

PHYSICAL DESCRIPTION: Lucy was thin, and taller than Nettie and Maria.

SPECIAL ABILITIES: She did not possess a quantifiable supernatural ability.

FAMILY/COVEN RELATIONSHIPS: Lucy was part of Maria's coven, along with Nettie.

PERSONAL HISTORY:

Lucy joined Maria and Nettie to further her ambitions. Her former coven—just her and her mate—had come under attack from another coven that was expanding its territory into northern Texas. Her mate was killed, but she escaped. She wanted a new hunting range, and the power to keep it. Maria had a good vision for how to accomplish that, so Lucy followed her lead.

After Lucy's new coven had established itself, Lucy and Nettie began to feel that Maria had too much power. They did not want to surrender their territory to her and seek another place, so they tried to kill her and her right-hand man, Jasper, instead. They underestimated Jasper's abilities, and Maria was able to surprise them with a preemptive attack. Lucy and Nettie were both killed.

⇥ MARIA

NAME: Maria

DATE OF BIRTH: Unknown

DATE OF TRANSFORMATION: 1800s or earlier, at age 19

SOURCE OF TRANSFORMATION: Unknown

PLACE OF ORIGIN: Mexico

HAIR COLOR: Black

EYE COLOR: Red/black (vampire)

HEIGHT: 5'1"

PHYSICAL DESCRIPTION: Maria is very short and small-boned. She has long black hair and a slight olive tone to her pale skin, denoting a darker skin pigmentation in her human life.

SPECIAL ABILITIES: She does not possess a quantifiable supernatural ability.

FAMILY/COVEN RELATIONSHIPS: She formed a coven with Nettie and Lucy in the 1850s, and later added Jasper

Whitlock after she transformed him in 1863. Eventually she killed Nettie and Lucy, and Jasper left her coven.

PERSONAL HISTORY:

Before Maria's time, a young vampire named Benito, from Dallas, used the strength of newborn vampires on a massive scale to wipe out neighboring covens and take over their land. Once other covens realized what was happening, they, too, created armies of newborns, to try to defeat Benito. The Volturi eventually had to step in to clean up the havoc these reckless armies had created in the South, destroying every newborn they could find. To serve as a deterrent to future newborn armies, anyone associated with the newborns was also executed.

When the Volturi returned to Italy, the survivors in the South quickly laid claim to the land. Before long, the covens began having border disputes and the wars resumed, but on a smaller scale. Newborns were used again, but more quietly. No one wanted to give the Volturi a reason to return.

It was during one of these battles that Maria lost her coven, which included her mate and two older vampires who were — for all intents and purposes — her parents. Along with them she lost control over Monterrey, Mexico, and the surrounding area. Defeated and alone, she looked for allies to help her get revenge. She found Nettie and Lucy, both of whom were survivors of other battles, and together they formed a coven. Maria's goal was to reclaim her land and exact vengeance; Nettie and Lucy hoped to gain more hunting territory.

Maria took newborn armies to a new level by choosing humans with combat potential and giving them more training than anyone had bothered to do before. When Maria met a young Confederate officer named Jasper Whitlock, she hoped

Maria grew fond of Jasper, depending on him more and more.

his physical stature and military experience would make him a helpful addition to her army. She also sensed that there was something special about him, and her instincts were on target. After assessing his abilities, she put Jasper in charge of her other newborns. He was able to facilitate cooperation between the members of the group. Casualties dropped, and Maria's army swelled to around twenty newborns—a large number for that time. Even Nettie, Lucy, and Maria were able to work together more easily with Jasper around.

Thanks to her planning and Jasper's gifts, Maria's army was very successful. Maria grew fond of Jasper, depending on him more and more. Eventually Nettie and Lucy betrayed their alliance with Maria and planned to turn against her. Jasper was able to give Maria early warning, and she killed them both. Jasper became her only ally. However, she never treated him as an equal or thought of him as her mate. As was normal for the vampire temperament, Maria never forgot her deceased mate or moved on.

Several decades passed, and Maria noticed Jasper growing depressed. He was no longer interested in their lifestyle of conflict and acquisition. Maria grew paranoid that he might turn on her the way Nettie and Lucy had, and she made plans to destroy him first. She selected a few of the older, more promising newborns and plotted secretly with them, offering them Jasper's position and perks if they got him out of the way. Jasper was well aware of her shift in feelings toward him, and began making similar defensive plans against her with the newborns he most trusted. Before it came to that, however, Jasper found an alternative and left her coven for a new way of life in the North. Maria eventually forgave Jasper for his defection, and considers herself to be on good terms with him. She continues to zealously defend her territories in Mexico against interlopers.

FAMOUS QUOTE

"I truly hope you survive, Jasper. I have a good feeling about you."
Eclipse, Chapter 13

 NETTIE

NAME: Nettie

DATE OF BIRTH: Unknown

DATE OF TRANSFORMATION: Unknown

SOURCE OF TRANSFORMATION: Unknown

PLACE OF ORIGIN: Arkansas

HAIR COLOR: White blond

EYE COLOR: Red/black (vampire)

HEIGHT: 5'3"

PHYSICAL DESCRIPTION: Nettie was petite, but taller than Maria.

SPECIAL ABILITIES: She did not possess a quantifiable supernatural ability.

FAMILY/COVEN RELATIONSHIPS: Nettie was part of Maria's coven, along with Lucy.

PERSONAL HISTORY:

Like Lucy and Maria, Nettie was the sole survivor of a lost battle. The two older males in her coven were destroyed, and

Nettie was driven out of Arkansas. Maria and Lucy approached her and offered an alliance. Nettie wanted the safety of numbers, and she liked Maria's plan for a special newborn army. However, Nettie had less self-control than either Lucy or Maria, so she was not very involved with the creation of the newborns. It was Nettie who originally suggested to Lucy that they kill Maria and Jasper and take over the coven.

Riley's Coven

This coven of newborns was created by Victoria but controlled by Riley. Riley was the only authority figure the newborns knew. They lived in and around the city of Seattle and existed as a coven for less than a year. In their final organization as a newborn army, they became an illegal creation. None of the newborns knew of the Volturi laws that prohibited their lifestyle. While Riley knew of the newborns' ultimate fate as an army, none of the other newborns were aware of this fact until a few days before the attack that ended in the demise of the coven. There were three survivors of the coven, who went on to become nomads; none of them were present for the attack against the Cullens.

Riley was the only
authority figure
the newborns knew.

NAME: Riley Biers

DATE OF BIRTH: October 8, 1986

DATE OF TRANSFORMATION: April 13, 2005, at age 18

SOURCE OF TRANSFORMATION: Victoria

PLACE OF ORIGIN: Santa Fe, New Mexico

HAIR COLOR: Blond

EYE COLOR: Brown (human); red/black (vampire)

HEIGHT: 6'3"

PHYSICAL DESCRIPTION: Riley was muscular and tall.

SPECIAL ABILITIES: He did not possess a quantifiable supernatural ability.

FAMILY/COVEN RELATIONSHIPS: Riley managed a coven of newborns created by Victoria.

PERSONAL HISTORY:

Riley was born in Santa Fe and lived in several places in the Southwest and along the Pacific coast during his childhood and adolescence. He lived with his parents and siblings—an older sister and a younger brother. He attended Oregon State University. One night near the end of his freshman year, Victoria saw him playing soccer with his intramural team. Victoria was panicked and seeking protection; Riley looked large and strong. She attacked him on his way home from the game. When he was lucid, she told him that she'd been watching him and had fallen in love with him. Riley was awed by Victoria; he bought her story and quickly returned her perceived feelings for him.

> Victoria told Riley many stories, half-truths, and outright lies, and Riley had no reason to disbelieve her.

Victoria told Riley many stories, half-truths, and outright lies, and Riley had no reason to disbelieve her. It was true that Victoria was scared and on the defensive; he could see that with his own eyes. She told him about her enemies, the Cullens, but gave him a false story about why they wanted to kill her, claiming she and her older sister, Anne, had trespassed on their territory, so they had killed Anne and hunted her still. She told him about the talents the Cullens possessed. Though this was the truest part of her story, Riley found it the hardest to believe.

When she decided to create more vampires to protect herself, Riley was initially jealous. However, when she explained her plan, told him that the new vampires would never see her face or know her name, and asked him to choose them for her, he was appeased. Clearly, she had no desire for any romantic companionship besides Riley; she didn't even want any particular kind of human. She asked only that he choose humans who wouldn't be missed, or whose disappearance could be easily attributed to another source. The original plan, as Riley understood it, was for the new vampires to eventually be trained as a guard for himself and Victoria, after they were past their newborn wildness and were teachable. Victoria had the idea to tell the newborns that the sun could kill vampires, as was commonly believed by humans. She thought this would make them easier to control during the first year.

Victoria was very aware of the laws of the Volturi, and while she did not inform Riley of all of them, she did tell Riley about their existence, and about the necessity of keeping a low profile. She did not have him instruct the newborns about the Volturi; they agreed that until the newborns were old enough, there was no reason to overwhelm them with information. Riley never realized how similar he was to the other newborns, both in Victoria's opinion of him and in her treatment of him.

When Victoria sensed that she was being tracked, she decided to run rather than hope her unskilled newborns could protect her. She left Riley with instructions to keep the newborns as quiet as possible, and she disappeared.

Riley wanted to go with her and was unhappy to be left behind. He worried that she would be killed, and he also worried that she would lose interest and never return for him. But he accepted her logic that, in the long run, the guard was worth the time investment. He grew friendly with some of the newborns in her absence; he enjoyed Diego's company in particular, though he was always entirely loyal to Victoria. Of course he did not find Fred easy to be around. He thought little of Raoul personally, but found him useful in organizing newcomers to the coven.

When Victoria returned, Riley was overjoyed. To Riley, her return meant that she really did love him. He was enthusiastic about her idea to act offensively by creating an army, rather than maintaining a guard for an indefinite amount of time while she waited for her enemies to come after her again. She told him of the necessity of not making decisions and instructed him to keep watch for any possible talents in their army.

Newborn production went into high gear, which meant that Riley was not with Victoria as often. He was busy containing the newborns and searching out more humans whose disappearances would attract little notice. Riley was unaware of Victoria's trip to see Laurent, or of her repeated attempts to get into Forks. Victoria did not tell him about the werewolf problem she'd observed.

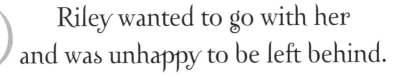

Riley wanted to go with her
and was unhappy to be left behind.

As the army stabilized at around twenty members, Riley felt like the time had come to strike. He was frustrated that Victoria still wavered. He wanted to train the newborns, particularly the older ones, so that they could fight more effectively. He and Victoria discussed training methods, but she was afraid that putting the training into action would alert Alice. Her hesitance to strike upset Riley; until they got rid of the Cullens, they couldn't really be together. He wondered how committed to him Victoria actually was.

Victoria sent him to Forks to obtain the scent of the Cullens' pet human for a few reasons. First, if she did decide to attack, it would mark her true target. Second, she knew of Riley's impatience and felt this assignment would make him think they were moving forward. Third, and most important, she wanted to test Alice's ability without putting herself in danger. If Riley was instructed to make no contact with the Cullens or any humans in Forks, if he was committed to doing no damage and remaining unseen, would Alice know he was coming? Victoria was thrilled to find out that the answer was no. The more she could learn about Alice's ability — and the flaws in her visions — the better she could know how to proceed.

When the Volturi visited, Riley was terrified but also relieved. He did not understand that he and Victoria were in trouble not just for the attention the newborns had gotten in the news, but also for a truly illegal creation. He just knew that now he would get to act. And once the Cullens were destroyed, he wouldn't have to take care of newborns all the time; he could be with Victoria.

Over the course of his time as warden to the newborns, two vampires, Doug and Adam, had discovered the truth about the sun. Victoria had told him to bring any newborns who knew the truth to her. At first he was shocked and a little frightened when he learned that the penalty for this knowledge was death. However, once Victoria explained what it would do to the coven if all the newborns knew the truth, it made sense. He used the disappearance of Doug and Adam to reinforce the idea that the sun was deadly. He did the same with the disappearances of Steve and Shelly, though those two had simply run away together. When Diego came to Riley and told him about the sun, Riley was disturbed. He hoped that, given the situation with the Volturi, Victoria might reconsider and let Diego live. He knew Diego could keep the secret. However, Victoria's response was even worse than he'd feared.

The next few hours changed Riley. Victoria made him choose between being with her and saving Diego's life. Riley chose Victoria and refused to acknowledge the feeling that he had chosen wrong. Victoria was high-strung and paranoid after the Volturi's visit. She insisted on extracting as much information as possible from Diego. In the end, Diego told her everything that he and Bree suspected. Riley was horrified by her actions and the things she made him do, but because he loved her he had to find a way to reconcile who she was with what he loved. He had to close himself off to his feelings of pity and humanity. He tried to enjoy Diego's pain the way she obviously did. Victoria was pleased with the change. Now that she felt Riley had proven himself, she told him the truth — mostly — about the coming battle. The majority of the newborns would be slaughtered before the Cullens were destroyed. She would not join the fight; she would observe to make sure the right members of the Cullen clan were destroyed. If a chance presented itself, she would act. After it was over she and Riley would run fast and far, until the Volturi got tired of chasing them. She lied about only a few things — including who her real target was, and that Riley would be escaping with her.

Riley did well in his last days with the newborns. He was able to manipulate them into exactly the mindset Victoria wanted. He did not entirely understand why the focus should be on the human girl — Victoria said the Cullens would be less effective if they were trying to protect the human — but he primed them perfectly. His only failure was in losing Fred; of course, in the end, he couldn't remember that he'd lost him. After sending the newborns on their way, he met up with Victoria at the rendezvous point she'd chosen. She told him that a key member of the coven had hidden to avoid the fight, and together they were going to make sure he didn't survive.

After it was over she and Riley would run fast and far, until the Volturi got tired of chasing them.

✈ DIEGO

NAME: Diego

DATE OF BIRTH: November 1987

DATE OF TRANSFORMATION: July 2005, at age 17

SOURCE OF TRANSFORMATION: Victoria

PLACE OF ORIGIN: Los Angeles, California

HAIR COLOR: Black

EYE COLOR: Brown (human); bright red/black (newborn vampire)

HEIGHT: 6'0"

PHYSICAL DESCRIPTION: Diego had thick, curly hair and a faint olive tone to his vampire skin. He was lean but muscular.

SPECIAL ABILITIES: He did not possess a quantifiable supernatural ability.

FAMILY/COVEN RELATIONSHIPS: Diego belonged to Riley's coven of newborns.

PERSONAL HISTORY:

Diego grew up in a lower-class, single-parent home in Los Angeles. He lived with his mother and younger brother. When he was sixteen, his mother relocated to Portland for a job that then fell through. Diego worked part-time jobs to help out while he went to school. He was determined to go to college, and to help his younger brother get an education as well. Diego had some trouble with a gang at his high school, but he did his best to avoid them. He was furious when he found out that the same gang was pursuing his younger brother. He tried to convince his brother to stay away from them, and he talked with his mother about switching his brother to a different school. Before they could come up with a plan to remove his brother from the situation, his brother was killed in an initiation ritual.

Diego went crazy with grief. He stole a gun from the house of one of the gang members. He'd learned who was actually responsible for his brother's death, and he tracked him down and fatally shot him. The other members of the gang came after Diego. They had him cornered when Riley interceded.

FRED

NAME: Fred; nickname: "Freaky Fred"

DATE OF BIRTH: April 1985

DATE OF TRANSFORMATION: August 2005, at age 20

SOURCE OF TRANSFORMATION: Victoria

PLACE OF ORIGIN: Vancouver, British Columbia

HAIR COLOR: Blond

EYE COLOR: Blue (human); bright red/black (newborn vampire)

HEIGHT: 6'2"

PHYSICAL DESCRIPTION: Fred is tall and broad-shouldered.

SPECIAL ABILITIES: He has the ability to make anyone feel physically repulsed. He can use this ability to make someone unable to think of him for a period of time.

FAMILY/COVEN RELATIONSHIPS: Fred belonged to Riley's coven of newborns; he is currently a nomad.

PERSONAL HISTORY:

Fred grew up with his father; his parents divorced when Fred was ten. His mother remarried and had three children, half-siblings whom Fred rarely saw. Fred's father was not very expressive, and Fred found that the only way to communicate with his father was through logic rather than emotion. Fred had a natural inclination toward the sciences, which his father encouraged. In elementary school he was bullied occasionally because he was thin and wore thick glasses. In high school Fred grew very tall, but he was awkward and gangly. He embraced being

He embraced being a science nerd and related to others academically but not socially.

a science nerd and related to others academically but not socially. He tried to avoid attention, and hated to be singled out except in the classroom. Eventually, Fred received a scholarship to Stanford University. Physically, he had gotten past his awkward stage and was quite attractive, but he was oblivious to this. After his sophomore year, he volunteered for a special research project offered by his favorite marine biology professor. Fred spent the majority of the summer on remote beaches along the Oregon and Washington coast, camping for the most part. It was a solitary trip, and he went several days at a time without seeing another person. Riley found him on one of those beaches and imagined that Fred's disappearance would seem quite explicable. He asked Fred if he was interested in some excitement. Fred said no, but Riley didn't take no for an answer.

Fred is one of three newborns who survived the rest of the coven's demise; he went on to become a solitary nomad.

 RAOUL

NAME: Raoul

DATE OF BIRTH: October 8, 1988

DATE OF TRANSFORMATION: September 2005, at age 16

SOURCE OF TRANSFORMATION: Victoria

PLACE OF ORIGIN: El Paso, Texas

HAIR COLOR: Black

EYE COLOR: Brown (human); bright red/black (newborn vampire)

HEIGHT: 5'10"

PHYSICAL DESCRIPTION: Raoul was wiry.

SPECIAL ABILITIES: He had a limited ability to make others view him as their leader. It worked best on those who were directionless.

FAMILY/COVEN RELATIONSHIPS: Raoul belonged to the coven of newborns managed by Riley.

PERSONAL HISTORY:

Raoul grew up in southern Texas. He lived with his mother and five siblings. He became very involved in an expanding drug-running gang. Despite his youth, he rose quickly through the gang's ranks. When he was fifteen, he shot three members of a competing gang. To keep him from falling into the hands of the law, his gang sent him to Seattle to manage a new branch of the organization. There he excelled, particularly at recruiting new members. Riley found him beating a client who was behind on payments. Riley asked Raoul if he was interested in some real power. Wary but intrigued, Raoul answered yes.

➵➵ BREE TANNER

NAME: Bree Tanner

DATE OF BIRTH: March 11, 1990

DATE OF TRANSFORMATION: March 11, 2006, at age 16

SOURCE OF TRANSFORMATION: Victoria

PLACE OF ORIGIN: Las Vegas, Nevada

HAIR COLOR: Dark brown

EYE COLOR: Brown (human); bright red/black (newborn vampire)

HEIGHT: 5'1"

PHYSICAL DESCRIPTION: Bree had a slight build.

SPECIAL ABILITIES: She did not possess a quantifiable supernatural ability.

FAMILY/COVEN RELATIONSHIPS: Bree belonged to Riley's coven of newborns.

PERSONAL HISTORY:

Bree was born in Nevada, but lived in Idaho for most of her life. Bree believed that her mother left her abusive father when Bree was four; in fact, Bree's father murdered her mother. He buried the body in the desert, then packed up and moved to Idaho with his young daughter. Because of the abuse, Bree felt isolated from her peers. She was a quiet, withdrawn girl. No one ever noticed the signs of her abusive home life, despite some physical evidence. Finally, Bree ran away from home a few weeks before her sixteenth birthday. She had enough money for the bus ride to Seattle, but nothing more. She tried unsuccessfully to get a job, and began stealing in order to eat. She slept in parks and alleys — wherever she could find a place that felt a little bit safe. Her biggest fear was that the police would catch her and send her home to her father. She'd been on the run for less than three weeks when Riley found her digging through a trash bin behind a restaurant.

What Bree never knew was that her mother's body had been discovered outside of Las Vegas, and the police tracked down her father a few months after she ran away. When he could not produce Bree, he was tried and found guilty of both murders.

Bree believed that her
mother left her abusive father when
Bree was four; in fact, Bree's father
murdered her mother.

ADAM After discovering that the sun does not injure vampires, Adam revealed his discovery to Riley. He was killed by Victoria.

CASEY Known to Bree as the "Spider-Man kid," Casey was a recruit suggested to Riley by Raoul, who had worked with him when they were human.

DOUG Doug was the first newborn to discover that the sun did not harm vampires. He went to Riley with his breakthrough and was killed by Victoria.

JEN Jen was Kristie's closest colleague.

KEVIN A member of Raoul's faction, Kevin was Raoul's second in command. Kevin was a part of Raoul's human gang, too, and was taken by Riley upon Raoul's suggestion. Riley asked Kevin if he wanted to join Raoul.

KRISTIE Kristie was Raoul's main competitor in the newborn coven. She did not have his ability to gain followers through magnetism alone, but she was smarter than Raoul, and better able to manipulate others.

SARAH Sarah did not like working closely with any of the other newborns, but she preferred Kristie's crowd to Raoul's.

SHELLY AND STEVE Shelly and Steve formed a romantic attachment in the early weeks of their newborn life. After a few months, they decided to abandon the newborn coven. They are currently nomads.

OFTEN REFERRED TO AS "DRACULA'S CASTLE," BRAN CASTLE
IS A NATIONAL MONUMENT AND LANDMARK IN ROMANIA.
IT WAS BUILT IN 1377 — HUNDREDS OF YEARS AFTER THE
ROMANIAN COVEN WAS DEFEATED BY THE VOLTURI.

The Romanian Coven

The Romanian coven dominated the vampire world until it was overthrown by the Volturi, between 400 and 500 A.D. Only two members of the original Romanian coven survive.

STEFAN

NAME: Stefan

DATE OF BIRTH: Unknown

DATE OF TRANSFORMATION: Before 1000 B.C.

SOURCE OF TRANSFORMATION: Unknown

PLACE OF ORIGIN: Dacia (Proto-Romania)

HAIR COLOR: Dark brown

EYE COLOR: Red/black (vampire)

HEIGHT: 5'3"

PHYSICAL DESCRIPTION: Stefan is slight and short. He has powdery skin like that of the Volturi, but his eyes are not clouded.

SPECIAL ABILITIES: He does not possess a quantifiable supernatural ability.

FAMILY/COVEN RELATIONSHIPS: He and Vladimir are the last surviving members of their coven.

PERSONAL HISTORY:

Stefan was one of the original twelve ruling members of what is now known as the Romanian coven. (Romania did not exist as a country at the time of the coven's inception; that area of Eastern Europe was known as Dacia.)

The Romanians were formed in a way similar to the Volturi: A group of ambitious vampires called a truce to the usual squabbling between small covens and then joined forces for the purpose of gaining power. This prevailing desire to rule allowed them to overcome their competitive drives and cooperate.

The eventual downfall of the Romanians was their focus on physical strength. They created a guardlike entity—a pattern later copied by the Volturi—composed entirely of vampires like Felix and Emmett. Perhaps because none of the ruling members of the coven possessed supernatural abilities themselves, they underestimated the advantage such abilities could give them in battle. They ignored talented vampires in favor of brute strength. This blind spot was understandable, as no one had ever used talents the way the Volturi eventually did. Talents have also grown stronger over the centuries; the talents exhibited by vampires during the Romanian rule were not as potent as the talents that developed in modern times. Much of that is due to vampires learning to seek out talented humans to transform, and also understanding how to focus and improve their talents after the transformation. Aro's innovative focus on talent over strength was the reason the Volturi were able to defeat the Romanians, though it took them more than a century, and they never wiped them out completely.

> Stefan and Vladimir both lost mates to the Volturi—Stefan during the third decade of the initial battle—ensuring that their drive for vengeance would never fade.

Stefan and Vladimir both lost mates to the Volturi — Stefan during the third decade of the initial battle — ensuring that their drive for vengeance would never fade. They are always searching for ways to discomfit or damage the Volturi. They are particularly bitter toward Jane and Alec, who were not involved in the original war but strengthened the Volturi to the point of invincibility, making it impossible for the Romanians to exact their revenge.

Every few decades, the Volturi send Demetri and others after the remaining Romanians, so Stefan and Vladimir are constantly on the move and always on their guard. If the Volturi focused their efforts, they would be able to wipe Stefan and Vladimir out, but since the two pose little threat, the Volturi have never committed their assets to a drawn-out chase.

FAMOUS QUOTE

"We've been waiting a millennium and a half for the Italian scum to be challenged. If there is any chance they will fall, we will be here to see it." Breaking Dawn, Chapter 32

 VLADIMIR

NAME: Vladimir
DATE OF BIRTH: Unknown
DATE OF TRANSFORMATION: Before 1000 B.C.
SOURCE OF TRANSFORMATION: Unknown
PLACE OF ORIGIN: Dacia (Proto-Romania)
HAIR COLOR: Ashy blond
EYE COLOR: Red/black (vampire)

HEIGHT: 5'4"

PHYSICAL DESCRIPTION: Vladimir is slight and short. He has papery skin similar to that of the Volturi, and his hair is so blond it appears almost white. Unlike the Volturi, his eyes are a clear, dark red.

SPECIAL ABILITIES: He does not possess a quantifiable supernatural ability.

FAMILY/COVEN RELATIONSHIPS: He is part of a coven with Stefan.

PERSONAL HISTORY:

Like Stefan, Vladimir was one of the original twelve ruling members of the Romanian coven. Vladimir was the head of a coven of four — large by normal vampire standards — when he joined forces with the other Romanian vampires. His big, successful coven was one of the inspirations for the notion of coexistence to pursue power.

> They ruled over humans and vampires alike, demanding slave labor and copious human sacrifice.

During their rule — which lasted nearly a thousand years — the Romanians lived brazenly and decadently. For thousands of miles in every direction, they were known and feared. They ruled over humans and vampires alike, demanding slave labor and copious human sacrifice. Occasionally humans would create armies to try to overthrow what they considered to be beautiful demon overlords, but of course all such attacks were futile, resulting in an easy feast for the Romanians. Obedient humans were spared death, if not labor, and a few lucky individuals pleased the Romanians enough to earn immortality.

Vampires were a well-known fact in the human world

when the Volturi began to rise. Their contention that vampires should conceal their existence was scoffed at.

After the Volturi had defeated the Romanians, the Volturi copied many aspects of the Romanians' way of life—the formation of a permanent guard, the stationary home, and the eschewing of hunting in favor of prey being rounded up and delivered to them. The difference was that they did all of these things while remaining invisible to humans.

Unlike Stefan's, Vladimir's mate survived the initial overthrow of the Romanians. She was killed around 810 A.D., during the last of many attempts the Romanians made during the centuries to regroup, repopulate, and topple the Volturi. The Romanians had amassed an army of more than a hundred new recruits and were confident that the Volturi would fall. This ill-fated assault occurred a decade after Aro had acquired Jane and Alec. It was the first time Aro displayed their talents in battle. The Romanians were decimated. Only Stefan and Vladimir, who were planning to spring a trap for the expected Volturi retreat, escaped. After this, Vladimir and Stefan made no further attempt to create more vampires for their coven. They decided to disappear until the Volturi weakened or another power presented itself.

> Only Stefan and Vladimir, who were planning to spring a trap for the expected Volturi retreat, escaped.

FAMOUS QUOTE

"Now the Volturi's eyes are filmed with dusty scum, but ours are bright. I imagine that will give us an advantage when we gouge theirs from their sockets." Breaking Dawn, Chapter 33

The Nomads

Many vampires prefer to roam the world on their own or with a single partner. These vampires are known as nomads.

→ ALISTAIR

NAME: Alistair

DATE OF BIRTH: Around 1300

DATE OF TRANSFORMATION: Around 1320, at approximately 20

SOURCE OF TRANSFORMATION: George

PLACE OF ORIGIN: England

HAIR COLOR: Black

EYE COLOR: Red/black (vampire)

HEIGHT: 6'2"

PHYSICAL DESCRIPTION: Alistair is tall and slender.

SPECIAL ABILITIES: Alistair can track both people and things. He can sense the general direction of whatever he is looking for, but it takes him a long time to narrow this feeling down to a specific location. If whatever he's seeking is on the move, he may never catch up.

FAMILY/COVEN RELATIONSHIPS: He prefers to wander alone.

PERSONAL HISTORY:

Alistair grew up in England during the turbulent reign of Edward II, considered the weakest of the Plantagenet kings.

Alistair's father was one of the barons who continually fought against Edward's attempts to limit the power of the British Peerage. Throughout Alistair's youth, his father and older brother were embroiled in conspiracy after conspiracy as they tried to protect the rights of the aristocracy while also trying to gain a place of preeminence over the other barons.

Alistair lived quietly at the family's country estate with his mother and sisters. He had no interest in his father's schemes. Alistair loved to hunt for sport and was considered the best hunter in the county. He was also an avid falconer. He kept many falcons, and training them was his favorite pursuit. He loved his birds and spent more time with them than with people.

Unknown to Alistair, his father formed an alliance with two other barons after the banishment of the king's favorite counselor. Their object was to get Alistair's older brother placed in that vacated position, and thereby control the weak king. Some of the other barons had the same idea, but with their own champions. After multiple betrayals on all sides, Alistair's brother was implicated in a plot to overthrow the king, and he and a few others were executed for treason. The charges were mostly false, created by another powerful aristocrat with an agenda that differed from Alistair's father's.

Losing his precious heir pushed Alistair's father over the edge. The baron's anger against the king became deeply personal and slightly deranged. He began plotting to actually do what his son had been executed for. He felt he could no longer trust his old allies. He began to explore ever darker sources of aid, becoming deeply involved with the occult.

Alistair knew nothing about his father's designs. Of course he knew of his brother's execution; he, his mother, and his sisters grieved privately and withdrew from society entirely. The mark of treason on the family was a hard blow for his sisters, who would have more difficulty making good matches. Alistair, who had never particularly wanted to inherit, was resigned to his duty, and planned to care for his sisters if they wished to remain unmarried.

Then, late one night, Alistair's father came for him. Alistair obediently went with his father, though he was not allowed to bid his mother farewell and had no idea why he was needed. Alistair's father told him nothing until they arrived in London. Alistair grew more and more concerned as his father led him through secret tunnels under the city, exchanging cryptic signs with masked men along the way. Finally, they reached a council room. Around a large round table were many minor aristocrats, some of whom Alistair knew. His father outranked them all and was clearly in charge. He sat Alistair at the head of the table, bolted the door, and explained his plan.

Alistair listened in horror, shocked at the change that had come over his father. It was apparent his father was mad. The baron had created a plan to set Alistair on the throne of

> Alistair listened in horror, shocked at the change that had come over his father.

England, and swore Alistair would be the next Charlemagne. Alistair tried to leave but was restrained. The baron ranted that he had sold his soul and paid an unthinkable price to make Alistair invincible. Alistair tried to reason with his father, to no avail. He entreated the other men present for help, but they seemed to believe the baron's story absolutely.

Shortly thereafter there was a quiet knock on the barred door. Every man in the room, including the baron, blanched. Some clutched at crosses. One man scurried to throw the door open. A man entirely enveloped in a dark red hooded cloak glided silently into the room. Every-one bowed to him. He was greeted as Astaroth by the baron. Quietly, Astaroth asked for the room to be emptied. The aristocrats ran to the exit. Only the baron stayed. Astaroth thanked the baron for his offering. The baron looked sick, but nodded and left, leaving Alistair alone with the hooded man.

Astaroth, whose name was actually George, threw off his cloak. Alistair was surprised to see a very handsome man who had long blond curls and wore modern clothes. The man was not much older than Alistair. Astaroth laughed casually and told Alistair that his father was certainly mad, but that it was true Alistair could be king if he wanted. Astaroth would give him power to stand against any man — even an army. Alistair could do what he wished with the power, but he might think about honoring his father's wishes, as his father had indeed paid a great price to buy this honor for his son.

> Astaroth laughed casually and told Alistair that his father was certainly mad, but that it was true Alistair could be king if he wanted.

Astaroth/George was a vampire not unlike Boris, the vampire who changed Laurent. George also enjoyed entertaining himself with humans; he just had a darker idea of fun than did Boris. He led on humans in love with the occult, asking them to sacrifice everything they held most dear in exchange for his supernatural assistance. He liked to see how far humans would go to get what they wanted. Of course, he could always have taken their sacrifices without their consent, but he liked to watch them struggle with the dilemma. He pretended to be one of the princes of hell because it impressed the mortals.

George gave Alistair a few pointers: Stay out of the sun, and don't attract too much attention. Of course, Alistair had no idea what George was talking about. George then bit Alistair, wished him good luck, and disappeared.

When Alistair's transformation was complete, he found himself surrounded by a large group of terrified peasants bound together with manacles. Unable to restrain himself, Alistair slaughtered most of them. When he was totally sated, there were still a few left living. It was then that his father entered the bloody council room; Astaroth had given him advice on how to stay alive when dealing with his indestructible new son.

The baron was prepared for Alistair's thirst, but not for his anger. He tried to explain the next steps to Alistair, but Alistair was furious with him—horrified by what he'd just been through, followed by the murders he'd committed. He shoved his father out of his way, accidentally killing him.

> Unable to restrain himself, Alistair slaughtered most of them.

Alistair was surprised by many things that night: his super strength, his sharp senses, his speed—none of which he expected. Escaping the underground maze was child's play, as he quickly discovered he could break through the stone walls. He wasn't able to ride a horse—he found his father's and tried to mount it, but the poor beast broke its own neck trying to escape him—but once he tried running he found that horses were unnecessary. He raced home to find his house empty, his mother and sisters vanished. In a burst of insight, Alistair realized what his father's offering to Astaroth must have been. Totally devastated, Alistair sought refuge with his falcons, only to find that they could bear his presence no more than the horse could.

Alistair left civilization that night. He avoided all contact with humans, except when he hunted. He mistrusted everyone from that point on, assumed conspiracies existed everywhere, and was paranoid about authority figures.

Alistair met Carlisle in the seventeenth century. Carlisle had already discovered a way to exist without the traditional vampire diet, but had not yet gone to Italy or met the Volturi. Alistair was a total recluse at that point, and had no interest in conversation. Carlisle was lonely, though, and so enthusiastic about finding someone to talk to that eventually he got Alistair to respond a little bit before he left. Carlisle was concerned about Alistair's isolated life; every few decades, Carlisle would visit to see how Alistair was doing. Against Alistair's wishes, they ended up as friends of a sort.

FAMOUS QUOTE

"I can't believe I got myself sucked into this mess. What a fine way to treat your friends." Breaking Dawn, Chapter 32

NAME: Charles

DATE OF BIRTH: 1922

DATE OF TRANSFORMATION: 1949, at age 27

SOURCE OF TRANSFORMATION: Makenna

PLACE OF ORIGIN: Denmark

HAIR COLOR: Dark blond

EYE COLOR: Red/black (vampire)

HEIGHT: 6'0"

PHYSICAL DESCRIPTION: Charles is thin, but muscular.

SPECIAL ABILITIES: Charles can sense when someone is lying to him.

FAMILY/COVEN RELATIONSHIPS: Charles's mate is Makenna.

PERSONAL HISTORY:

Charles was a law student in Barcelona when he met Makenna. They fell in love. After some time, Makenna told Charles that her family was unusual and she was approaching some big changes. Charles said he would be there through anything. Makenna told him she had to leave for a while, but would come back. If Charles wanted to wait, he could. If not, she would understand. When she returned more than a year later as a vampire, Charles was still waiting. After hashing through all the pros and cons together, Charles decided to join her. They waited three years so Makenna would be able to keep from killing him, and then he was successfully transformed.

Charles said he would be there through anything.

They live nomadically for the most part, but Makenna still visits her family often.

 CHARLOTTE

NAME: Charlotte

DATE OF BIRTH: Between 1920 and 1925

DATE OF TRANSFORMATION: Approximately 1938, at around age 18

SOURCE OF TRANSFORMATION: Maria

PLACE OF ORIGIN: Southern United States

HAIR COLOR: Pale blond

EYE COLOR: Red/black (vampire)

HEIGHT: 5'0"

PHYSICAL DESCRIPTION: Charlotte is very petite.

SPECIAL ABILITIES: Charlotte does not possess a quantifiable supernatural ability.

FAMILY/COVEN RELATIONSHIPS: Charlotte's mate is Peter.

PERSONAL HISTORY:

Charlotte was added to Maria's newborn army during a time when Maria was regrouping and not actively planning to conquer any more territories. Maria still kept a large number of newborns to protect herself, but she was not as picky about the newborns she selected. Jasper had just destroyed a large batch of newborns, and when Maria went hunting for more, Charlotte was in the wrong place at the wrong time.

Peter was in charge of babysitting the newborns on a day-to-day basis, keeping them from attacking one another, feeding them as inconspicuously as possible, and helping Jasper a little bit with their fight training. Peter was the first person to talk with Charlotte after her transformation. He was the only stable, sane thing she knew during her first weeks of vampire life. As Charlotte's first year of life passed, a deep bond formed between them.

Charlotte could tell something was wrong with Peter in those last weeks with Maria. He was tense and irritable with everyone. Though Peter idolized Jasper as if he were an older brother, Charlotte saw them arguing heatedly. A few times it seemed as though he wanted to discuss something with her, but he always changed his mind.

One night, Jasper was giving the newborns one-on-one instruction. He would call them out individually, but none came back before the next was called. Charlotte was the eighth to be selected. Jasper called for her and gestured for her to follow. But Peter was there, looking both furious and fearful. He yelled for Charlotte to run. She trusted him enough that she broke into a sprint without a second of doubt. She heard him running with her. She listened for some other pursuit, but heard nothing.

When they were very far away, Peter said they were safe, and Charlotte stopped running. Peter finally explained what was going on, and what he feared they were up against. However, they quickly learned that much of what they knew about life applied only to a limited geographic area. Soon they were comfortable with the new vampire world they'd discovered. Peter only had one lingering regret, and after five years, he decided to go back for Jasper. Charlotte wanted to go with him, but Peter told her that he could sneak in more easily alone.

Charlotte was surprised that Jasper chose to join them. She wasn't entirely thrilled with having him in their new coven. Certainly, he added to their strength. However, he was depressing to be around in those days. When he decided to leave them, she was relieved. She preferred to have Peter to herself. Peter always kept in touch with Jasper, and after Jasper found Alice, Charlotte enjoyed his company a lot more. If not for their dietary peculiarities, Charlotte would have been tempted to join Jasper and Alice.

 MAKENNA

NAME: Makenna
DATE OF BIRTH: 1920
DATE OF TRANSFORMATION: 1946, at age 26
SOURCE OF TRANSFORMATION: Luca
PLACE OF ORIGIN: Malta
HAIR COLOR: Black
EYE COLOR: Red/black (vampire)
HEIGHT: 5'2"
PHYSICAL DESCRIPTION: Makenna is short and thin.
SPECIAL ABILITIES: She does not possess a quantifiable supernatural ability.
FAMILY/COVEN RELATIONSHIPS: Makenna's mate is Charles.

Makenna comes from a Maltese family with a very unusual link to vampirism. One of her ancestors, Luca, was converted to vampirism around 400 B.C. Unlike most vampires, Luca did not leave his mortal family behind; he continued to look after his family's prosperity and safety. And, with a vampire on their side, the family prospered greatly. Everyone in the family was in on the secret and thought of Uncle Luca as a kind of personal family saint. The next generation grew up with an entirely different perception of vampirism than was usual. After several more generations had passed, one of Luca's relatives, a distant nephew, asked if he could join Luca. When he saw that the boy's parents were willing, Luca agreed. The nephew went his own way rather than staying a part of the family, and Luca was disappointed. He looked for another family member to help him protect the family line. He converted a few more of his relatives into vampires, two of whom became his constant companions. Others left the family for various reasons; Renata, for example, was adopted into the Volturi. It became the tradition that every other century, one child would be chosen to join Luca as a family protector. Makenna was one of the chosen ones, and she grew up knowing this would be her destiny. She looked forward to her fate, until she met Charles. Luca told her she could give up her heritage if she wanted to grow old and die with the human. Makenna did not want to give up either, so she chose immortality, always planning to go back for Charles.

When she went back to Charles, Makenna was honest with him. She explained to him all the drawbacks and advantages of vampirism. They discussed everything thoroughly before Charles chose to be with her. Knowing her uncle Luca would not change someone unrelated to the family, Makenna waited until she was sure she was strong enough to handle the temptation, and then she changed Charles herself.

Renata was the one who invited Makenna and Charles to accompany the Volturi to Forks to witness the crime the Cullens had committed. Because the Volturi were sure that Renesmee was an immortal child, Charles got no sense of dishonesty until they arrived in the clearing.

FAMOUS QUOTE

"We did not come here for a fight. We came here to witness. And our witness is that this condemned family is innocent."
Breaking Dawn, Chapter 37

 PETER

NAME: Peter
DATE OF BIRTH: Sometime between the 1860s and 1920s
DATE OF TRANSFORMATION: Sometime between the 1860s and 1920s
SOURCE OF TRANSFORMATION: Maria
PLACE OF ORIGIN: Southern United States
HAIR COLOR: Pale blond
EYE COLOR: Red/black (vampire)
HEIGHT: 6'3"
PHYSICAL DESCRIPTION: Peter is tall and lean.
SPECIAL ABILITIES: Peter does not possess a quantifiable supernatural ability.
FAMILY/COVEN RELATIONSHIPS: Peter's mate is Charlotte.

PERSONAL HISTORY:

Peter was created by Maria to fight in her newborn army. Jasper found a kindred spirit in Peter and was impressed with his abilities; he advised Maria that Peter might be worth keeping. Maria didn't care much either way, and so indulged Jasper in his preference.

Jasper enjoyed Peter's company, and they worked well as a team. Peter knew Jasper had saved his life, and he felt indebted; he would do anything Jasper asked. He cheerfully took on the responsibility of the other newborns. He was not concerned about their fate. Like Maria and Jasper, he viewed them as tools without individual personalities — until Maria brought Charlotte back.

> Peter knew Jasper had saved his life, and he felt indebted; he would do anything Jasper asked.

Charlotte was different from the other newborns. Usually Maria selected humans she thought would make good warriors, but during her brief interludes of peaceful living, she was less picky. There were some women, a few physically older individuals, and some who were too young to be of much use. They were just numbers. Charlotte was one of the vampires who did not have physical attributes or life experience that would lead to her being a good warrior. She was very small physically, and scholarly by nature. She was the most self-controlled of all the fresh newborns, which gained Peter's attention. She was able to carry on a conversation, a rarity for newborns, and Peter found himself spending more and more time with her.

At first Peter did not think he was in danger. Charlotte was interesting and oddly pleasant, but still just another newborn. She was also very pretty in a delicate way, but all the female recruits were beautiful. She was fun to talk to, but that was just killing time. It wasn't until nearly nine months had passed that Peter suddenly realized she would be destroyed soon — and it wasn't until he imagined her gone that he realized how much she'd come to mean to him.

Peter waited for a good moment, and then spoke to Jasper about maybe preserving a few of the newborns. Jasper brushed him off, saying Maria would make that decision. In truth, Jasper had seen nothing special about any of the group. They were poor soldiers; he wouldn't make any recommendations this time. Jasper could tell that Peter was agitated, but he assumed it was a similar emotion to his own depression. He thought Peter was opposed to the coming destruction in a general sense. Jasper knew Peter would need to get over that weakness in order to stay alive.

As the time for Charlotte's demise approached, Peter agonized over his options. To his understanding, the world was entirely made up of warring factions of strong vampires surrounded by newborn armies. He had powerful allies in Jasper and Maria; he was in as good a position as possible for a three-year-old vampire. His best option was to convince Jasper to leave Charlotte alive. Peter could barely conceive of trying to strike off on his own with Charlotte — they'd be massacred in no time.

Charlotte's time grew closer and Peter became more frantic. Again he tried to talk Jasper into letting him save the ones he wanted. He never said Charlotte's name, worried that drawing attention to her would prove dangerous for her. Jasper told him to relax and not worry about it — there was still plenty of time to make a decision. He promised to talk to Maria. Peter thought that sounded promising, so he waited. Jasper actually went to Maria to ask, for Peter's sake, but Maria felt that three permanent vampires were enough. She didn't want another Nettie/Lucy situation on her hands.

The night of the purge came a few weeks sooner than Peter had expected. As it began, he tried to control his panic.

He begged Jasper to let him keep one or two. Jasper was adamant; Maria said all of them had to go. Peter tried frantically to come up with an answer as, one by one, he helped Jasper destroy the newborns. Then Jasper brought Charlotte out. She had no idea what was going on; she smiled when she saw Peter there.

Though he absolutely believed he and Charlotte would be slaughtered on their own, it was the only option he could think of. He didn't want to live if Charlotte was dead. He yelled for her to run, worried that she would be confused and hesitate. She didn't. He bolted after her, expecting to feel Jasper's teeth at any second, but there was no pursuit. They ran hundreds of miles before Peter paused to explain.

They lived very cautiously in the beginning; it took them a while to figure out that not all vampires lived Maria's way. Over time, they grew very comfortable with their new world. Peter's only regret was leaving Jasper behind. He knew Jasper was his true friend because Jasper had not killed him for leaving. He also knew that Jasper was unhappy, and he was sure that, just like himself, Jasper had no idea of any other way of life.

Peter's only regret was leaving Jasper behind.

Peter decided to go back for Jasper. He told Charlotte he could move more inconspicuously alone, but in fact he was trying to protect her. Peter knew Charlotte felt no loyalty or friendship for Jasper; she should not have to risk her life to try to help him. Peter would take the risk alone.

Peter was shocked that Jasper was ready to leave after just one conversation. On the road, Jasper explained how things had changed with Maria. Peter was all for going back together and killing her, but Jasper was happy to not have to destroy her.

As pleased as Peter was to rescue his friend and have his

company, he couldn't miss the fact that Jasper wasn't much happier with him than he'd been with Maria. Peter tried to discover what was making Jasper so miserable, and he noticed how much worse Jasper's mood became after eating. This was a contrast to how he and Charlotte felt—relieved and well. He discussed this with Jasper, and Jasper recognized the source of his problems. He tried to go without hunting, but struggled. Peter could be of no help to him in this, so Jasper left.

Peter missed Jasper, but couldn't help but enjoy how much happier he and Charlotte were without him. They pursued a comfortable nomadic existence, mostly in the Americas. Peter kept tabs on his old friend and was thrilled when Jasper found Alice. The foursome traveled together for a while, but Peter and Charlotte's lifestyle did not help Jasper embrace the way of life he wanted to learn from Alice. Peter never understood the benefits of not hunting humans, but he was glad it made Jasper happier. He and Charlotte stayed on good terms with Jasper and all the Cullens.

✈ OTHER NOMADS

MARY A solitary nomad, Mary was born in Nova Scotia around 1890 and transformed just after her twenty-eighth birthday, in 1918.

RANDALL Randall was born in California in 1945 and became a vampire in 1963, at age eighteen. Carlisle was one of the first vampires he met, and he's always considered him a great friend.

Joham and
the Vampire Hybrids

Joham is the father of the four known human/vampire hybrids in existence aside from Renesmee. With four different human women, he fathered three daughters and one son, Nahuel. None of the human women survived. All of Joham's daughters are on relatively friendly terms with their father and consider him their coven leader for all intents and purposes, though they don't travel with him. Nahuel, the only hybrid capable of effecting a vampire transformation, lives with his aunt — a full vampire changed by him — Huilen. He is not on good terms with Joham.

 HUILEN

NAME: Huilen

DATE OF BIRTH: Mid-1830s

DATE OF TRANSFORMATION: Approximately 1850, at around age 17

SOURCE OF TRANSFORMATION: Nahuel

PLACE OF ORIGIN: Mapuche territory, considered to be Central and Southern Chile and Southern Argentina, particularly concentrated in the Araucanía Region

HAIR COLOR: Black

EYE COLOR: Red/black (vampire)

HEIGHT: 5'0"

PHYSICAL DESCRIPTION: She is short and slight, with an olive tone to her pale skin. She wears her long hair in a braid.

SPECIAL ABILITIES: She does not possess a quantifiable supernatural ability.

FAMILY/COVEN RELATIONSHIPS: She is Nahuel's aunt. Her sister, Pire, is Nahuel's deceased mother.

PERSONAL HISTORY:

Huilen was a member of the Mapuche tribe in the mid-1800s. Her people made their living farming and raising livestock.

Huilen's closest friend and confidante was her younger sister, Pire. Only twelve months separated them, and they were like fraternal twins in many ways, having their own shorthand language between them. Pire was the beautiful one, and Huilen was the strong, capable one. Because they were so close, Huilen knew immediately when something changed in Pire's life. However, Pire did not confide in Huilen immediately. Joham had asked Pire to keep their liaison a secret, and such was her infatuation with him that she refused to answer Huilen's pleas for information. Eventually, though, Huilen saw the bruises on Pire's skin and was able to guess most of what had happened. Huilen was sure that Pire's lover was the blood-sucking Libishomen of their legends. Pire refused to believe her or to try to leave Joham, though Huilen did not stop begging her sister to do so.

This situation did not last long. It was less than a month before Pire realized that she was pregnant. She told Joham,

Pire was the beautiful one, and Huilen was the strong, capable one.

who was very pleased. He told her he had to go away but would return soon, and urged her to run away until the child was born; they both knew that she would be in danger if the truth were known. However, Joham was only truly worried about the safety of the child.

Pire turned to Huilen for help. Huilen knew that their people, even their own parents, would insist on the child's immediate death, though this would mean Pire's death as well. Huilen and Pire left their people and took to the wild. Huilen was a good hunter and protector, and they did well on their own.

Pire's appetite for raw meat and blood confirmed Huilen's fears about the child Pire carried, but again Pire refused to hear anything negative about her lover or her child. Even when the fetus was strong enough to break her bones, Pire loved it and made her sister swear to protect it if Pire did not live. She called her unborn child Nahuel, for the jaguar, because of his strength.

Pire did not survive the birth. Huilen, having sworn to care for the baby, truly meant to honor her sister's wishes despite her own feelings toward it. But the baby boy bit Huilen as she tried to pick him up out of her sister's body. The pain of transformation hit her immediately and quickly incapacitated her. She was only able to drag herself a few feet from Pire and the baby before collapsing.

When Huilen recovered, she found the boy curled up against her side, fast asleep. She did not understand how a newborn child could have crawled even those few feet, but when he woke she quickly learned that Nahuel was amazingly developed and capable. She did not mean to love him—she blamed him for her sister's death—but Nahuel was adorable and endearing, and he resembled Pire quite a bit.

Huilen's appetite had changed, but not her hunting prowess. As a newborn, she became a terror in the area, and several tribes picked up and moved to avoid the new jungle demon. Huilen hunted for Nahuel until he was able to hunt for himself.

Both Huilen and Nahuel were totally unaware that they'd had a visitor in that first week after Nahuel's birth. Joham, knowing that there was no way Pire would survive the birth, sent his oldest daughter, Serena, to take the child and raise him until he was old enough to live on his own. Joham did not like the bother of dealing with a child. Serena found Nahuel as instructed, but was unsure how to proceed because of Huilen's existence. She knew better than to engage with a full vampire, and she mistook Huilen for the child's mother, though she had no idea how the transformation could have come about. She went back to report to Joham but was unable to find him for a few years. When he heard the unexpected news, he went to check on Nahuel himself. That contact was the first Nahuel and Huilen were aware of.

Joham was thrilled to have a son, excited and intrigued by his son's ability to create a full vampire, and ready to join forces with him. However, Joham's total lack of concern for Pire's fate quickly turned Huilen and Nahuel against him.

Huilen was happy when Nahuel showed no interest in Joham as a father figure and sent him away. Whenever Joham visits, Huilen is civil but unforgiving.

Huilen was happy when Nahuel showed no interest in Joham as a father figure and sent him away.

→→ JOHAM

NAME: Joham

DATE OF BIRTH: 1560s

DATE OF TRANSFORMATION: Early 1600s, at approximately age 40

SOURCE OF TRANSFORMATION: An unknown female vampire

PLACE OF ORIGIN: Portugal

HAIR COLOR: Black

EYE COLOR: Red/black (vampire)

HEIGHT: 5'10"

PHYSICAL DESCRIPTION: Wiry and slight

SPECIAL ABILITIES: Joham does not possess a quantifiable supernatural ability.

FAMILY/COVEN RELATIONSHIPS: He has one hybrid son, Nahuel, and three hybrid daughters.

PERSONAL HISTORY:

Joham was born in Portugal in the late 1560s. As a human, he was a scientist with a deep interest in the occult and how it could be proven or debunked by rational thought. He had an obsessive personality, and he found it impossible to let go of any pursuit until it was fully investigated. This obsession with the occult eventually resulted in his meeting a female vampire. This vampire was amused by his questions and offered to transform him as a way to satisfy his curiosity. Joham eagerly agreed.

After his transformation, Joham continued his scientific studies, mostly focusing on vampire abilities. Over time, he grew fascinated with the potential of a vampire-human hybrid. To test the possibility, he attempted to mate with a human female. His initial attempt was a failure, as were many subsequent attempts; he was unable to restrain himself from killing the women involved.

After much practice, Joham developed the ability to be intimate with a human woman without killing her. Still, there were many casualties. Despite his preparation, he sometimes lost control. Others died from injuries inflicted by the fetus before they could carry it to a viable age.

His first success was Serena, daughter to a Norwegian village girl of the same name. Joham stayed with the mother until the child was born, monitoring the effect of the pregnancy on the girl while doing his best to keep her alive. He paid similarly close attention to his first daughter, charting her progress and development carefully. Of all his children, Serena remains closest to Joham.

Serena was born around 1810, after sixty years of effort on Joham's part. After his success with Serena, things moved more quickly. His second daughter, Maysun, also named for her mother, was born in Algeria around 1820. Joham's curiosity about the gestation and early childhood of the hybrid was already satisfied; he abandoned his human lover as soon as he knew she was pregnant, and then sent Serena to collect the child and rear it until it was old enough to be interesting to him.

During the interim between Maysun's birth and Nahuel's around 1850, Joham fathered three hybrids who did not survive; their mothers died too early in their pregnancies.

Conceiving Nahuel was Joham's biggest challenge. For Joham, Nahuel's mother, Pire, was a "singer"—not as potent as Bella was for Edward, but strong enough to make the situation exceptionally

> Conceiving Nahuel was Joham's biggest challenge.

difficult. Joham chose her because he wanted to test a theory he was forming. He had noticed that the more appealing an individual woman smelled to him, the more likely she was to conceive quickly. Pire confirmed this theory; he fathered a child with her within their first two weeks together.

Once again, Joham deserted Pire shortly after he saw the signs of her pregnancy. He contacted Serena and asked her to take care of the child after Pire's death. He did not expect any complications, and left Serena with no way to contact him.

He came looking for Serena a few years later, when he assumed the child would be old enough to carry on an interesting conversation. He was disappointed to hear that another vampire had interceded, but was very pleased to have fathered a son. He tracked Nahuel and Huilen and introduced himself to his son. Already excited about the boy, he was even more thrilled when he learned that Nahuel was capable of transforming a human into a full vampire. However, he was unprepared for Nahuel's reverence for his dead mother, and handled the situation insensitively. Had he known what to expect, he would have had a convincing lie prepared; during his many courtships, Joham had become an expert in saying the right thing. Joham tried to reason with them — after all, humans were no more than food to them now, and surely Huilen and Nahuel could see how little they mattered as individuals — but they refused to see his side. Joham decided not to alienate his son further by killing the aunt. Instead, he waits for Nahuel to grow out of his strange regard for his human mother.

> Joham decided not to alienate his son further by killing the aunt.

Having successfully fathered both male and female off-spring, Joham left off his personal experimenting for a while and attempted to find another vampire to join him in his endeavor. The true test of the validity of the hybrid as a race would be its ability to reproduce itself, and it would be an imperfect experiment if there were no hybrids of a different genetic history for his own offspring to mate with. Joham had to proceed carefully; he knew the Volturi might object to his project, so he confided in relatively few vampires. A couple were taken by the novelty of his idea, but neither of them had the discipline to develop the necessary control. Joham went back to his own experimenting, hoping that in time he would meet another male vampire with a scientific nature like his own.

Joham's newest daughter is named Jennifer, after her mother. She was born in Ohio in 1991, and was raised mostly by Serena. Joham was more involved than with the others, careful to avoid another situation like that with Nahuel.

✈ NAHUEL

NAME: Nahuel
DATE OF BIRTH: Around 1850
DATE OF TRANSFORMATION: Born a vampire/human hybrid
PLACE OF ORIGIN: Mapuche territory, considered to be Central and Southern Chile and Southern Argentina, particularly concentrated in the Araucanía Region
HAIR COLOR: Black
EYE COLOR: Teak brown

HEIGHT: 5'7"

PHYSICAL DESCRIPTION: Nahuel has dark brown skin and, like his aunt, is short. He wears his hair in a braid.

SPECIAL ABILITIES: He does not possess a quantifiable supernatural ability.

FAMILY/COVEN RELATIONSHIPS: He lives with his mother's sister, Huilen. Pire, his mother, died during his birth. Joham, Nahuel's father, and Nahuel's three half-sisters live elsewhere.

PERSONAL HISTORY:

Nahuel's very first postbirth memory is of Huilen's scent, and of her face as she tried to lift him from his mother's body. After he found himself essentially alone and abandoned in the forest, he followed that scent to where Huilen lay, convulsed in pain, teaching himself to crawl in his first day of life.

When Huilen's transformation was complete, she and Nahuel began their nomadic life. Huilen was lonely without her sister, and she talked to Nahuel incessantly about Pire. She was only mildly surprised when Nahuel answered her back for the first time two weeks later; his startling development was already an accepted fact for her. Grieving for her sister, Huilen made sure that Nahuel knew exactly how wonderful his mother had been. She didn't intend for him to turn this knowledge into self-hatred, but despite the love she learned to feel for Nahuel, she did hold him responsible for Pire's death.

Nahuel and Huilen kept to themselves and became extremely close. They did occasionally run into other vampires, but Huilen never really trusted others, thanks to Joham's treatment of her sister. She kept Nahuel out of sight during these encounters, not sure how others would react to him.

Nahuel found it very easy to pass as a human. The only perceptible differences between himself and the humans were his physical abilities, which he could easily mask when necessary. He was much more of an anomaly in the vampire world. Visibly closer to human, Nahuel was also not quite as strong or as fast as a full vampire. His senses were also weaker, though exponentially stronger than human senses.

All of his sisters have visited him a time or two—on Joham's orders. Joham hoped the girls could soften Nahuel to his father. Nahuel found Serena too much like Joham, but liked Maysun and Jennifer quite a bit. Nahuel returned only Jennifer's visits; because she is the youngest sister, he feels protective toward her. He remains closest to her.

Huilen would prefer never to leave the traditional Mapuche lands, but Nahuel is more curious about the world at large. He's talked Huilen into several field trips, including his visits with Jennifer.

He was much more of an anomaly in the vampire world.

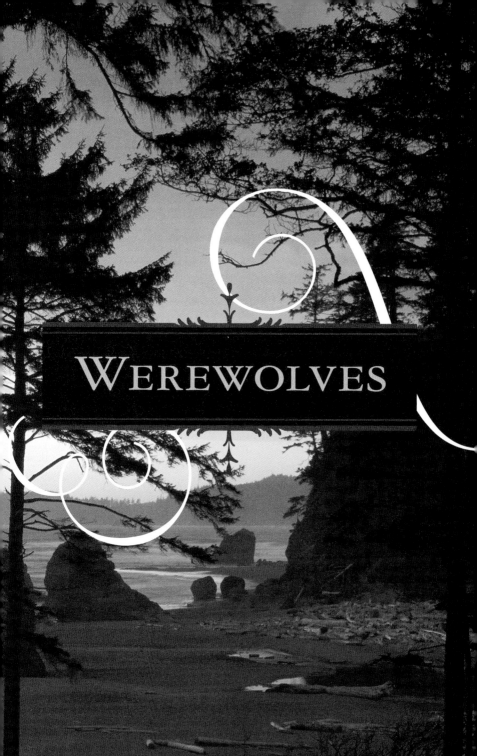

WEREWOLVES

There are two types of supernatural creatures referred to as werewolves in the Saga: those that pass on werewolf traits through a bite, and those that inherit werewolf traits from their parents. The first type, known as the Children of the Moon, are merely alluded to in the novels. The second type, the Quileute wolves, are the werewolves featured in the Twilight Saga.

The Children of the Moon

The Children of the Moon are creatures similar to the traditional werewolves of myth. They phase, or change form, in response to the cycles of the moon. In their changed form, they do not entirely resemble actual wolves: Their forelegs are more powerful than their hind legs, and they still have usable hands with opposable thumbs. In addition, their stance is more upright, making their movement somewhat apelike, rather than entirely canine.

Children of the Moon change form only at night, and during the fullest phase of the moon. While in their werewolf form, Children of the Moon are not aware of their human selves; they are feral rather than rational. Usually, they run alone, or with one companion of the opposite gender. Children of the Moon cannot breed in their animal form; they can spread their species only by infecting other humans through a bite. Infected humans who have children do not pass their abilities to their offspring.

> While in their werewolf form, Children of the Moon are not aware of their human selves; they are feral rather than rational.

"THE CHILDREN OF THE MOON HAVE BEEN OUR BITTER
ENEMIES FROM THE DAWN OF TIME."

—Caius (*Breaking Dawn*, Chapter 37)

In their animal form, Children of the Moon have heightened strength and speed that make them both deadly and difficult to kill; contrary to legend, these werewolves cannot be killed with a silver bullet, nor does silver repel them. Their amplified abilities make them capable of destroying a lone vampire; however, the vampire generally has the advantage due to the fact that he retains his logic and intelligence. One advantage the werewolf has in both his human and animal forms is immunity to vampire venom, both the transformative properties and the pain-producing properties.

Because vampires and Children of the Moon share the same food source and because each is an exception to the other's near indestructibility, they are natural enemies. Over time, however, the vampires have hunted the once populous werewolves into near extinction.

The Quileute Werewolves

Although the Quileutes call themselves werewolves, they are not werewolves in the traditional mythological sense. They are actually shape-shifters who take the form of a wolf. Unlike the Children of the Moon, mature Quileute werewolves are able to phase by choice. Another fundamental difference between Quileute werewolves and the Children of the Moon is that Quileutes in their wolf form retain their human minds, reasoning abilities, and personalities. The Quileute werewolves consider themselves the designated protectors of their human tribe. They see vampires as enemies to themselves and all humans.

INHERITANCE

Not every member of the Quileute tribe has the potential to transform into a werewolf. Only those who can trace a direct bloodline back to the first shape-shifter, Taha Aki, are born with the potential to become shape-shifters themselves. The first transformation occurs between the onset of puberty and approximately age twenty-five, and is based on two factors: heritage and the proximity of vampires.

The direct descendants of Taha Aki are born with twenty-four chromosomal pairs rather than the twenty-three pairs of a normal human. It was once believed that the extra chromosome could be passed down only to male descendants, but that has been proven false; in *Eclipse* we saw the first female tribe member transformed.

"I did quite a bit of research on the Quileutes. All of the legends in the books are part of their tradition. The only legend that is not a part of the Quileute tradition is the part I devised specifically to fit the Cullens."

— Stephenie

This extra chromosome will not have any effect on the carrier if he or she is not in close proximity to vampires during all or part of the critical time between the onset of puberty and the age of twenty-five. If the potential werewolf is not exposed to vampires within this window of time, transformation will never occur. It is the scent of the vampire that triggers the reaction; a potential werewolf would not have to actually see or touch a vampire, only cross his scent.

SIGNS OF IMMINENT TRANSFORMATION:

If a tribe member meets both conditions for transformation, he will go through a number of physical and psychological changes. First, a male will undergo a noticeable growth spurt, affecting both height and musculature. For a female, the physical changes are much more subtle, mainly denoted by the definition of muscle rather than bulk or height. Both males and females will then experience a drastic rise in body temperature, one that a typical human would be unable to survive. At the same time, he or she will begin to have dramatic mood swings and brief, sudden episodes of nearly uncontrollable rage. When the transformation is very close, he or she will begin to tremble and shake during these moments of rage.

Standing too close to a young werewolf during phasing can result in unintentional injury, or even death.

PHASING:

After the shaking begins, the first transformation, or phase, can happen within seconds if the affected person does not calm himself. All the initial transformations are triggered by rage, until the werewolf can learn to control his reactions. The actual act of phasing lasts only an instant. There is no gradual shift, no in-between form where the werewolf appears to be a mix of human and animal. Because the wolf has more than four times the mass of the human, to an observer the change looks explosive as the human expands to the size of the wolf. This impression can be intensified if the werewolf did not have time to remove his clothes before phasing; the clothes rip apart from the pressure of the expansion, adding a tearing sound to the otherwise soundless transformation.

Young werewolves are often unable to control their phasing, shifting forms whenever they feel anger. This unpredictability, combined with the massive size of the wolf form and the suddenness of the phasing process, makes werewolves dangerous to any humans in proximity to them during the change. Standing too close to a young werewolf during phasing can result in unintentional injury, or even death.

As young werewolves gain more control over their phasing, they have time to remove clothing, preventing it from being destroyed in the shape-shifting process. Most carry a leather strap with them so they can tie their clothes to their legs before phasing.

With experience, werewolves eventually master phasing and can control when they shape-shift.

PHYSICAL CHARACTERISTICS

APPEARANCE:

The Quileute werewolves are very similar to normal wolves, but are several times larger. An average Quileute werewolf would stand at about the height of a horse, but with greater body mass. Besides being bigger than a normal wolf, the werewolves are also supernaturally stronger and faster. Their teeth and claws are sharp and strong enough to be able to damage a vampire; they can also run as fast as vampires. (Just as with normal humans, there are individual wolves who are faster than other wolves.) In their human forms, werewolves are stronger and faster than humans, but not enough to take on a vampire without phasing.

The wolves' fur ranges in color, through many shades of brown, gray, and black. The length of a tribe member's hair in human form affects the length of his werewolf coat. For example, if someone has long human hair, the coat in wolf form will also be longer.

ABILITIES

SIGHT:

A werewolf's eyesight is more than ten times sharper than a normal human's, twice as sharp as the average bird of prey. Though a normal human can easily spot a vampire at a glance if she knows what she is looking for, a werewolf—even in his human form—sees much more than the pale skin and characteristic eye color. To werewolves, vampires look shiny and angular, almost like moving crystal.

SENSE OF SMELL:

Like wolves and other predators, werewolves have a heightened sense of smell. Of special note, vampires have a distinctive scent that werewolves are particularly aware of, in both their human and wolf forms. In general, for werewolves a vampire's scent is uncomfortable to the point of pain—a sickly sweet smell that burns. Individually, each vampire has his or her own personal scent, which is easily distinguishable to werewolves. They can pick up this scent from a good distance, or from any item a vampire has touched.

SPEED:

Quileute werewolves possess great speed. They can outrun motor vehicles. A fast werewolf can outrun an average vampire. In human form, they are faster and have greater endurance than all normal humans.

TELEPATHIC COMMUNICATION:

Werewolves are pack animals. They are at their most effective, whether hunting or fighting, when they work as a team. In their wolf forms, the werewolf pack shares a group mind; every member of the pack hears the thoughts of every other member.

When in wolf form, werewolves have no privacy.

This telepathic communication allows them to work as one, coordinating instantaneously and moving with perfect unity. The pack's true power isn't in each individual wolf's strength, but in this ability to work together as a cohesive group.

The ability to smoothly act as a team comes at a price. When in wolf form, werewolves have no privacy. All thoughts, no matter how fleeting or seemingly insignificant, are transmitted to other pack members who are also in wolf form. Feelings are transmitted, too — even those that are personal or potentially embarrassing.

When more than one wolf pack exists at a time, werewolves from one pack cannot communicate telepathically with werewolves from the other pack. The only exception is the Alpha, or leader, of each pack. The Alpha can decide whether to share his thoughts with another Alpha and can select which thoughts to send, in the same way that he would choose to speak aloud.

HEALING:

Quileute werewolves heal very quickly, in both human and wolf form. When they are wounded, they immediately begin to heal. Minor injuries heal in as little as a few seconds. More serious injuries, like broken bones, typically repair themselves in a matter of days. Quileute werewolves are not indestructible, and although killing one is easier than killing a vampire, it still takes supernatural strength or great skill to seriously wound a werewolf.

An exception to this rule is vampire venom. In a werewolf's system — whether he is in his human or wolf form — venom does not begin the process of transformation into a vampire. Rather, it acts as a poison that retards the healing abilities of the werewolf. Venom alone will not generally kill a healthy werewolf; however, in combination with other injuries, it can be fatal.

Once a werewolf transforms, his aging speeds up until he reaches the age of maturity, roughly twenty-five. At this point, as long as he continues to phase, he remains at that age. It's possible that a werewolf could choose to live this way forever and enjoy the same limited immortality as a vampire, but most Quileute werewolves give up phasing in order to grow old and die alongside their family and friends. Once a werewolf gives up phasing altogether, he slowly begins to age again until his aging reaches the normal human speed.

LIFESTYLE AND BEHAVIOR

TRIBE STRUCTURE:

The members of the Quileute tribe live as a group in the Quileute Nation on the La Push reservation and are governed by a council of elders. The tribe consists of everyone who is a descendant of another Quileute. The Quileute pack is a subset of the tribe; every member of the pack is a member of the tribe, but the majority of the tribe are not members of the pack. Moreover, most members of the tribe are not aware of the reality of werewolves. Only the members of the council and the pack are in on the secret. While the tribal elders work closely with the pack, only those individuals with the ability to phase are actually classified as members of the pack. The leader of the pack is referred to as the Alpha. The role of Alpha wolf is inherited; the oldest descendant of the previous Alpha has the rightful claim to the position. If, for any reason, the oldest descendant of the last Alpha refuses the position, the Alpha title can be claimed by either the next closest relative of the last Alpha or by the chronologically oldest member of the pack. In such a situation, each member of the pack must initially choose to support this Alpha candidate. After that support is given, the Alpha has the ability to impose control over the other members of the pack, and no member can refuse the Alpha's commands. According to tribal tradition, the Alpha wolf is not only the head of the pack, but also the chief of the entire tribe. As the tribe is now governed by council, the Alpha takes the position of the most senior tribe elder, despite his age.

One factor affecting which members of the tribe transform is the number of vampire scents in the area. Throughout Quileute history, the pack has usually consisted of three members. With most vampires traveling alone or in pairs, there was never a need for more than three werewolves to defend Quileute land. However, with a large vampire coven settled in the area, the tribe members with the strongest blood ties to the former pack are not the only ones who transform. Everyone in the tribe who has any relation to past wolves has a chance of joining the new pack. As more vampires enter the area in response to the resident coven, even more tenuous bloodlines result in new werewolves.

> *As more vampires enter the area in response to the resident coven, even more tenuous bloodlines result in new werewolves.*

Recently, as a result of the size of the Quileute werewolf population and the accompanying tension, the pack split into two separate groups. For the first time in Quileute history, there are currently two Alphas, each with his own pack. There are presently seventeen members of the two werewolf packs.

RANK:

The wolf pack has a very complex system of rank that helps keep them organized and prepared for all eventualities. The Alpha's absolute authority over the pack makes them

an effective fighting force, and if something happens to the Alpha, there is no debate about how to proceed. The pack does not lose effectiveness due to confusion.

Every Alpha has a second in command — referred to as his Second — who immediately assumes control if the Alpha is incapacitated. Ranking under the Second is the Third, who is next in line to act as Alpha.

In the case of a large pack, each Second and Third has his own Second and Third, and so on down, so that each wolf has someone in line to step into his responsibilities within the pack if something should happen to him. In a large pack, during a fight the wolves tend to operate in three-wolf pods.

IMPRINTING:

Some werewolves experience a bonding incident called imprinting, in which they become unconditionally tied to a human of the opposite sex. There are several theories on why imprinting occurs: Some believe that imprinting ensures the passing on of the werewolf gene; others believe that imprinting happens to produce larger, stronger wolves in the next generation. The werewolves do not know the answer for certain.

Imprinting occurs only after a werewolf's first phasing. It can happen with anyone, regardless of previous personal feelings. Imprinting happens the first time a werewolf sees the human object of his imprinting; if the werewolf does not react to a human the first time he sees her after he phases, he will never imprint on that human. If the werewolf does imprint, he is forever changed. From the second he sees the object of his imprinting, he will do anything to please and protect her. All other commitments in his life become secondary, even his commitment to the pack.

The relationship between the imprinting werewolf and

the human imprinted upon is one of total acceptance and support on the werewolf's part. No matter the age or living conditions of the human, the werewolf automatically becomes whatever the human wants him to be, at the loss of his personal free will. If the human is young, the werewolf becomes the perfect platonic playmate and protector. As the human ages and changes, the werewolf instinctively switches roles to fulfill the human's needs.

It is against pack law for any werewolf to kill the object of another werewolf's imprinting. Such an act would be devastating not only to the wolf who suffered the loss, but to the entire pack. Given the telepathic ability of the pack, each pack member would suffer the pain of the wolf whose mate had been killed. Even if the death of a wolf's mate was an accident, the two wolves involved would fight to the death.

ANCIENT QUILEUTE HISTORY

The Quileutes have a detailed history of how they came to be shape-shifters, and how that aspect of their nature was focused by their first contact with vampires. Essentially, the early Quileutes had the ability to use astral projection. When this ability led to a coup, the rightful chief put his spirit into the body of a wolf. His progeny were able to assume wolf form as well. The first time a vampire — or "cold one," as the Quileutes called them — entered the Quileutes' land, the tribe discovered that their wolf protectors were able to kill vampires, but it was an almost evenly matched contest. Vampires became the main focus of the Quileute wolves. Over time, the Quileute warriors gained the ability to assume wolf form only if a vampire triggered the reaction.

This history was passed down through oral storytelling. Originally the entire tribe would learn the account; in the last century, however, the sharing became more secretive, passed only from werewolf descendants to the next generation of potential werewolves. All tribe members know the basics, but think of the stories as myths rather than facts.

HISTORY WITH THE CULLENS

In 1936, cold ones again entered Quileute land. They were different from the vampires who had come before. Their coven was larger — three males and two females — and the eyes of all the members were golden rather than red. The leader, Carlisle Cullen, somehow knew that the wolves had human intelligence. He told the wolves that the Cullens meant no harm to the wolves, the Quileute tribe, or any other humans. He claimed that they did not drink human blood, and offered a treaty between his coven and the werewolves. The three werewolves in the pack were outnumbered, so Carlisle had no need to make this offer other than an honest desire to refrain from killing the wolves. For this reason, Alpha wolf Ephraim Black believed Carlisle was making a genuine offer.

Ephraim insisted on two main points to the treaty: The vampires could not injure any humans (either by hunting them for food or by transforming them into vampires, as the Quileutes viewed this transformation as equal to murder), and the vampires were never to trespass on Quileute land. Carlisle agreed to these terms and proposed adding the concept of mutual secrecy: The Quileutes would not be able to tell anyone the true nature of the Cullens, and vice versa. Ephraim agreed, and they worked out the boundary lines for their respective lands. The Quileute territory covered all of the reservation, plus some of the land that had traditionally belonged to the Hohs and the Makahs. In some places, the boundary line followed the main road, now Highway 101, but in others it followed the old tribal lines. In turn, the werewolves would not cross into Cullen land. The town of Forks, along with a few other surrounding towns, and the highway were "truce areas" where both the Quileute werewolves and the Cullens were allowed to venture.

As the years passed and the Cullens moved elsewhere, the younger members of the Quileute tribe began to think of the treaty between the cold ones and the werewolves as part of a legend, not factual truth. The Cullens returned to the area in 2003, and Jacob Black later told human Bella Swan that the Cullens were vampires who had made a treaty with his werewolf great-grandfather, Ephraim. He thought he was only telling her a scary story, but in fact, he unknowingly broke the treaty.

The Cullens' return had a huge impact on the tribe, especially those who had inherited the extra chromosome and who were in the right age range to transform. Werewolves hadn't existed in the Quileute tribe since Ephraim's pack. But the number of vampires in the Cullen coven caused an unusually large number of tribe members to become werewolves. The result was the largest wolf pack the tribe had seen since the days of the first shape-shifter.

As the years passed and the Cullens moved elsewhere, the younger members of the Quileute tribe began to think of the treaty between the cold ones and the werewolves as part of a legend, not factual truth.

The Quileute Packs
and Tribe

Quileute Genealogy Trees

KEY:

Symbol	Meaning
▲	Ateara family werewolf gene carrier
◆	Black family werewolf gene carrier
■	Uley family werewolf gene carrier
/	Married
---	Imprinted, not married
‖	Immediate family not known
●	Werewolf

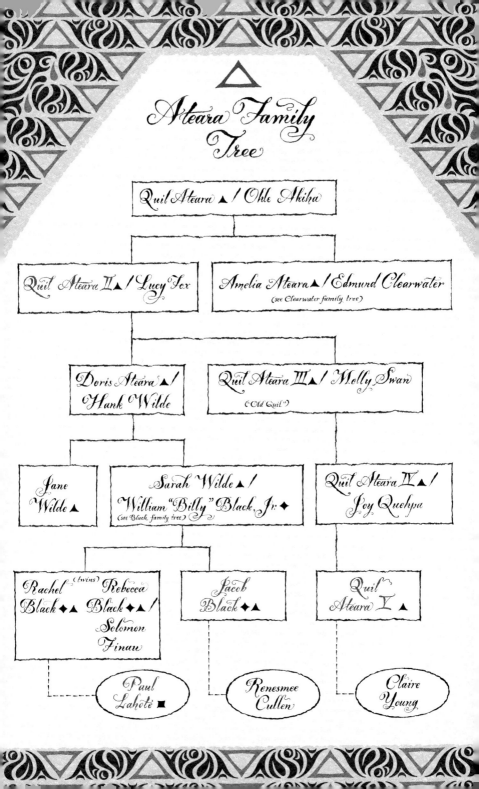

Ateara Family Tree

Quil Ateara ▲ / Ohle Akiha

Quil Ateara II ▲ / Lucy Fox

Amelia Ateara ▲ / Edmund Clearwater
(see Clearwater family tree)

Doris Ateara ▲ / Hank Wilde

Quil Ateara III ▲ / Molly Swan
("Old Quil")

Jane Wilde ▲

Sarah Wilde ▲ / William "Billy" Black, Jr. ◆
(see Black family tree)

Quil Ateara IV ▲ / Joy Quehpa

Rachel Black ◆▲ (twins) Rebecca Black ◆▲ / Solomon Finau

Jacob Black ◆▲

Quil Ateara V ▲

Paul Lahote ■

Renesmee Cullen

Claire Young

Black Family Tree

Jacob Black ◆ / Alice Fox

Lape Huautah / Joanna Black ◆

Joseph Black ◆ / Jane Clearwater (sister of Moses Clearwater)

Lorraine Huautah ◆

Alice Huautah ◆ / Caleb Uley ■

Dorothy Black ◆

Ephraim Black ◆ / Martha Young

Deborah Black ◆ (twins) **Susanah Black ◆**

William Black, Sr. ◆ / Judith Peterson

Mary Black ◆ (twins) **Jane Black ◆**

Nora Black ◆

William "Billy" Black, Jr. ◆ / Sarah Wilde ▲ (see Ateara family tree)

Jennie Black ◆ (twins) **Connie Black ◆ / Kevin Littlesea**

Emmie Black ◆

Jared Cameron ◆

Rachel Black ◆▲ (twins) **Rebecca Black ◆▲ / Solomon Finau**

Jacob Black ◆▲

Collin Littlesea ◆

Kim

Paul Lahôte ■

Renesmee Cullen

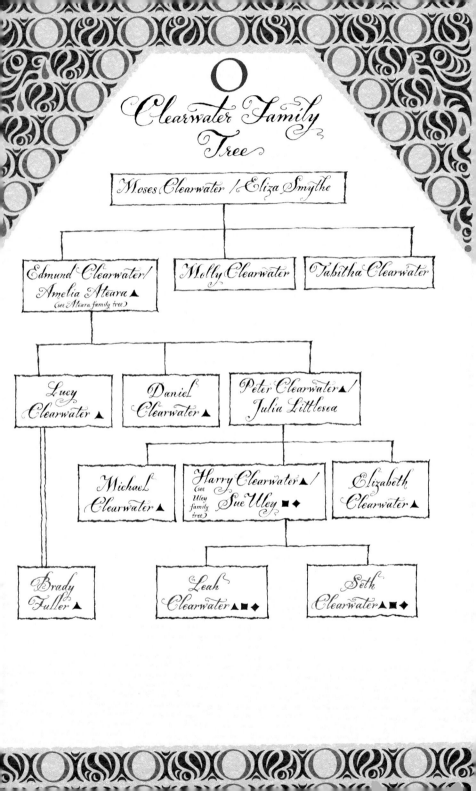

Clearwater Family Tree

Moses Clearwater / Eliza Smythe

Edmund Clearwater / Amelia Ateara ▲ (see Ateara family tree)

Molly Clearwater

Tabitha Clearwater

Lucy Clearwater ▲

Daniel Clearwater ▲

Peter Clearwater ▲ / Julia Littlesea

Michael Clearwater ▲

Harry Clearwater ▲ / Sue Uley ■ ◆ (see Uley family tree)

Elizabeth Clearwater ▲

Brady Fuller ▲

Leah Clearwater ▲ ■ ◆

Seth Clearwater ▲ ■ ◆

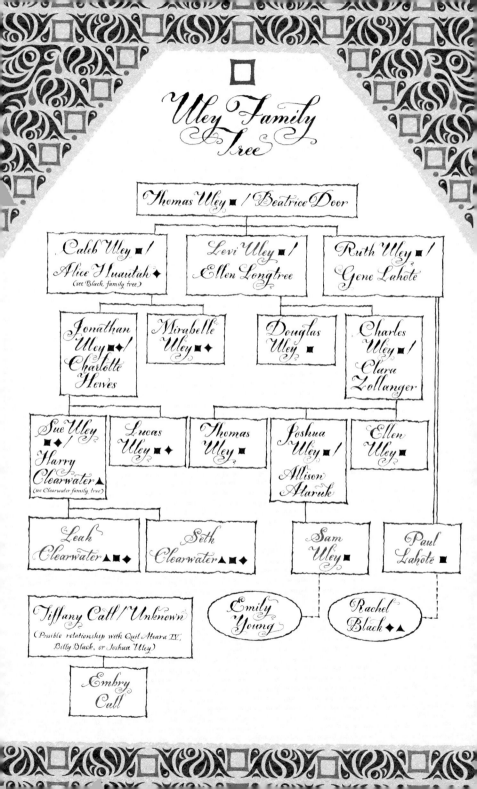

The Black Pack

➻ JACOB BLACK

NAME: Jacob Black; nickname: Jake

DATE OF BIRTH: January 14, 1990

QUILEUTE STATUS: Werewolf Alpha

WEREWOLF GENE SOURCE: Black and Ateara lines

HUMAN HAIR COLOR: Black

WOLF COAT COLOR: Rusty brown

EYE COLOR: Brown

HEIGHT: 5'10" at age 15; 6'7" after transformation

PHYSICAL DESCRIPTION: When Jacob first met Bella, he looked older than he was because he was tall for his age, although he had a hint of childish roundness to his chin. He had a lanky build and wore his long, glossy black hair in a ponytail. As he got closer to transforming, he went through a series of growth spurts. By the time he phased for the first time, he had reached 6'7" in height and had achieved his current imposing, muscular build. He cut his hair very short after his transformation but soon started letting it grow again.

EDUCATION/OCCUPATION: He attends the tribal high school at La Push. Although he is currently on "sabbatical," he plans to return soon. In the past, he has worked at the store on the La Push reservation to earn extra money. Since his transformation his main focus has been protecting tribal lands and Bella Swan.

HOBBIES: He enjoys rebuilding automotive vehicles.

VEHICLES: Red Volkswagen Rabbit and a classic black Harley Sprint motorcycle

FAMILY MEMBERS: Jacob's mother, Sarah, is deceased. He has older twin sisters named Rachel and Rebecca. He lives with his father, Billy Black. He has imprinted on Renesmee Cullen.

PERSONAL HISTORY:

Jacob Black was born in La Push, Washington. He grew up with his father, Billy; his mother, Sarah; and his older twin sisters, Rachel and Rebecca. Jacob's best friends throughout his childhood and adolescence were Embry Call and Quil Ateara V. All three attended school on the La Push reservation.

When Jacob was nine, his mother was killed in a car accident on the highway between La Push and Forks. This loss was hard on Jacob, but he recovered better than his sisters did, thanks in part to his sisters filling the role of mother for him as much as they were able. When his father became wheelchair-bound due to complications from diabetes, Jacob became Billy's legs. He did not resent taking care of his father; in fact, Jacob enjoyed spending so much time with him. Jacob looked up to Billy and thought he was a great dad, his only real flaw being his superstitious beliefs. Billy constantly tried to indoctrinate Jacob in the traditions and histories of the tribe, but Jacob stopped listening at an early age.

Jacob and his father were on their own as soon as Jacob's sisters were out of high school. Both Rachel and Rebecca had a difficult time living in the place where their mother had lived; it made them miss her even more. Rebecca married a Samoan surfer right out of high school, and traveled with him around the world to his many competitions. Rachel went to Washington State University and worked through her breaks and holidays.

Jacob noticed the change in his father when the Cullens moved to Forks, but he didn't understand it. He found his father's aversion to the new doctor very embarrassing, and

"I think being a teenager is such a compelling time period in your life—it gives you some of your worst scars and some of your most exhilarating memories. It's a fascinating place: old enough to feel truly adult, old enough to make decisions that affect the rest of your life, old enough to fall in love, yet, at the same time too young (in most cases) to be free to make a lot of those decisions without someone else's approval. There's a lot of scope for a novel in that." —Stephenie

"THE BLACKS' HOUSE WAS VAGUELY FAMILIAR, A SMALL
WOODEN PLACE WITH NARROW WINDOWS, THE DULL RED
PAINT MAKING IT RESEMBLE A TINY BARN."

—Bella (*New Moon*, Chapter 5)

the increased emphasis on the Quileute traditions annoying. After a while, he began tuning out most of what his father said.

Jacob was the fifth person to join the current crop of were-wolves. Genetically, he was the rightful Alpha. However, he did not assume that title until later, when he formed a separate pack from Sam's. He continued to live with only his father until his sister Rachel returned home and was imprinted on by Paul Lahote.

FAMOUS QUOTES

"Do you like scary stories?" Twilight, Chapter 6

"I guess I just violated the treaty." Twilight, Chapter 6

"'We'll be watching.'" Twilight, Epilogue

"What are you, forty?" New Moon, Chapter 5

"Sometimes you're a little strange, Bella. Do you know that?"
New Moon, Chapter 7

"Well, I'm so sorry that I can't be the right *kind of monster for you, Bella. I guess I'm just not as great as a bloodsucker, am I?"*
New Moon, Chapter 13

"You really, honestly don't mind that I morph into a giant dog?"
New Moon, Chapter 13

"We're a pretty messed-up pair, aren't we? Neither one of us can hold our shape together right." New Moon, Chapter 15

"Bye, Bella. I really hope you don't die." New Moon, Chapter 16

"He's at the funeral." New Moon, Chapter 18

"The treaty is quite specific. If any of them bite a human, the truce is over. Bite, *not kill."* New Moon, Epilogue

"I don't have any leeches on my speed dial." *Eclipse*, Chapter 3

"Normal humans run away from monsters, Bella. And I never claimed to be normal. Just human." *Eclipse*, Chapter 4

"It's more like . . . gravity moves. When you see her, suddenly it's not the earth holding you here anymore. She does. And nothing matters more than her. And you would do anything for her, be anything for her. . . . You become whatever she needs you to be, whether that's a protector, or a lover, or a friend, or a brother." *Eclipse*, Chapter 8

"Does my being half-naked bother you?" *Eclipse*, Chapter 10

"Bella, I love you. And I want you to pick me instead of him." *Eclipse*, Chapter 14

"She's in love with me, too, you know." *Eclipse*, Chapter 22

"That *should have been our first kiss. Better late than never.*" *Eclipse*, Chapter 23

"I'm not going to cut you in half anymore, Bella." *Eclipse*, Chapter 26

"Make Bella see sense? What universe do you live in?" *Breaking Dawn*, Chapter 9

"Bella! What was the point of me loving you? What was the point of you loving him? When you die how is that ever right again? What's the point to all the pain? Mine, yours, his! You'll kill him, too, not that I care about that. So what was the point of your twisted love story, in the end? If there is any sense, please show me, Bella, because I don't see it." *Breaking Dawn*, Chapter 10

"Ephraim Black's son was not born to follow Levi Uley's." *Breaking Dawn*, Chapter 11

"You know how you drown a blonde, Rosalie? Glue a mirror to the bottom of a pool." *Breaking Dawn*, Chapter 14

"Thanks, anyway, Alice, but I don't want to eat something Blondie's spit in. I'd bet my system wouldn't take too kindly to venom."
Breaking Dawn, Chapter 15

"I gotta say it, Bells. You're a freak show." Breaking Dawn, Chapter 22

"Jeez, Bells. You didn't used to be so melodramatic. Is that a vampire thing?" Breaking Dawn, Chapter 25

"Say what you want, I still think Dracula One and Dracula Two are creep-tacular." Breaking Dawn, Chapter 33

"IT WAS AMAZING THE AMOUNT OF DETAIL INVOLVED IN
THE LITTLE FIGURINE — THE MINIATURE WOLF WAS UTTERLY
REALISTIC. IT WAS EVEN CARVED OUT OF SOME RED-BROWN
WOOD THAT MATCHED THE COLOR OF HIS SKIN."
— Bella, on the charm Jacob gives her (*Eclipse*, Chapter 17)

"THE WATER WAS DARK GRAY, EVEN IN THE SUNLIGHT, WHITE-CAPPED AND
HEAVING TO THE GRAY, ROCKY SHORE. ISLANDS ROSE OUT OF THE STEEL HARBOR
WATERS WITH SHEER CLIFF SIDES, REACHING TO UNEVEN SUMMITS,
AND CROWNED WITH AUSTERE, SOARING FIRS."

—Bella, on La Push Beach (*Twilight*, Chapter 6)

➤ LEAH CLEARWATER

DATE OF BIRTH: 1986

QUILEUTE STATUS: Werewolf Alpha Second, under Jacob

WEREWOLF GENE SOURCE: Ateara, Black, and Uley lines

HUMAN HAIR COLOR: Black

WOLF COAT COLOR: Gray

EYE COLOR: Brown

HEIGHT: Around 5'10"

PHYSICAL DESCRIPTION: Leah is beautiful. She has perfect copper skin, shiny black hair, and long, thick eyelashes. In her wolf form, she is the smallest of the pack, and also the fastest.

EDUCATION/OCCUPATION: She graduated from the high school on the reservation. She is a protector of La Push.

FAMILY MEMBERS: Leah's father, Harry, is deceased. She lives with her mother, Sue, and her younger brother, Seth.

PERSONAL HISTORY:

As a freshman in high school, Leah began dating, and then fell in love with, Sam Uley. They were involved in a serious relationship for three years.

During her junior year of high school, Leah's life was thrown into upheaval when Sam disappeared. The police and forest rangers were involved, but could find no trace of him.

Two weeks later, Sam reappeared. He gave no explanation for his absence, and from that time forward he was a changed person. Leah knew there was something big he wasn't telling her, but she had no idea what it could be. She tried to give him space to resolve whatever the problem was, and continued to love and support him.

Not long after that, Leah's second cousin Emily Young

came to La Push. Emily was Leah's closest girlfriend — almost a sister — and a frequent visitor. She had met Sam several times before this visit. But this time, when Sam came over to see Leah, he saw Emily for the first time since his disappearance. Leah didn't understand his bizarre behavior. He left very quickly, but came back later that night to break up with Leah. She could tell he was truly devastated, but she didn't understand what could have happened to change him so completely. She understood more when Emily came to her and told her — with dismay — that Sam was pursuing her. Leah, who had wanted to give Sam the benefit of the doubt, because clearly something very odd was going on with him, could no longer imagine that he had any excuse. She became furious with him. Emily supported her, and Leah relied on Emily's refusal of Sam's pursuit.

Leah started to realize that Emily was spending a great deal of time with Sam, ostensibly rejecting him. She became suspicious. Then she heard that Emily had been mauled by a bear and that Sam was inconsolable about it. Initially, she was mostly concerned about Emily's well-being. However, it became clear shortly after the accident that Sam and Emily were a couple, and Leah's concern turned into bitterness. Part of her felt like Emily had gotten what she deserved.

Leah kept her distance from Emily and Sam as much as possible. Emily asked for forgiveness, but Leah wouldn't speak to her.

Time passed, and Leah found herself growing angrier than she had been before, though there was no new catalyst for her feelings. She flew into a rage

> Emily asked for forgiveness, but Leah wouldn't speak to her.

over the smallest irritants, sometimes getting so angry that she would physically shake. Privately, she worried about this change in her nature, and wondered if she needed counseling or medication. Before she had time to think it over more, she phased for the first time. She was arguing with her mother about her mood swings, and her father joined the conversation in support of her mother. Leah was so angry that her whole body started shaking, and then she exploded into a werewolf in their small living room. She didn't touch either of her parents in the process, though she did destroy a couch. However, the shock of Leah phasing triggered her father's fatal heart attack. Harry was aware of the reality of werewolves, and expected to someday deal with that issue with Seth, but he was so secure in his belief that only male ancestors had the potential to phase that he missed the signs with Leah. He was completely shocked. Reacting to the chaos and horror of the moment, Leah's little brother, Seth, also phased, though he was younger than the usual age.

It was extremely difficult for Leah to deal with her first weeks as a werewolf. She'd just lost her father and blamed herself for his death, though of course she'd done nothing to hurt him intentionally. Sam was the usual guide for the new wolves, the one who explained everything to the newcomers and assigned the roles in the pack; there couldn't have been a harder person for Leah to have to face. It was even worse because now, knowing the whole truth, she could no longer blame him for his actions. There was no choice but to forgive both him and Emily, and that took so much that Leah had few emotional resources left to deal gracefully with any other problem. She did agree to support Emily by being a bridesmaid at the wedding. She tried not to show how much that hurt her, but as a wolf, there was no way for her to keep secrets.

The shared-thoughts aspect of being a wolf was definitely the hardest part for Leah. The second hardest was trying to understand the changes in her human body — the halt of her menstrual cycle, specifically — and what that might mean for her future. The only thing she really enjoyed was being faster than the others.

FAMOUS QUOTES

"This is making me sick, Jacob. Can you imagine what this feels like to me? I don't even like Bella Swan. And you've got me grieving over this leech-lover like I'm in love with her, too. Can you see where that might be a little confusing? I dreamed about kissing her last night! What the hell am I supposed to do with that?"
Eclipse, Epilogue

"You think I'm just going to sit home while my little brother volunteers as a vampire chew toy?" Breaking Dawn, Chapter 12

"Give me a break, Jacob. You can phase in front of me. Despite my best efforts, I've seen you naked before — doesn't do much for me, so no worries." Breaking Dawn, Chapter 13

"I'm a genetic dead end and we both know it."
Breaking Dawn, Chapter 16

➤ EMBRY CALL

NAME: Embry Call

DATE OF BIRTH: 1990

QUILEUTE STATUS: Werewolf Alpha Third, under Jacob

WEREWOLF GENE SOURCE: Unknown

HUMAN HAIR COLOR: Black

WOLF COAT COLOR: Gray with dark spots

EYE COLOR: Brown

HEIGHT: 6'4"

PHYSICAL DESCRIPTION: Embry is almost as tall as Jacob, but more slender. Until his transformation, his hair was chin length. After that, he cropped it short.

EDUCATION/OCCUPATION: He attends the high school on the reservation. He is a protector of La Push.

FAMILY MEMBERS: He lives with his mother, Tiffany.

PERSONAL HISTORY:

Tiffany Call moved to La Push while she was pregnant with Embry. Tiffany was of Makah descent, with no known connection to anyone in La Push, and people wondered why she would relocate. However, as time passed she became an established member of the community and people stopped speculating about her past.

Embry grew up with Jacob Black and Quil Ateara. He was especially close to Jacob. They both were interested in automotives and liked to ride dirt bikes together.

Embry was the fourth werewolf to join the present-day pack. His transformation was a shock to the rest of the wolves: Only descendants of Taha Aki had the ability to become werewolves. Because Embry's mother had no genetic connection to the Quileute Tribe, Embry's ability to transform had to have been inherited from his father. The men with the strongest connection to the last pack were therefore the men most likely to be Embry's father. Those men were Billy Black, Joshua Uley, and Quil Ateara IV—all three of whom were married at the time of Embry's conception—making Quil, Jacob, or Sam Embry's half-brother.

This information caused some strain in the tribe, but for the most part the wolves ignored it. Embry wanted to ask his mother for the truth—she had always said his father was someone she had not known well and had lost track of before Embry was born. Now Embry knew this story wasn't true, but he was unable to tell his mother why he knew. Because he had to keep his werewolf heritage a secret, he was unable to confront her.

FAMOUS QUOTES

"Well, the wolf's out of the bag now." New Moon, Chapter 14

"I bet she's tougher than that. She runs with vampires."
New Moon, Chapter 14

His transformation was a shock to the rest of the wolves: Only descendants of Taha Aki had the ability to become werewolves.

NAME: Seth Clearwater

DATE OF BIRTH: 1992

QUILEUTE STATUS: Werewolf pack member

WEREWOLF GENE SOURCE: Ateara, Black, and Uley lines

HUMAN HAIR COLOR: Black

WOLF COAT COLOR: Sandy

EYE COLOR: Brown

HEIGHT: Nearly 6'0"

PHYSICAL DESCRIPTION: Seth has a very long, gangly build. His face is youthful, and his huge grin is reminiscent of Jacob's when he was younger.

EDUCATION/OCCUPATION: He attends the high school on the reservation. He is a protector of La Push.

FAMILY MEMBERS: Seth's father, Harry, is deceased. He lives with his mother, Sue, and his older sister, Leah.

PERSONAL HISTORY:

When Seth's older sister, Leah, phased in front of the family one night, the shock caused their father, Harry, who already had a weak heart, to have a fatal cardiac arrest. The upheaval all around him catalyzed Seth's own transformation, earlier than it would normally have happened; he phased that night, too.

Although Seth was deeply saddened by the death of his father, he accepted his transformation far better than Leah did hers. He didn't have the same challenges to deal with. Seth enjoyed being a werewolf. He saw being a pack member as a cool kind of magic that made him special, rather than viewing it as a curse. He is known in the pack for having the best hearing.

Seth is the most open-minded of the wolves. He sees the

Cullens not as monsters, but as individuals who have chosen to live in a way that makes them good guys.

FAMOUS QUOTE

"Lucky thing Ness — Renesmee's not venomous. 'Cause she bites Jake all the time." Breaking Dawn, Chapter 23

✈ QUIL ATEARA V

NAME: Quil Ateara V

DATE OF BIRTH: 1990

QUILEUTE STATUS: Werewolf pack member

WEREWOLF GENE SOURCE: Ateara and Black lines

HUMAN HAIR COLOR: Black

WOLF COAT COLOR: Chocolate brown

EYE COLOR: Brown

HEIGHT: Over 6'0"

PHYSICAL DESCRIPTION: Quil is shorter than Embry, but is more muscular. He has an impish grin, and he wears his hair in a near buzz cut.

EDUCATION/OCCUPATION: He attends the high school on the reservation. He is a protector of La Push.

FAMILY MEMBERS: He is the son of the late Quil Ateara IV and Joy Quehpa Ateara. Quil Ateara III, also known as Old Quil, is his grandfather.

PERSONAL HISTORY:

Quil's great-grandfather was Quil Ateara II, who helped form the treaty with the Cullen family. His father, Quil IV, died when Quil was a young child, leaving his mother, Joy, to raise him on her own. She had the help of her father-in-law, Quil Ateara III, commonly known as Old Quil, who functioned more like a father than a grandfather to Quil. Quil is one of Jacob Black's best friends, as well as his second cousin.

Quil was the sixth person to join the Quileute werewolf pack. For some time, he'd been aware of the drastic changes in his close friends' lives, without knowing the reason for those changes. He was relieved to learn the truth and pleased to be with his friends again. His easy transition was challenged when he became the third member of the tribe to imprint on a human female. Unlike Sam and Jared, who had imprinted on girls of roughly their own age, the object of Quil's imprinting was a young child. This caused much upheaval in the pack.

Of lesser concern was the fact that so many members of the pack were imprinting; according to legend, imprinting was a rare event that the majority of werewolves would never experience. The other members of the pack began to worry that they would all imprint, and should therefore eschew normal relationships for fear of hurting an innocent bystander the way Leah had been hurt by Sam. The pack theorized that the increase in imprinting frequency was due to the continued presence of the large Cullen coven; their genetic subconscious was compensating for the constant vampire threat, pushing

According to legend, imprinting was a rare event that the majority of werewolves would never experience.

all of them toward paths that would result in a strengthened werewolf presence. Of course, that theory was dependent upon the truth of their first theory — that imprinting existed in order to pass on the werewolf gene. A theory that, in light of Jacob's imprinting experience, has been called into question.

The bigger concern was, of course, Claire's age; she was two at the time. Though there were ancient legends that told of such situations, the werewolves had discounted them as empty stories. That this myth could be true seemed more horrific than the rest of the legends they'd come to accept. From the outside it looked depraved, as they were well aware. However, from the inside, there could be nothing more pure than Quil's feelings for Claire. That he would never do anything to hurt her in any way, mentally or physically, was mandated by the bond between them. All the wolves could experience the nature of his feelings for her, so they knew exactly how deep it was — and also how platonic it was. But they knew it was something that outsiders would not be able to understand, so they kept the imprinting as secret as possible.

Quil could only be content with his situation. As long as Claire was happy and safe, he was satisfied with life.

> Quil could only be content with his situation. As long as Claire was happy and safe, he was satisfied with life.

FAMOUS QUOTE

"You know, Jake, maybe you should think about getting a life." Breaking Dawn, Chapter 8

The Uley Pack

SAM ULEY

NAME: Sam Uley

DATE OF BIRTH: 1986

QUILEUTE STATUS: Werewolf Alpha

WEREWOLF GENE SOURCE: Uley line

HUMAN HAIR COLOR: Black

WOLF COAT COLOR: Black

EYE COLOR: Brown

HEIGHT: 6'6"

PHYSICAL DESCRIPTION: Sam is very tall, with cropped black hair.

EDUCATION/OCCUPATION: He attended the high school on the reservation. He is currently the leader of the original wolf pack.

FAMILY MEMBERS: He is the only child of Joshua and Allison Uley. He has imprinted on Emily Young.

PERSONAL HISTORY:

Sam was raised on the Quileute reservation by his mother, Allison. The stress of providing for a family was too much for his father, who left when Sam was very young. Sam took on most of what should have been his father's responsibilities, and as a result, he was always mature for his age. He had been taught the old werewolf legends about his great-grandfather, Levi Uley, but like everyone else of his generation, Sam believed they were myths.

When he was a senior in high school, Sam became the first of his generation to phase into a werewolf. He had no idea what had happened to him. Totally panicked, he hid deep in the forest for two weeks. Finally, he calmed down enough that he turned back into a human while he slept. He snuck home and told no one about his experience. He wouldn't talk to his mother or to his long-term girlfriend, Leah Clearwater. He believed he'd gone insane and was having delusions.

Sam lived in fear of another attack until the day Old Quil Ateara stopped by to see Allison and happened to shake Sam's hand. Old Quil had been taught to recognize the signs of a werewolf who has already phased, or is about to. Sam's high body temperature and recent unexplained disappearance made the situation clear to Old Quil. He called an emergency meeting with the other tribal elders, Billy Black and Harry Clearwater. They were the last surviving members of the tribe who had seen an actual werewolf transformation. That night they went to Sam's house and asked him to attend their council meeting. Sam respected them enough to go with them, though he assumed they were only going to castigate him for his strange behavior. Instead, they were able to tell him exactly what he'd just been through. He was stunned to realize that he'd known the explanation all along. The elders gave him as much information as they could, but, as none of them had ever personally experienced being a werewolf, their instruction was incomplete. They told Sam that he could expect new werewolves to join him as they became old enough, and that he would have to keep everything he now knew a secret. They also told him that vampires were

> Sam's high body temperature and recent unexplained disappearance made the situation clear to Old Quil.

real, living just a few miles from the tribe, and responsible for what was happening to him.

Sam was relieved to know he wasn't insane, and comforted by the fact that at least three people understood. But being a literal werewolf seemed to him only slightly better than being insane. He took his responsibility toward the tribe very seriously from the outset. The idea that his friends and family were in danger from real-life vampires made him furious. He started practicing his phasing and trying to control it, but coming at it blind and alone, he made only slow progress.

His relationship with his mother and Leah remained difficult because he couldn't give them any information about what had happened or where he was now spending his time. His mother was somewhat reassured because he was with the elders so often; she felt he was in good hands, at least. Leah, on the other hand, refused to be placated. She demanded answers that Sam couldn't give. The relationship was very strained, but not broken. They loved each other too much to let a fight, no matter how serious, come between them. Hundreds of times Sam was tempted to just tell her the truth. The knowledge that she would never believe him helped him keep his secret. He swore to her that he was not involved in anything criminal, and also that there was no other woman. They still spent as much time together as possible, though it was less than before. The elders warned him to keep his distance, but he didn't fully understand the danger; he'd never seen the transformation from the outside.

Not long after his own transformation, Jared Cameron and then Paul Lahote also phased for the first time. The elders

> The idea that his friends and family were in danger from real-life vampires made him furious.

kept watch over the tribe and called Sam whenever they thought there was something going on. For example, when Jared failed to come home one night, Jared's father called Billy for help. Billy contacted Sam; Sam phased and located Jared. Sam was able to coach Jared and Paul through the difficult transition. They bonded through shared experience and their mutual secret. They became extremely close and spent most of their time together. They were able to help one another when one of them got angry.

Then Leah's cousin Emily Young came for a weekend visit. It wasn't an unusual event; Sam had met Emily several times during his years with Leah. He liked Emily, and he liked that Emily was a good friend to Leah. Sam knew the stories about imprinting, and he now believed that — like the were-wolf stories — they were based in fact. However, he never imagined that imprinting would affect his own life. When he arrived at the Clearwaters' that night, Leah met Sam at the front door and led him to the yard, where the rest of the family was chatting while Harry barbecued. He was still holding hands with Leah when he saw Emily.

> That one second of staring into Emily's eyes changed his life more than anything he'd ever experienced — including phasing into a werewolf for the first time.

That one second of staring into Emily's eyes changed his life more than anything he'd ever experienced — including phasing into a werewolf for the first time. His first impulse was to go to Emily's side. As he dropped Leah's hand and walked toward Emily, he started to realize what had just happened and began to process the consequences. Before he could reach

out and touch Emily's hand, which he felt compelled to do, he
turned abruptly and left without a word.

He wasn't able to go far. Every step he took away from
Emily was physically painful. He paced the block, trying to
understand and to formulate a plan. He knew
for certain that the way he felt about
Emily would never change, and
that his life would not be bearable
without her near. He also knew
that while he still loved Leah the
same way he had before, it was
irrelevant compared to how he
felt about Emily. And it broke
his heart that he was going to have
to break Leah's. In that moment, he
began to truly loathe the Cullens. They had turned him into a
traitor and a liar. At the same time, he couldn't bring himself
to hate his feelings for Emily; they felt too right, too pure.

Sam returned to the Clearwaters' several hours later. Getting closer to Emily was a physical relief, though he was consumed with guilt over what he had to do. He asked Sue to
send Leah outside; he was afraid of how he would react to
seeing Emily again, although he wanted nothing more. When
Leah came out, he was direct. He told her he had to break
up with her. He cried. Leah assumed it had something to do
with Sam's many secrets, and while she was devastated, she
had hope for the future. She told him she wasn't giving up on
him. He told her she needed to. But he couldn't bring himself
to mention Emily.

Sam spent the longest two days of his life waiting for
Emily to return to her home in Neah Bay. He forced himself to keep his distance while she was with Leah, determined
to keep from hurting Leah any more than was absolutely

**They
had turned
him into a traitor
and a liar.**

unavoidable. Emily was very surprised to see Sam, having heard about the breakup. She was horrified when he explained that he had broken up with Leah in order to be with her. She told him to leave. He did what she wanted, but was unable to stay away for long. He tried to talk to her again, and Emily heard him out. He told her all his secrets, because she wanted to know them. She didn't believe any of it, and demanded that he show her. So he followed her into the forest and phased. At that point, she had to believe everything, but she told him she still couldn't accept his feelings for her. But she didn't order him to leave and never come back. So he returned, and they continued to argue. Emily wanted him to go back to Leah and try to make it work; Sam said that would be living a lie, that he would be hurting Leah more—did Emily want that?

Many of these conversations took place in the woods outside of Neah Bay. While Emily continued to have many problems with Sam's behavior, she respected the secrecy he had to maintain, so they discussed these things only in private. And Emily was fascinated by the fantasy of it all—the reality of the legends, the danger of the vampires, all of it.

> Emily was fascinated by the fantasy of it all—the reality of the legends, the danger of the vampires, all of it.

Sam, thrilled to please her, described everything in detail. She even met the other members of the pack. But then she heard that rumors were circulating about her behavior. She realized how much time she'd been spending with Sam, and recognized what that would look like to Leah. Furious with herself, she lashed out at Sam. She met him in the woods and told him that he had to stay away from her. Knowing he would have to obey if it would make her happy, Sam despaired. Next she ordered him to go back to Leah. This Sam could not agree to; he would not hurt Leah further by pretending. He told Emily it was impossible for him to love Leah the way he loved Emily, and he wouldn't ask Leah to settle that way. Emily couldn't doubt that Sam truly cared for Leah's well-being, but that only made her angrier about her own behavior. She called him a liar and shoved him away. She told him that he was just like his father, that he was running away from his responsibilities like Joshua had.

This was a more sensitive issue than Emily had imagined. Sam had lived his whole life trying to be the opposite of his father. Just hearing his father's name threw him into a rage. Sam had never perfected his control of phasing. He tried to remain calm all the time, but he lacked the ability to calm himself once the fury hit. He realized what was happening with less than a second to react. He tried to move away from Emily, throwing his hand up to warn her away. Emily didn't understand; she thought he was trying to avoid her words. She stepped forward, refusing to let him back away from her accusations. When Sam burst into his wolf form, he took up much more space than he had as a human. His hand, still extended to warn Emily, turned into massive claws, which raked down her face and right arm. Emily was knocked unconscious by the blow. Sam, believing that he had killed her, was frantic. He could not control himself enough to phase back into human form. Luckily, Jared was in his wolf form at the time and heard Sam's hysteria. He swiftly contacted Paul, and then Sue Clearwater, who, as a nurse, was the

> Sam had lived his whole life trying to be the opposite of his father.

perfect person to help. Paul drove Sue to the scene while Jared went on foot, in wolf form. Jared revived Emily and Sam paced and hovered while they waited for Sue. Sue stabilized Emily and then got her to the nearest hospital.

She told the attending doctor that Emily had been mauled by a bear. Sam couldn't calm down enough to go with Sue to the hospital, and he hated that, as he was already racked with guilt.

Sam eventually calmed down enough to become human again. He was desolate and wanted to die. Jared kept him updated on Emily's condition, which was not critical. The next afternoon, Jared told Sam that Emily was asking for him. Sam went into Emily's hospital room and saw her face covered with bandages. They both already knew that she was scarred for life. Sam asked her to tell him to kill himself so that he could escape the misery; he couldn't even commit suicide without knowing for certain that this was what she wanted. But Emily had asked for him to visit because she knew how horrified he would be and how unintentional his action had been. She didn't want him to blame himself for what was truly an accident. She had already forgiven him. She also had realized, as she lay there in the hospital, that the one person she really wanted there with her was Sam. She felt lonely and incomplete without him.

Sam was never able to forgive himself entirely, but he put those feelings aside as much as possible to make Emily happy. Emily no longer fought the relationship. She called Leah to tell her about the change in her feelings; due to the need for secrecy, she was not able to explain herself well. She begged

> Sam couldn't calm down enough to go with Sue to the hospital, and he hated that, as he was already racked with guilt.

for forgiveness, but Leah refused. Leah's pain was a difficult thing for both Emily and Sam, but their relationship progressed easily from that point; they found it effortless to be close both emotionally and physically.

Embry Call joined the pack, and then Jacob Black. Embry was a surprise to everyone, but Jacob was expected, as he was descended straight from the last Alpha wolf, Ephraim Black, and Sam had been waiting for him to take his place as the new Alpha. Jacob was opposed to leading the pack, and insisted that Sam stay in charge. Sam, who had been the acting Alpha up to this point due to being the first to phase, was now the official Alpha, with all the power that entailed. As the pack grew, Sam struggled with his role, sometimes being too slow to take command, other times going too far with his authority. He tried hard to balance his leadership and do the best for his pack.

> As the pack grew, Sam struggled with his role, sometimes being too slow to take command, other times going too far with his authority.

FAMOUS QUOTES

"The Cullens don't come here." Twilight, Chapter 6

"This is not something our treaty anticipated. This is a danger to every human in the area." Breaking Dawn, Chapter 10

JARED CAMERON

NAME: Jared Cameron

DATE OF BIRTH: 1990

QUILEUTE STATUS: Werewolf Alpha Second, under Sam

WEREWOLF GENE SOURCE: Black line

HUMAN HAIR COLOR: Black

WOLF COAT COLOR: Brown

EYE COLOR: Brown

HEIGHT: At least 6'0"

PHYSICAL DESCRIPTION: Jared is tall and muscular, but not as big as Sam or Jacob.

EDUCATION/OCCUPATION: He attends the high school on the reservation. He is a protector of La Push.

FAMILY MEMBERS: He has imprinted on Kim. His great-great-great-grandfather was the first Jacob Black.

PERSONAL HISTORY:

Jared was born in La Push and grew up there. He was a casual friend to Sam Uley, though Sam was ahead of him in school. Jared had an experience similar to Sam's the first time he phased; he panicked completely and ran. But he had Sam, who quickly explained things and helped him through the rough beginning. As a consequence, Jared was able to resume his human form in just a few days. He and Sam became very tight after Jared joined the pack, and remain best friends. Jared is known in the pack for having the best vision.

> Jared is known in the pack for having the best vision.

Jared was the second wolf to imprint. His journey was much easier; he imprinted on a girl who already had a crush on him. Kim was only too pleased to have Jared interested in her. She took the werewolf aspect in stride, and the two are nearly always together.

PAUL LAHOTE

NAME: Paul Lahote

DATE OF BIRTH: 1990

QUILEUTE STATUS: Werewolf Alpha Third, under Sam

WEREWOLF GENE SOURCE: Uley line

HUMAN HAIR COLOR: Black

WOLF COAT COLOR: Dark silver

EYE COLOR: Brown

HEIGHT: At least 6'0"

PHYSICAL DESCRIPTION: Paul is shorter than Jacob and leaner than Quil.

EDUCATION/OCCUPATION: He attends the high school on the reservation. He is a protector of La Push.

FAMILY MEMBERS: He has imprinted on Rachel Black. His great-great-grandfather was Thomas Uley.

PERSONAL HISTORY:

Paul was born in Tacoma and lived there until he was eight. When his parents split up, his father took him back to La Push, where Paul spent the rest of his childhood and teenage years. He was not close to either Sam or Jared, though he was in the same year of school as Jared. He had his own circle of friends, so when he abruptly stopped hanging out with them and instead became inseparable from Sam, it drew attention. People began to notice the wolf pack and speculate about it being a gang.

Paul had a great deal of difficulty controlling his temper. More than Sam or Jared, Paul frequently phased accidentally. Sam had to stay very close to Paul to make sure these out-of-control moments happened in private. After Emily was injured by Sam, Paul began to take his temper problems more seriously and improved some-what, though he still found control more difficult than did any of the others.

Sam had to stay very close to Paul to make sure these out-of-control moments happened in private.

Paul was the fourth wolf to imprint. After he imprinted, the rest of the pack became truly worried that they would all share the same fate. Paul imprinted on Jacob's sister Rachel, which caused a bit of drama in the pack; Jacob wasn't excited about Paul joining his family. Rachel had not been comfortable in La Push since the death of her mother, so she had a difficult time choosing whether to stay there with Paul. She had just graduated from college with a degree in computer engineering and had been offered a job she could do from home. She'd planned to look around for an apartment in Seattle or Portland, but she decided to stay in La Push for a while to see how things worked out with Paul. At that point, restraint became much more important to Paul. After the vampire situation was under control, he wanted to be able to give up phasing so he could travel with Rachel.

"I'm sure the leech-lover is just dying to help us out!"
New Moon, Chapter 14

"You're such a pain, Jacob. I swear, I'd rather hang out with Leah."
Breaking Dawn, Chapter 8

➵ BRADY FULLER

NAME: Brady Fuller

DATE OF BIRTH: 1993

QUILEUTE STATUS: Werewolf pack member

WEREWOLF GENE SOURCE: Ateara line

HUMAN HAIR COLOR: Black

WOLF COAT COLOR: Dark, ashy brown that almost appears gray

EYE COLOR: Brown

HEIGHT: Nearly 6'0"

EDUCATION/OCCUPATION: Brady attends the high school on the reservation. He is a protector of La Push.

FAMILY MEMBERS: He is related to the Clearwaters and the Atearas through his grandmother.

PERSONAL HISTORY:

Brady is one of the youngest members of the pack, along with Collin Littlesea. Both were thirteen years old when the pack decided to help the Cullens fight against Victoria's newborn army. Considered too young to fight, both Brady and Collin stayed behind in La Push to protect the tribe while the others participated in the battle.

⇥ COLLIN LITTLESEA

NAME: Collin Littlesea

DATE OF BIRTH: 1993

QUILEUTE STATUS: Werewolf pack member

WEREWOLF GENE SOURCE: Black line

HUMAN HAIR COLOR: Black

WOLF COAT COLOR: Reddish brown, with his legs, face, and tail a darker color

EYE COLOR: Brown

HEIGHT: Nearly 6'0"

EDUCATION/OCCUPATION: Collin attends the high school on the reservation. He is a protector of La Push.

FAMILY MEMBERS: His parents are Connie Black and Kevin Littlesea. Connie is Billy Black's younger sister. Jacob and Collin are first cousins.

PERSONAL HISTORY:

Collin is one of the younger members of the tribe, who phased after Seth and Leah Clearwater. Collin was only thirteen at the time he joined the pack. Collin is very loyal to Sam, and thinks Leah is the most beautiful woman in the world.

Considered too young
to fight, both Brady and Collin
stayed behind in La Push
to protect the tribe while the others
participated in the battle.

The Tribe

✈ BILLY BLACK

NAME: Billy Black

DATE OF BIRTH: Late 1950s

QUILEUTE STATUS: Tribal elder — non-werewolf

WEREWOLF GENE SOURCE: Black line

HAIR COLOR: Black

EYE COLOR: Black

PHYSICAL DESCRIPTION: Billy is heavyset, with a deeply wrinkled face and dark russet skin. He is currently wheelchair-bound as a result of nerve damage due to complications from diabetes.

EDUCATION/OCCUPATION: Formerly a commercial fisherman, he is currently on disability. Billy is one of the tribal elders and was considered the unofficial chief of the tribe because he was the direct descendant of the last chief. When Sam Uley transformed, Sam became the most senior tribe elder and unofficial chief.

FAMILY MEMBERS: He has three children: twin daughters Rebecca and Rachel, and son Jacob. His wife, Sarah, is deceased. It is also possible that he is Embry Call's biological father.

PERSONAL HISTORY:

Billy Black has lived in La Push his entire life. One of his earliest childhood memories is being held in his father's arms while he watched his wrinkled, stooped grandfather explode into a giant russet-colored wolf along with his two best friends, Quil Ateara and Levi Uley. All three seemed ancient to Billy;

their wolf forms were ancient, too, with grizzled muzzles and stiff joints. Yet Billy remembers them making a noise like laughter as they went for one last run through the woods.

Because of this experience, Billy grew up in a different world than most—a world where magic was absolutely real and lived in his blood. It was a world where evil was real, too. As a teenager, Billy always hoped a vampire would be foolish enough to cross Quileute land. He dreamed of being a powerful wolf, a savior to his tribe. Around the time he turned twenty he realized that he would probably never have the chance to be

"IN THE BEGINNING, THE TRIBE SETTLED IN THIS HARBOR AND BECAME SKILLED SHIPBUILDERS AND FISHERMEN."
—Billy Black (*Eclipse*, Chapter 11)

a superhero, and for many years that was a hard thing for him to accept. Most of the time, however, he was happy. After all, it was a good thing that vampires had learned to stay away from La Push. He became a man with a family, and he learned to treasure the peace of his small town and the safety it promised his wife and daughters. When Jacob was born, he saw the curse of his wolf heritage for the first time, and he fervently hoped that vampires would never trouble the Quileute tribe again. He wanted his son to have the same peaceful life that he'd had.

His wife, Sarah, died in a car accident nine years later. Rachel and Rebecca had a very difficult time living around the memories of their mother, and both of them found ways to leave La Push as soon as they were old enough. Billy wouldn't leave; he felt like his children, his young son particularly, needed the stability of the place where they'd grown up. Billy was away working on his fishing boat so often, and he wanted Jacob to be with people he could trust. In the back of his mind, Billy always worried about accidentally taking Jacob away to a place where he might encounter vampires. The same thing could happen in La Push someday, of course, but at least then Jacob would have the support of a pack, and tribal elders who understood. A few years later, Billy had to quit his job because of the progression of his diabetes. It was difficult for him to lose mobility, but it gave him more time with his children. With his daughters more active socially, it was Jacob who cared for his father most often. They became very close.

Billy was always a social person; he had many friends. Harry Clearwater and Quil Ateara IV were his closest friends, almost his brothers. They, too, grew up in a world with magic, and also spent a few years wishing for the chance to be super-heroes. If the vampires had come, Harry and Quil would have been his packmates. When Quil's small boat was destroyed in a storm, killing Quil, it was hard for both Harry and Billy; if Quil had been a shape-shifter, he would have been able to survive the accident.

Billy was also close with Charlie Swan, despite the fact that Charlie could know nothing about Billy's secrets. Charlie did know about losing a wife, though not in the same circumstances, and they both had daughters who were often mysteries to their fathers. Billy and Charlie also shared a love for fishing.

When the Cullens returned to Forks, it was a dark time for the tribe. Billy knew exactly what this would mean for his son, and he mourned for the safe and commonplace life Jacob would lose. The elders had taught the histories to their sons, but the entire tribe had begun to believe that the stories were only legend. Billy had warned Jacob about the signs of the werewolf—the heat, the growth spurt, the anger—but Jacob had totally ignored him, thinking Billy no more than superstitious. Billy knew that his son was unprepared for what was coming.

Billy knew the Cullens were vampires. He had no history with them, only the tales of his grandfather, as passed to him by his father. He did not believe that the Cullens were as

The elders had taught the histories to their sons, but the entire tribe had begun to believe that the stories were only legend.

harmless as they presented themselves to be. He feared that without a strong wolf pack to enforce the treaty, the Cullens would take advantage. He worried for his tribe, and for his friends in Forks. He tried to warn Charlie to stay away from the Cullens, but his warning backfired. Charlie had already taken a liking to Carlisle, and he was upset about Billy's prejudice against the newcomers. When Charlie learned that members of the Quileute tribe were boycotting the hospital, it caused a rift between Billy and Charlie for a few years.

Watching Sam deal with the blows his werewolf heritage had forced upon him, Billy was even more concerned for Jacob. He was glad, though, that Jacob had struck up a friendship with Charlie's daughter. Billy missed Charlie and was glad for the excuse to visit him again. However, in the course of that visit, he was shocked and horrified to learn of Bella's relationship with one of the local vampires. Now he had more specific worries for his friend and his friend's family.

FAMOUS QUOTE

"You seem . . . well informed about the Cullens. More informed than I expected." Twilight, Chapter 17

⤳ QUIL ATEARA III

NAME: **Quil Ateara III; nickname: Old Quil**
DATE OF BIRTH: **Early 1940s**
QUILEUTE STATUS: **Tribal elder — non-werewolf**
WEREWOLF GENE SOURCE: **Ateara line**
HAIR COLOR: **White**

EYE COLOR: Black

PHYSICAL DESCRIPTION: Old Quil is a frail man with a deeply wrinkled face and a thin tenor of a voice.

EDUCATION/OCCUPATION: He is an elder on the tribal council. He used to be a fisherman.

FAMILY MEMBERS: He married Molly Swan (very distantly related to Charlie Swan), now deceased. They had one son, Quil Ateara IV, who died in his twenties. Old Quil now lives with his daughter-in-law, Joy Ateara, and his grandson, Quil Ateara V.

PERSONAL HISTORY:

Quil Ateara III, commonly known as Old Quil, is one of the few living tribe members who knew the last generation of werewolves. Old Quil was born just after the Cullens left the La Push area the first time, and he saw his father make the transformation.

Old Quil married Molly Swan, making him Billy Black's uncle, and they had one child, Quil Ateara IV. Both Old Quil and Molly were alive to see their only son marry Joy Quehpa and to see their grandchild, Quil Ateara V, born.

In the years that followed, Old Quil lost both his wife and his son. Quil IV was killed during a bad storm when his boat capsized off the coast of La Push; his body washed ashore later. After Quil IV's death, Old Quil moved in with Joy and Quil V. He acted as both grandfather and father to young Quil.

> Old Quil was the first to discover that a new generation of werewolves had begun transforming.

Old Quil was the first to discover that a new generation of werewolves had begun transforming. During a visit to Sam Uley's mother, Old Quil shook the young man's hand and recognized the extreme body heat that was the hallmark of a werewolf in human form. Sam's recent disappearance was easily understood now. Old Quil, along with Harry Clearwater and Billy Black, met with Sam and revealed what they knew. They explained that all the tribal legends about werewolves were true, and let Sam know at least some of what he could expect.

Old Quil knew that his grandson would soon transform, too. He tried to prepare Quil V, but like his friends, Quil believed the stories were pure legend.

✈ SUE ULEY CLEARWATER

NAME: Sue Uley Clearwater

DATE OF BIRTH: Mid-1960s

QUILEUTE STATUS: Tribal elder—non-werewolf

WEREWOLF GENE SOURCE: Black and Uley lines

HAIR COLOR: Black

EYE COLOR: Black

PHYSICAL DESCRIPTION: Sue has a thin face, and her hair is cut in a short, severe style.

EDUCATION/OCCUPATION: She is a registered nurse and an elder on the tribal council.

FAMILY MEMBERS: She lives with her two children, Leah and Seth Clearwater. Her husband, Harry Clearwater, is deceased. She is currently dating Charlie Swan.

Sue Clearwater and her husband, Harry Clearwater, knew that the legends about the Quileute werewolves were true. Harry had passed the wolf gene to his children from the Ateara line, while Sue carried both the Black and Uley lines. Once the Cullens returned to Forks, Sue knew that her son would one day become a werewolf. However, the shock of seeing their daughter, Leah, phase in front of them caused Harry, who had a weak heart, to go into cardiac arrest. As an RN, Sue knew Harry's condition was critical. She called Billy Black and Sam Uley for help because they, too, knew the truth about werewolves. By the time Sue called him, Sam had already learned about Harry's condition; he'd heard what happened when Leah entered into the pack mind. They were unable to save Harry, and the turmoil of the ordeal caused Sue's son, Seth, to transform that night, too, at a younger age than was normal. After Harry passed away, Sue took over his position on the tribal council, joining Quil Ateara III and Billy Black.

 EMILY YOUNG

NAME: Emily Young

DATE OF BIRTH: Late 1980s

QUILEUTE STATUS: Non-werewolf. Imprinted on by a pack member. Originally from the Makah tribe, she is Quileute on her mother's side.

HAIR COLOR: Black

EYE COLOR: Black

PHYSICAL DESCRIPTION: Emily has long, dark hair and satiny copper skin. One side of her mouth is distorted due to injury. She also has a trio of scars on the right side of her face from her hairline to her chin, and more scars extend down her right arm to her hand.

EDUCATION/OCCUPATION: She has graduated high school. She teaches weaving and traditional Makah and Quileute arts at the local high school and nearby community colleges.

FAMILY MEMBERS: She is a cousin of the Clearwaters. She is engaged to Sam Uley.

PERSONAL HISTORY:

From early childhood, Emily Young and her second cousin Leah Clearwater were like sisters. They grew up together and were always best friends. Emily was very involved in Leah's life, and vice versa. Emily was friends with Leah's boyfriend, Sam, and approved of him. Leah did not approve of Emily's serious boyfriend as much, and Leah was right; Emily got tired of his self-absorbed behavior and broke up with him. Things like romantic interference did not come between them. After Emily dumped the narcissistic boyfriend, she dated a few boys casually. Most of her time was taken up with learning traditional native arts and languages, something she was very passionate about. She and Leah kept in constant contact.

Emily was one of the first people Leah told about Sam's disappearance. Emily stayed with Leah through the first week, and then helped organize searches in the area around her home after her return. She shared Leah's relief when Sam came home, and then Leah's frustration when Sam wouldn't confide in her. Emily was Leah's shoulder to cry on throughout the whole experience. Busy with school, Emily was not able to visit Leah during the

> She shared Leah's relief when Sam came home, and then Leah's frustration when Sam wouldn't confide in her.

difficult time after Sam returned, but she went to see her as soon as she could.

Sam showed up late to the Clearwaters' barbecue. Emily intended to watch him closely; she was suspicious of his recent behavior and how it would affect her cousin. Sam walked in, taller and bigger than Emily remembered, and stared right at her with an expression she couldn't define; it might have been shock, or it might have been amazement. Emily felt like Sam had something important to tell her. He began to walk toward her, and she had a strange feeling that he would not keep his big secret from her as he was keeping it from Leah. But then Sam turned quickly and walked away. Emily felt oddly unsettled by Sam's behavior, though she tried to hide it. It was Leah's confusion and upset that mattered, not Emily's. That night, Sam came back for Leah. Emily expected Leah to be out for the evening, but she returned only ten minutes later, sobbing — Sam had broken up with her. Emily found herself unsurprised, though she was not sure why she felt that way. She told herself it was just a predictable consequence of Sam's bizarre behavior and silence.

Emily was disturbed when she left Leah that Sunday night to head home. She told herself she was upset by her best friend's heartbreak, but she knew there was something more to it. The next day after class, Sam was waiting for Emily at her house. Emily knew she should be shocked to see him, but she wasn't; his appearance felt somehow inevitable. What he told her next also should have been surprising, but felt just as inevitable. Sam told Emily that he loved her and had left Leah to be with her. Emily thought of Leah's tears and was furious. She knew she'd done nothing wrong, but knowing that Sam had chosen her over Leah made her feel guilty. She told Sam to leave. Looking tormented, Sam walked away without another word. As she watched him go, Emily felt like she'd done something wrong, though she knew it was right. She also realized that she should have told him to never come back.

She called Leah immediately to tell her, feeling horrible about what the news would do to Leah and because she felt that she was somehow betraying Sam's trust. Of course, that shouldn't matter at all. Leah was beside herself with rage, and Emily agreed that Sam was a horrible person, though deep down she had some doubts about that. She supported Leah as best she could.

She knew Sam would return, and when he did—the next day—she was prepared. She demanded that he tell her everything, all the secrets he'd kept from Leah. Where he'd disappeared to, and why. She thought he would leave; instead, he told her everything—that he was a shape-shifter, that all the stories were true, that he had imprinted on her. Emily had some Ateara blood on her mother's side, and she'd heard the myths before, but she laughed at him, surprised that he thought her so gullible. He told her he could prove it, so she led him into the forest on the outskirts of town and told him to show her. He did, and Emily was shaken to her core. She struggled to wrap her head around this new world of magic. Though now she could not doubt anything he'd told her, she knew it shouldn't change anything. He belonged to Leah, and she would not accept Sam's feelings for her. She told him to go away again, and she went home.

Emily told Leah that Sam had been back, but mentioned

nothing of what had happened. Instinctively, she knew she could not betray Sam's secret.

He returned the next day, as Emily expected. They went to the forest again. Emily decided it was her job to convince Sam to go back to Leah. Sam tried to describe what imprinting felt like, and how impossible it was for him to have a relationship with Leah under the circumstances. They were both frustrated. Sam defused the situation by telling Emily about other things — all the lore and magic that was a part of his life now. Emily couldn't hide her fascination.

They met again, several times. Emily continued to push him to forget about her and return to Leah. Sam was honest, insisting that would never happen. He continued to tell her all about his new life, even bringing his two packmates to meet her. Emily was captivated by the wolves, but adamant in her purpose: Sam must return to Leah.

Emily was so wrapped up in this new world that she was unaware that others were watching her — until her mother told her that people were talking. Word had gotten back to Leah, and another cousin had called. Emily's mother didn't know what to say. She asked her daughter what she was doing. How could she treat her best friend this way? Emily was aghast. She realized that she should have refused to see Sam after that first afternoon. She couldn't explain her behavior to herself or to her mother.

Emily went to her and Sam's usual place in the woods, ashamed at the thought that they *had* a usual place. She admitted to herself that she had desired his company, that she thought about him too much. She acknowledged that it wasn't just about the magic — it was also Sam himself. She had betrayed Leah, and this could go on no longer. When Sam appeared after looking for her at her home, Emily was sickened to see how strongly she responded to his presence. Her anger was at herself, but she took it out on him. She ordered him to go back to Leah. It was the only thing he was able to refuse her; he still loved Leah enough that he would not act out a charade with her. That Sam's feelings for Leah were in some ways more honorable than her own infuriated Emily. She called him a liar, though she knew she was the one who was lying. She shoved him away from her. Because of Leah, she knew a great deal about Sam; she knew his most vulnerable spot. She used this knowledge, accusing him of being like his father, Joshua, a coward who had run away from his family.

Emily was pleased to see that her insult had struck home; she'd never seen Sam's face angry before. She had just a fraction of a second to enjoy that pettiness. Sam stumbled back from her, suddenly afraid. She intended to push her point; she moved toward him. He raised his hand, warning her away, but she kept on. She didn't understand what the shaking meant. Then Sam expanded into his wolf form so quickly that Emily had no time to react. His hand was close to her face; it became a huge claw that slashed her as he tried to get away from her.

The pain and shock sent her into unconsciousness. When she woke, Jared was there. He held her, keeping her warm so that she wouldn't go into shock. Though Emily barely knew Jared, his face was as tormented as if he held his own

The pain and shock
sent her into unconsciousness.

sister. Emily, though disoriented, realized the bond Sam felt for her through his packmate's agony. Then Sam was there, in his huge black wolf form. Emily was surprised that there was nothing frightening at all about him. She understood clearly how the accident had happened, and tried to tell him so, but her mouth was injured and Jared discouraged her from talking. Sue arrived, and even though she was in a great deal of pain, Emily was still able to feel mortified; how much Leah's mother must hate her! But Sue's face was kind and understanding. Emily realized that Sue must understand about imprinting. She wasn't judging Emily or Sam. Sue and Paul took Emily to the Neah Bay hospital. Emily went along with the story that she'd been mauled by a black bear, though she worried that this story would hurt Sam.

> ## She realized that Sam was the one person she wanted with her.

Sedated, Emily was still aware and surprised that Sam did not come to her immediately. Jared, however, was constantly at her side. This comforted her; she knew she was being watched over. But it was not the same as having Sam there. She realized that Sam was the one person she wanted with her. The next day, when she was more lucid, she asked Jared where Sam was. She was not surprised to hear that Sam was devastated; she had an intuitive sense of how he would react to the accident. She told Jared to send Sam to her.

When Sam entered the room, Emily could see how right she was about his mindset. He looked at her for one long moment, and then knelt at the side of her bed and asked Emily to tell him to kill himself. Emily fully realized in that moment how bound Sam was by her wishes and needs, how little free will he had outside of that, and she pitied him greatly. She told him that what she wanted was for him to forgive himself, as she had already forgiven him. She told him the realization she had the night before.

Emily could feel that being with Sam would be a very easy thing. On the other hand, it would require a very hard thing first—she had to tell Leah. Sam asked her to wait until she was more fully recovered, and Emily agreed, though she knew she was chickening out. Later, she wished she had acted more swiftly. When Emily did call, Leah already knew what she was going to hear. Leah refused to ever forgive her cousin. Emily felt horrible, but she knew there was nothing she could do to make things easier for Leah.

Emily was surprised by how happy she was with Sam. She'd never dreamed of such an easy, joyful relationship. She also loved his pack; she never forgot how Jared had cared for her, and she began to think of them all as her younger brothers. Because few of their parents knew about their real lives, Emily took it on herself to care for the boys as much as possible—feeding their immense appetites, finding replacement clothes for them, giving them a place to hang out when they were keeping odd hours. She felt that in some ways, she was preserving the most important Quileute tradition of all.

When Leah joined the pack, it healed her relationship with Emily, on the surface at least. Emily knew that Leah no longer held her responsible for what had happened, but she also knew that it hurt Leah to be near Emily. Emily did her best to protect Leah from extra pain, and hoped fervently that Leah would find a way to be happy again.

FAMOUS QUOTE

"So, you're the vampire girl." New Moon, Chapter 14

✈ OTHER TRIBE MEMBERS

QUIL ATEARA IV Quil Ateara IV was the son of Old Quil Ateara and Molly Swan. He married Joy Quehpa, and they had a son, Quil Ateara V. As a descendant of the previous werewolf pack through both parents, he passed the shape-shifting gene on to his son. It is also possible that he was Embry Call's biological father and passed the chromosome on to him as well. He died before he was thirty years old, when his fishing boat capsized during a big storm.

SARAH BLACK Sarah Black was the granddaughter of Quil Ateara II, the wife of Billy Black, and the mother of Rachel, Rebecca, and Jacob Black. She was a full-time mother and a part-time artist, working mostly with watercolors. She died in a car accident when her daughters were thirteen and her son was nine. She knew the truth about the Quileute wolves, but hoped that her son would never have to live that life.

RACHEL BLACK Rachel is the daughter of Billy and Sarah Black, and the sister of Jacob and Rebecca Black. She and her twin sister had a difficult time dealing with the death of their mother. Rachel left La Push as soon as she was old enough, and rarely returned home to visit. However, when she returned home after graduating from Washington State University with a degree in computer engineering, Paul Lahote imprinted on her. Though she had intended to leave again soon, she was very drawn to Paul. He told her the truth about the Quileute wolves, and so she understood his dilemma. She decided to work from home in La Push until Paul was able to leave with her.

REBECCA BLACK Rebecca is the daughter of Billy and Sarah Black, and the sister of Jacob and Rachel Black. She lives in Hawaii for most of the year with her husband, a professional surfer; they travel frequently for his competitions. Like her mother, Rebecca is an artist, though Rebecca prefers oils. She does not know of the existence of wolves in La Push.

HARRY CLEARWATER Harry Clearwater was the father of Leah and Seth Clearwater. He was a tribal elder and a very good friend of both Billy Black and Charlie Swan, often accompanying them on fishing trips. He was a descendant of the Ateara werewolf line and extended that lineage to his children.

KIM Kim was one of Jared Cameron's classmates. She'd had a secret crush on him for a while, so she was thrilled when he imprinted on her.

JOSHUA ULEY Joshua Uley is Sam Uley's father. He disappeared when Sam was very young, leaving abruptly when he realized he couldn't cope with the responsibility of having a family. It is possible that he is also Embry Call's biological father.

CLAIRE YOUNG Claire Young is the young cousin of Emily Young. When Claire was two, Quil Ateara V imprinted on her during a visit to the La Push reservation. Claire considers Quil a big brother.

"THERE ARE LOTS OF LEGENDS, SOME OF THEM CLAIMING TO DATE
BACK TO THE FLOOD — SUPPOSEDLY, THE ANCIENT QUILEUTES
TIED THEIR CANOES TO THE TOPS OF THE TALLEST TREES ON THE
MOUNTAIN TO SURVIVE — LIKE NOAH AND THE ARK."
— Jacob (*Twilight*, Chapter 6)

HUMANS

The vast majority of the people living in and around the town of Forks, Washington, do not believe that either vampires or werewolves exist in reality. Bella's family, her classmates, and other members of the community live their lives oblivious to the occasional hints of the supernatural world that surrounds them.

Family and Friends of Bella

 CHARLIE SWAN

NAME: Charlie Swan

DATE OF BIRTH: 1964

PLACE OF ORIGIN: Forks, Washington

HAIR COLOR: Brown

EYE COLOR: Brown

HEIGHT: 6'0"

PHYSICAL DESCRIPTION: Charlie is fairly tall and has an average build.

EDUCATION/OCCUPATION: He is the chief of police.

HOBBIES: He enjoys fishing.

VEHICLE: A police cruiser

FAMILY MEMBERS: His parents were Geoffrey and Helen Swan. His ex-wife is Renée Dwyer, and his daughter is Isabella "Bella" Swan. He is currently dating Sue Clearwater.

PERSONAL HISTORY:

Charlie was born and raised in Forks, Washington, by his parents, Geoffrey and Helen Swan. Geoffrey and Helen were both in their mid-forties when Charlie was born; they had thought they were unable to have children, so Charlie was a huge — but very welcome — surprise. He remained an only child and stayed close to both his parents. Billy Black, Harry Clearwater, and Quil Ateara IV were his close friends since childhood. During his teenage years, Charlie always felt a little bit on the

"EVENTUALLY WE MADE IT TO CHARLIE'S.
HE STILL LIVED IN THE SMALL, TWO-BEDROOM HOUSE
THAT HE'D BOUGHT WITH MY MOTHER
IN THE EARLY DAYS OF THEIR MARRIAGE."

—Bella (*Twilight*, Chapter 1)

outside of this circle of friends. He attributed that distance to the fact that the others all belonged to the Quileute tribe and he did not. In reality, Billy, Harry, and Quil were caught up in the secret world they were forbidden to tell Charlie about, hoping that a vampire would come their way so they could all become superheroes.

As an adult, Charlie joined the Forks Police Department. He wanted to go to college, but his parents' health began deteriorating at that time and he felt that he needed to stay close to home. His mother was in the early stages of Alzheimer's and his father's mobility was being curtailed by severe arthritis. Charlie did everything he could to help care for them.

During Charlie's first summer as a cop, he met Renée Higginbotham. She was driving up the Pacific Highway with a group of her girlfriends, and they stopped to camp at First Beach in La Push. Charlie was visiting Billy when he met Renée on the beach. There was an instant attraction between the two. They spent a few days together before her friends were ready to continue their journey. Renée promised to visit Charlie on the return trip. In her absence, Charlie realized just how much he had fallen for Renée. She returned as promised, and he convinced her to stay when her friends left. Renée was impetuous and romantic by nature, and she loved the passionate whirlwind relationship. Charlie quickly proposed, and Renée accepted. They were married at the courthouse in Port Angeles, Washington, just a few weeks later.

> Renée was impetuous and romantic by nature, and she loved the passionate whirlwind relationship. Charlie quickly proposed, and Renée accepted.

Charlie bought a small house down the street from his parents' home. For a little while, he and Renée were deliriously happy. Charlie was even happier when he found out Renée was pregnant with their first child a few months later.

Charlie's life took a downturn during Renée's pregnancy. Both his parents' conditions worsened. His father needed Charlie's help with his mother every day. At the same time, depression began to take a major toll on Renée. She wanted Charlie to leave Forks with her and start over somewhere sunnier, but Charlie couldn't do that. Renée had the baby, and her depression was only compounded by the postpartum hormones.

A few months after Bella was born, Renée decided she couldn't live in Forks anymore. She left with Bella, leaving Charlie devastated. Charlie wanted to follow her, but he couldn't leave his parents. He didn't contest the divorce or the child support. All he asked for was time with Bella. He did not stop loving Renée.

Four years later, within six months of each other, Geoffrey and Helen Swan died. Charlie was alone, aside from his summer visits with Bella. He devoted himself to his job and worked his way up through the ranks to become the chief of police in Forks. He maintained his longtime friendship with Billy Black and Harry Clearwater, and the three friends spent a lot of their free time fishing together. Billy in particular

Charlie always felt awkward with Bella, and was never sure how to express his love for her.

was a great support to Charlie during the difficult years following his divorce and the loss of his parents; they became even closer. Later, when Billy lost his wife, Sarah, to a car accident, Charlie was able to be there for Billy as Billy had been for him.

Charlie always felt awkward with Bella, and was never sure how to express his love for her. He did recognize that Bella was much more like him than she was like Renée, despite her living with Renée year-round. He was truly thrilled when Bella decided to live with him for her last year and a half of high school.

FAMOUS QUOTES

"You aren't turning into a tree-hugger on me, are you?"
New Moon, Chapter 12

"It's not normal, Alice, and it . . . it frightens me. Not normal at all. Not like someone . . . left her, but like someone died."
New Moon, Chapter 17

"Isn't Edward up for a little healthy competition?" Eclipse, Chapter 1

"Maybe I'm just feeling . . . superstitious after hanging out with Billy while he was being so strange all day. But I have this . . . hunch. I feel like . . . I'm going to lose you soon." Eclipse, Chapter 26

"You're pregnant! You're pregnant, aren't you?"
Breaking Dawn, Chapter 1

"I don't want to know everything, but I'm done with the lies!"
Breaking Dawn, Chapter 25

"I would have tried to protect you, too, if I'd known how. But I guess you've never fit into the fainthearted category, have you?"
Breaking Dawn, Chapter 26

NAME: Renée Higginbotham Dwyer (previous married name: Swan)

DATE OF BIRTH: 1968

PLACE OF ORIGIN: Unknown

HAIR COLOR: Brown

EYE COLOR: Blue

HEIGHT: Around 5'4"

PHYSICAL DESCRIPTION: Renée looks a lot like Bella, but she has short hair, blue eyes, and laugh lines.

EDUCATION/OCCUPATION: She is a teacher; she has taught kindergarten, first grade, and second grade. She has also worked as a substitute.

HOBBIES: Renée has had too many hobbies to list. She doesn't stick with any of them for very long.

FAMILY MEMBERS: She is currently married to Phil Dwyer. Her daughter is Isabella "Bella" Swan, and Bella's father, Charlie Swan, is her ex-husband. Her mother was Marie Higginbotham.

PERSONAL HISTORY:

Renée was born in Downey, California. Her parents divorced when she was still a child, and she never had much contact with her father. Her mother, Marie, was a difficult, bitter woman, but hardworking and loyal. Renée had a very different personality: fun-loving and artistic, but flighty and inconstant. Renée did not do well in school, despite the fact that she tested well. During her teenage years she was never able to hold a job for long, though she always interviewed very well.

The first year after high school, Renée worked several temporary jobs, making enough money to move in with a girlfriend who had space available in her small apartment. Renée couldn't take living with her pessimistic mother any longer. The next summer, one of her girlfriends decided to take a month off and travel the length of the Pacific coast, camping along the way. This was exactly the kind of adventure that Renée loved. She went on the trip with a few other girls, having no idea where she would live when she got back, if her roommate rented the space to someone else.

On First Beach, Renée met Charlie Swan. She was very attracted to him; he was different from her usual boyfriends, so serious and responsible, but funny and kind. She fell head over heels. She thought about Charlie for the rest of the trip north, and when she returned to Forks, she was easily convinced to stay for a little while longer. Renée loved being in love, and she loved feeling like she was living an adventure. When Charlie proposed, getting married sounded like the perfect cap to the whirlwind romance. They were married by a justice of the peace, with only Charlie's parents and three best friends in attendance. Renée sent her mother a picture from the wedding, but Marie didn't respond.

For a while, Renée enjoyed the novelty of being married. Charlie was a much easier person to live with than her mother had been, and his passionate adoration of her was very pleasant. She had a great deal of fun decorating the little house. She liked Charlie's kind, quiet parents. The tiny, quaint town was very different from L.A. She worked as a waitress for a while, and she liked meeting new people.

> Renée loved being in love, and she loved feeling like she was living an adventure.

When Renée found out she was having a baby, it seemed like the next big adventure. She learned to knit and started decorating the nursery. She wrote to her mother again, and this time Marie sent a gift: her own mother's handmade quilt. Renée was touched.

However, after a few months, everything seemed to get stale. The rain didn't let up for even an afternoon; Renée had never gone so long without seeing the sun. Charlie was busy with work and his parents, and Renée felt trapped and unhappy. She still loved Charlie, but there was no adventure left in their now staid relationship.

When Bella was born, it changed Renée in some ways, but not in others. She became more responsible, better able to focus on what had to be done. But she still felt trapped by the sunless small town. She hated the thought of letting her baby grow up in the gloom. She begged Charlie to leave with her, though she knew that was not a kind thing to ask. Finally, she decided that she needed to leave on her own and get her life in order, for Bella's sake. She realized that she had made some life-altering decisions without much thought, and she wanted to start over and proceed more carefully.

Renée went back to her mother, who was still difficult, but who doted on Bella. She enrolled in school and got her elementary education degree — spending time with Bella had made her realize that she was good with children and enjoyed them. Once she had her degree and a job, she moved a little distance away from her mother, to Riverside, California. There she began teaching kindergarten. Bella grounded Renée, who found ways to be satisfied with small changes in her hobbies and recreational activities. She made many close friends among the other teachers, and she got a lot of sunshine.

Renée's life was still more than a little chaotic, however. She was always getting herself into messy situations. As Bella got older, she began to assume many of the adult responsibilities in the home, simply because she was better suited to them than Renée was. When she took over the bookkeeping at age ten, it made both of their lives much easier.

After living in Riverside, California, for six years, Renée decided that she wanted to try living in a new place. She ended up getting a job in Phoenix, where she and Bella lived for five years. Renée's mother, Marie, died when Bella was twelve, after which Renée did not visit Califonia as often as she had when Bella's grandmother was alive.

Renée missed Charlie, but always thought of him as a childish infatuation. She recognized that she was not well suited for serious relationships, and she did her best to keep herself from becoming entangled romantically, worried about the impact such a relationship would have on Bella. When Bella was in her teens, she encouraged Renée to date more, sensing that her mother was a little lonely. After a few relationships that didn't take, Renée met Phil and fell hard. Phil had an adventurous spirit, too, though he was a little more practical than Renée. They married when Bella was seventeen.

> "I rarely write about just humans. You can get humans anywhere."
>
> —Stephenie

Shortly after they were married, Phil went on the road with his minor-league baseball team. It was difficult for Renée to stay behind, for multiple reasons. She missed Phil a lot, and he was off having the kinds of adventures she still craved. Renée never considered leaving Bella, however. But when Bella suddenly announced her intention to live with Charlie for her last year and a half of high school, Renée did not fight her decision as much as she would have before Phil.

FAMOUS QUOTES

"*I think that boy is in love with you.*" Twilight, Chapter 24

"*The way he watches you—it's so…protective. Like he's about to throw himself in front of a bullet to save you or something.*"
Eclipse, Chapter 3

"*You've never been a teenager, sweetie. You know what's best for you.*"
Breaking Dawn, Chapter 1

→→ ANGELA WEBER

NAME: Angela Weber

DATE OF BIRTH: 1988

PLACE OF ORIGIN: Forks, Washington

HAIR COLOR: Light brown

EYE COLOR: Light brown

HEIGHT: 6'1"

PHYSICAL DESCRIPTION: Angela is tall and has honey-colored highlights in her hair.

EDUCATION/OCCUPATION: She is a graduate of Forks High School.

FAMILY MEMBERS: She lives with her mother and father and her nine-year-old twin brothers, Joshua and Isaac Weber.

PERSONAL HISTORY:

Angela Weber was born and raised in Forks. She is the only daughter of a Lutheran minister and his wife. Her twin brothers, Joshua and Isaac, are eight years younger than she is and are very loud and demanding of attention, but Angela dotes on them. Angela's unusual height made her self-conscious, and she developed into a shy, reserved person. She was a good all-around student and well liked despite her shyness, thanks to her kind, sweet nature. Angela started dating Ben Cheney during her junior year. She was accepted to the University of Washington, where Ben also planned to attend.

FAMOUS QUOTE

"Edward's only human, Bella. He's going to react like any other boy." Eclipse, Chapter 6

DATE OF BIRTH: 1988
PLACE OF ORIGIN: Sacramento, California
HAIR COLOR: Pale blond
EYE COLOR: Clear blue
HEIGHT: 5'11"
PHYSICAL DESCRIPTION: Mike is good-looking. He was baby-faced when Bella first met him, but his face lost some of that roundness in his senior year of high school. He originally wore his hair in spikes, then started to grow it out, in a look inspired by Edward Cullen's hairstyle.
EDUCATION/OCCUPATION: He is a graduate of Forks High School. He currently works at his parents' store, Newton's Olympic Outfitters.
FAMILY MEMBERS: He lives with his mother, Karen Newton, and his father.

He originally wore his hair in spikes, then started to grow it out, in a look inspired by Edward Cullen's hairstyle.

"THAT MUST BE
MIKE NEWTON.
NICE KID — NICE
FAMILY. HIS
DAD OWNS THE
SPORTING GOODS
STORE JUST
OUTSIDE
OF TOWN."
—Charlie, to
Bella (*Twilight*,
Chapter 2)

PERSONAL HISTORY:

Mike Newton was born in California. He is an only child. When he was ten, his parents moved to Forks and opened Newton's Olympic Outfitters. During high school Mike worked for his parents, selling camping and hiking gear. He was very popular at school, and he dated the most popular girls, including Lauren and, later, Jessica.

FAMOUS QUOTES

"So, did you stab Edward Cullen with a pencil or what?"
Twilight, Chapter 1

"He looks at you like . . . like you're something to eat."
Twilight, Chapter 11

✈ JESSICA STANLEY

NAME: Jessica Stanley

DATE OF BIRTH: 1988

PLACE OF ORIGIN: Austin, Texas

HAIR COLOR: Brown

EYE COLOR: Blue

HEIGHT: 5'1"

PHYSICAL DESCRIPTION: Jessica is quite short, but her voluminous curly hair and outgoing personality make her seem bigger than she is.

EDUCATION/OCCUPATION: She is a graduate of Forks High School.

FAMILY MEMBERS: She is an only child and lives with her parents.

PERSONAL HISTORY:

Jessica was born in Austin, Texas. Her parents relocated to Forks when Jessica was still a small child, but Jessica has always thought of herself as being less provincial than the locals. Jessica was a good student and fairly popular, though she wasn't as sought after by boys as Lauren. Jessica thinks of Lauren and Angela as her best friends, though she's not loyal to either of them. She dated Mike briefly during their sophomore year, and always wanted to get back together with him. She was happy when that wish was later fulfilled, though their relationship was sporadic.

FAMOUS QUOTES

"That's Edward. He's gorgeous, of course, but don't waste your time. He doesn't date. Apparently none of the girls here are good-looking enough for him." Twilight, Chapter 1

"Edward Cullen is staring at you." Twilight, Chapter 2

"Does he mean you?" Twilight, Chapter 5

 BEN CHENEY

NAME: Ben Cheney

DATE OF BIRTH: 1987

PLACE OF ORIGIN: Forks, Washington

HAIR COLOR: Black

EYE COLOR: Dark brown

HEIGHT: 5'7"

PHYSICAL DESCRIPTION: Ben is of Asian descent and wears glasses.

EDUCATION/OCCUPATION: He is a graduate of Forks High School.

HOBBIES: Ben enjoys graphic novels, comics, indie rock, and action movies.

VEHICLES: Dodge Neon

PERSONAL HISTORY:

During high school Ben's best friend was Austin Marks. The two shared an interest in comic books, action movies, and indie rock music. Toward the end of his junior year, Ben developed a crush on Angela Weber. He eventually got up the courage to ask her to the prom, and she agreed to go with him. They dated each other exclusively throughout their final year of high school. They were still together after graduation, and both went on to study at Washington State University.

⤙ TYLER CROWLEY

NAME: Tyler Crowley

DATE OF BIRTH: 1988

PLACE OF ORIGIN: Forks, Washington

HAIR COLOR: Brown

EYE COLOR: Brown

HEIGHT: 6'1"

PHYSICAL DESCRIPTION: Tyler has an athletic build.

EDUCATION/OCCUPATION: He is a graduate of Forks High School.

HOBBIES: He was on the Forks High football, basketball, and track teams.

VEHICLES: An old full-size van and a Nissan Sentra

FAMILY MEMBERS: He lives with his mother, Beth Crowley.

Tyler Crowley grew up in Forks and attended Forks High School. He was popular in high school, and what he lacked in academic ability he made up for in athletic talent. He was the quarterback of the football team and the pitcher on the baseball team, and he ran the fastest mile on the track team. He was good friends with Mike Newton, Austin Marks, and Ben Cheney. He and Mike both enjoyed camping.

FAMOUS QUOTE

"That's cool. We still have prom." Twilight, Chapter 4

✈ LAUREN MALLORY

NAME: Lauren Mallory
DATE OF BIRTH: 1988
PLACE OF ORIGIN: Forks, Washington
HAIR COLOR: White-blond
EYE COLOR: Green
HEIGHT: 5'6"
PHYSICAL DESCRIPTION: Lauren has silky, straight, silvery blond hair, which she initially wore long. Just before senior year, she cut her hair very short.
EDUCATION/OCCUPATION: She is a graduate of Forks High School.

PERSONAL HISTORY:

Before Bella Swan moved to Forks, Lauren Mallory was the most sought-after girl in school. She had dated Tyler Crowley and Mike Newton in her sophomore year. When Bella started attending Forks High, it was difficult for Lauren. Despite the fact that Lauren was in fact much prettier than Bella, many of the guys at school were intrigued by a new face.

Sometime during the summer following her junior year, Lauren was approached by an alleged modeling agent in a mall in Victoria, British Columbia, Canada. He told her she was a natural model, and Lauren agreed with him. The agent told her that if she cut her long hair into a shorter, edgier look and had some high-quality headshots taken, her future would be assured. Lauren followed his instructions—spending three hundred dollars on a haircut and fifteen grand on pictures taken by the agent's partner—and never heard from the agent again.

✈ ERIC YORKIE

NAME: Eric Yorkie
DATE OF BIRTH: 1988
PLACE OF ORIGIN: Forks, Washington
HAIR COLOR: Black
EYE COLOR: Brown
HEIGHT: 6'1"
PHYSICAL DESCRIPTION: Eric is tall and gangly, with a poor complexion and greasy hair.
EDUCATION/OCCUPATION: He is a graduate of Forks High School.

PERSONAL HISTORY:
Somewhat awkward, Eric was generally acknowledged as the class geek. He wanted to be part of Mike's popular crowd, so he tended to hang around them at lunch. After a while, he was considered one of the group. During his senior year, he

and Katie Marshall started dating. Eric graduated as the vale-dictorian of Forks High School and planned to attend college the following fall.

"THE SCHOOL WAS, LIKE MOST OTHER THINGS, JUST OFF THE HIGHWAY.
IT WAS NOT OBVIOUS THAT IT WAS A SCHOOL; ONLY THE SIGN, WHICH
DECLARED IT TO BE THE FORKS HIGH SCHOOL, MADE ME STOP."

—Bella (*Twilight*, Chapter 1)

Teachers at Forks High School

MR. BANNER Mr. Banner is the science teacher at Forks High School.

MR. BERTY Mr. Berty teaches English at Forks High School.

COACH CLAPP Coach Clapp is the gym teacher at Forks High School.

MRS. COPE Mrs. Cope is the red-haired secretary at Forks High School.

MR. GREENE Mr. Greene is the principal of Forks High School.

MR. JEFFERSON Mr. Jefferson is the government teacher at Forks High School.

MR. VARNER Mr. Varner teaches math at Forks High School.

Other Students at Forks High School

CONNER Conner is a friend of Mike Newton's.

LEE Lee was in the same class at Forks High School as Mike, Jessica, and the others. He dated Samantha.

AUSTIN MARKS Austin Marks is Ben Cheney's best friend.

KATIE MARSHALL Katie Marshall was Eric Yorkie's girlfriend during his senior year. She has red hair and lives around the corner from Charlie Swan.

SAMANTHA Samantha was in the same class at Forks High School as Mike, Jessica, and the others. She dated Lee and was friends with Lauren Mallory.

Other Residents of Forks

BETH CROWLEY Beth Crowley is Tyler Crowley's mother. She is friends with Mike Newton's mother.

DR. GERANDY Dr. Gerandy is Carlisle Cullen's friend and colleague.

KAREN NEWTON Karen Newton is the mother of Mike Newton. Her coiffed blond hair, perfect manicure and pedicure, and stiletto-heeled shoes make her seem out of place as the co-owner of Newton's Olympic Outfitters.

MR. NEWTON Mr. Newton is Mike Newton's father and the co-owner of Newton's Olympic Outfitters.

MRS. STANLEY Mrs. Stanley is Jessica Stanley's mother and the town gossip. She works at the local bank. She and her family live west of Forks, in a house that is very large for the area. The view from her attic extends all the way to the coast.

MRS. WEBER Mrs. Weber is Angela Weber's mother, and the mother of twin boys Joshua and Isaac Weber. She comes from a very large family.

MR. WEBER Mr. Weber is the father of Angela Weber and twin boys Joshua and Isaac Weber. He is a Lutheran minister.

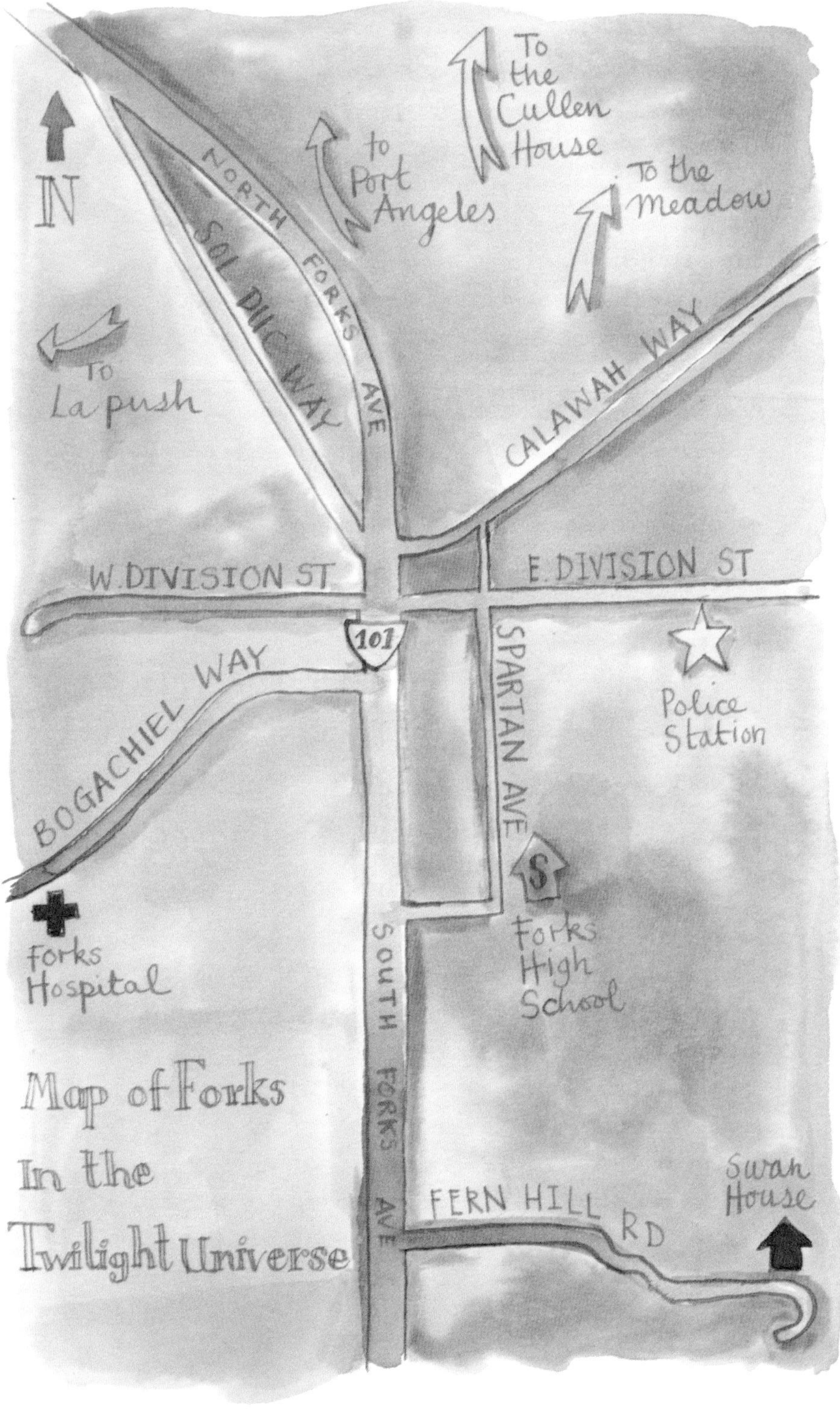

N
To the Cullen House
to Port Angeles
To the meadow
NORTH FORKS AVE
SOL DUC WAY
To La push
CALAWAH WAY
W. DIVISION ST
E. DIVISION ST
101
BOGACHIEL WAY
SPARTAN AVE
Police Station
S
Forks High School
Forks Hospital
SOUTH FORKS AVE
Map of Forks
In the
Twilight Universe
FERN HILL RD
Swan House

> "More fiercely than I would have dreamed I was capable of, I wished for the green, protective forests of Forks…of home."
>
> —Bella (*Twilight*, Chapter 22)

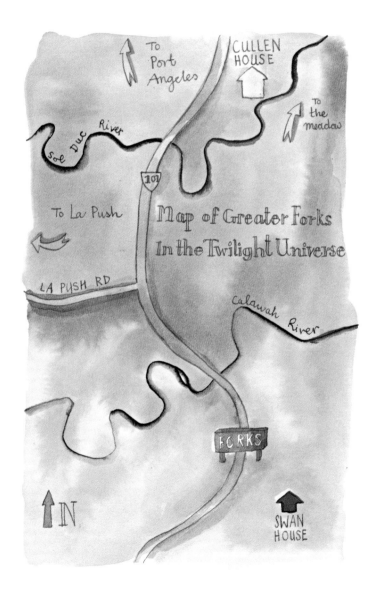

"J.'s USUAL CLIENTS . . . JUST GO STRAIGHT UP TO HIS
FANCY OFFICE IN THE SKYSCRAPER."

—Max, to Bella (*Breaking Dawn*, Chapter 33)

Residents of Seattle

NAME: J. Jenks (also known as Jason Jenks and Jason Scott)

DATE OF BIRTH: 1950s

PLACE OF ORIGIN: Seattle, Washington

HAIR COLOR: Medium brown, balding

EYE COLOR: Brown

PHYSICAL DESCRIPTION: J. is short and balding, and has a paunch. He wears expensive clothing.

EDUCATION/OCCUPATION: He is an attorney, but he also provides illegal services for clients willing to pay his prices.

PERSONAL HISTORY:

J. Jenks is a full-time lawyer and a part-time criminal. He is known in certain circles as being one of the best document forgers available. He learned the art from his mentor and former partner, who originally worked with the Cullens. J. prefers not to use an office for most of his illegal clients; instead, he uses a run-down place in the ghetto as a contact point. He also conducts legitimate business as Jason Jenks, an attorney with a fancy office in a skyscraper in Seattle, and as Jason Scott, an attorney with a modest practice in the suburbs.

> He is known in certain circles as being one of the best document forgers available.

J. started working for Jasper Hale and the rest of the Cullen family in the late 1980s. He doesn't know that the Cullens are vampires, but he does know he is dealing with the supernatural, thanks to the fact that Jasper never ages. Because he is paid well — and because Jasper has manipulated his emotions to make sure he fears the Cullens —J. always gives Jasper top priority and does not talk about the Cullens to others.

FAMOUS QUOTE

"If you could just assure me that you are not planning to kidnap the little girl from her father, I would sleep better tonight."
Breaking Dawn, Chapter 35

✈ MAX

NAME: Max

PLACE OF ORIGIN: Seattle, Washington

HAIR COLOR: Black

PHYSICAL DESCRIPTION: Max has crinkly black hair; dark, smooth skin; and straight white teeth. He wears fine clothing underneath a rumpled duster.

EDUCATION/OCCUPATION: He works for J. Jenks, at his downtown office.

PERSONAL HISTORY:

Max assists J. Jenks in his underhanded business dealings. His primary duty is to sit on the porch of an old, run-down building and relay messages back to his boss.

"Well, she looks like a freaking supermodel, that's what she looks like. Rocking body, pale as a sheet, dark brown hair almost to her waist, needs a good night's sleep—any of this sounding familiar?"
Breaking Dawn, Chapter 33

Residents of Brazil

GUSTAVO Gustavo is a Brazilian who was also hired as a caretaker of Isle Esme. He is embarrassed by Kaure's superstitions and wants her to be more modern.

KAURE Kaure, a Ticuna native, is a resident of Rio de Janeiro, Brazil, and one of the caretakers of Isle Esme. She was raised to believe in the traditions of her people—traditions that include vampires and the reality of vampire-human procreation. She believes vampires are real, and that she is working for some of them.

She believes vampires are real, and that she is working for some of them.

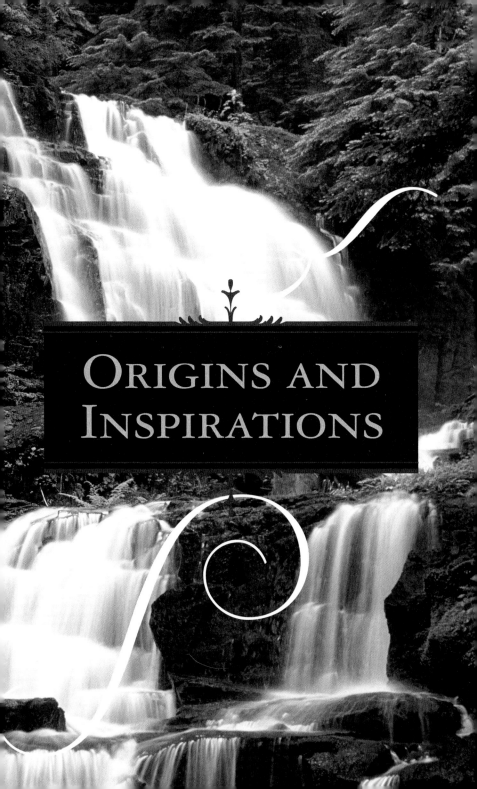

ORIGINS AND INSPIRATIONS

Timeline

The history of the Saga's vampires and werewolves encompasses hundreds of thousands of years. This timeline notes key events that occurred over the eras, from the creation of the first Quileute werewolf and the formation of the Volturi all the way through the birth of Renesmee Cullen and the near war that followed.

1400–1200 B.C.	Aro, Caius, and Marcus are born in Greece during the Mycenaean civilization. They form the Volturi coven with their wives.
1000 B.C.	Aro kills his sister, Didyme.
•	Dacia (proto-Romania) is the power center of the vampire world, ruled by the coven that would later be called the Romanian coven.
•	The Volturi found the city of Volterra in pre-Roman Etruscan Italy.
400–500 A.D.	The Volturi overthrow the Romanian coven.
500	The Volturi begin introducing vampire law.
•	Immortal children are executed on a case-by-case basis.
750	Immortal children outlawed.
800	Jane and Alec changed to vampires by the Volturi.
1000	Practice of creating immortal children mostly eradicated.
•	Kaheleha and his spirit warriors use their magic to vanquish intruders.
1230–1250	Hohs and Makahs make treaties with Quileutes.
•	Taha Aki becomes first Quileute shape-shifter.
1265	The first of Taha Aki's sons inherits ability to shape-shift.

1400–1410	Three Quileute shape-shifters killed by vampire.
•	Quileute shape-shifters kill their first vampire.
•	The Cold Woman comes to the Quileute village to avenge her mate; the third wife dies to save the tribe.
1640s	Carlisle Cullen born in London, England.
1663	Carlisle changed to a vampire.
EARLY 1700s	Carlisle migrates to the continent and meets the Volturi.
1720s	Carlisle leaves the Volturi, goes to America.
1750s	Joham begins experimenting with vampire hybrids.
1820s	First army of newborns created by Benito; the Southern Wars begin.
1830s	The death toll from the Southern Wars reaches epidemic proportions; the Volturi wipe out all newborn armies in the southern parts of North America.
1844	Jasper Whitlock born in Texas.
1861	Jasper joins the Confederate Army.
1863	Jasper changed to a vampire by Maria.
1895	Esme Anne Platt born in Columbus, Ohio.
1901	June 20 Edward Anthony Masen born in Chicago, Illinois.
•	Mary Alice Brandon born in Biloxi, Mississippi.
1905	Carlisle moves to Columbus, Ohio, where he practices medicine as a country doctor.
1911	Carlisle meets Esme Platt.
1912	Carlisle leaves Columbus.

1915	Rosalie Lillian Hale born in Rochester, New York.
	Emmett McCarty born in Tennessee.
1917	Esme marries Charles Evenson.
	Carlisle moves to Chicago, Illinois, where he practices medicine in a hospital.
1918	SEPTEMBER
	Edward changed to a vampire by Carlisle.
1920	Alice institutionalized in a mental asylum by her father and stepmother.
	Alice changed to a vampire by a worker at the mental asylum.
	Esme becomes pregnant; leaves her husband and moves to Ashland, Wisconsin.
1921	Carlisle and Edward move to Ashland, Wisconsin, and establish themselves as uncle and nephew. Carlisle begins working in a small hospital.
	Esme jumps off a cliff after losing her son to disease.
	Carlisle changes Esme to a vampire.
	Carlisle and Esme marry. The Cullen family leaves Ashland. Edward now poses as Esme's younger brother.
1927	Edward leaves Carlisle to try a traditional vampire/vigilante life.
1931	Edward returns to the Cullens and they reestablish their family in Rochester, New York.
	Rosalie changed to a vampire by Carlisle.
1935	Emmett changed to a vampire by Carlisle.
	Rosalie and Emmett have their first wedding.
1936	The Cullens move to Hoquiam, Washington, and make a treaty with the Quileutes.
1938	Jasper leaves Maria.

1948	Alice finds Jasper in Philadelphia, Pennsylvania; they become companions.
1950	Alice and Jasper join the Cullens.
•	Alice and Jasper get married.
1987	September 13 Isabella "Bella" Marie Swan born in Forks, Washington.
	December Renée Swan and Bella move to Riverside, California.
1990	January 14 Jacob Black born.
1993	Renée and Bella move to Phoenix, Arizona.
1996–2001	Bella visits Charlie Swan in Forks for one month in the summer.
2003	August The Cullens move to Forks.
2005	JANUARY
•	January 17 Bella moves back to Forks.
•	January 18 Bella's first day of school; Bella meets Edward; Edward leaves Forks for Alaska.
•	Edward comes back to school.
•	Edward stops Tyler Crowley's van from crushing Bella.
	MARCH
•	Mike asks Bella to the spring dance; Edward spends the night in Bella's room for the first time.
•	Bella sits with Edward at lunch; Bella nearly passes out in Biology.
•	Edward ditches school to hunt with Emmett.
•	Bella goes to First Beach and becomes reacquainted with Jacob Black; Jacob tells Bella the history of the cold ones.
•	Bella is nearly attacked in Port Angeles; Edward rescues her; Edward confirms that he is a vampire.
•	Edward takes Bella to the meadow.

- Edward introduces Bella to his family; the Cullens play baseball; James starts his hunt for Bella.
- Alice, Jasper, and Bella arrive in Phoenix, Arizona.
- James lures Bella to the ballet studio; the Cullens kill James before he can kill Bella.
- Bella awakens in the hospital with many injuries.

MAY

- Edward and Bella attend the Forks High School prom.

SEPTEMBER

- September 13 Bella's eighteenth birthday; Jasper nearly attacks her when she gets a paper cut.
- Edward breaks up with Bella; the Cullens disappear.

OCTOBER–DECEMBER

- Bella exists in a zombielike state.

2006   JANUARY

- Bella and Jessica see a movie in Port Angeles.
- Bella takes broken motorcycles to Jacob.
- Bella visits the empty Cullen house.
- Bella and Jacob see Sam Uley's gang cliff diving; they ride their repaired motorcycles.
- Bella and Jacob begin their search for the meadow.

FEBRUARY

- Bella, Jacob, and Mike Newton go to the movies; Jacob transforms into a werewolf for the first time.
- Jacob tells Bella he is sick and she should stay away.

MARCH

- Bella finds the meadow; she sees Laurent and five huge wolves.

- Bella finds Jacob with Sam's pack and confronts him; Jacob sneaks into her room at night and reminds her about the "scary stories."
- Bella realizes Jacob is a werewolf; she sees Paul and Jacob phase.
- Bella dives off the cliff, Harry dies, and Alice returns to Forks.
- Edward calls Bella's house and Jacob answers the phone; Alice and Bella race to Italy to stop Edward from killing himself.
- Bella, Edward, and Alice meet the Volturi.
- Alice shows Aro that Bella will become a vampire.
- Bella, Edward, and Alice return to Forks.
- Bella asks the Cullens to vote on her mortality.

APRIL
- Jacob reminds Edward about the treaty.

MAY
- Edward and Bella visit Renée in Florida.
- The Cullens and the Quileutes clash while hunting Victoria.
- Jacob confronts Edward in front of Forks High School.
- Bella sneaks out to visit Jacob.
- Bella is kidnapped by Alice; Rosalie tells her story to Bella.

JUNE
- Edward realizes another vampire has been in Bella's bedroom.
- Bella goes to La Push and hears the tribe's history.
- Jacob kisses Bella.
- June 11 Bella graduates; Alice throws her graduation party.
- The Cullens and Quileutes train to fight the newborn army.
- June 13 Bella and Edward become officially engaged.
- Jacob carries Bella to the campsite, where Edward meets them.

- Bella asks Jacob to kiss her before the battle with the newborns; Edward kills Victoria; Jacob is wounded; the Volturi visit.
- Jacob receives an invitation to Bella's wedding and runs away as a wolf.

AUGUST

- August 13 Edward and Bella are married.
- AugusT 30 Bella discovers she is pregnant and returns to Forks with Edward.

SEPTEMBER

- Jacob breaks away from Sam's pack to protect Bella.
- September 11 Renesmee Cullen born; Bella begins transformation into a vampire; Jacob imprints on Renesmee.
- September 13 Bella completes transformation into a vampire.
- Jacob phases in front of Charlie.

DECEMBER

- Irina sees Renesmee.
- Irina decides to go to the Volturi; Alice sees a vision of the Volturi's attack; Alice and Jasper leave the Cullens.
- The Denali coven and Peter and Charlotte agree to support the Cullens.
- The Amazons, Irish, Egyptians, nomads, and Romanians arrive.
- Bella visits J. Jenks.
- December 25 Bella, Edward, and Renesmee spend Christmas with Charlie, Jacob, and the pack.
- December 31 The Volturi arrive; Caius kills Irina; Bella discovers the true power of her shield; Alice arrives with Nahuel; the Volturi retreat; Edward hears Bella's thoughts for the first time.

Key Plot Points

he following pages note key plot points that
occur in *Twilight*, *New Moon*, *Eclipse*, and *Breaking
Dawn*, from Bella's move to Forks to the finale of
Breaking Dawn.

Twilight

Seattle that day; Edward speaks to Bella again, telling her it is better if they aren't friends; Edward laughs as Eric and Tyler ask Bella to the dance; the next morning Edward offers to drive Bella to Seattle; Edward reminds Bella it would be more prudent for her not to be his friend

CHAPTER 5

- Edward invites Bella to sit with him at lunch
  Edward and Bella decide to be "friends"; Bella tells Edward her theory about him being a superhero; Edward hints that he might be "the bad guy"
- Bella has to do blood typing in Biology class
  In class, Bella gets queasy at the sight of blood; Mike escorts her to the nurse's office; Edward rushes to her and takes over from Mike, carrying her to the nurse's office; Bella explains that the smell of blood makes her sick; Edward drives Bella home, and they talk about their families; Bella invites Edward to the upcoming party at La Push

CHAPTER 6

- Bella is lonely when Edward misses the next day of school

- Bella goes to the party at First Beach in La Push
  The group is joined by some of the Quileute boys; Bella meets Jacob Black; she remembers his older sisters; one of the Quileute boys tells Bella the Cullens don't come to La Push
- Bella flirts with Jacob to get him to tell her about the Cullens
  Jacob tells her the Quileute legends about wolves and vampires; Jacob says the Cullens are supposedly vampires

CHAPTER 7

- Bella does research about vampires; the facts don't add up
- Bella decides to go with Jessica and Angela to pick out their dresses in Port Angeles

CHAPTER 8

- Bella goes dress shopping in Port Angeles
  Bella is distracted while the other girls try on dresses; she decides to go find a bookstore, telling them she will meet them later
- Bella walks in the wrong direction and is threatened by four drunk men
  She tries to remember self-defense moves
- Edward drives up just in time

Bella gets in his car and they speed away; Edward needs time to calm down; Bella remembers that she is supposed to meet Jessica and Angela; Edward drives to the right restaurant without asking which one

- The girls have already eaten so Edward takes Bella to dinner
  Edward doesn't notice the hostess or the waitress; Bella tells Edward he shouldn't "dazzle" people, and he asks if he dazzles her; she tells him he does, frequently; Edward makes Bella eat while they talk "hypothetically" about his ability to hear thoughts

CHAPTER 9

- On the drive home from Port Angeles, they are past all the evasiveness
  Bella tells Edward about her talk with Jacob Black and about the Quileute

legends; Edward realizes that Bella knows the truth; Bella asks why Edward's family doesn't drink human blood; Edward tells her he doesn't want to be a monster; Edward promises to show her why he doesn't go out in the sunlight

- Bella knows that Edward is a vampire, that part of him thirsts for her blood, and that she is unconditionally and irrevocably in love with him

CHAPTER 10

- Edward offers Bella a ride to school
  Edward points out that he's breaking the rules
- Edward listens as Jessica quizzes Bella about her relationship with him
  Edward is upset when he hears Bella say she likes him more than he likes her; at lunch Edward tells her she is wrong, that he'd

"ABOUT THREE THINGS I WAS ABSOLUTELY POSITIVE. FIRST, EDWARD WAS A VAMPIRE. SECOND, THERE WAS A PART OF HIM — AND I DIDN'T KNOW HOW POTENT THAT PART MIGHT BE — THAT THIRSTED FOR MY BLOOD. AND THIRD, I WAS UNCONDITIONALLY AND IRREVOCABLY IN LOVE WITH HIM."

— Bella (*Twilight*, Chapter 9)

"I REACHED THE EDGE OF THE POOL OF LIGHT AND
STEPPED THROUGH THE LAST FRINGE OF FERNS INTO THE LOVELIEST
PLACE I HAD EVER SEEN. THE MEADOW WAS SMALL, PERFECTLY ROUND,
AND FILLED WITH WILDFLOWERS—VIOLET, YELLOW, AND SOFT WHITE."
—Bella (*Twilight,* Chapter 12)

hurt himself if that meant
keeping her safe
- Edward invites Bella to
spend Saturday togther so she
can see him in the sunlight
- Edward tells Bella about his
hunting trip with Emmett

CHAPTER 11

- Edward and Bella watch
a movie in Biology class;
Bella is hyperaware of
Edward sitting next to her
  Mike tells Bella he doesn't
  like the idea of her and
  Edward; Edward quizzes
  Bella about all her favorite
  things; Billy and Jacob
  Black see Edward with
  Bella

CHAPTER 12

- Bella is afraid Billy Black
will tell Charlie about
Edward
- Sitting with Edward at
lunch, Bella sees Rosalie
glaring at her
  Edward explains that it
  will be dangerous for his
  whole family if, after he
  spends time with her
  publicly, things end badly;
  Bella tells her friends she
  is not going to Seattle
  with Edward after all
- Edward meets Bella Saturday morning and she drives
to the trailhead
  They hike five miles to the
  meadow

CHAPTER 13

- In the sunshine Edward's
skin sparkles like diamonds
  Bella gazes at his beauty
  and touches his hand and
  forearm; Bella leans in to
  smell Edward's breath and
  he is caught off guard;
  Edward is gone in a
  moment; when he calms
  down he demonstrates his
  deadly speed and strength;
  Edward promises not to
  hurt Bella; he tries to
  explain why it is so difficult for him; Edward and
  Bella try slowly and carefully to be close to each
  other; Edward is surprised
  at his control
- Edward carries Bella back to
the truck piggyback
- Edward carefully kisses
Bella for the first time

CHAPTER 14

- On the drive home from the
meadow, Edward tells Bella
how Carlisle created the rest
of his family; he explains
that Alice and Jasper joined
them later, and tells Bella
about Alice's special talent
  Edward admits that
  he watches Bella sleep;
  Edward stays that night
  with Bella, tells her about
  the talents of his other
  family members; Edward
  sings Bella to sleep

"HE LED ME A FEW FEET THROUGH THE TALL, WET FERNS AND
DRAPING MOSS, AROUND A MASSIVE HEMLOCK TREE . . . ON THE
EDGE OF AN ENORMOUS OPEN FIELD IN THE LAP OF THE OLYMPIC
PEAKS. IT WAS TWICE THE SIZE OF ANY BASEBALL STADIUM."

—Bella, on going to the baseball field with Edward (*Twilight*, Chapter 17)

taking her to the prom
Bella doesn't want to
go—she can't dance, plus
she's wearing a cast on one
leg; Edward lifts her onto
his feet and they dance
- Jacob Black shows up
Billy Black has paid
Jacob to give a message to

Bella—they want her to
break up with Edward
- Bella dances again with
Edward
- She wants him to change
her into a vampire right
away; he wants her to stay
human; she says being with
him is enough for now

New Moon

CHAPTER 3
- Edward is remote and silent; Bella is frightened
  Alice and Jasper have gone away; Edward doesn't stay with her the next two nights
- Edward takes Bella to the edge of the woods to have a talk
  Edward says his family is leaving; he makes Bella promise not to do anything reckless or foolish, in return promising that after he leaves, it will be as if he never existed; Bella tries to follow him into the forest but gets lost and collapses; hours later Bella is found by Sam Uley
- October – November – December – January: Bella is like a zombie

CHAPTER 4
- Charlie threatens to send Bella to her mother in Florida
  Bella is lifeless; she screams in her sleep; Charlie thinks maybe Renée can help
- To placate Charlie, Bella asks Jessica to go to a movie with her
- Bella and Jessica walk down the street to get some food
  They pass a bar and see four men standing outside; Bella approaches them; they seem familiar; she

feels a rush of adrenaline
- Bella hears Edward's voice, angry and concerned
  Bella comes out of the lifeless haze, her senses awake
- That night Bella feels the nightly pain like a huge hole punched through her chest — it is hard to breathe

CHAPTER 5
- Bella is out of the numbness, but still has nightmares of nothingness; she holds herself tightly together
- Bella realizes that she doesn't need to keep her promise to Edward
  Bella wants to be reckless and stupid; she finds two free, broken-down motorcycles and takes them to Jacob Black to be repaired

CHAPTER 6
- Bella starts spending time with Jacob
  Bella is surprised to hear herself laugh; Jacob carries happiness like an aura — an earthbound sun; Charlie is cautiously relieved to see her happy
- Bella makes a comment at lunch in the cafeteria; her friends are stunned

CHAPTER 7
- Bella drives to Edward's house to see if she will hear his voice again — nothing

- Jacob finishes the motorcycles

  While driving the bikes
  out to a secluded riding
  place, Bella sees four
  boys on a cliff overlooking
  the water; one jumps off;
  Jacob explains that the
  boys are just cliff diving,
  that it's an adrenaline
  rush; Bella wants
  to give cliff diving a try;
  Jacob says the boys are
  Sam Uley's gang;
  he seems worried and
  frightened

- Bella realizes that Jacob
likes her as more than just a
friend

CHAPTER 8

- Jacob instructs Bella how to
ride the motorcycle

- As soon as Bella lets go
of the clutch, she hears
Edward's angry voice

  The motorcycle falls on
  top of her, but she is eager
  to try again; the second
  attempt goes better; she
  hears Edward's voice several times; she crashes and
  cuts her head; she apologizes to Jacob for bleeding

- After several days of acci-
dents and injuries, Bella
and Jacob decide to try
hiking — Bella wants to see
Edward's meadow again

CHAPTER 9

- Bella's time is filled with
school, work, and Jacob

- Mike invites Bella to a
movie; she turns it into a
group activity; she invites
Jacob and Quil

  Everyone backs out or
  comes down with the flu
  except Mike and Jacob;
  Mike gets sick during the
  movie

- Jacob tells Bella he will
always be there for her

  Bella doesn't want to lead
  Jacob on; she feels she has
  nothing left to give

- Jacob doesn't feel well; Bella
gets sick

CHAPTER 10

- Jacob never calls to say he is
better; Billy won't let Bella
talk to Jacob

  Bella is told that Jacob has
  mono and can't have visitors for a month

- Bella doesn't handle "alone"
well; the hole in her chest is
worse than ever

  Charlie is worried

- Bella decides to find Edward's
meadow on her own

  When she does, the memories there are too painful

- Laurent shows up in the
meadow

  Laurent knows the Cul-
  lens are gone; Bella hears
  Edward's warning voice;

Laurent is thirsty; he says he'll kill Bella quickly, that it will be better than what Victoria has planned for her, that Victoria wants to torture Bella in revenge for Edward killing James
- Five huge wolves appear; Laurent runs away; the wolves follow

CHAPTER 11
- Bella is terrified to know that Victoria is coming for her; she is worried about Charlie
- Bella realizes what has happened to Jacob — Sam has gotten to him
    Bella drives to La Push to see Jacob; she talks first to Quil, who is worried he will be next
- Jacob is angry; he says his problem is all the bloodsuckers' fault; he is not good enough to be Bella's friend anymore
- Bella is alone again

CHAPTER 12
- That night Bella hears a sound outside her window; she is sure Victoria has come to kill her, but it is Jacob
    Jacob has come to apologize for breaking his promise; Bella is tired and upset; Jacob cannot tell her his secret but hopes she can guess; he tells her she needs

"I KNEW WE WERE BOTH IN MORTAL DANGER. STILL, IN THAT INSTANT, I FELT *WELL*. WHOLE. I COULD FEEL MY HEART RACING IN MY CHEST, THE BLOOD PULSING HOT AND FAST THROUGH MY VEINS AGAIN. MY LUNGS FILLED DEEP WITH THE SWEET SCENT THAT CAME OFF HIS SKIN. IT WAS LIKE THERE HAD NEVER BEEN ANY HOLE IN MY CHEST. I WAS PERFECT — NOT HEALED, BUT AS IF THERE HAD NEVER BEEN A WOUND IN THE FIRST PLACE."
—Bella (*New Moon*, Chapter 20)

to remember the Quileute legends he talked about
- In a dream Bella sees Jacob turn into a werewolf
    Bella realizes that her only human friend isn't human after all
- Charlie goes out with a group of men to kill the wolves

CHAPTER 13
- Bella goes to warn Jacob and to ask if he can try not to be a werewolf
- Jacob is relieved that Bella doesn't hate him
    Jacob explains that the wolves protect people from vampires; they killed Laurent, and they're trying to catch Victoria, but they don't know what she is after; Bella tells Jacob that Victoria is after her

"I WAS PROUD OF MYSELF AS I PLUNGED
DEEPER INTO THE FREEZING BLACK WATER.
I HADN'T HAD ONE MOMENT OF TERROR—
JUST PURE ADRENALINE."

—Bella (*New Moon*, Chapter 15)

- Jacob calls a meeting with the wolves; Bella learns that wolves hear one another's thoughts

  Bella says Edward can also read minds

CHAPTER 14

- Bella meets the wolf pack

  Paul loses control; Jacob phases on the fly; they fight; Jared and Embry take a shaken Bella to Emily's house
- Jacob, Paul, and Sam return; they make plans to protect Bella and Charlie, and to kill Victoria

CHAPTER 15

- Bella spends most of spring break in La Push, while the wolves patrol the area

  Jacob tells Bella the good things about being a wolf: warmth, fast healing, speed; Bella tells Jacob about her scar, about how Edward saved her from James, and about Alice's and Jasper's talents
- It hurts Bella to talk about the Cullens

  Jacob promises to take Bella cliff diving for some fun but ends up having to follow a new trail left by Victoria
- Bella is lonely and frustrated; she decides to cliff jump alone

  She hears Edward's voice,

then jumps; the fall is exhilarating—the water is the danger; Bella is tossed around beneath the surface; Edward's voice commands her to keep swimming, keep fighting; Bella senses she is going to die and is happy to have Edward's voice with her at the end; Bella's last thought is *Goodbye, I love you.*

CHAPTER 16

- Jacob pulls Bella from the water and resuscitates her

  Sam is there, but Jacob tells him to get back to the hospital; Jacob tells Bella that Harry Clearwater has had a heart attack
- Jacob takes Bella to his house; they both rest

  Bella remembers *Romeo and Juliet*: If Romeo left Juliet, could she love Paris? Wouldn't Romeo want her to be happy?
- Billy Black comes home; Harry has died

  Jacob takes Bella home, embraces her; Bella wonders if she can love Jacob enough, and make him happy; she knows if she kisses him, the decision will be made
- Jacob smells a vampire and rushes to get Bella away

  Bella sees Carlisle's car and demands to go back; Jacob feels betrayed

CHAPTER 17

- Bella goes into her house, sees Alice and runs into her arms

  Alice is confused—she saw Bella throw herself off a cliff; Bella assures Alice she was not trying to kill herself, just having fun cliff diving; Bella explains that Jacob Black saved her; Alice did not see Jacob in her vision
- Bella tells Alice that Jacob is a werewolf and that Victoria is trying to kill her
- Bella makes Alice stay with her

  Bella overhears Charlie telling Alice how bad it was for Bella when Edward left
- Alice tells Bella she has found out her real name; she had a sister, and she has a niece
- Harry Clearwater's funeral is the next day

CHAPTER 18

- Jacob comes over before the funeral to see how long Alice is staying; he can't be around vampires
- Jacob is getting ready to kiss Bella when the phone rings

  Jacob answers the phone and says Charlie is not there, he's at the funeral
- Alice rushes in to say

it was Edward on the phone—Rosalie has told Edward about Bella jumping off the cliff

  Edward thinks the funeral is for Bella and is going to the Volturi
- Alice and Bella hurriedly leave for the airport and Italy

  Jacob begs Bella to stay with him

CHAPTER 19

- On the plane, Alice tells Bella it is too dangerous for any of the family to come with them—she can't lose Jasper

  Alice tells Bella Edward needs to see her to believe she is alive; she explains about the Volturi, their guard, their law enforcement, and their eating arrangements
- Alice closes her eyes and follows Edward's actions in her mind
- In Italy, Alice steals a Porsche and she and Bella race to Volterra

  It is St. Marcus Day; Edward plans to enter the main plaza when the sun is at its brightest, at noon

CHAPTER 20

- The roads around Volterra are crowded

  Alice drops off Bella and

tells her which direction to run; there are people everywhere; Bella is afraid she'll be too late

- The clock is tolling and Bella sees Edward at the edge of the light

  She cries his name but he is not listening — his eyes are closed, his face peaceful; Bella slams into him; Edward believes that he's dead

- Bella finally makes Edward see that they are not dead, but Felix and Demetri are already there; there is a confrontation; Alice joins them

  Jane arrives and Edward's defensive stance relaxes in defeat; they follow Jane through a long, cold alley to meet the Volturi; Edward holds Bella, caresses her face, kisses her hair

CHAPTER 21

- Jane finally leads them into what seems an unremarkable office; they pass through long halls with many doors, into a round, cavernous room filled with several vampires
- Aro cheerfully talks to them about their talents; he wonders how Edward can stand so close to Bella
- Aro knows that Bella is the one exception to Edward's gift; he wonders if she is also an exception to his own

  Bella gives him her hand — nothing; Aro asks Jane to see if Bella is immune to her talent as well; Edward launches himself toward Jane but ends up on the floor writhing in pain; Aro redirects Jane toward Bella — again, nothing

- Aro asks Edward, Alice, and Bella to join his guard; they all say no

  Aro notes that Bella knows their secrets; she must become a vampire or die; Alice gives her hand to Aro and shows him a vision of Bella as a vampire; Aro is satisfied; they are free to go

- A group of tourists is led into the room; their screams of terror begin before Bella, Edward, and Alice can make it down the hall

CHAPTER 22

- Bella stays awake all that day and through both plane flights — she doesn't want to miss a second of her time with Edward

  In Edward's arms, it is easy for Bella to fantasize that he still wants her

- All the Cullens meet them

at the airport and thank
Bella for saving Edward
  Rosalie apologizes for
  her part in the misunder-
  standing
- At Bella's home, a wor-
  ried Charlie is furious with
  Edward

CHAPTER 23
- After a long sleep, Bella
  wakes to find Edward with
  her; she's convinced she's
  still asleep
- Edward tells Bella that
  Charlie has forbidden him
  to ever walk through his
  door again
- Edward is in agony over the
  dangers he left Bella to face
    Edward tries to explain
    that he lied to Bella
    about not wanting her;
    he is astonished that she
    believed the lie after the
    thousands of times he
    told her he loved her;
    Bella answers that it
    never made sense for him
    to love her
- Edward tries to convince
  Bella that he loves her and
  will never leave her
    Bella reminds Edward that
    she will grow old and die
    unless he changes her into
    a vampire; Edward refuses
- Bella decides to put her
  mortality up for a vote by
  Edward's family

CHAPTER 24
- On the way to Edward's
  house, Bella says her worst
  fear is that Edward will
  leave her
    Edward tells her that her
    hold on him is permanent
    and unbreakable; Bella
    has an epiphany: Edward
    loves her
- The Cullens congregate
  in the dining room; Bella
  explains that her mortality
  involves all of them
    Bella asks them if they
    want her to join their
    family; all but Rosalie and
    Edward say yes; Rosalie
    tells Bella that she wishes
    there had been someone to
    vote no for her; Alice says
    she can't change Bella,
    and Carlisle says he can
    do it; Edward bargains for
    more time — he suggests
    that they wait until after
    graduation; Edward says
    he will change Bella him-
    self on one condition: if
    she marries him first

EPILOGUE
- Almost everything is back
  to normal
    Bella is grounded; Jacob
    won't return her phone
    calls
- Edward drives Bella home
  from school to find her
  motorcycle in the driveway

- Jacob is waiting to talk to Edward in the woods
  Jacob had hoped the motorcycle would get Bella grounded, and away from Edward; Edward thanks Jacob for keeping Bella alive; Jacob reminds Edward the treaty forbids a vampire from biting a human
- Bella and Jacob part in sadness; Bella vows to see him smile again

Eclipse

CHAPTER 1

- Jacob sends Bella a note saying that he misses her, but that doesn't change anything
  Charlie tells Bella she is not grounded anymore if she will balance her time among her friends, especially Jacob
- Edward brings over a stack of college applications
- Bella and Edward see a newspaper article about a killing spree in Seattle
  Edward says the Cullens are monitoring the situation — they think it involves newborn vampires
- Bella wants to go see Jacob; Edward says it is too dangerous

CHAPTER 2

- Bella is no longer grounded so she offers to help Angela address her graduation announcements

- Alice has a vision; Edward is evasive about it
- Edward suggests that Bella should use the nearly expired airplane tickets Carlisle and Esme gave her for her birthday: They should fly to Florida this weekend
  Bella knows Charlie won't want her to go; Edward manipulates an argument between Charlie and Bella that makes Bella insist she will go to Florida; Charlie tries to give Bella the sex talk

CHAPTER 3

- Bella and Edward fly to visit Renée in Florida; Edward stays indoors
  Renée is insightful — she observes that Bella and Edward are more serious than she had supposed
- As soon as Bella gets home Jacob calls to see if she is going to be in school the next day

Bella assumes he is checking to see if she is still human, if the treaty has been broken
- The next day Jacob comes to Bella's school to talk to Edward; they argue
  Bella figures out from their conversation that Victoria has been in Forks; Alice saw it in her vision; Edward took Bella away to keep her out of danger; there was some problem between the Quileutes and the Cullens

CHAPTER 4
- Bella is again frightened because of Victoria
  The Cullens don't seem worried; Edward goes to hunt
- Bella goes to her Saturday job but isn't needed
  She drives quickly to La Push, before Alice can see what she's doing
- Jacob is overjoyed to see her
  The conversation turns to Bella's trip to Italy, the Volturi, Victoria's appearance, and the confrontation between the wolves and the Cullens
- Jacob wishes the vampires had never come back
  Jacob wonders what Bella sees in Edward and tries to convince Bella that he would be better for her

CHAPTER 5
- Bella and Jacob continue their talk
  Quil is happy to have become a werewolf; Jacob tells Bella what Sam went through when he changed, then imprinted on Emily and broke Leah's heart; he explains to Bella that werewolves don't age
- Bella promises to come back as soon as she can

CHAPTER 6
- Bella leaves Jacob and drives straight to Angela's house, not stopping even when she sees Edward's car behind her
  Bella enjoys the afternoon with Angela
- Edward is waiting in her room; he is worried and angry
  Edward says Bella can never see Jacob again — it is too dangerous; Bella says she *will* see him
- Edward goes hunting again for two days; he bribes Alice to kidnap Bella for a slumber party; his room now has a bed, but Bella uses the couch

CHAPTER 7
- Rosalie comes to talk with Bella
  Rosalie tells Bella about

the awful events that led
to her becoming a vam-
pire; explains why she
doesn't like Bella; says
that Bella is making the
wrong choice; tells Bella
how she found Emmett
- The next day at school
Jacob shows up and races
away with Bella on his
motorcycle

CHAPTER 8
- Bella and Jacob spend the
afternoon on the beach talking
  Quil has imprinted on
  a two-year-old; Jacob
  explains that it's not a
  romantic thing — more
  like gravity; Bella wonders
  when Jacob will see someone and imprint; Jacob
  tells Bella that he'll only
  ever see her
- Jacob finds out that Bella
intends to become a vam-
pire very soon
  Jacob tells her she'd be
  better off dead; Bella
  leaves, angry and hurt; she
  goes back to Alice's slumber party
- Edward returns in the night
  He is not angry; he trusts
  her judgment, and she
  can see Jacob whenever
  she likes; Bella says she
  doesn't think she's welcome in La Push anymore

CHAPTER 9
- Bella goes home; Jacob has
called to apologize, but she
won't call him back
- Bella's bedroom seems
unusually tidy, and some of
her clothes are missing
  Edward comes and smells
  that a vampire has been
  there; Edward takes Bella
  to his house and has
  Emmett and Jasper check
  the vampire's trail; Alice
  has not seen the intruder;
  Bella is frightened again
- Bella calls Jacob and he
apologizes profusely
- Edward talks to Jacob, tells
him about the unknown
vampire in Bella's room
  Edward and Jacob agree to
  work together to protect
  Bella

CHAPTER 10
- Jacob comes to Bella's
house to get the scent of
the vampire
  Bella wonders why Jacob
  wears so little clothing; he
  explains the problem of
  clothes and phasing
- Jacob accidentally cuts his
hand with a knife; it heals
in minutes
- Bella gets an acceptance
letter from Dartmouth
- Bella mentions the missing
clothes to Edward
  Edward realizes the

intruder took things with
Bella's scent, as evidence of
having found her
- There are more newspaper
headlines about killings in
Seattle
- Bella decides to go to La
Push for a bonfire party
Edward drives her to the
boundary line and hands
her off to Jacob

CHAPTER 11

- Bella and Jacob go to the
bonfire
The wolf pack is there,
along with Billy Black,
Old Quil, and Sue Clear-
water
- A council meeting begins;
Billy Black recites the
Quileute history:
Spirit warriors defend
the Quileute land; Taha
Aki, the last Spirit Chief,
was betrayed by the evil
Utlapa; Taha Aki and a
great wolf joined; the cold
ones came to Quileute
land; the third wife sacrificed herself to save Taha
Aki; the yellow-eyed cold
ones came and made a
treaty with the Quileutes
- Billy notes that the sons
of the tribe now carry the
burden of their ancestors

CHAPTER 12

- Graduation is near; Bella is
not ready to change

Edward doesn't want
Bella to become a vampire
just because she is afraid;
Edward reiterates why he
wants Bella to stay human;
Bella explains her problem
with getting married
- There are more headlines
about killings in Seattle; the
Cullens wonder what they
should do

CHAPTER 13

- Jasper relates the story of his
human years and his vam-
pire life
- Jasper recognizes the killings in Seattle as the result
of a newborn army
Jasper thinks that perhaps
the Volturi are encourag-
ing someone to destroy the
Cullens' coven
- The Denali clan refuses to
come help because the werewolves killed Laurent, who
was involved with Irina

CHAPTER 14

- Alice makes preparations for
Bella's graduation party
- The Cullens feel they must
go to Seattle to take care of
the problem
Edward goes hunting to
be strong; Bella is dropped
off to spend the afternoon
with Jacob
- Bella invites Jacob to her
graduation party
Jacob tells Bella he loves

her and wants her to
choose him over Edward

"IN THE DEAD SILENCE,
ALL THE DETAILS SUDDENLY FELL INTO PLACE FOR ME
WITH A BURST OF INTUITION.
SOMETHING EDWARD DIDN'T WANT ME TO KNOW.
SOMETHING THAT JACOB WOULDN'T HAVE KEPT FROM ME . . .
IT WAS NEVER GOING TO END, WAS IT?"
—Bella (*Eclipse*, Chapter 3)

learn how to kill newborns

The wolf pack has grown to ten members; the vampires and werewolves are wary of one another; Jasper explains and demonstrates the newborns' strengths and weaknesses

- Edward and Jacob discuss how to best protect Bella

Jacob will carry Bella to a secluded spot; his scent will mask hers

CHAPTER 19

- Edward notices the bracelet and charm Jacob gave Bella and asks if he can give her a charm, just a hand-me-down
- Edward muses about listening to the pack mind

Leah Clearwater is one of the wolves now — the only female; she makes everyone miserable; Edward is surprised to learn about imprinting

- Bella informs Edward that she must be with him during the fight

Bella asks Edward to sit out the fight

- The wolves and vampires undergo another night of training and instruction

Bella feels guilty about her selfishness

CHAPTER 20

- After ensuring that Charlie

will be safe in La Push for the weekend, all the Cullens except Edward go hunting; Bella spends the night with Edward

Edward gives Bella the hand-me-down charm, a heart-shaped crystal that was his mother's

- Bella worries about what she will be like as a vampire, fearing that she will only be interested in blood, that she won't want Edward the same way she does now

Bella wants to be physically intimate now, but Edward resists — it's too dangerous; Edward swears they will try after she marries him; Bella thinks he is worried about his virtue; Edward admits he would like to leave one commandment unbroken

- Edward shows Bella the wedding ring — the ring Edward's father gave his mother

Bella hesitantly tries the ring on; it fits perfectly; Edward is exultant

- Edward gets down on one knee and asks Bella to marry him

CHAPTER 21

- Alice sees that Bella is going to marry Edward

Alice is hurt because Bella

wants to go to Las Vegas
to get married
- Edward takes Bella to the
clearing so the newborns
will find her scent
    She falls and scrapes her
    palm; she smears blood on
    rocks and ferns
- Jacob comes to carry Bella
to the campsite
    Jacob thinks Bella should
    ask him to kiss her — he's
    sure he's a better kisser
    than Edward
- Bella tells Jacob that she has
asked Edward not to be in
the fight
    Bella is afraid that if
    anyone gets hurt, it will
    be her fault; she's worried
    about Jacob; Jacob asks
    Bella when she'll admit
    that she loves him, too

CHAPTER 22

- A frigid storm hits the
campsite
    Inside the tent, Bella is
    freezing, and Edward
    cannot warm her; Jacob
    comes into the tent to act
    as a space heater; he crawls
    into the sleeping bag with
    Bella; Edward is furious
    and jealous, but he sees
    the necessity of keeping
    Bella warm
- With the wind howling
outside and Bella finally
asleep, Edward and Jacob

discuss Bella, and their
competition for her love
    Edward asks about the
    legend of the third wife
    that Bella mentioned in
    her sleep
- They forge a tenuous truce
for the night

CHAPTER 23

- The storm ends, as does the
truce between Edward and
Jacob; Jacob leaves
- Bella and Edward compare
their top ten nights; Jacob
can hear them; he howls in
agony and runs off
    Bella feels terrible that she
    has hurt Jacob; Edward
    goes to bring Jacob back;
    Bella realizes she has also
    hurt Edward
- Bella talks privately with
Jacob and apologizes for all
the pain she has caused him
    Jacob apologizes, too, and
    says he can redeem him-
    self by letting himself get
    taken out in the battle;
    Bella begs him to stay
    with her; she asks him to
    kiss her
- Jacob kisses Bella; the kiss
is eager, nearly violent;
Bella resists
    Jacob urges her to let her-
    self go; Bella *does* feel love
    for Jacob; she kisses him
    back; she envisions what
    might have been

- Jacob leaves cheerfully for the fight; Edward returns and hears from the pack mind what has happened Bella is miserable
- The fight begins; Edward narrates as he hears the action through Seth's mind; everything sounds positive until Edward senses danger
- Victoria and Riley walk into the campsite
  Seth attacks Riley while Edward takes on Victoria; Bella watches the battle, listens to the metallic snaps and tears, gasps and hisses; Riley flings Seth into the rock wall; Seth falls, limp
- Bella needs to create a diversion; she grips a sharp stone and slashes her arm
  Victoria loses her focus and Edward finishes her off; Seth dismantles Riley

CHAPTER 25

- Edward and Seth gather the pieces of Victoria and Riley and set them on fire
- Bella is frozen in place; Edward thinks she is afraid of him and approaches her carefully
- The main battle is over; everyone is fine
  Suddenly Seth howls and Edward gasps; Jacob has been hurt while trying to protect Leah; Bella faints
- Back in the clearing, Bella revives; Carlisle assures her Jacob is already healing
  There is another bonfire here; one young vampire with wild red eyes is sitting on the ground — she has surrendered; the young vampire wails and thrashes — she wants Bella
- Jane and other members of the Volturi arrive
  Jane tortures the young vampire, Bree, for more information; Carlisle offers to take responsibility for Bree; Jane refuses the offer; Felix kills Bree

CHAPTER 26

- Bella goes home to Charlie; she needs to go see Jacob
  Charlie says Carlisle is treating Jacob; Charlie feels like he is going to lose Bella soon; he asks for advance notice before she leaves with Edward
- Bella goes to see the injured Jacob
  Bella and Jacob talk about her knowing that she is in love with him, but still choosing Edward; Jacob is her soul mate in this world, but Bella knows she cannot live without Edward

Breaking Dawn

destination a secret; Alice and Rosalie work all day on Bella's makeup and hair; Charlie and Renée give Bella a set of silver hair combs; Charlie escorts Bella down the stairs

- As soon as Bella sees Edward at the altar, all her fears are gone

CHAPTER 4

- The reception is in the backyard, at twilight
  Edward and Bella greet their guests
- Jacob steps out from the woods; Edward leaves so he and Bella can talk alone
- Jacob is horrified to hear that Bella is planning a "real" honeymoon before she becomes a vampire; he grabs Bella and shakes her
  Edward is instantly there; Jacob is ready to kill him; Seth and two wolves shove Jacob back into the woods
- Bella composes herself and they go back to the reception
- Bella says a tearful, loving

goodbye to Renée and Charlie

CHAPTER 5

- Bella and Edward leave for their honeymoon: they take a plane to Houston, a second one to Rio de Janeiro, and then a boat to Isle Esme
- Edward carries Bella across the threshold; he goes for a midnight swim, waits for Bella in the water
  Bella takes a shower to calm down
- Edward is afraid of hurting Bella
- In the morning, Bella wakes to a feeling of pure happiness
  Edward is angry at himself—he points out the bruises all over Bella's body; he berates himself for hurting Bella; she tries to convince him that she is fine, she is happy
- Edward gets up to fix breakfast for Bella, and she asks him if he plans to avoid touching her for the rest of the honeymoon

"THEY WERE YOUR GRANDMA SWAN'S. . . . WE HAD A JEWELER REPLACE THE PASTE STONES WITH SAPPHIRES."

—Charlie, on the wedding present he and Renée give Bella (*Breaking Dawn*, Chapter 3)

CHAPTER 6
- Edward keeps Bella busy with snorkeling, hiking, swimming, exploring, and sunsets

  Bella tries to seduce Edward with lingerie, bribes, and compromises
- Bella has nightmares about the Volturi and a vampire child, and wakes up crying

  Bella wants Edward so much; she pleads with him, kisses him; they make love; Edward and Bella are both happy in the morning; Bella gets woozy; the Brazilian cleaning people come; the native woman suspects what Edward is and she is frightened for Bella

CHAPTER 7
- Bella awakes from another dream about the Volturi and the child

  Edward has gone hunting; Bella fixes herself fried chicken but it tastes wrong so she throws it out
- When Edward gets home Bella starts throwing up; the pieces fall into place; she realizes she must be pregnant
- Bella touches her stomach and feels a little nudge; Edward is stunned
- Alice calls; Bella talks to Car-

lisle, tells him her theory; he asks some medical questions and agrees she is pregnant
- Edward starts making travel arrangements while hurriedly packing; Bella doesn't understand why Edward seems furious
- Bella feels another nudge; she is surprised at how much she already loves her little nudger
- Edward tells her not to be afraid, that he won't let the "thing" hurt her
- Bella sneaks a phone call to Rosalie to ask for help

CHAPTER 8, BOOK TWO— JACOB
- Paul has imprinted on Jacob's sister Rachel, and no one is pleased; Paul is annoying everyone
- Jacob is waiting to hear about Bella

  Jacob spends an afternoon with Quil and Claire
- Sam calls·a meeting of the pack; Edward and Bella have returned

  Jacob feels the treaty has been broken and the wolves should attack; Sam declares that the Cullens are not a danger

CHAPTER 9
- Jacob decides to kill Edward on his own

  Carlisle meets Jacob at

the door, and Bella calls to Jacob from inside; Jacob sees Edward, who looks like he's in agony, half-crazed; Bella is still human but looks sick and haggard — she is pregnant

- Edward takes Jacob outside to talk

  Edward looks like a man being burned at the stake; he knows it's all his fault; he had no idea this could happen; Rosalie is protecting Bella; Edward asks Jacob to talk to Bella, to tell her she can have a baby with him; Jacob knows Bella will reject him; Edward promises Jacob that the moment Bella's heart stops beating, he will beg Jacob to kill him; Jacob tells him they have a deal

CHAPTER 10

- Jacob and Bella speak privately

  Bella believes Jacob will imprint on someone and everything will make sense; Bella doesn't expect to survive as a human; Bella understands what Edward has sent Jacob to offer, and won't consider it; Jacob feels an addiction to be with Bella, but he wants to leave

- The pack decides the risk of this new creature is too great — they will attack the Cullens

  Sam plans their strategy, and uses the Alpha voice to ensure obedience

CHAPTER 11

- Jacob struggles against Sam's order to obey

  Jacob is the true Alpha — he was not born to kneel to Sam

- Jacob breaks from the pack; he will stand between the pack and the Cullens

- Jacob leaves to warn the Cullens

  Seth breaks from the pack and joins Jacob; they patrol the Cullens' land

- Bella's condition worsens

CHAPTER 12

- Leah also breaks from the pack and joins Jacob

  Leah is irritating; Jacob doesn't want to lead a pack; Leah wants to be free of Sam

- Carlisle and Jacob talk; Carlisle is frustrated because he can't figure out what the fetus wants; Jacob has a thought about blood, and Edward hears the thought and shares it with the others; Bella agrees to give blood a try

CHAPTER 13

- Jacob stays with Bella—he doesn't want to miss the last few minutes of her life
  Jacob feels that his presence helps Bella
- Bella drinks a cup of blood; it tastes good, and she immediately feels stronger
- Jacob is called to a meeting with some of Sam's pack; they want Jacob, Seth, and Leah to rejoin them, but all three say no; Jacob thinks the Alpha bond is permanent

CHAPTER 14

- Bella is better; her whole face lights up when she sees Jacob
- Jacob starts taunting Rosalie with blonde jokes
- The fetus breaks one of Bella's ribs
- Alice gets headaches around Bella; she feels better near Jacob
- The Cullens give food and clothes to the now homeless wolves; Jacob and Seth accept, but Leah doesn't

CHAPTER 15

- Bella and Charlie talk on the phone; neither Edward nor Jacob condones this
- Bella asks for Jacob; her face lights up again when she sees him
  Jacob sits next to Bella to

keep her warm; Rosalie brings Jacob food in a dog dish

- Bella says Carlisle thinks the baby will be born within four days
  Jacob feels his ties to Bella get even stronger; Bella thinks that Jacob is supposed to be in her life, but not like this—like they got off track somehow
- Edward tells Jacob about old myths that say vampire babies chew their way out of the womb

CHAPTER 16

- Jacob's pack is still protecting the Cullens' land
  Jacob congratulates Leah on being less annoying than Paul; Leah thinks Jacob makes a good Alpha; Jacob teaches Leah how to better enjoy eating as a wolf
- All the Cullens go hunting except Edward and Rosalie
- Edward hears the baby's thoughts: The baby is happy and adores Bella
  Jacob now sees Bella and Edward as a happy little family; he feels alone and in pain
- Edward hears Jacob's pain and gives Jacob the car keys and tells him to get away

CHAPTER 17

- Jacob races away toward Seattle

  Jacob hopes he can imprint on someone so he won't hurt over Bella anymore; he compares everyone to Bella; he goes back to be with her

- Edward tells Jacob they want to deliver the baby early — tomorrow

- Edward asks Jacob, the true Alpha, to grant him permission to save Bella

  In anguish, Jacob consents

- Bella bends and there is a ripping sound followed by a shriek of pain

CHAPTER 18

- Bella is semiconscious; her body jerks and twitches; there is a wild thrashing in her body, and sharp snaps and cracks

  Edward injects Bella with morphine; Rosalie uses a scalpel to cut Bella's skin; blood gushes out, and Rosalie's eyes glint with thirst; Jacob knocks Rosalie out the door, hitting her in the face and gut; Alice drags Rosalie away; Rosalie does not fight back

- Jacob performs CPR

- Edward uses his teeth to get to the baby; Jacob doesn't look away from Bella's face

  Bella sees the baby, Renesmee, then gasps; Edward snatches the baby away

- Jacob continues CPR as Bella's eyes roll back; her heart falters

  Edward injects a syringe of his venom into Bella's heart; he bites her in more places to force venom into her body

- Jacob sees there is no life in Bella — she is a broken, bled-out corpse

"'DON'T BE AFRAID,' I MURMURED.
'WE BELONG TOGETHER.'
I WAS ABRUPTLY OVERWHELMED BY THE TRUTH
OF MY OWN WORDS. THIS MOMENT WAS SO PERFECT,
SO RIGHT, THERE WAS NO WAY TO DOUBT IT.
HIS ARMS WRAPPED AROUND ME, HOLDING ME
AGAINST HIM. . . . IT FELT LIKE EVERY NERVE ENDING
IN MY BODY WAS A LIVE WIRE.
'FOREVER,' HE AGREED."

— Bella (*Breaking Dawn*, Chapter 5)

Bella's dead body has no draw for Jacob now, so he leaves; Jacob gave everything to save Bella, but she sacrificed herself to be torn apart by a monster
- Jacob hears Rosalie downstairs, cooing to the monster, feeding it blood

    Pain and hatred wash through Jacob—the thing must be destroyed; Jacob can feel the pull tugging him toward the abomination
- Rosalie turns around and Jacob looks into the baby's eyes

    Everything that made Jacob what he was floats away and the universe swirls around only one point: Renesmee

CHAPTER 19, BOOK THREE—BELLA
- Bella is bewildered by the pain and darkness

    The morphine keeps Bella paralyzed while the venom burns; Bella wants to stay alive for Edward, Jacob, and Renesmee; Bella burns but forces herself to remain silent to lessen Edward's anguish
- After two days Bella's heart stops; she opens her eyes

CHAPTER 20
- All of Bella's senses are magnified: sight, smell, taste, hearing, touch

    A touch sends Bella into a defensive crouch, until she sees it was Edward; Bella gasps at the beauty of Edward's face, voice, and scent
- Bella looks in a mirror and doesn't recognize herself; she has red eyes
- Jasper is perplexed by Bella's self-control

CHAPTER 21
- Edward takes Bella hunting before letting her see Renesmee
- Bella can run and jump like Edward; she now has raw, massive power

    Everything physical is easy, but it's hard for her to focus the expanded capacity of her mind
- Bella catches the scent of deer, but then smells something more fragrant and turns toward it

    Bella hears a pursuer behind her, so she turns and snarls—it's Edward; Bella realizes the fragrant smell is human and runs away
- Bella kills a mountain lion and feeds

CHAPTER 22
- Edward and Bella race home to see Renesmee

Jacob meets them outside to test Bella's control; Bella is happy that Jacob is still her friend

- Bella sees Renesmee; she looks two months old

    Everyone, including Jacob, is afraid to let Bella hold Renesmee; Edward tells everyone about Bella's control on their hunting trip

- Renesmee touches Bella's face; Bella sees Renesmee's thoughts and memories
- Bella sees how Jacob stares at Renesmee

    Bella is angry that Jacob has imprinted on Renesmee;

Jacob calls the baby Nessie and Bella lunges for his throat

CHAPTER 23

- Because Jacob has imprinted on Renesmee, the pack cannot hurt her; the treaty is reinstated
- Renesmee is growing at an alarming rate
- Jasper is discomfited by Bella's control — he wonders if super-self-control is her gift
- Renesmee shows Bella every happening of her day

    Renesmee wants Bella to know all about her

"THERE, NESTLED INTO A SMALL CLEARING IN THE FOREST, WAS A TINY STONE COTTAGE, LAVENDER GRAY IN THE LIGHT OF THE STARS."

—Bella (*Breaking Dawn*, Chapter 24)

- Alice hands Bella a key — today is Bella's nineteenth birthday

CHAPTER 24

- The birthday present is a house for Bella and Edward: a storybook stone cottage
  Bella and Edward spend a romantic night together

CHAPTER 25

- Jacob thinks he can help Bella stay in Forks by having Charlie see her and let him make the wrong assumptions
  Jacob phases in front of Charlie, then tells Charlie that Bella has changed, that she and Edward are caring for a special baby; Jacob starts to tell Charlie more, but Charlie wants to hear as little as possible — he'd like to remain on a need-to-know basis; everyone is angry with Jacob, but Jacob didn't realize the danger or the pain he was causing Bella; Alice has colored contacts for Bella, to fool Charlie; Bella gets a crash course in acting human; Bella instructs Renesmee not to touch or bite Charlie
- Charlie arrives and sees Bella; he feels shock, disbelief, fear, anger
  Edward introduces Renes-

mee as his orphaned niece; Charlie sees the resemblance to Bella and himself

CHAPTER 26

- Charlie spends the day with the family
  Bella explains her daughter's name: Renesmee = Renée + Esme; Carlie = Carlisle + Charlie; Charlie acknowledges that Bella looks good and tells her he'll get used to the change in her
- Bella is angry about Emmett's embarrassing comments
  Bella beats Emmett at arm-wrestling

CHAPTER 27

- Renesmee speaks at one week, walks at three weeks; at this rate she will be an adult in four years
  Edward and Carlisle plan a trip to South America to find answers
- Aro sends Bella a wedding gift
  Bella needs to go see Aro alone in order to protect Renesmee
- Irina comes to apologize but sees Renesmee from a distance and assumes she is an immortal child; Irina runs away

CHAPTER 28

- Alice has a vision of the

Volturi and warns the others
that they're coming
  Irina has gone to the
  Volturi with her mistaken
  assumption; the Volturi
  plan to destroy the Cullens
• The Cullens need friends to
  witness for them, to make
  the Volturi hesitate
• Alice and Jasper leave hurriedly
• Bella tells Jacob that it's
  over, that they've all been
  sentenced to die

CHAPTER 29

• Alice and Jasper are gone
• Alice leaves a note listing
  the friends the Cullens need
  as witnesses
• Alice also leaves a secret
  note for Bella, in a copy of
  The Merchant of Venice, about
  J. Jenks; Bella realizes she
  needs to keep the note from
  Edward
• The Cullens split up to find
  their witnesses; Edward and
  Bella stay home to let their
  expected visitors see Renesmee for themselves

CHAPTER 30

• Bella wants to learn to fight
  so she can defend herself
  and her family
  Edward explains the
  Volturi's strengths; Bella
  hopes she is immune to
  some of their gifts
• The Denalis arrive and are

horrified to see Renesmee,
who they think is an immortal child
  Edward convinces them
  that Renesmee is half-
  vampire, half-human; they
  each let Renesmee touch
  them and show them her
  story
• The Denalis agree to witness, and feel sad that Irina
  is the cause of the danger

CHAPTER 31

• Eleazar, who has the gift of
  sensing the gifts of others,
  mentions that Bella is a
  shield
  Bella and Edward are
  surprised; Kate wonders
  if Bella can project her
  shield onto others
• Under the circumstances,
  Eleazar has to rethink his
  opinion of the Volturi
  Eleazar thinks the Volturi
  are coming not to punish,
  but to acquire
• More witnesses arrive; the
  explanations start again

CHAPTER 32

• The Cullens' house is
  crowded with visitors: the
  Denalis, Peter and Charlotte,
  the Irish clan, the Egyptians,
  a few nomads, the Amazons,
  the Romanians
  A few refuse to touch
  Renesmee, but agree to
  witness

"ON HER WRIST WAS AN INTRICATELY BRAIDED QUILEUTE VERSION OF A PROMISE RING. EDWARD HAD GRITTED HIS TEETH OVER THAT ONE. . . ."
—Bella, on the bracelet Jacob gives Renesmee
(*Breaking Dawn*, Chapter 34)

- The wolves, now numbering seventeen, join the Cullens; the Volturi halt
- Edward reads their layers of strategy for finding guilt
- Carlisle greets Aro, and explains that no law has been broken

  Aro wants to hear from Edward; Bella is so angry that she flings her shield across the field with no effort; Aro next wants to see Renesmee
- Aro is convinced that Renesmee is not an immortal child

  Aro wonders if the werewolves could be loyal to him

CHAPTER 37

- Aro confers with Caius; the Volturi's witnesses grow uneasy

  Bella inspects her shield, wraps it closer around her allies
- Caius proclaims that an alliance with werewolves is against their law

  Edward explains that the wolves are shape-shifters, not true werewolves
- Caius calls for Irina

  Irina refuses to make a formal complaint, and takes responsibility for her mistake; Caius executes Irina; Carlisle and Garrett restrain Irina's sisters, Tanya and Kate
- The Volturi witnesses are suspicious; Aro's need for an audience has backfired; the Romanians murmur in glee

  Aro speaks with a few of the Cullens' witnesses; the Volturi drift closer; Aro declares that they need to know with absolute certainty what Renesmee will become if she is to live; Garrett gives a speech about tyranny and freedom; Aro is amused
- More of the Volturi's witnesses retreat

  Aro, Caius, and Marcus counsel together
- Bella sees the danger coming; she kisses Renesmee goodbye and instructs Jacob to run away with her as soon as the Volturi are distracted

  Carlisle acknowledges that there's no hope; there are goodbyes and murmured expressions of love

CHAPTER 38

- While Aro, Caius, and Marcus "counsel," Chelsea tries to break the Cullens' emotional ties but can't find them

  Edward asks Bella if she's shielding them, and she confirms that she is; Jane

sends sharp jabs at Bella's shield, but the shield remains undamaged; Jane is furious; Alec takes over; a strange haze oozes toward the shield, but swirls harmlessly around the edges
- Aro calls for a vote
  Caius votes to destroy Renesmee; Marcus sees no immediate danger; Aro must cast the deciding vote
- Edward asks to clarify one point; he asks Aro if they'll be forgiven if they can prove that Renesmee is not a threat; Aro agrees
- Edward invites Alice into the clearing
  Alice has returned from South America with an olive-skinned female vampire named Huilen and her nephew, Nahuel
- Huilen tells their story; Nahuel is half-vampire, half-human; he matured at seven years and has not changed since; he can drink blood or eat human food
  Nahuel has sisters, all of whom are nonvenomous

- Aro declares that he sees no threat
- The Volturi leave
- Cheers erupt from the Cullens and friends
  Bella promises Renesmee that they'll be together forever

CHAPTER 39
- All the Cullens' friends return to their homes
  The Romanians are extremely disappointed but have enjoyed the Volturi's cowardice; Garrett leaves with Kate; the Cullens have a joyous reunion with Alice and Jasper
- Edward explains that the Volturi's confidence has been shattered
  They have never before been outnumbered, the wolves frightened them, and they were terrified of Bella's power; Alice gave them an excuse to get out of the fight
- Bella pushes her shield away from her mind, and Edward is able to read her thoughts for the first time
- The "happily ever after" begins

Cars

T hough, unlike Bella, I do speak Car and Driver to an extent, I would never classify myself as an expert. I wanted this section to offer a rundown on each of the vehicles appearing in the Twilight Saga, so I turned to my usual adviser on all things automotive: my younger brother—and car enthusiast—Jacob Morgan. Jacob wrote the following piece, which sheds light not only on the characters' views of vehicles themselves—describing them in more detail than I'm capable of—but also the way those vehicles reflect the personalities of the characters who drive them. Enjoy! (And never let a mechanic talk down to you.)

CARLISLE'S MERCEDES
S55 AMG

"I MIGHT BE THE FURTHEST
THING FROM AN AUTOPHILE,
BUT I COULD TELL YOU EVERYTHING
ABOUT THAT PARTICULAR CAR. IT WAS A
MERCEDES S55 AMG.... IT WAS CARLISLE'S CAR."
—Bella (New Moon, Chapter 16)

CARLISLE: MERCEDES S55 AMG

COLOR: Black
ENGINE: 5.4-liter supercharged V8
HORSEPOWER: 469 hp at 6100 rpm
TORQUE: 516 ft.-lbs. at 2650 rpm
0–60: 4.5 seconds

Carlisle's choice of car reveals his controlled and reserved personality. Most will recognize the S-class as the pinnacle of luxury cars, but only a few will understand the meaning of the AMG badging on the vehicle. Few differences are apparent from the outside, but the supercharged V8 under the hood produces enough power to shame most of the super exotics offered by legitimate sports-car brands. Mercedes engineers did not stop at the engine; they enhanced all elements of driving, including a stiffer suspension and larger brakes. Despite having sports-car capabilities, this S55 AMG travels mainly unnoticed, being recognized with its more obtainable S-class relatives. The S55 allows Carlisle to cover ground as quickly as any of his children do, and is certainly as expensive as his children's impressive cars, but does not stand out like any of his children's cars—with the notable exception of Edward's S60R. Showcasing his uniquely strong personality, this car represents Carlisle's extreme abilities hidden by his eloquent, yet humble, actions and words.

EDWARD: VOLVO S60R

COLOR: Silver
ENGINE: 2.5-liter turbocharged I-5
HORSEPOWER: 300 hp at 5500 rpm
TORQUE: 295 ft.-lbs. at 1950 rpm
0–60: 5.5 seconds

Most often overlooked, yet also one of the most illuminating of all the cars in the story, is the Silver Volvo S60R. The perfect car for Edward's lifestyle and personality, an S60R is the ideal choice for him. Bearing almost no marks to set this simple Volvo apart from its more sedate siblings, the S60R brings no attention to its sports-sedan intent. With 300 horsepower

"THE SILVER CAR WAS ALREADY THERE, WAITING IN CHARLIE'S
SPOT ON THE DRIVEWAY. I BOUNDED DOWN THE STAIRS AND
OUT THE FRONT DOOR, WONDERING HOW LONG THIS BIZARRE
ROUTINE WOULD CONTINUE. I NEVER WANTED IT TO END."
—Bella (*Twilight*, Chapter 11)

on tap from the doubled pressure of the turbocharger, and an advanced six-speed manual transmission providing power to all four wheels, the silver car is more capable than anyone would guess, assuming that anyone would notice the car in the first place. With a higher lateral acceleration than even Rosalie's BMW M3, Edward views the Volvo S60R as capable of cutting through the narrow, winding Washington roads better than all but two of the vehicles in the books: Edward's Aston Martin V12 Vanquish and Bella's Ferrari F430, shown later. This vehicle was chosen by Edward as an extension of his personality—someone always desiring to blend in, while offering more under the skin than anyone could imagine.

EDWARD: ASTON MARTIN V12 VANQUISH

COLOR: Silver
ENGINE: 5.9-liter V12
HORSEPOWER: 460 hp at 6500 rpm
TORQUE: 400 ft.-lbs. at 5000 rpm
0–60: 4.4 seconds

The Aston Martin V12 Vanquish is the English company's response to the world-renowned grand touring cars offered by Ferrari and Mercedes. Splitting those two dissimilar personalities down the middle is the Vanquish, a car that has the looks, performance, and competence of a true sports car, while offering enough luxury to call into question its sporting nature. While capable on a racetrack, this Aston is more comfortable in high-performance cruising, transporting its occupants in the utmost style and comfort.

While the Volvo S60R is the outward expression of Edward's inner personality, the silver Aston Martin is more the automotive equivalent to the story's hero. While technically a sports car, the British-made Aston is the proper gentleman of the group, just as the Ferrari F430 is the cocky hero. Made in true British style, every ounce of this car alludes to old-world money, power, and manners. The Vanquish stands as a supreme offering from the sports-car world for the reserved driver.

EDWARD'S ASTON
MARTIN V12
VANQUISH

"IT WAS ANOTHER CAR—A STANDOUT EVEN IN THE
LONG LINE OF VEHICLES THAT WERE MOSTLY ALL
DROOL-WORTHY IN THEIR OWN WAYS."
—Jacob (*Breaking Dawn*, Chapter 17)

ROSALIE'S BMW M3
CONVERTIBLE

ROSALIE: BMW M3 CONVERTIBLE

COLOR: Red
ENGINE: 3.2-liter Inline 6
HORSEPOWER: 333 hp at 7900 rpm
TORQUE: 262 ft.-lbs. at 4900 rpm
REDLINE: 8000 rpm
0–60: 4.8 seconds

Rosalie's choice of car is limited by the necessity to seat her siblings. Though her personality is best captured by a Lamborghini Murcielago, the M3 represents the most extreme sports car that can fit her constraints. The BMW M3 is recognized as one of the best all-around sports cars in the world. While Edward's S60R has an all-wheel-drive advantage, and certain offerings from Mercedes-Benz outpower the bimmer, the M3 is recognized as a purist sports car, providing greater driving feel than nearly anything on the road.

With a front-biased weight distribution, rear-wheel drive, and aggressive dry-weather treaded tires, the M3 is not an ideal choice for wet-weather, high-speed driving. These factors, however, are outweighed by its dry-weather performance. And, of course, how good it looks in red.

EMMETT: JEEP WRANGLER

COLOR: Red
ENGINE: 5.7-liter V8
HORSEPOWER: 400 hp
TORQUE: 600 ft.-lbs.
0–60: 4.5 seconds

Emmett's Jeep started life as a 4.0-liter inline 6-powered Wrangler Rubicon. That quickly changed in Rosalie's hands, as the brand-new engine was tossed in favor of a heavily modified Chevrolet small-block V8. Every piece of the already new and capable suspension was replaced to provide several inches of lift and enough strength to take anything the Washington terrain can throw at it.

The bulletproof power train features a five-speed manual transmission, a 4:1 low-range transfer case, 4.10 differential gears, and Dana 44 axles front and rear. Coupled with the high-torque small block, this setup allows Emmett to scale

EMMETT'S JEEP
WRANGLER

"THERE, BEHIND MY TRUCK, WAS
A MONSTER JEEP. ITS TIRES WERE
HIGHER THAN MY WAIST."
—Bella (*Twilight*, Chapter 17)

slopes that send other four-wheel-drive vehicles looking for friendlier routes.

Not satisfied with mechanical superiority, Rosalie added everything from massive KC lights to aggressively treaded all-terrain tires to safety harnesses. All of these modifications create a Jeep that is not only the most capable off-road vehicle money can buy, but one that looks equally menacing, acting as the automotive equivalent to the character whose immense strength is easily seen.

ALICE: PORSCHE 911 TURBO

COLOR: Yellow
ENGINE: 3.6-liter Flat 6
HORSEPOWER: 415 hp at 6000 rpm
TORQUE: 415 ft.-lbs. at 2700 rpm
0–60: 4.0 seconds

When a fast car is needed to negotiate the tight and often twisting roads of the Italian countryside, Alice turns to, or rather steals, the Porsche 911 turbo. While beautiful, the 911 turbo bears a striking resemblance to its siblings, the base 911 Carreras. Should onlookers miss the large side scoop air intake or the wider body stance over the rear wheels, the turbo could be mistaken for a car not nearly as capable. The 911 turbo is nimble and balanced, making the most of its turbocharged engine by sending power to all four wheels through a complicated all-wheel-drive system. Performing better than even its numbers would suggest, this high-performance 911 variant was engineered on the racetrack, and every piece was purpose-built to allow it to pass much more powerful and expensive cars. Porsche engineers focused on the entire package, ensuring that the engine, suspension,

"A BRIGHT YELLOW PORSCHE SCREAMED TO A STOP A FEW
FEET IN FRONT OF WHERE I PACED, THE WORD *TURBO*
SCRAWLED IN SILVER CURSIVE ACROSS ITS BACK. EVERYONE
BESIDE ME ON THE CROWDED AIRPORT SIDEWALK STARED."
—Bella (*New Moon*, Chapter 19)

brakes, tires, and every other piece of the puzzle fit together seamlessly.

It is fitting that Alice would fall in love with this car, which offers the same characteristics that she possesses. The Porsche is generally the smallest in the exotic race, offering fewer cylinders and less power in a package that is seemingly less race inspired, yet its subsequent agility allows it to beat its flashier competitors.

JASPER: DUCATI 848

COLOR: Silver

ENGINE: 849-cc V-twin

HORSEPOWER: 134 hp at 10000 rpm

TORQUE: 72 ft.-lbs. at 8400 rpm

0–60: 4.5 seconds

Edward's motorcycle of choice, which he gave to Jasper, is a stark contrast to those belonging to Bella and Jacob. The Ducati 848 is a lightweight, high-powered street bike designed to out-accelerate and outmaneuver all things automotive. This sport bike is the lighter Ducati, offering increased agility compared to its heavier, higher-powered siblings.

Easily going beyond most drivers' capabilities, this bike is ideally suited for a vampire's quickened reflexes, as it requires constant attention to minute angles and positions. This is one of the very few vehicles in the novels that can perform to the level vampires demand, acting as an extension of their natural faculties.

JASPER'S
DUCATI 848

"TO CALL THIS OTHER VEHICLE A MOTORCYCLE HARDLY
SEEMED FAIR. . . . IT WAS BIG AND SLEEK AND SILVER
AND — EVEN TOTALLY MOTIONLESS — IT LOOKED FAST."
—Bella (*Eclipse*, Chapter 10)

BELLA: CHEVROLET PICKUP TRUCK

COLOR: Red
ENGINE: 216.5-cubic-inch Inline 6 cylinder
HORSEPOWER: 92 hp at 3400 rpm
TORQUE: 176 ft.-lbs. at 1000 rpm

The main automotive character in the Twilight Saga is the 1953 reddish Chevrolet pickup truck driven by Bella. As the highest-selling truck for its entire eight-year run (1947–1954), this post–World War II Advance Design Series truck is still common enough to be found in its original condition. With its stock engine churning out a robust 92 horsepower and a three-speed manual transmission powering just the rear wheels, it is easy to understand Jacob's joy in his father's sale of this truck. Not fast even by standards of its day, Bella's '53 did, however, boast state-of-the-art features for the time, such as a fresh-air heater system and a larger, two-piece windshield for increased visibility.

BELLA'S CHEVY
PICKUP TRUCK

"IT WAS A FADED RED COLOR, WITH BIG, ROUNDED
FENDERS AND A BULBOUS CAB. TO MY INTENSE
SURPRISE, I LOVED IT. I DIDN'T KNOW IF IT WOULD
RUN, BUT I COULD SEE MYSELF IN IT."
—Bella (*Twilight*, Chapter 1)

As the most simplistic car with perhaps the most unique styling and driving character, this vehicle correctly identifies with the main character, serving as a vehicular analogy to give readers an increased understanding of Bella's personality.

BELLA: MERCEDES GUARDIAN

COLOR: Black
ENGINE: 5.5-liter twin turbo V12
HORSEPOWER: 469 hp at 6100 rpm
TORQUE: 516 ft.-lbs. at 2650 rpm
0–60: 4.6 seconds

While some of its features are based on the actual Mercedes S600 Guard, the Mercedes Guardian does not exist in reality and is the only fictional car in the Twilight Saga. As its name suggests, the focus of Edward's choice for Bella's pre-vampiric conversion was entirely on safety. Built from the ground up with protection in mind, the car offers its occupants security

BELLA'S MERCEDES
GUARDIAN

"BECAUSE I WAS SO FRAGILELY HUMAN, SO ACCIDENT-PRONE, SO MUCH
A VICTIM TO MY OWN DANGEROUS BAD LUCK, APPARENTLY I NEEDED A
TANK-RESISTANT CAR TO KEEP ME SAFE. HILARIOUS."
—Bella (*Breaking Dawn*, Chapter 1)

from everything that automotive engineers could dream up. Armor designed to resist military-standard small-arms projectiles, hand-grenade fragments, and various other explosive charges lies beneath the car's skin, while run-flat tires, a self-sealing fuel tank, and a fire-extinguishing system allow the driver to get out of bad situations. Should assailants switch to a gaseous attack, the Guardian provides occupants with a fresh oxygen supply while completely sealing off the car from all outside air. No doubt understanding Bella's limited human reflexes, Edward would also have welcomed the car's driving aids, including everything from night vision to electronic brake distribution.

This car highlights the inherent differences in how Edward views Bella and how Bella views herself. Bella is content with her seat belt–lacking Chevy, while Edward puts her in a car generally reserved for land mine–avoiding oil sheiks, sparing no effort, or expense, to protect her in every way possible.

BELLA: FERRARI F430

COLOR: Red
ENGINE: 4.3-liter V8
HORSEPOWER: 483 hp at 8500 rpm
TORQUE: 343 ft.-lbs. at 5250 rpm
0–60: 3.5 seconds

The Ferrari F430, hidden until after Bella transforms, is the most stand-out car of the series. This car choice was unencumbered by the normal compromises necessary in the characters' car decisions. The Ferrari F430 is the pinnacle of sports-car engineering. Though many ultra exotics have a higher price tag, this car outperforms almost all. In addition, the car's beautifully defined lines and curves remind the viewer more

BELLA'S
FERRARI F430

"I HADN'T
SEEN THE
'AFTER' CAR YET.
IT WAS HIDDEN
UNDER A SHEET IN THE
DEEPEST CORNER OF THE
CULLENS' GARAGE. I KNEW
MOST PEOPLE WOULD HAVE PEEKED BY
NOW, BUT I REALLY DIDN'T WANT TO KNOW."
—Bella (*Breaking Dawn*, Chapter 1)

of classical Italian sculpture than anything related to trans-
portation. Though it plays only a minor role in the books, it
identifies Edward's true feelings for Bella. The majority of
the cars in the series show Edward as overly obsessed with her
safety, but small moments, like revealing the identity of this
car, show that his feelings for Bella are much more involved
than just a need to protect her.

JACOB: VOLKSWAGEN RABBIT

COLOR: Red
ENGINE: 1.8-liter Inline 4
HORSEPOWER: 90 hp at 5500 rpm
TORQUE: 107 ft.-lbs.
0–60: 10.5 seconds

Perhaps the most obtainable vehicle in the series, Jacob's daily
driver is the cult classic Volkswagen Rabbit. With a modest

1.8-liter engine offering just 90 horsepower when it was originally rolling off the factory line, before Jacob was born, this car's force of acceleration is not its strong suit. The lightweight front driver makes up for this, though, with remarkably communicative steering, engaging the driver without the use of massive amounts of tire-shredding power.

The VW Rabbit has been accepted by car nuts since its inception as an easily modded driver's car. It was the most attractive option for Jacob, with its low cost of entry, ease of repair, and fun return on investment. While worth less than a wheel from Edward's Aston Martin, the Rabbit is still capable of putting the same smile on Jacob's face.

Highlighting the accessible nature of Jacob's character, this car proves that driving enjoyment does not require hundreds of thousands of dollars and looks to match the price tag. Jacob shows himself as equally endearing despite constant comparisons to Bella's perfect vampire love.

JACOB'S
VOLKSWAGEN RABBIT

"IT'S AN OLD RABBIT — 1986, A CLASSIC."
—Jacob (*New Moon*, Chapter 5)

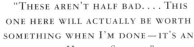

Jacob's
Harley Sprint

Jacob and Bella:
Harley Sprint/Honda XL250

COLOR: Black/red
ENGINE: 1-cylinder 250-cc 4-stroke
HORSEPOWER: 50 hp at 10,000 rpm/24 hp

These are two motorcycles that were nursed back to life by
Jacob. Despite their origins an ocean apart, these two-wheeled
vehicles have striking similarities.

Bearing little resemblance to the Harleys of today, the
Sprint was offered under the Harley name after the manufac-
turer bought a 50-percent stake in a small Italian motorcycle
firm. The motorcycle was offered as competition to the tech-
nologically superior Japanese motorcycles that were beginning
to gain popularity in America. The Sprint was developed with
motorcycle racing in mind, and offered impressive performance from the 4-stroke engine.

The 1-cylinder engine allowed the bike to be made with relative simplicity, which meant the mechanically minded, though inexperienced, Jacob would be able to bring the dying bike to life.

Bella's Honda was similar to Jacob's Harley in a number of respects. A 250-cc 1-cylinder, making power through the then less than common 4-stroke cycle, pulled the bike on road or dirt. Designed as less of a racer than the Harley Sprint, the XL250 was a more well-rounded bike, ready for any ground conditions it might encounter.

BELLA'S
HONDA
XL250

"WHEN I WALKED INTO THE GARAGE, I WAS SHOCKED
TO SEE THE RED BIKE STANDING UP, LOOKING LIKE A
MOTORCYCLE RATHER THAN A PILE OF JAGGED METAL.
'JAKE, YOU'RE AMAZING,' I BREATHED."
—Bella (*New Moon*, Chapter 7)

Inspirations

THE TWILIGHT SAGA PLAYLIST

*E*xplaining a playlist — especially in writing — is a problem. I've tried to do it before, and what comes out is a lot of "this goes here" and "that goes there." Not exciting to read, but still, people want to know where a certain song fits into the story, and what it means to the characters. So what I've done is assign a quote from the series to each song. This will give you the general location of the song, and the specific feeling or issue I was thinking of while listening. I hear all of the songs from Bella's perspective, except where otherwise noted. In a few cases (like "Sing for Absolution" on the **New Moon** playlist) the song is part of a situation that is taking place "offscreen," so to speak. In those cases, I've tried to find a quote that identifies the situation even though Bella's not around to see it.

Twilight

1. TRAVIS, "WHY DOES IT ALWAYS RAIN ON ME?"

Chapter 1 When I landed in Port Angeles, it was raining. I didn't see it as an omen — just unavoidable. I'd already said my goodbyes to the sun.

2. RADIOHEAD, "CREEP" [RADIO EDIT]

Chapter 4 My stomach twisted as I realized what he must have meant. He must see how absorbed I was by him; he must not want to lead me on ... so we couldn't even be friends . . . because he wasn't interested in me at all.

Of course he wasn't interested in me, I thought angrily, my eyes stinging — a delayed reaction to the onions. I wasn't *interesting*. And he was. Interesting ... and brilliant ... and mysterious ...

and perfect… and beautiful… and possibly able to lift full-sized vans with one hand.

Well, that was fine. I could leave him alone. I *would* leave him alone. I would get through my self-imposed sentence here in purgatory, and then hopefully some school in the Southwest, or possibly Hawaii, would offer me a scholarship.

3. COLDPLAY, "IN MY PLACE"
Chapter 5   "I decided as long as I was going to hell, I might as well do it thoroughly."

4. MY CHEMICAL ROMANCE, "I'M NOT OKAY (I PROMISE)"
Chapter 5   "What if I'm not a superhero? What if I'm the bad guy?"

5. LINKIN PARK, "WITH YOU" {REANIMATION REMIX}
Chapter 7   And I knew in that I had my answer. I didn't know if there ever was a choice, really. I was already in too deep. Now that I knew — if I knew — I could do nothing about my frightening secret. Because when I thought of him, of his voice, his hypnotic eyes, the magnetic force of his personality, I wanted nothing more than to be with him right now.

6. LINKIN PARK, "BY MYSELF"
Chapter 8   It seemed to take forever for me to get to the corner. I kept my pace steady, the men behind me falling ever so slightly farther behind with every step. Maybe they realized they had scared me and were sorry. I saw two cars going north pass the intersection I was heading for, and I exhaled in relief. There would be more people around once I got off this deserted street. I skipped around the corner with a grateful sigh.

And skidded to a stop.

The street was lined on both sides by blank, doorless, windowless walls. I could see in the distance, two intersections down, streetlamps, cars, and more pedestrians, but they were all too far away. Because lounging against the western building, midway down the street, were the other two men from the group, both watching with excited smiles as I froze dead on the sidewalk. I realized then that I wasn't being followed.

I was being herded.

7. OMD, "DREAMING"

Chapter 12 He was too perfect, I realized with a piercing stab of despair. There was no way this godlike creature could be meant for me.

He stared at me, bewildered by my tortured expression.

"Do you want to go home?" he said quietly, a different pain than mine saturating his voice.

"No." I walked forward till I was close beside him, anxious not to waste one second of whatever time I might have with him.

8. DAVID GRAY, "PLEASE FORGIVE ME"

Chapter 13 "Be very still," he whispered, as if I wasn't already frozen.

Slowly, never moving his eyes from mine, he leaned toward me. Then abruptly, but very gently, he rested his cold cheek against the hollow at the base of my throat. I was quite unable to move, even if I'd wanted to. I listened to the sound of his even breathing, watching the sun and wind play in his bronze hair, more human than any other part of him.

With deliberate slowness, his hands slid down the sides of my neck. I shivered, and I heard him catch his breath. But his hands didn't pause as they softly moved to my shoulders, and then stopped.

His face drifted to the side, his nose skimming across my collarbone. He came to rest with the side of his face pressed tenderly against my chest.

Listening to my heart.

"Ah," he sighed.

"Music is my one necessary tool. I put on music that fits the mood of what I'm writing, to help me stay in the zone and get the emotional tone right."

— Stephenie

9. DIDO, "HERE WITH ME"

Chapter 15 "I love you," I whispered.

"You are my life now," he answered simply.

There was nothing more to say for the moment. He rocked us back and forth as the room grew lighter.

10. MUSE, "TIME IS RUNNING OUT"

Chapter 21 Slowly, slowly, my thoughts started to break past that brick wall of pain. To plan. For I had no choices now but one: to go to the mirrored room and die. I had no guarantees, nothing to give to keep my mother alive. I could only hope that James would be satisfied with winning the game, that beating Edward would be enough. Despair gripped me; there was no way to bargain, nothing I could offer or withhold that could influence him. But I still had no choice. I had to try.

I pushed the terror back as well as I could. My decision was made. It did no good to waste time agonizing over the outcome. I had to think clearly, because Alice and Jasper were waiting for me, and evading them was absolutely essential, and absolutely impossible.

11. COLLECTIVE SOUL, "TREMBLE FOR MY BELOVED"

Chapter 24 "You don't know what you're asking." His voice was soft; he stared intently at the edge of the pillowcase.

"I think I do."

"Bella, you don't know. I've had almost ninety years to think about this, and I'm still not sure."

12. THE CRANBERRIES, "DREAMS"

Chapter 24 "I'll be the first to admit that I have no experience with relationships," I said. "But it just seems logical . . . a man and woman have to be somewhat equal . . . as in, one of them can't always be swooping in and saving the other one. They have to save each other equally."

He folded his arms on the side of my bed and rested his chin on his arms. His expression was smooth, the anger reined in. Evidently he'd decided he wasn't angry with me. I hoped I'd get a chance to warn Alice before he caught up with her.

"You *have* saved me," he said quietly.

"I can't always be Lois Lane," I insisted. "I want to be Superman, too."

13. BILLY JOEL, "LULLABY (GOODNIGHT, MY ANGEL)"

Epilogue "I love you more than everything else in the world combined. Isn't that enough?"

"Yes, it is enough," he answered, smiling. "Enough for forever."

And he leaned down to press his cold lips once more to my throat.

New Moon

1. THE FLAMING LIPS, "DO YOU REALIZE"

Chapter 1 I'd been dreading this day for months.

All through the perfect summer — the happiest summer I had ever had, the happiest summer anyone anywhere had ever had, and the rainiest summer in the history of the Olympic Peninsula — this bleak date had lurked in ambush, waiting to spring.

And now that it had hit, it was even worse than I'd feared it would be. I could feel it — I was older. Every day I got older, but this was different, worse, quantifiable. I was eighteen.

And Edward never would be.

2. LINKIN PARK, "PAPERCUT"

Chapter 1 Dazed and disoriented, I looked up from the bright red blood pulsing out of my arm — into the fevered eyes of the six suddenly ravenous vampires.

3. MUSE, "HYPER MUSIC"

Chapter 3 "You...don't...want me?" I tried out the words, confused by the way they sounded, placed in that order.

"No."

I stared, uncomprehending, into his eyes. He stared back without apology. His eyes were like topaz — hard and clear and very deep. I felt like I could see into them for miles and miles, yet nowhere in their bottomless depths could I see a contradiction to the word he'd spoken.

4. MUSE, "APOCALYPSE PLEASE"

Chapter 3 With shaky legs, ignoring the fact that my action was useless, I followed him into the forest. The evidence of his path had disappeared instantly. There were no footprints, the leaves were still again, but I walked forward without thinking. I could not do anything else. I had to keep moving. If I stopped looking for him, it was over.

5. THE ALL-AMERICAN REJECTS, "TIME STANDS STILL"

Chapter 4 Time passes. Even when it seems impossible. Even when each tick of the second hand aches like the pulse of blood behind a bruise. It passes unevenly, in strange lurches and dragging lulls, but pass it does. Even for me.

6. MARJORIE FAIR, "EMPTY ROOM"

Chapter 4 I sat down on the bench outside the theater door and tried very hard not to think of the irony. But it was ironic, all things considered, that, in the end, I would wind up as a zombie. I hadn't seen that one coming.

Not that I hadn't dreamed of becoming a mythical monster once — just never a grotesque, animated corpse. I shook my head to dislodge that train of thought, feeling panicky. I couldn't afford to think about what I'd once dreamed of.

It was depressing to realize that I wasn't the heroine anymore, that my story was over.

7. MATCHBOX TWENTY, "UNWELL"

Chapter 6 Charlie stared at me during breakfast, and I tried to ignore him. I supposed I deserved it. I couldn't expect him not to worry. It would probably be weeks before he stopped watching for the return of the zombie, and I would just have to try to not let it bother me. After all, I would be watching for the return of the zombie, too. Two days was hardly long enough to call me cured.

Not that I hadn't dreamed of becoming a mythical monster once — just never a grotesque, animated corpse.

8. JIMMY EAT WORLD, "PAIN"

Chapter 7 I turned my back on the gaping emptiness and hurried to my truck. I nearly ran. I was anxious to be gone, to get back to the human world. I felt hideously empty, and I wanted to see Jacob. Maybe I was developing a new kind of sickness, another addiction, like the numbness before. I didn't care. I pushed my truck as fast as it would go as I barreled toward my fix.

9. THE VINES, "RIDE"

Chapter 8 I'd left my stomach back at the starting point; the adrenaline coursed through my body, tingling in my veins.

10. COLDPLAY, "FIX YOU"

Jacob's perspective

Chapter 9 "It's just that, I know how you're unhappy a lot. And, maybe it doesn't help anything, but I wanted you to know that I'm always here. I won't ever let you down—I promise that you can always count on me. Wow, that does sound corny. But you know that, right? That I would never, ever hurt you?"

11. ROONEY, "BLUESIDE"

Chapter 9 I was in deeper than I'd planned to go with anyone again. Now I couldn't bear for him to be hurt, and I couldn't keep from hurting him, either. He thought time and patience would change me, and, though I knew he was dead wrong, I also knew that I would let him try.

He was my best friend. I would always love him, and it would never, ever be enough.

12. THE FRAY, "OVER MY HEAD (CABLE CAR)"

Chapter 11 I'd thought Jake had been healing the hole in me—or at least plugging it up, keeping it from hurting me so much. I'd been wrong. He'd just been carving out his own hole, so that I was now riddled through like Swiss cheese.

13. EVANESCENCE, "GOING UNDER"

Chapter 15 I smiled and raised my arms straight out, as if I were going to dive, lifting my face into the rain. But it was too ingrained from years of swimming at the public pool—feet first, first time. I leaned forward, crouching to get more spring. . . .

And I flung myself off the cliff.

14. BRAND NEW, "TAUTOU"

Chapter 15 My ears were flooded with the freezing water, but his voice was clearer than ever. I ignored his words and concentrated on the sound of his voice. Why would I fight when I was so happy where I was? Even as my lungs burned for more air and my legs cramped in the icy cold, I was content. I'd forgotten what real happiness felt like.

Happiness. It made the whole dying thing pretty bearable.

15. RELIENT K, "BE MY ESCAPE"

Chapter 16 What if Paris had been Juliet's friend? Her very best friend? What if he was the only one she could confide in about the whole devastating thing with Romeo? The one person who really understood her and made her feel halfway human again? What if he was patient and kind? What if he took care of her? What if Juliet knew she couldn't survive without him? What if he really loved her, and wanted her to be happy?

And...what if she loved Paris? Not like Romeo. Nothing like that, of course. But enough that she wanted him to be happy, too?

Jacob's slow, deep breathing was the only sound in the room—like a lullaby hummed to a child, like the whisper of a rocking chair, like the ticking of an old clock when you had nowhere you needed to go. . . . It was the sound of comfort.

If Romeo was really gone, never coming back, would it have mattered whether or not Juliet had taken Paris up on his offer? Maybe she should have tried to settle into the leftover scraps of life that were left behind. Maybe that would have been as close to happiness as she could get.

16. THE VERVE PIPE, "NEVER LET YOU DOWN"

Chapter 16 "I know you don't feel exactly the way I do, Bells. I swear I don't mind. I'm just so glad you're okay that I could sing—and that's something no one wants to hear." He laughed his throaty laugh in my ear.

17. MUSE, "SING FOR ABSOLUTION"

Edward's perspective

Chapter 18 "I saw him going to the Volturi...and asking to die."

18. FATBOY SLIM, "YA MAMMA"

Chapter 20 She drove in quick spurts and sudden stops, and the people in the crowd shook their fists at us and said angry words that I was glad I couldn't understand. She turned onto a little path that couldn't have been meant for cars; shocked people had to squeeze into doorways as we scraped by. We found another street at the end. The buildings were taller here; they leaned together overhead so that no sunlight touched the pavement — the thrashing red flags on either side nearly met. The crowd was thicker here than anywhere else. Alice stopped the car. I had the door open before we were at a standstill.

She pointed to where the street widened into a patch of bright openness. "There — we're at the southern end of the square. Run straight across, to the right of the clock tower. I'll find a way around — "

Her breath caught suddenly, and when she spoke again, her voice was a hiss. "They're *everywhere*!"

I froze in place, but she pushed me out of the car. "Forget about them. You have two minutes. Go, Bella, go!" she shouted, climbing out of the car as she spoke.

I didn't pause to watch Alice melt into the shadows. I didn't stop to close my door behind me. I shoved a heavy woman out of my way and ran flat out, head down, paying little attention to anything but the uneven stones beneath my feet.

19. FOO FIGHTERS, "DOA"

Chapter 20 I wished I could ask him exactly what was going to happen now. I wanted desperately to know how we were going to die — as if that would somehow make it better, knowing in advance.

20. MARJORIE FAIR, "STARE"

Chapter 22 I couldn't keep my eyes off of Edward's face for long. I stared at him, wishing more than anything that the future would never happen. That this moment would last forever, or, if it couldn't, that I would stop existing when it did.

Edward stared right back at me, his dark eyes soft, and it was easy to pretend that he felt the same way. So that's what I did. I pretended, to make the moment sweeter.

21. COLDPLAY, "THE SCIENTIST"

Edward's perspective

Chapter 23 "You weren't going to let go," he whispered. "I could see that. I didn't want to do it — it felt like it would kill me to do it — but I knew that if I couldn't convince you that I didn't love you anymore, it would just take you that much longer to get on with your life. I hoped that, if you thought I'd moved on, so would you."

"A clean break," I whispered through unmoving lips.

"Exactly. But I never imagined it would be so easy to do! I thought it would be next to impossible — that you would be so sure of the truth that I would have to lie through my teeth for hours to even plant the seed of doubt in your head. I lied, and I'm so sorry — sorry because I hurt you, sorry because it was a worthless effort. Sorry that I couldn't protect you from what I am. I lied to save you, and it didn't work. I'm sorry."

22. SUGARCULT, "MEMORY"

Chapter 23 "Don't promise me anything," I whispered. If I let myself hope, and it came to nothing . . . that would kill me. Where all those merciless vampires had not been able to finish me off, hope would do the job.

23. ARMOR FOR SLEEP, "THE TRUTH ABOUT HEAVEN"

Edward's perspective

Chapter 23 "Before you, Bella, my life was like a moonless night. Very dark, but there were stars — points of light and reason. . . . And then you shot across my sky like a meteor. Suddenly everything was on fire; there was brilliancy, there was beauty. When you were gone, when the meteor had fallen over the horizon, everything went black. Nothing had changed, but my eyes were blinded by the light. I couldn't see the stars anymore. And there was no more reason for anything."

24. BLUE OCTOBER, "SOUND OF PULLING HEAVEN DOWN"

Edward's and Bella's perspectives

Chapter 24 "Your epiphany?" he asked, his voice uneven and strained.

"You love me," I marveled. The sense of conviction and rightness washed through me again.

Though his eyes were still anxious, the crooked smile I loved best flashed across his face. "Truly, I do."

My heart inflated like it was going to crack right through my ribs. It filled my chest and blocked my throat so that I could not speak.

New Moon ALTERNATES

1. PLACEBO, "DRAG"

Chapter 3 The last was the picture of Edward and me standing awkwardly side by side. Edward's face was the same as the last, cold and statue-like. But that wasn't the most troubling part of this photograph. The contrast between the two of us was painful. He looked like a god. I looked very average, even for a human, almost shamefully plain. I flipped the picture over with a feeling of disgust.

2. BLUE OCTOBER, "HATE ME" {RADIO EDIT}

Edward's perspective

Chapter 3 "Bella, I don't want you to come with me." He spoke the words slowly and precisely, his cold eyes on my face, watching as I absorbed what he was really saying.

There was a pause as I repeated the words in my head a few times, sifting through them for their real intent.

"You . . . don't . . . want me?" I tried out the words, confused by the way they sounded, placed in that order.

"No."

I stared, uncomprehending, into his eyes. He stared back without apology. His eyes were like topaz — hard and clear and very deep. I felt like I could see into them for miles and miles, yet nowhere in their bottomless depths could I see a contradiction to the word he'd spoken.

3. WEEZER, "THE WORLD HAS TURNED AND LEFT ME HERE"

Chapter 4 The thick haze that blurred my days now was sometimes confusing. I was surprised when I found myself in my room, not clearly remembering the drive home from school or even opening the front door. But that didn't matter. Losing track of time was the most I asked from life.

4. VERTICAL HORIZON, "BEST I EVER HAD"

Chapter 5   I wondered how long this could last. Maybe someday, years from now—if the pain would just decrease to the point where I could bear it—I would be able to look back on those few short months that would always be the best of my life. And, if it were possible that the pain would ever soften enough to allow me to do that, I was sure that I would feel grateful for as much time as he'd given me. More than I'd asked for, more than I'd deserved. Maybe someday I'd be able to see it that way.

> The contrast between the two of us was painful. He looked like a god. I looked very average, even for a human, almost shamefully plain.

5. EVANESCENCE, "MY IMMORTAL"

Chapter 5   *As if he'd never existed,* I thought in despair. What a stupid and impossible promise to make! He could steal my pictures and reclaim his gifts, but that didn't put things back the way they'd been before I'd met him. The physical evidence was the most insignificant part of the equation. I was changed, my insides altered almost past the point of recognition.

6. KEANE, "EVERYBODY'S CHANGING"

Chapter 6   I was beginning to get annoyed with myself. I might as well have been packed in Styrofoam peanuts through the last semester.

7. AUDIOSLAVE, "LIKE A STONE"

Chapter 7   I didn't go any closer. I didn't want to look in the windows. I wasn't sure which would be harder to see. If the rooms were bare, echoing empty from floor to ceiling, that would certainly hurt. Like my grandmother's funeral, when my mother had insisted that I stay outside during the viewing. She had said that I didn't need to see Gran that way, to remember her that way, rather than alive.

But wouldn't it be worse if there were no change? If the couches sat just as I'd last seen them, the paintings on the walls—worse still, the piano on its low platform? It would be second only to the house disappearing all together, to see that there was no physical possession that tied them in anyway. That everything remained, untouched and forgotten, behind them.

Just like me.

8. U2, "STUCK IN A MOMENT YOU CAN'T GET OUT OF"
Chapter 7 I'd come full circle, and now everything felt like an echo—an empty echo, devoid of the interest it used to have.

9. SALIVA, "REST IN PIECES"
Chapter 9 How could I explain so that he would understand? I was an empty shell. Like a vacant house—condemned—for months I'd been utterly uninhabitable. Now I was a little improved. The front room was in better repair. But that was all—just the one small piece. He deserved better than that—better than a one-room, falling-down fixer-upper. No amount of investment on his part could put me back in working order.

10. COLLECTIVE SOUL, "NOT THE ONE"
Chapter 13 "Is that what happened? Why the Cullens left?"

"I'm nothing but a human, after all. Nothing special," I explained, shrugging weakly.

11. BLINK 182, "I MISS YOU"
Chapter 15 "Bella."

I smiled and exhaled.

Yes? I didn't answer out loud, for fear that the sound of my voice would shatter the beautiful illusion. He sounded so real, so close. It was only when he was disapproving like this that I could hear the true memory of his voice—the velvet texture and the musical intonation that made up the most perfect of all voices.

"Don't do this," he pleaded.

You wanted me to be human, I reminded him. *Well, watch me.*

"Please. For me."

"I'm nothing but a human, after all. Nothing special."

But you won't stay with me any other way.

"Please." It was just a whisper in the blowing rain that tossed my hair and drenched my clothes—making me as wet as if this were my second jump of the day.

12. MUSE, "UNINTENDED"

Chapter 16   I couldn't imagine my life without Jacob now—I cringed away from the idea of even trying to imagine that. Somehow, he'd become essential to my survival. But to leave things the way they were... was that cruel, as Mike had accused?

I remembered wishing that Jacob were my brother. I realized now that all I really wanted was a claim on him. It didn't feel brotherly when he held me like this. It just felt nice—warm and comforting and familiar. Safe. Jacob was a safe harbor.

I could stake a claim. I had that much within my power.

13. DIDO, "WHITE FLAG"

Chapter 20   I'd never seen anything more beautiful—even as I ran, gasping and screaming, I could appreciate that. And the last seven months meant nothing. And his words in the forest meant nothing. And it did not matter if he did not want me. I would never want anything but him, no matter how long I lived.

> I would never want anything but him, no matter how long I lived.

14. HOOBASTANK, "THE REASON"

Edward's perspective

Chapter 23   "I only left you in the first place because I wanted you to have a chance at a normal, happy, human life. I could see what I was doing to you—keeping you constantly on the edge of danger, taking you away from the world you belonged in, risking your life every moment I was with you. So I had to try. I had to do something, and it seemed like leaving was the only way. If I hadn't thought you would be better off, I could have never made myself leave. I'm much too selfish. Only you could be more important than what I wanted... what I needed. What I want and need is to be with you, and I know I'll never be strong enough to leave again."

Eclipse

1. ELBOW, "MEXICAN STANDOFF"

Jacob's perspective

Chapter 1 "What part of 'mortal enemies' is too complicated for you...?"

2. COLDPLAY, "CLOCKS"

Chapter 1 "I thought the timing was still undecided," Edward reminded me softly. "You might enjoy a semester or two of college. There are a lot of human experiences you've never had."

"I'll get to those afterward."

"They won't be *human* experiences afterward. You don't get a second chance at humanity, Bella."

3. BLUE OCTOBER, "OVERWEIGHT" [RADIO EDIT]

Jacob's perspective

Chapter 1 "Please just listen for a minute. This is so much more important than some whim to drop in on an old friend. Jacob is in pain." My voice distorted around the word. "I can't not try to help him—I can't give up on him now, when he needs me. Just because he's not human all the time... Well, he was there for me when I was... not so human myself. You don't know what it was like...." I hesitated. Edward's arms were rigid around me; his hands were in fists now, the tendons standing out. "If Jacob hadn't helped me... I'm not sure what you would have come home to. I owe him better than this, Edward."

"If Jacob hadn't helped me... I'm not sure what you would have come home to. I owe him better than this, Edward."

4. KEANE, "HAMBURG SONG"

Jacob's perspective

Chapter 3 Jacob dropped the antagonistic façade completely. It was like he'd forgotten Edward was there, or at least he was determined to act that way. "I miss you every day, Bella. It's not the same without you."

5. THE ALL-AMERICAN REJECTS, "STAB MY BACK"

Jacob's perspective

Chapter 8 "Don't worry about me," he insisted, smiling with deliberate cheer, too brightly. "I know what I'm doing. Just tell me if I'm upsetting you."

6. MUSE, "THE SMALL PRINT"

Jacob's perspective

Chapter 8 "Will you never forgive me, Jacob?" I whispered. As soon as I said the words, I wished I hadn't. I didn't want to hear his answer.

"You won't be Bella anymore," he told me. "My friend won't exist. There'll be no one to forgive."

7. THE KILLERS, "MR. BRIGHTSIDE"

Edward's perspective

Chapter 10 As I turned away from him, I thought I saw a flash of something in his eyes that I wasn't supposed to see. I couldn't tell for sure what it was exactly. Worry, maybe. For a second I thought it was panic. But I was probably just making something out of nothing, as usual.

Chapter 22 "The jealousy . . . it has to be eating at you. You can't be as sure of yourself as you seem. Unless you have no emotions at all."

"Of course it is," Edward agreed, no longer amused. "Right now it's so bad that I can barely control my voice. Of course, it's even worse when she's away from me, with you, and I can't see her."

"Do you think about it all the time?" Jacob whispered. "Does it make it hard to concentrate when she's not with you?"

"Yes and no," Edward said; he seemed determined to answer honestly. "My mind doesn't work quite the same as yours. I can think of many more things at one time. Of course, that means that I'm always able to think of you, always able to wonder if that's where her mind is, when she's quiet and thoughtful."

8. MUSE, "NEWBORN"

Chapter 13 "Benito had created an army of newborn vampires. He was the first one to think of it, and, in the beginning, he was unstoppable. Very young vampires are volatile, wild, and almost impossible to control. One newborn can be reasoned with, taught to restrain himself, but ten, fifteen together are a nightmare."

9. THE MAGIC NUMBERS, "LOVE ME LIKE YOU"

Jacob's and Edward's perspectives

Chapter 15 "One more thing," Edward said slowly. "I'll be fighting for her, too. You should know that. I'm not taking anything for granted, and I'll be fighting twice as hard as you will."

"Good," Jacob growled. "It's no fun beating someone who forfeits."

"She is mine." Edward's low voice was suddenly dark, not as composed as before. "I didn't say I would fight fair."

"Neither did I."

10. DASHBOARD CONFESSIONAL, "VINDICATED"

Jacob's perspective

Chapter 21 He laughed with me, and then his eyes were sad. "When are you finally going to figure out that you're in love with me, too?"

"Leave it to you to ruin the moment."

"I'm not saying you don't love him. I'm not stupid. But it's possible to love more than one person at a time, Bella. I've seen it in action."

11. MUSE, "HYSTERIA"

Chapter 23 My brain disconnected from my body, and I was kissing him back. Against all reason, my lips were moving with his in strange, confusing ways they'd never moved before—because I didn't have to be careful with Jacob, and he certainly wasn't being careful with me.

My fingers tightened in his hair, but I was pulling him closer now.

He was everywhere. The piercing sunlight turned my eyelids

"The most solid example of songs on the playlists being the ones that shaped the book was when I was working on *Eclipse*. I was in the car with my sister listening to 'Hysteria' by Muse — we were out of town and I had my *Absolution* CD because I don't travel without it. We were listening to 'Hysteria' and the kiss scene between Bella and Jacob choreographed itself in my mind, down to the number of steps. I can hear him in the beat as he's walking toward her. The scene is not everybody's favorite, but I certainly enjoy it." — Stephenie

red, and the color fit, matched the heat. The heat was everywhere. I couldn't see or hear or feel anything that wasn't Jacob.

12. ALANIS MORISSETTE, "UNINVITED"

Chapter 23 Jacob was right. He'd been right all along. He was more than just my friend. That's why it was so impossible to tell him goodbye — because I was in love with him. Too. I loved him, much more than I should, and yet, still nowhere near enough. I was in love with him, but it was not enough to change anything; it was only enough to hurt us both more. To hurt him worse than I ever had.

13. PLACEBO, "INFRA-RED"

Edward's perspective

Chapter 24 "Don't go, Victoria," he murmured in that same hypnotic tone as before. "You'll never get another chance like this."

She showed her teeth and hissed at him, but she seemed unable to move farther away from me.

"You can always run later," Edward purred. "Plenty of time for that."

14. MUSE, "YES PLEASE"

Bree's perspective

Chapter 25 After a second of fruitless searching, my gaze crept back to the young female vampire. She was still watching me, her eyes half-mad.

I met the girl's stare for a long moment. Chin-length dark hair framed her face, which was alabaster pale. It was hard to tell if her features were beautiful, twisted as they were by rage and thirst. The feral red eyes were dominant—hard to look away from. She glared at me viciously, shuddering and writhing every few seconds.

15. BRAND NEW, "THE BOY WHO BLOCKED HIS OWN SHOT"

Jacob's perspective

Chapter 26 "You know that story in the Bible?" Jacob asked suddenly, still reading the blank ceiling. "The one with the king and the two women fighting over the baby?"

"Sure. King Solomon."

"That's right. King Solomon," he repeated. "And he said, cut the kid in half...but it was only a test. Just to see who would give up their share to protect it."

"Yeah, I remember."

He looked back at my face. "I'm not going to cut you in half anymore, Bella."

16. & 17. TRAVIS, "LUV" AND MUSE, "BLACKOUT"

Jacob's and Bella's perspectives

Chapter 26 With a sigh, he turned his cheek toward me.

I leaned in and kissed his face softly. "Love you, Jacob."

He laughed lightly. "Love you more."

He watched me walk out of his room with an unfathomable expression in his black eyes.

18. OK GO, "IT'S A DISASTER"

Chapter 27 My hindsight seemed unbearably clear tonight. I could see every mistake I'd made, every bit of harm I'd done, the small things and the big things. Each pain I'd caused Jacob, each wound I'd given Edward, stacked up into neat piles that I could not ignore or deny.

And I realized that I'd been wrong all along about the magnets. It had not been Edward and Jacob that I'd been trying to force together, it was the two parts of myself, Edward's Bella and Jacob's Bella. But they could not exist together, and I never should have tried.

I'd done so much damage.

19. MUSE, "FALLING AWAY WITH YOU"
ALTERNATES:
ARCADE FIRE, "THE WELL AND THE LIGHTHOUSE"
MY CHEMICAL ROMANCE, "SLEEP"
MY CHEMICAL ROMANCE, "THIS IS HOW I DISAPPEAR"

Jacob's perspective

Epilogue *Come home when you can.* The words were faint, trailing off into blank emptiness as he left, too. And I was alone.

So much better. Now I could hear the faint rustle of the matted leaves beneath my toenails, the whisper of an owl's wings above me, the ocean — far, far in the west — moaning against the beach. Hear this, and nothing more. Feel nothing but speed, nothing but the pull of muscle, sinew, and bone, working together in harmony as the miles disappeared behind me.

If the silence in my head lasted, I would never go back. I wouldn't be the first one to choose this form over the other. Maybe, if I ran far enough away, I would never have to hear again. . . .

I pushed my legs faster, letting Jacob Black disappear behind me.

Hear this, and nothing more.
Feel nothing but speed, nothing but the
pull of muscle, sinew, and bone,
working together in harmony as the miles
disappeared behind me.

1. BILLY IDOL, "WHITE WEDDING"

Chapter 1 I briefly contemplated my issues with words like *fiancé, wedding, husband,* etc.

I just couldn't put it together in my head.

On the one hand, I had been raised to cringe at the very thought of poofy white dresses and bouquets. But more than that, I just couldn't reconcile a staid, respectable, dull concept like *husband* with my concept of *Edward*. It was like casting an archangel as an accountant; I couldn't visualize him in any commonplace role.

2. THE BEACH BOYS, "WOULDN'T IT BE NICE"

Chapter 1 "Getting married, though? What's the rush?" He eyed me suspiciously again.

The rush was due to the fact that I was getting closer to nineteen every stinking day, while Edward stayed frozen in all his seventeen-year-old perfection, as he had for over ninety years. Not that this fact necessitated marriage in my book, but the wedding was required due to the delicate and tangled compromise Edward and I had made to finally get to this point, the brink of my transformation from mortal to immortal.

These weren't things I could explain to Charlie.

3. MUSE, "CAN'T TAKE MY EYES OFF OF YOU"

Chapter 4 And when the music started, Edward pulled me into his arms for the customary first dance; I went willingly, despite my fear of dancing — especially dancing in front of an audience — just happy to have him holding me. He did all the work, and I twirled effortlessly under the glow of a canopy of lights and the bright flashes from the cameras.

4. BLUE OCTOBER, "CONGRATULATIONS"

Jacob's perspective

Chapter 4 "You'd think I'd be used to telling you goodbye by now," he murmured.

I tried to swallow the lump in my throat, but I couldn't force it down.

Jacob looked at me and frowned. He wiped his fingers across my cheek, catching the tears there.

"You're not supposed to be the one crying, Bella."

"Everyone cries at weddings," I said thickly.

"This is what you want, right?"

"Right."

"Then smile."

5. PLAIN WHITE T'S, "TAKE ME AWAY"

Jacob's perspective

Chapter 4 "I'll kill you," Jacob said, his voice so choked with rage that it was low as a whisper. His eyes, focused on Edward, burned with fury. "I'll kill you myself! I'll do it now!" He shuddered convulsively.

The biggest wolf, the black one, growled sharply.

"Seth, get out of the way," Edward hissed.

Seth tugged on Jacob again. Jacob was so bewildered with rage that Seth was able to yank him a few feet farther back. "Don't do it, Jake. Walk away. C'mon."

Sam — the bigger wolf, the black one — joined Seth then. He put his massive head against Jacob's chest and shoved.

The three of them — Seth towing, Jake trembling, Sam pushing — disappeared swiftly into the darkness.

6. JACK'S MANNEQUIN, "DARK BLUE"

Edward's perspective

Chapter 5 I half-smiled, then raised my free hand — it didn't tremble now — and placed it over his heart. White on white; we matched, for once. He shuddered the tiniest bit at my warm touch. His breath came rougher now.

"I promised we would try," he whispered, suddenly tense. "If . . . if I do something wrong, if I hurt you, you must tell me at once."

I nodded solemnly, keeping my eyes on his. I took another step through the waves and leaned my head against his chest.

"Don't be afraid," I murmured. "We belong together."

7. COLDPLAY, "NO MORE KEEPING MY FEET ON THE GROUND"

Chapter 5 The sun, hot on the bare skin of my back, woke me in the morning. Late morning, maybe afternoon, I wasn't sure. Everything besides the time was clear, though; I knew exactly where I was — the bright room with the big white bed, brilliant sunlight streaming through the open doors. The clouds of netting would soften the shine.

I didn't open my eyes. I was too happy to change anything, no matter how small. The only sounds were the waves outside, our breathing, my heartbeat....

8. FUEL, "HEMORRHAGE"

Edward's perspective

Chapter 7 When I could no longer bear the violent energy radiating out of him, I quietly left the room. His manic concentration made me sick to my stomach — not like the morning sickness, just uncomfortable. I would wait somewhere else for his mood to pass. I couldn't talk to this icy, focused Edward who honestly frightened me a little.

Breaking Dawn BOOK TWO

Jacob's perspective

9. NINE INCH NAILS, "DOWN IN IT"

Chapter 8 I wondered — would a bullet through my temple actually kill me or just leave a really big mess for me to clean up?

I threw myself down on the bed. I was tired — hadn't slept since my last patrol — but I knew I wasn't going to sleep. My head was too crazy. The thoughts bounced around inside my skull like a disoriented swarm of bees. Noisy. Now and then they stung. Must be hornets, not bees. Bees died after one sting. And the same thoughts were stinging me again and again.

10. AEROSMITH, "WHAT IT TAKES"

Chapter 9 I saw her at the same moment that I caught her scent.

Her warm, clean, human scent.

Bella was half-hidden behind the arm of the sofa, curled up in a loose fetal position, her arms wrapped around her knees. For a long second I could see nothing except that she was still the Bella that I loved, her skin still a soft, pale peach, her eyes still the same chocolate brown. My heart thudded a strange, broken meter, and I wondered if this was just some lying dream that I was about to wake up from.

11. INCUBUS, "EARTH TO BELLA" (PART 1)

Chapter 10 "If you think that imprinting could ever make sense of this insanity . . ." I struggled for words. "Do you really think that just because I might someday imprint on some stranger it would make this right?" I jabbed a finger toward her swollen body. "Tell me what the point was then, Bella! What was the point of me loving you? What was the point of *you* loving *him*? When you die"— the words were a snarl — "how is that ever right again? What's the point to all the pain? Mine, yours, his! You'll kill him, too, not that I care about that." She flinched, but I kept going. "So what was the point of your twisted love story, in the end? If there is any sense, please show me, Bella, because I don't see it."

12. INTERPOL, "NO I IN THREESOME"

Chapter 10 She knew what I was offering, and she wasn't going to think twice about it. I'd known that she wouldn't. But it still stung.

"There isn't much you wouldn't do for me, either, is there?" she whispered. "I really don't know why you bother. I don't deserve either of you."

"It makes no difference, though, does it?"

"Not this time."

13. KORN, "TWISTED TRANSISTOR"

Leah's perspective

Chapter 12 Seth doesn't want or need your protection. In fact, no one wants you here.

Oooh, ouch, that's gonna leave a *huge* mark. *Ha,* she barked. Tell me who *does* want me around, and I'm outta here.

So this isn't about Seth at all, is it?

Of course it is. I'm just pointing out that being unwanted is not a first for me. Not really a motivating factor, if you know what I mean.

14. MY CHEMICAL ROMANCE, "THE SHARPEST LIVES"

Chapter 15 Two weeks to a day, the days flying by. Her life speeding by in fast-forward. How many days did that give her, if she was counting to forty? Four? It took me a minute to figure out how to swallow.

"You okay?" she asked.

I nodded, not really sure how my voice would come out.

Edward's face was turned away from us as he listened to my thoughts, but I could see his reflection in the glass wall. He was the burning man again.

15. MOTION CITY SOUNDTRACK, "POINT OF EXTINCTION"

Chapter 15 "It feels...complete when you're here, Jacob. Like all my family is together. I mean, I guess that's what it's like — I've never had a big family before now. It's nice." She smiled for half a second. "But it's just not whole unless you're here."

"I'll never be part of your family, Bella."

I could have been. I would have been good there. But that was just a distant future that died long before it had a chance to live.

"You've always been a part of my family," she disagreed.

My teeth made a grinding sound. "That's a crap answer."

"What's a good one?"

"How about, 'Jacob, I get a kick out of your pain.'"

I felt her flinch.

"You'd like that better?" she whispered.

"It's easier, at least. I could wrap my head around it. I could deal with it."

Our minds were more closely linked than they had ever been before, because we both were trying to think together.

16. TV ON THE RADIO, "WOLF LIKE ME"

Chapter 16 She hesitated for a second, but then, tentatively, she seemed to reach out with her mind and try to see my way. It felt very strange — our minds were more closely linked than they had ever been before, because we both were trying to think together.

Strange, but it helped her. Her teeth cut through the fur and skin of her kill's shoulder, tearing away a thick slab of streaming flesh. Rather than wince away as her human thoughts wanted to, she let her wolf-self react instinctively. It was kind of a numbing thing, a thoughtless thing. It let her eat in peace.

It was easy for me to do the same. And I was glad I hadn't forgotten this. This would be my life again soon.

Was Leah going to be a part of that life? A week ago, I would've found that idea beyond horrifying. I wouldn't've been able to stand it. But I knew her better now. And, relieved from the constant pain, she wasn't the same wolf. Not the same girl.

17. R.E.M., "ACCELERATE"

Chapter 16 And I was all alone with my hatred and the pain that was so bad it was like being tortured. Like being dragged slowly across a bed of razor blades. Pain so bad you'd take death with a smile just to get away from it.

The heat unlocked my frozen muscles, and I was on my feet.

All three of their heads snapped up, and I watched my pain ripple across Edward's face as he trespassed in my head again.

"Ahh," he choked.

I didn't know what I was doing; I stood there, trembling, ready to bolt for the very first escape that I could think of.

Moving like the strike of a snake, Edward darted to a small end table and ripped something from the drawer there. He tossed it at me, and I caught the object reflexively.

"Go, Jacob. Get away from here." He didn't say it harshly — he threw the words at me like they were a life preserver. He was helping me find the escape I was dying for.

The object in my hand was a set of car keys.

18. JIMMY GNECCO FEATURING BRIAN MAY, "SOMEONE TO DIE FOR"

Chapter 18 Everything inside me came undone as I stared at the tiny porcelain face of the half-vampire, half-human baby. All the lines that held me to my life were sliced apart in swift cuts, like clipping the strings to a bunch of balloons. Everything that made me who I was — my love for the dead girl upstairs, my love for my father, my loyalty to my new pack, the love for my other brothers, my hatred for my enemies, my home, my name, my *self* — disconnected from me in that second — *snip, snip, snip* — and floated up into space.

I was not left drifting. A new string held me where I was. Not one string, but a million. Not strings, but steel cables. A million steel cables all tying me to one thing — to the very center of the universe.

I could see that now — how the universe swirled around this one point. I'd never seen the symmetry of the universe before, but now it was plain.

The gravity of the earth no longer tied me to the place where I stood.

It was the baby girl in the blond vampire's arms that held me here now.

Renesmee.

Breaking Dawn BOOK THREE

19. SMASHING PUMPKINS, "TODAY"

Chapter 20 Everything was so clear.

Sharp. Defined.

The brilliant light overhead was still blinding-bright, and yet I could plainly see the glowing strands of the filaments inside the bulb. I could see each color of the rainbow in the white light, and, at the very edge of the spectrum, an eighth color I had no name for.

20. RIGHT SAID FRED, "I'M TOO SEXY"

Chapter 20 My first reaction was an unthinking pleasure. The alien creature in the glass was indisputably beautiful, every bit as beautiful as Alice or Esme. She was fluid even in stillness, and her flawless face was pale as the moon against the frame of her dark, heavy hair. Her limbs were smooth and strong, skin glistening subtly, luminous as a pearl.

21. THE TEMPER TRAP, "SWEET DISPOSITION"

Chapter 27 And I was euphoric the vast majority of the time. The days were not long enough for me to get my fill of adoring my daughter; the nights did not have enough hours to satisfy my need for Edward.

22. LINKIN PARK, "PTS.OF.ATHRTY"

Chapter 28 "The Volturi," Alice moaned.

"All of them," Edward groaned at the same time.

"Why?" Alice whispered to herself. "How?"

"When?" Edward whispered.

"Why?" Esme echoed.

"When?" Jasper repeated in a voice like splintering ice.

Alice's eyes didn't blink, but it was as if a veil covered them; they became perfectly blank. Only her mouth held on to her expression of horror.

"Not long," she and Edward said together. Then she spoke alone. "There's snow on the forest, snow on the town. Little more than a month."

23. 3 DOORS DOWN, "DUCK AND RUN"

Chapter 29 "I'm not going down without a fight," Emmett snarled low under his breath. "Alice told us what to do. Let's get it done."

The others nodded with determined expressions, and I realized that they were banking on whatever chance Alice had given us. That they were not going to give in to hopelessness and wait to die.

Yes, we all would fight. What else was there? And apparently we would involve others, because Alice had said so before she'd left us. How could we not follow Alice's last warning? The wolves, too, would fight with us for Renesmee.

We would fight, they would fight, and we all would die.

> We would fight, they would fight, and we all would die.

24. SIMON AND GARFUNKEL, "HAZY SHADE OF WINTER"

Chapter 33 And then my smile faded. Alice had sent me here for a reason, and I was sure it was to protect Renesmee. Her last gift to me. The one thing she would know I needed...

It was as I had suspected. We couldn't win. But we must have a good shot at killing Demetri before we lost, giving Renesmee the chance to run.

My still heart felt like a boulder in my chest — a crushing weight. All my hope faded like fog in the sunshine. My eyes pricked.

25. DEATH CAB FOR CUTIE, "I WILL FOLLOW YOU INTO THE DARK"

Chapter 35 Edward cocked one eyebrow as I approached, but otherwise did not remark on my accessory or Renesmee's. He just put his arms tight around us both for one long moment and then, with a deep sigh, let us go. I couldn't see a goodbye anywhere in his eyes. Maybe he had more hope for something after this life than he'd let on.

26. MUSE, "INTRO {ABSOLUTION}"

Chapter 35 Another minute ticked by, and I found myself straining to hear some sound of approach.

And then Edward stiffened and hissed low between his clenched teeth. His eyes focused on the forest due north of where we stood.

We stared where he did, and waited as the last seconds passed.

27. MUSE, "TAKE A BOW"

Chapter 36 They came with pageantry, with a kind of beauty.

They came in a rigid, formal formation. They moved together, but it was not a march; they flowed in perfect synchronicity from the trees—a dark, unbroken shape that seemed to hover a few inches above the white snow, so smooth was the advance.

The outer perimeter was gray; the color darkened with each line of bodies until the heart of the formation was deepest black. Every face was cowled, shadowed. The faint brushing sound of their feet was so regular it was like music, a complicated beat that never faltered.

At some sign I did not see—or perhaps there was no sign, only millennia of practice—the configuration folded outward. The motion was too stiff, too square to resemble the opening of a flower, though the color suggested that; it was the opening of a fan, graceful but very angular. The gray-cloaked figures spread to the flanks while the darker forms surged precisely forward in the center, each movement closely controlled.

Their progress was slow but deliberate, with no hurry, no tension, no anxiety. It was the pace of the invincible.

Their progress was slow but deliberate, with no hurry, no tension, no anxiety.

28. MUSE, "ASSASSIN"

Chapter 37 "We have the answer to all these questions. We heard it in Aro's lying words—we have one with a gift of knowing such things for certain—and we see it now in Caius's eager smile. Their guard is just a mindless weapon, a tool in their masters' quest for domination.

"So now there are more questions, questions that you must answer. Who rules you, nomads? Do you answer to someone's will besides your own? Are you free to choose your path, or will the Volturi decide how you will live?

"I came to witness. I stay to fight. The Volturi care nothing for the death of the child. They seek the death of our free will."

He turned, then, to face the ancients. "So come, I say! Let's hear no more lying rationalizations. Be honest in your intents as we will be honest in ours. We will defend our freedom. You will or will not attack it. Choose now, and let these witnesses see the true issue debated here."

29. OK GO, "INVINCIBLE"

Chapter 38 I could taste it as soon as it touched my shield—it had a dense, sweet, cloying flavor. It made me remember dimly the numbness of Novocain on my tongue.

The mist curled upward, seeking a breach, a weakness. It found none. The fingers of searching haze twisted upward and around, trying to find a way in, and in the process illustrating the astonishing size of the protective screen.

There were gasps on both sides of Benjamin's gorge.

"Well done, Bella!" Benjamin cheered in a low voice.

My smile returned.

I could see Alec's narrowed eyes, doubt on his face for the first time as his mist swirled harmlessly around the edges of my shield.

And then I knew that I could do this. Obviously, I would be the number-one priority, the first one to die, but as long as I held, we were on more than equal footing with the Volturi. We still had Benjamin and Zafrina; they had no supernatural help at all. As long as I held.

30. TRAVIS, "SAFE"

Chapter 38 "Forever," I promised her.

We had forever. And Nessie was going to be fine and healthy

and strong. Like the half-human Nahuel, in a hundred and fifty years she would still be young. And we would all be together.

Happiness expanded like an explosion inside me—so extreme, so violent that I wasn't sure I'd survive it.

31. ELBOW, "ONE DAY LIKE THIS"

Chapter 39 "Bella!" Edward whispered in shock.

I knew it was working then, so I concentrated even harder, dredging up the specific memories I'd saved for this moment, letting them flood my mind, and hopefully his as well.

Some of the memories were not clear—dim human memories, seen through weak eyes and heard through weak ears: the first time I'd seen his face... the way it felt when he'd held me in the meadow... the sound of his voice through the darkness of my faltering consciousness when he'd saved me from James... his face as he waited under a canopy of flowers to marry me... every precious moment from the island... his cold hands touching our baby through my skin...

And the sharp memories, perfectly recalled: his face when I'd opened my eyes to my new life, to the endless dawn of immortality... that first kiss... that first night...

"I *heard* you," he breathed. "How? How did you do that?"

"Zafrina's idea. We practiced with it a few times."

He was dazed. He blinked twice and shook his head.

"Now you know," I said lightly, and shrugged. "No one's ever loved anyone as much as I love you."

> And the sharp memories, perfectly recalled: his face when I'd opened my eyes to my new life, to the endless dawn of immortality... that first kiss... that first night...

The Short Second Life of Bree Tanner

1. MUSE, "YES PLEASE"

Page 55 It was impossible to mistake the noise. The *boom boom boom* of the bass, the video-game soundtrack, the snarling. Totally our crowd.

Page 83 The sound of the thudding music that greeted my approach was accompanied by the unmistakable sweet, smoky scent of a burning vampire. My panic went into overdrive. I could just as easily die inside the house as outside.

2. YEAH YEAH YEAHS, "HEADS WILL ROLL"

Page 9 I turned off my brain. It was time to hunt. I took a deep breath, drawing in the scent of the blood inside the humans below. They weren't the only humans around, but they were the closest. Who you were going to hunt was the kind of decision you had to make before you scented your prey. It was too late now to choose anything.

3. WHITE RABBITS, "MIDNIGHT AND I"

Page 13 I followed him up the alley wall, and then we swung across the girders under the freeway. The lights from the cars below didn't touch us. I thought how stupid people were, how oblivious, and I was glad I wasn't one of the clueless.

4. THE THERMALS, "NOW WE CAN SEE"

Page 35 We sat in silence, pondering this. I mostly thought about how much I didn't know. And why hadn't I worried about everything I didn't know before now? It was like talking to Diego had cleared my head. For the first time in three months, *blood* was not the main thing in there.

5. HA HA TONKA, "FALLING IN"

Diego's perspective

Pages 49-50 Diego grinned at me, his face beautiful with light, and suddenly, with a deep lurch in my stomach, I realized that the whole BFF thing was way off the mark. For me, anyway. It was just that fast.

His grin softened a little bit into just the hint of a smile. His eyes were wide like mine. All awe and lights. He touched my face, the way he'd touched my hand, as if he was trying to understand the shine.

"So pretty," he said. He left his hand against my cheek.

6. THE DEAD WEATHER, "ROCKING HORSE"

Pages 57-58 "I see the little girl made it, too," said a new voice, and I shuddered because it was Raoul. I felt a little bit of relief that he didn't know my name, but mostly I just felt horrified that he'd noticed me at all.

"Yeah, she followed me." I couldn't see Diego, but I knew he was shrugging.

"Aren't you the savior of the hour?" Raoul said snidely.

"We don't get extra points for being morons."...

"Interesting attitude you got, Diego. You think that Riley likes you so much he's gonna care if I kill you. I think you're wrong. But either way, for tonight, he already thinks you're dead."

7. REFUSED, "NEW NOISE"

Page 113 Riley had better control of them than I had thought possible.

Still, it was mostly repetition. I noticed Riley saying the same things over and over and over again. *Work together, watch your back, don't go at her head-on; work together, watch your back, don't go at him head-on; work together, watch your back, don't go at her head-on.* It was kind of ridiculous, really, and made the group seem exceptionally stupid. But I was sure I would have been just as stupid if I'd been in the thick of the fight with them rather than watching calmly from the sidelines with Fred.

It reminded me in a way of how Riley had drilled into us our fear of the sun. Constant repetition.

8. BLUE OCTOBER, "WHAT IF WE COULD"

Pages 89-90 And I suddenly realized something stupendously obvious. It was the solution that had tickled the edges of my understanding before, when I was tracking the vampire herd to this place with Diego....

We didn't have to come back the other night! We *shouldn't* have! Why hadn't I thought of it then? . . .

We could disappear, and Riley would have to make do with nineteen vampires, or make some new ones quick. Either way, not our problem.

I couldn't wait to tell Diego my plan. My gut instinct was that he would feel the same. Hopefully.

9. QUEENS OF THE STONE AGE, "SICK, SICK, SICK"

Pages 105-106 His face was not twisted in rage, the way it usually was when he was angry; it was calm and cold, smooth and beautiful, his mouth curled at the edges into a small smile. I suddenly had the impression that this was a new Riley. Something had changed him, hardened him, but I couldn't imagine what could have happened in one night to create that cruel, perfect smile.

10. SILVERSUN PICKUPS, "THE ROYAL WE"

Page 115 Kristie and Raoul growled, and both of their companies followed suit immediately. I was surprised to see it, but they did look like an army in that moment. Not that they were marching in formation or anything, but there was just something uniform about the response. Like they all were part of one big organism.

Pages 133-134 It took them a minute, but everyone started to realize that this was it, and they got quieter and more fierce. I could see that the idea of a real fight — of being not only allowed but encouraged to rip and burn — was almost as exciting as hunting. It appealed to people like Raoul and Jen and Sara.

> I could see that the idea of a real fight— of being not only allowed but encouraged to rip and burn — was almost as exciting as hunting.

11. MEESE, "COUNT ME OUT"

Fred's perspective

Pages 136-137 "You're not going?"

Fred shook his head. "Of course not. It's obvious we're not being told what we need to know. I'm not going to be Riley's pawn. . . . I'm out. I'm going to explore on my own, see the world."

12. METRIC, "BLINDNESS"

Page 143 But it didn't feel like I had a choice. I headed south in a flat-out sprint again. I had to go get Diego. Drag him away if it came to that. We could catch up with Fred. Or take off on our own. We needed to run. I would tell Diego how Riley had lied. He would see that Riley had no intention of helping us fight the battle he'd set up. There was no reason to help him anymore....

And then I heard the snarling and screaming and screeching explode from ahead and I knew the fight was happening and I was too late to beat Diego there. I only ran faster. Maybe I could still save him.

13. DAN MANGAN, "SET THE SAILS"

Pages 162-163 I was of two minds about survival anyway. I didn't want to die, I didn't want pain, but what was the point? Everyone else was dead. Diego had been dead for days.

His name was right on my lips. I almost whispered it aloud. Instead, I gripped my skull with both hands and tried to think about something that wouldn't hurt.

Fan Art Gallery

One of the things I most enjoy about Twilight fans is their creativity. I remember the first time I saw a piece of original artwork inspired by my book. . . .I was speechless. I was so flattered and impressed by the talent and effort that had been spent on illustrating my story. Since then, I've seen thousands of original drawings, paintings, and even videos, and I always love getting to experience what the fans are seeing in their heads when they read. Here is just a small sample of the talent and imagination that the fans bring to the Twilight world.

THE CULLENS
RINIAN

BELLA SWAN

JESSICA TANNER

("Silivrenstar")

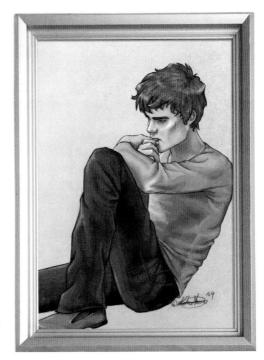

EDWARD CULLEN

KATRINA YOUNG

("Rohanelf")

YOUNG JACOB BLACK
KIM KINCAID

BELLA x JACOB—*ECLIPSE*
LEEN ISABEL ("Lenity")

**JACOB AND BELLA—
SUNNY DAYS**
ALLYA KOESOEMA
("Alizarin")

**BELLA x
EDWARD—
*TWILIGHT***
LEEN ISABEL
("Lenity")

HOW TO SAVE
A LIFE (CARLISLE)
ANGELINA CARILLO
("SHIRE22")

ESME CULLEN
SAYEH GORJIFARD
("LAMPOONA")

ROSALIE
VALERIA BOGADO
("Palnk")

BRUTE FORCE (EMMETT CULLEN)
KIM KINCAID

**JASPER
WHITLOCK**

KATRINA YOUNG
("Rohanelf")

ALICE POPISH

VALERIA BOGADO
("Palnk")

THE UPSTAIRS WINDOW (BELLA, EDWARD, AND JACOB)
DARCY RIPLEY
("Tainted Tea")

HEADACHE (ALICE)
DARCY RIPLEY
("Tainted Tea")

International Cover Gallery

The Twilight Saga has been translated into forty-eight languages and counting, so this guide would not be complete without a gallery of covers from around the world. While some international publishers used the original U.S. covers, others went in completely different directions. Here is a sampling of international interpretations of the Twilight Saga covers.

CZECH REPUBLIC

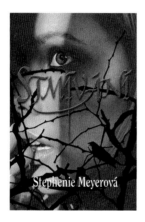

TITLE TRANSLATION: *Twilight*, *New Moon*, *Eclipse*: exact translations; *Breaking Dawn*: "Daybreak." © Egmont

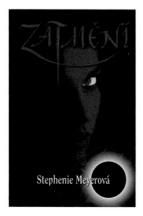
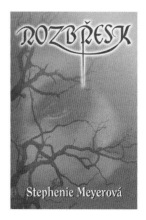

TITLE TRANSLATION: *Twilight*: "Twilight Volume 1" and
"Twilight Volume 2" © Forlaget Sesam/Carlsen;
Cover design: Thomas Scoeke-Eyelab.dk

FRANCE

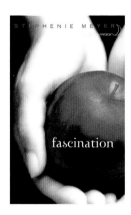

TITLE TRANSLATION: *Twilight*: "Fascination"; *New Moon*:
"Temptation"; *Eclipse*: "Hesitation" © Hachette Livre

TITLE TRANSLATION: *Twilight*: "Until the Break of Dawn" or "Bite at the Break of Dawn"; *New Moon*: "Until Noon" or "Bite at Noon"; *Eclipse*: "Until the Evening Glow" or "Bite at the Evening Glow"; *Breaking Dawn*: "Until the End of the Night" or "Bite at the End of the Night." Carlsen Verlag.

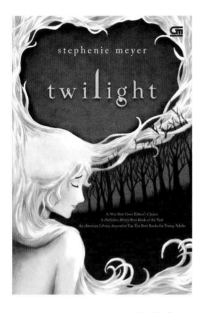

TITLE TRANSLATION: *Twilight*: exact translation; *New Moon*: "Two Loves"; *Eclipse*: exact translation; *Breaking Dawn*: "A New Beginning." © PT Gramedia Pustaka Utama. Illustrator: Dianing Ratri

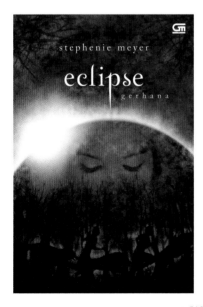

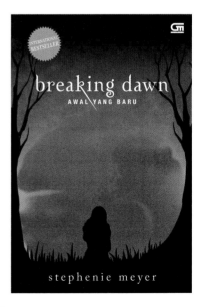

TITLE TRANSLATION: *Twilight*, volume 1: "Whom I Loved Was
a Vampire"; volume 2: "Blood Is a Taste of Sorrow"; volume 3:
"Vampire Family in Darkness." © Gotsubo X Ryuji 2005

TITLE TRANSLATION: *New Moon*, volume 4: "Tusk Speaks Sweetly";
volume 5: "Moon of Wolf"; volume 6: "Grief of Falling Angel."
© Gotsubo X Ryuji 2006

TITLE TRANSLATION: *Eclipse*, volume 7: "Red Mark";
volume 8: "Give Me a Cold Kiss"; volume 9: "Time of Monsters."
© Gotsubo X Ryuji 2007

TITLE TRANSLATION:
Breaking Dawn,
volume 10:
"Bride of Vampire";
volume 11:
"Guardian Deity of Dawn";
volume 12:
"Immortal Child";
volume 13:
"Embracing Forever."
Volumes 11–12
© Gotsubo X Ryuji 2008;
Volumes 12–13
© Gotsubo X Ryuji 2009

TITLE TRANSLATION: *Twilight, New Moon, Eclipse, Breaking Dawn*: exact translations © Bookfolio

TITLE TRANSLATION: *Twilight*, *New Moon*, *Eclipse*, *Breaking Dawn*:
exact translations. © AST Publishers

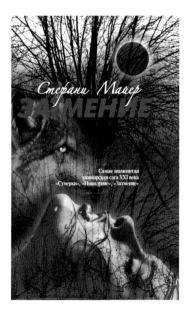 

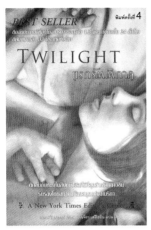  

TITLE TRANSLATION: *Twilight*: "First Night";
New Moon: exact translation; *Eclipse*: "Eclipse Blessing";
Breaking Dawn, volume 1: "First Blush"; *Breaking Dawn*,
volume 2: "Next Blush." © Book Innovation Co., Ltd.

Outtakes

As in moviemaking, during the process of writing and editing a book, some scenes are cut. This section includes several scenes that were once part of the Twilight Saga. Think of them as similar to the outtakes in the special-features section of a DVD. (Other outtakes and materials are available at www.stepheniemeyer.com.)

"BADMINTON"

This is an outtake from chapter 11 of *Twilight*. The scene gives a vivid picture of Bella's legendary clumsiness, and an extra peek at Mike Newton.

I walked into the gym, light-headed, wobbly. I drifted to the locker room, changing in a trancelike state, only vaguely aware that there were other people surrounding me. Reality didn't fully set in until I was handed a racket. It wasn't heavy, yet it felt very unsafe in my hand. I could see a few of the other kids in class eyeing me furtively. Coach Clapp ordered us to pair up into teams.

Mercifully, some vestiges of Mike's chivalry still survived; he came to stand beside me.

"Do you want to be a team?" he asked cheerfully.

"Thanks, Mike — you don't have to do this, you know." I grimaced.

"Don't worry, I'll keep out of your way." He grinned. Sometimes it was so easy to be fond of Mike.

It didn't go smoothly. I tried to stay clear of Mike so that he could keep the birdie in play, but Coach Clapp came by and ordered him to remain on his side of the court so I could participate. He stayed, watching, to enforce his words.

With a sigh, I stepped into a more central place on

the court, holding my racket upright, if still gingerly. The girl on the other team sneered maliciously as she served the birdie — I must have injured her during the basketball section — lobbing it just a few feet past the net, directly toward me. I sprung gracelessly forward, aiming my swing in the direction of the little rubber pest, but I forgot to take the net into account. My racket bounced back from the net with surprising strength, popping out of my hand and glancing off my forehead before whacking Mike in the shoulder as he rushed forward to get the birdie I had completely missed.

Coach Clapp coughed, or muffled a laugh.

"Sorry, Newton," he mumbled, ambling away so we could return to our former, less dangerous, positions.

"Are you okay?" Mike asked, massaging his shoulder, just as I was rubbing my forehead.

"Yeah, are you?" I asked meekly, retrieving my weapon.

"I think I'll make it." He swung his arm in a circle, making sure he still had full range of motion.

"I'll just stay back here." I walked to the back corner of the court, holding my racket carefully behind my back.

My racket bounced back from the net with surprising strength, popping out of my hand and glancing off my forehead before whacking Mike in the shoulder as he rushed forward to get the birdie I had completely missed.

"EMMETT AND THE BEAR"

Originally this piece was to be in the *Twilight* epilogue. Although Emmett's backstory is touched on in chapter 14 of *Twilight*, this scene gives Emmett's take on his encounter with the bear—and first meeting with Rosalie—in his own words.

I was surprised to find a strange kinship growing between myself and Emmett, especially since he had once been the most frightening to me of them all. It had to do with how we had both been chosen to join the family; we'd both been loved—and had loved in return—while we were human, though very briefly for him. Only Emmett remembered—he alone really understood the miracle that Edward remained to me.

We spoke of it for the first time one evening as the three of us lounged on the light sofas of the front room, Emmett quietly regaling me with memories that were better than fairy tales, while Edward concentrated on the Food Network—he'd decided he needed to learn to cook, to my disbelief, and it was rough going without the proper sense of taste and smell. After all, there *was* something that didn't come naturally to him. His perfect brow furrowed as the celebrity chef flavored yet another dish according to taste. I repressed a smile.

"He was finished playing with me then, and I knew I was about to die," Emmett remembered softly, winding up the tale of his human years with the story of the bear. Edward paid us no attention; he'd heard it before. "I couldn't move, and my consciousness was slipping away, when I heard what I thought was another bear, and a fight—over which would get my carcass, I supposed. Suddenly it felt like I was flying. I figured I'd died, but I tried to open my eyes anyway. And then I saw *her*"—his face was incredulous at the memory; I empathized entirely—"and I *knew* I was dead. I didn't even mind the pain. I fought to keep my eyelids open—I didn't want to miss one second of the angel's face. I was delirious, of course, wondering why we hadn't gotten to heaven yet, thinking it must be farther away than I'd expected. I kept waiting for her to take flight. And then she brought me to God." He laughed his deep, booming laugh. I could easily comprehend anyone making that assumption.

"I thought what happened next was my judgment. I'd had a little too much fun in my twenty human years, so I wasn't surprised by the fires of hell." He laughed again, and I shivered; Edward's arm tightened around me unconsciously. "What surprised me was that the angel didn't leave. I couldn't understand how something so beautiful would be allowed to stay in hell with me—but I was *grateful*. Every time God came to check on me, I was afraid he would take her away, but he never did. I started to think maybe those preachers who talked about a merciful God might have been right after all. And then the pain went away... and they explained things to me.

> "I'd had a little too much fun in my twenty human years, so I wasn't surprised by the fires of hell."

"*They* were surprised at how little disturbed I was over the vampire issue. But if Carlisle and Rosalie, my angel, were vampires, how bad could it be?" I nodded, agreeing completely, as he continued. "I had a bit more trouble with the rules...." He chuckled. "You had your hands full with me at first, didn't you?" Emmett's playful nudge to Edward's shoulder set us both rocking.

Edward snorted without looking away from the TV.

"So you see, hell's not so bad if you get to keep an angel

with you," he assured me mischievously. "When he gets around to accepting the inevitable, you'll do fine."

Edward's fist moved so swiftly that I didn't see what knocked Emmett sprawling over the back of the couch. Edward's eyes never left the screen.

"Edward!" I scolded, horrified.

"Don't worry about it, Bella." Emmett was unruffled, back in his seat. "I know where to find him." He looked over me toward Edward's profile. "You'll have to put her down sometime," he threatened. Edward merely snarled in response, without looking up.

"Boys!" Esme's reproving voice called sharply down the stairs.

"*Romeo and Juliet*"

This quote was the original epigraph for *New Moon*. The quote actually used, also from *Romeo and Juliet*, foreshadows more of the danger and potential heartbreak in the book, while the original choice emphasized the romance of the story.

Come, gentle night; come, loving, black-browed night;
Give me my Romeo; and, when I shall die,
Take him and cut him out in little stars,
And he will make the face of heaven so fine
That all the world will be in love with night. . . .

—*Romeo and Juliet*, Act III scene ii

"Old Quil"

The following excerpt was the original first introduction to Old Quil. It takes place in chapter 12 in *New Moon* after Jacob tells Bella to stay away from him (in the rough draft, Jacob didn't come to her window that night).

Charlie was at the breakfast table with a plate of scrambled eggs in front of him. He looked up, seeming surprised to see me.

"You're up early," he said, examining my face carefully.

I glanced at the clock; I was actually running late. "I've only got fifteen minutes," I disagreed.

His face was wary. "It's Saturday, honey. You don't have work for another hour."

"Oh." He was still scrutinizing my face. "Well, that's good. I didn't want to go to school much anyway."

I turned away from him, feeling his eyes on my back, and went to search in the fridge. The pizza was right on top.

We ate in silence as I wondered what to do with my day. I regretted trading my Saturday hours at Newton's. It would have been a nice distraction.

But I knew that I wasn't giving up on Jacob, and I wondered what angle to approach him from.

"So you're really worried about this Sam thing, aren't you?" Charlie was done with his food before I was, and his thoughts were in the same place.

I swallowed. "Yes, I really am."

"Do you think he's involved with something bad? Drugs or crime or something?"

"I don't know. I can't think of anything else, but I just can't see Jacob changing for something like that." I shrugged.

"I'm sorry I didn't listen to you before," he said quietly.

"Don't worry about it. I'm used to people thinking I'm crazy." It slipped out before I could think, and Charlie's eyes flashed up to mine.

"I don't think you're crazy."

"Yeah, I know. I was kidding."

He nodded, but there was no agreement in the motion.

"Anyway, what were you supposed to think? Billy supports this." I shook my head. "It's too weird. It's like Quil said yesterday... something stinks."

"Quil Ateara?" he asked quickly.

I nodded. "He's not in the cult. He's scared, like Jacob was."

"Cult?" Charlie repeated in a sharp tone.

"That's what Quil called it, and Jacob, too, before they beamed him up," I said morosely. "Jacob also said something about tribe pride and tribe lands...."

Charlie's eyes narrowed. "I wonder if that's why Billy and the others seem to approve? I talked to Billy yesterday—"

I nodded knowingly, and he broke off for a second, looking uncomfortable. He was probably trying to remember what all he'd said about me.

"Anyway," he started again, "he was acting pretty strange himself. Billy's always been a straightforward person. Yesterday...well, it seemed like he was hiding something." His voice was full of disbelief, as if this were the most ridiculous of theories.

"Dad, I think that's *exactly* what he's doing."

Charlie looked at me unhappily. "What are we going to do?"

"I think I'm going to La Push—Mrs. Newton traded shifts with me for today."

He frowned. "I don't know if I want you down there, Bella. This is a little bit disturbing."

"It's a lot disturbing," I told him. "But I don't think it's dangerous disturbing — at least not for me. Maybe for Quil, though. By the way, I offered Quil our couch if he wants to get away. Is that all right?"

He blinked twice. "Um, sure." He paused. "Are you good friends with Quil Ateara?"

"I think I've talked to him twice," I admitted.

"Okay." Charlie pursed his lips. Life was spinning out of Charlie's comfort zone. I knew the feeling well.

I got up from the table.

"Bella?"

"Yeah?"

"If anything looks...weird, don't stay. I'll be at the station. And call me, either way."

"Sure, Dad."

I felt sort of guilty as I retraced the familiar road to La Push. I was going to do something that I knew was wrong, and that maybe was a slight overreaction, too.

I was going to do my best to convince Quil Ateara to run away from home.

Jacob had thought Sam was after him, and he'd been right. Now Quil felt the same way. I was going to trust Quil's gut instinct and assume that he was next in line for the brainwashing. But if they wanted him, they were going to have to get through the Chief and me. Maybe Quil would be the key to finding out what was really happening to Jacob, and getting him out.

My mood was more hopeful, now that I had a goal.

La Push was empty. It was almost sultry out today, warm and close under the thick clouds. No rain to drive anyone

Life was spinning out of Charlie's comfort zone.

indoors. The vacant yards and sidewalks seemed suspicious, but I was probably being paranoid. La Push was never a bustling hot spot.

I was glad that Quil's family lived on the opposite side of the village from the Blacks. I didn't want anyone to guess what I was up to and target Quil earlier than expected. I wished my truck were much quieter. It was the loudest thing in town—so much for stealth.

There was no sign of life outside the Ateara home. I couldn't tell if the lights were on inside the store in front of it.

I shut the truck off and hurried up the short dirt path to the front door. I couldn't help looking over my shoulder every other second, though it made me feel ridiculous. I rapped my knuckles hard and fast against the faded blue door, then listened, waiting for a response. Nothing. I beat my fist against the wood twice again, this time generating a muffled thud that seemed to shiver in the walls.

As I waited—discouragement beginning to conquer hope—I was reminded of those movies on the sci-fi channel that I always flipped through quickly, the movies where someone finds herself all alone, the only person left on the planet. I shivered.

I raised my fist for one last, futile attempt, and the door swung open under my hand. I nearly punched the shriveled white-haired man in the face.

"Oh," I gasped, quickly dropping my hand.

"Hey, you're Chief Swan's girl," the little man accused.

"Yes," I admitted.

"You hang out with Billy's kid."

"Sometimes." I wondered if he treated all visitors this way. Maybe just the ones who almost assaulted him.

"What do you want? He's not here." He shut the door halfway.

"Um, Mr. Ateara?" I guessed, easing my foot surreptitiously around the doorjamb so he couldn't shut me out until I wanted him to.

"Yeah, that's right." He seemed displeased that I knew his name.

"Is your grandson Quil here?"

"No."

A few seconds passed.

"Could you tell me where I can find him?" I prompted.

"Can't tell you what I don't know. He's out."

"Do you know if he's with Jacob?" I asked anxiously. There hadn't been enough time for that, had there? Did they guess what I was up to? Was Sam taking preemptive action against me?

"Don't think so," the old man said reluctantly. "He goes off on his own now."

Relief rushed through me. "Okay, I guess I'll just come back later."

The only answer I got was a sour look as he slammed the door. I yanked my foot out of the way, barely avoiding some broken toes.

Well, that was welcoming.

I decided I would drive around and hope to find Quil walking along the road, as I had yesterday. I'd much rather talk to him without his grandfather present.

Did they guess what I was up to? Was Sam taking preemptive action against me?

This outtake shows another approach to the scene at the end of *New Moon*'s chapter 2.

I collapsed back onto my pillow, gasping, my head spinning. My arm didn't hurt anymore, but I didn't know whether that was due to the painkillers or the kiss. Something tugged at my memory, elusive, on the edges. . . .

"Sorry," he said, and he was breathless, too. "That was out of line."

To my own surprise, I giggled. "You're funny," I mumbled and giggled again.

He frowned at me in the darkness. He looked so serious. It was hysterical.

I covered my mouth to muffle the laughter so Charlie wouldn't hear.

"Bella, have you ever had Percocet before?"

"I don't think so." I giggled. "Why?"

He rolled his eyes, and I couldn't stop laughing.

"How's your arm?"

"I can't feel it. Is it still there?"

He sighed as I giggled on. "Try to sleep, Bella."

"No, I want you to kiss me again."

"You're overestimating my self-control."

I snickered. "Which is bothering you more, my blood or my body?" My question made me laugh.

"You're overestimating my self-control."

"It's a tie." He grinned in spite of himself. "I've never seen you high. You're very entertaining."

"I'm not high." I tried to choke back the giggles to prove it.

"Sleep it off," he suggested.

I realized that I was making a fool of myself, which wasn't uncommon, but it was still embarrassing, so I tried to follow his advice. I put my head on his shoulder again and closed my eyes. Every now and then another giggle would escape. But that became more infrequent as the drugs lulled me toward unconsciousness.

*   *   *

I felt absolutely hideous in the morning. My arm burned and my head ached. Edward said I had a hangover, and recommended Tylenol rather than the Percocet before he kissed my forehead casually and ducked out my window.

It didn't help my outlook that his face was smooth and remote. I was so afraid of the conclusions he might have come to during the night while he watched me sleep. The anxiety seemed to ratchet up the intensity of the pounding in my head.

I took a double dose of Tylenol and threw the little bottle of Percocet into the bathroom trash.

Frequently Asked Questions

Q. WHAT DO THE COVERS OF THE BOOKS REPRESENT?

A. The apple on the cover of *Twilight* represents the knowledge of good and evil. Eve ate this forbidden fruit in Genesis, and *Twilight* has an epigraph from this book of the Bible: "But of the tree of the knowledge of good and evil, thou shalt not eat of it: for in the day that thou eatest thereof thou shalt surely die." The question inherent in the apple is "Do you want to know?" It asks if you are going to bite in and discover the frightening possibilities around you or refuse and stay safe in the comfortable world you know.

Unlike the other covers, Stephenie was not involved in choosing the cover for *New Moon*. The author originally proposed a clock image, as time is such a key theme in the book. But ultimately the team that chose the tulip focused on the theme of loss. The image of the flower losing its petal was chosen to reflect that. They felt the fallen petal could also be interpreted to represent the drop of blood from Bella's paper cut in the first chapter.

The not-quite-broken ribbon on the cover of *Eclipse* is a metaphor for Bella trying to leave her human life behind her, but being unable to make a clean break. There are some threads she is unable to cut — she can't completely divorce herself from her past.

The two chess pieces on the cover of *Breaking Dawn* both represent Bella. They show her moving from the least significant player, the pawn, at the beginning of the Saga to the most important player, the queen, at the end of the series. The chessboard also hints at *Breaking Dawn*'s resolution, where the battle with the Volturi is one of wits and strategy, not physical violence.

The image on *The Official Guide* cover represents all

the "pieces of the puzzle" of the Twilight Saga coming together in one place.

The hourglass on the cover of *The Short Second Life of Bree Tanner: An Eclipse Novella* symbolizes the theme of time and represents the fact that it is running out for Bree and her fellow newborns.

Q. WHEN EDWARD ATE THE PIZZA IN *TWILIGHT*, WHAT HAPPENED TO THE BIT OF FOOD HE SWALLOWED?

A. Vampires cannot digest food, but they sometimes find themselves in a situation where eating human food is unavoidable to keep up a human façade. The food that they consume sits in their stomach until they can find a private place to cough it up.

Q. WAS EDWARD SECRETLY WATCHING BELLA IN *TWILIGHT* WHILE SHE WAS READING JANE AUSTEN?

A. Yes. In secret, Edward used to pay very close attention to everything Bella did before they began their relationship.

Q. WHY WAS BELLA'S WINDOW SO EASY TO OPEN IN *TWILIGHT*?

A. The window was stuck and made a groaning sound the first time Edward opened it. While Bella didn't wake up, Edward promised himself he'd bring some oil for the window the next time, which he did.

Q. WHAT CAUSES EDWARD TO WARN BELLA ABOUT BEING ALONE IN THE WOODS IN *TWILIGHT*?

A. There was no specific threat on Edward's mind when he warned Bella to stay out of the woods. (Peter and Charlotte had been visiting Jasper, but they didn't hunt in Forks, and they were already gone when Edward cautioned Bella.) It was more of a general sense of Bella's vulnerability that motivated the warning. He had tracked her scent in the woods after he came back from his hunting trip in the Goat Rocks Wilderness, and found himself unnerved by the image of her alone and unprotected. After all, Bella regularly attracted catastrophes.

Q. HOW WAS EDWARD ABLE TO DRINK BELLA'S BLOOD AT THE END OF *TWILIGHT* AND NOT INFECT HER WITH MORE VENOM?

A. Edward drank with his lips puckered, as if using a straw, and never touched her with his "saliva."

Q. IF VAMPIRES ARE SOLID LIKE GRANITE, DOESN'T THAT MEAN THEY MUST WEIGH A LOT?

A. It is possible for things to be really durable, but not weigh a tremendous amount. Polymers are a good example of this. Vampires do, however, weigh more than humans of the same size.

Q. CAN ANIMALS BE TURNED INTO VAMPIRES?

A. No, only humans can be turned into vampires. Venom is deadly to animals.

Q. HOW IS EDWARD ABLE TO BE AROUND BELLA WHEN SHE HAS HER MONTHLY CYCLE?

A. Edward is aware of what's going on physiologically with Bella, but he is too much of a gentleman to ever say anything about it, and Bella would be too embarrassed to ask if he noticed or was bothered by it. The blood from a woman's period isn't the same as a cut; it's not freshly oxygenated, not flowing from the heart.

Q. WHY DO ALICE'S AND JASPER'S SUPERNATURAL POWERS WORK ON BELLA, BUT EDWARD'S, ARO'S, JANE'S, ALEC'S, CHELSEA'S, AND HEIDI'S POWERS DON'T AFFECT HER?

A. Bella has a shield that protects only her mind. Edward and Aro both have the ability to read minds, but their gifts are blocked by this shield. Jane, Alec, Chelsea, and Heidi also work inside the head. For example, Jane doesn't actually inflict pain on someone's body; she just puts the illusion of pain inside her victim's head. It's a very effective form of torture. Conversely, what Jasper does is no illusion. He affects the physical body, slowing the pulse and upping the endorphin levels to calm someone, for example, or raising the pulse and pumping out the adrenaline to excite people. Alice also works outside the mind, in the realm of possible realities. She doesn't see the thought process behind the decisions — just the outcomes.

Q. DID BELLA REALLY HEAR EDWARD'S VOICE IN *NEW MOON*? WAS HE HIDING IN THE BUSHES, OR WAS HE SOMEHOW COMMUNICATING WITH BELLA TELEPATHICALLY?

A. Edward was in England, Texas, and Brazil for most of *New Moon*. What Bella heard in her head was all imagined. Her subconscious was powerfully trying to correct the erroneous belief that her conscious mind was so absolutely sure of — that Edward didn't care about her. The proof that Edward couldn't know what was happening to Bella comes when she is almost killed by Laurent. Had Edward even had an inkling that Victoria or Laurent was back in Forks, he would have returned immediately to protect Bella.

Q. HOW COULD BELLA FALL IN LOVE WITH JACOB ALL OF A
SUDDEN IN *ECLIPSE*?

A. Bella actually falls in love with Jacob in *New Moon*.
It's understandable why this fact doesn't occur to her:
Bella has fallen in love only one other time, and it
was a very sudden, dramatic, sweep-you-off-your-feet,
change-your-world, magical, passionate, all-consuming
thing (see *Twilight*). She didn't recognize the much
more subtle falling-in-love she experienced with Jacob.
She was aware only that she preferred being with him
over everyone else, that he was constantly on her mind,
and that his happiness was essential to her own. She also
enjoyed being physically close to him in a way that she
didn't with her other friends. But it took her a while to
add up all the pieces.

Q. IS THE CRYSTAL HEART THAT EDWARD GIVES BELLA
REALLY A CRYSTAL?

A. No, it's an actual diamond that once belonged to
Edward's mother.

Q. WHAT IS *FOREVER DAWN*?

A. *Forever Dawn* is the original title of the book that eventually became *Breaking Dawn*. Initially it was planned
as an immediate sequel to *Twilight*, but it was decided
that the book skipped too much that was interesting in
Bella's last year of high school, and didn't have enough
space for all the development the characters were crying
out for. Still, the basic plotline of *Forever Dawn*, including Renesmee and Jacob and the Volturi, was always
the end toward which the series was written.

ILLUSTRATION CREDITS